'With its high-voltage blend of drama, intrigue and suspense,
and a storyline full of twists and turns, there is no question
of betrayal here. Miller delivers again.'
Irish Independent

'Blends passion, drama, glamour and intrigue'
The Bookseller

'Zoë Miller's done it again. A hot page-turner with
a shiver of sensuality'
Evening Herald

'Intriguing and fun. Contains a great cast of characters, a beautiful
setting and a storyline that will keep you guessing'
Chloe's Chick Lit Reviews

'A good, solid story with romance, glamour and deep emotion'
Chick Lit Club

Zoë Miller was born in Dublin, where she now lives with her husband. She began writing stories at an early age. Her writing career has also included freelance journalism and prize-winning short fiction. She has three children.

Also by Zoë Miller

Guilty Secrets
Sinful Deceptions
Rival Passions
A Family Scandal
The Compromise
A Husband's Confession
A Question of Betrayal

www.zoemillerauthor.com
Twitter:@zoemillerauthor
Facebook.com/zoemillerauthor

Zoë MILLER

Someone New

HACHETTE
BOOKS
IRELAND

A CIP catalogue record for this title is available from the British Library.

ISBN 978 1 473607262

Printed and bound by Clays Ltd, St Ives plc
Typeset in Garamond by redrattledesign.com

Hachette Books Ireland policy is to use papers that are natural, renewable and recyclable products and made from wood grown in sustainable forests. The logging and manufacturing processes are expected to conform to the environmental regulations of the country of origin.

Hachette Books Ireland
8 Castlecourt Centre
Castleknock
Dublin 15, Ireland

Dedicated with love to Derek,

who has always encouraged me

to dream big.

PROLOGUE

Sometimes Grace still saw him standing in her doorway, exactly as he'd stood before he'd left that evening; other times he drifted through her dreams, smiling back at her from the divide between them, but for once she wasn't thinking of him as she arrived home from the office and let herself into the apartment block.

She picked up the small padded envelope from her post box in the foyer, along with a mobile phone advertisement, shoving both of them into her tote bag as she hurried across to the waiting lift. The doors snapped closed just as she reached it, so she took the stairs to the second floor, walking briskly down the corridor to her apartment, mildly curious as to what the envelope might contain. The advertisement went straight into the bin – no, she didn't need the latest in smartphone technology, no matter how many mega pixels it had.

The padded envelope was addressed to her in block capitals with a black felt pen. At first she didn't know what to make of the small pieces of paper that were tucked inside. She poked them out with her finger and spread them across the table, turning them coloured side up. Then from one of the pieces, his eyes looked up at her, from another, his mouth. Another piece showed the top of his head. And a fourth was a part of his hips. She sifted through the fragments, her hand shaking as she turned them this way and that, fitting them together.

She was by now used to the empty feel of her apartment, but this evening the silence seemed to take on a life of its own, resonating around her. Even though a square of warm May sunshine slanted across the far wall, illuminating the life-affirming posters like some kind of beacon, she felt chilly inside. She scooped up the torn photograph, shoved it back into the envelope and rammed it into the bin.

She had no idea who might have sent this, but as if he or she was still lurking around, she glanced out the kitchen window and down to the landscaped courtyard that was situated in the small space between three identical apartment blocks. It was shadowed from the sun by the height of the five-storey blocks, and the courtyard was deserted save for a discarded plastic bag caught in a tree branch, flapping like a small, forgotten ghost.

She went across to the big picture window in the living area, and rested her forehead against the glass, hoping her chill might evaporate as she stood in the last rays of sunshine before it slid away westwards behind the adjacent apartment block. From the second floor of Rathbrook Hall, there wasn't much to see except the glint of glass and chrome off evening traffic streaming down the link road towards the M50, and oncoming traffic heading up towards the retail parks and the village of Rathbrook.

After she plugged in the kettle, she ran her fingertips through the long, flowing tail of the kite secured to the tall kitchen press. It was shaped like a butterfly, and it was a lively blaze of yellow and red against the cream press. It floated out onto the air under the touch of her hand, twirling around for her before settling back down again. Although she'd be thirty years of age in a few months' time, it usually had the power to make her smile.

It was impossible to summon a smile this evening.

Up to now it had been a gut feeling, an odd sense that something wasn't quite right. But there was no denying the malice behind this photograph. It had been sent to rattle her and it worked, because it deepened her unease, and the evening imploded around her as all the joy and heartache of the last few months came rushing back.

Chapter One

Five months earlier

Christmas was two weeks away, and every inch of the gastropub was alive with flashing decorations and festive party-goers singing out-of-tune carols. Framed by the big picture windows, and adding to the frenzied sparkle, the length of the Royal Hibernian Way outside was ablaze with incandescent streams of twinkly lights. Sitting in a seat by the window, Grace felt marooned, surrounded on all sides by an abundance of Christmas cheer, but in contrast to the cheerful glitter of it all, Grace's heart was sinking lower and lower.

Agreeing to meet Gavin for a drink had not been a good idea.

'You look great …' Gavin said. She thought there was a hint of mild surprise in his voice as though he'd expected her to look unhappy or discontented, or – God forbid – heartbroken that they were finished.

'Thank you,' she said. She'd come straight from the office, swopping her black jacket and white shirt for a floaty, red chiffon top over a matching vest. She'd worn it on purpose because it best covered her generous cleavage, something Gavin used to like seeing on display – but only when he was with her.

'So do you,' she added, closing her mind to the white lie. He'd also come from the office and had taken off his overcoat to reveal

4

a sharp grey suit and white shirt with a striped tie. He'd ordered a bottle of wine, pouring a generous glass for Grace, and a half glass for himself. His clothes looked like a perfectly arranged uniform, but his face looked pale, his eyes red-rimmed with exhaustion and lines that hadn't been there before.

'You're joking,' he said. 'I look wrecked. Thanks to a party last night, I didn't hit the sack until four, and I don't know how I crawled through today in the office. Then there was a cheese and wine event this afternoon. I could have done without that.' He sounded like it was a boast of sorts. The words 'wrecked' and 'party' had rarely occurred together in any of Gavin's sentences, never mind references to four in the morning.

'Out until four? You've turned over a new leaf,' Grace said, marvelling at the understatement.

'I was out with some accountancy heads I knew from college. Turns out one of them works in that building where you got stuck in the lift that day.' Gavin said it casually enough but she imagined that his eyes were keener than usual as he gazed at her.

'Really?' She said, equally casually. Her mind spun back to the October day when she'd called to a dressmaker to collect a dress that had been in for repair, and had got stuck in a lift between floors for almost an hour. She hoped Gavin hadn't guessed that it had been the very day she'd started to visualise what her life could be like without him in it.

Her hopes faded when he went on to say, sounding as if he was choosing his words carefully, 'Things were never … the same between us after that, Grace. God knows what you were thinking about, stuck in a dark lift, all alone, for the guts of an hour.' He raised an inquisitive eyebrow and his blue eyes held hers with a questioning glint.

Grace said, crossing her fingers against the lie under the table, 'I was far too panicked to think about anything except getting out in one piece.'

'I think it had a bigger effect on you than you realised.' She thought his eyes narrowed slightly but then he went on, changing the subject, saying quite casually, and not as if this was a whole new language for him, 'And I've more punishment lined up for tomorrow night, the new place in South William Street this time.'

'Hey, you've turned into a right party animal,' Grace said. 'The break has been good for both of us.'

'So in other words,' he said, tilting his head quizzically to one side, 'You haven't changed your mind. About us?' He smiled as he spoke, but there was a tightness in his face.

Grace felt on edge. She'd nothing to say to Gavin that he wanted to hear. The realisation that she'd rather be anywhere else but sitting across the table from him, struggling to make meaningless small talk, crept through her like a paralysis of sorts. She tried to pull herself together. It was over. She was free of him; free of the hundred and one things about him that had begun to aggravate her immensely in recent months. This was just a friendly Christmas drink for old times' sake. It had been a casual suggestion, tossed out for good measure the evening Gavin had moved out after they'd agreed to go their separate ways. It had suddenly hit Grace that after three years of being in a relationship, including six months of living together, this was actually it. He was about to walk out the door of her apartment and out of her life. So as a way of easing the parting, besides soothing her waves of guilt, Grace had heard herself say, without really meaning it, 'Meet you for a Christmas drink …?'

Gavin had responded, hesitating in the doorway, 'Are you sure?'

'Yes,' she'd said, managing to half convince herself. 'It'll be good to catch up and see how we're getting on …' Surely it was the least she could do?

'You mean in case all this is a mistake?'

'It'll be a chance to wish you a Happy Christmas, if nothing else …' She'd known even then that breaking up wasn't going to be a mistake.

Then earlier that day, four weeks after he'd moved out, Gavin had texted her suggesting they meet for that drink, and despite the drop of her heart, she'd agreed.

The crowd of young women at the next table were joined by more party-goers, who grabbed extra chairs and drew them across. One of the women bumped into Gavin's chair, and the impact caused the glittery Christmas tiara she was wearing to fall off her head. Gavin smiled good-humouredly as he picked it up, handing it to her with a funny quip and moving his own chair a little closer to Grace to give the women more space. Typical of mannerly Gavin, Grace thought. Even so, manners hadn't been enough for her.

A habit, was what she'd said, when she'd first begun to talk very tentatively about a break. She'd gone straight from college into Arcadia, a big insurance firm, where she still worked. Although she'd had casual dates, Gavin had been her first serious relationship, she'd pointed out gently. She hadn't really lived her life at all, she'd said. Neither had he. He *really* hadn't, continuing with evening studies after he'd gone straight from college to start his career in his uncle's accountancy firm. They were too dependent on each other and needed some breathing space. How did they know what they wanted out of life, the kind of people they could really be, when they hadn't really stretched their wings?

These were the words and phrases that she'd begun to drop into their conversations, as benignly as possible. Then somehow, when her suggestion of a temporary break – 'to see how it would feel' – hadn't met undue resistance, it had tentatively morphed into a total break. After all, she'd said, treading very carefully, it was the only way they'd learn to stand on their own feet, leaving them both free to find their rightful place in the world. They'd never do that if they were still looking back over their shoulders at each other, or planning on having a great reunion. Which wasn't to say it might never happen for them again, she'd said falteringly in the face of his sad smile.

To her utter relief, he'd agreed with her. In lots of ways, Gavin was too nice for his own good. Too mindful of Grace, far too attentive when it came to her needs, acutely observant of every move she made. But the day he'd left her apartment, it was as if a huge suffocating cloud had lifted from her life, something intangible and formless that she couldn't explain to anyone. Never one to interfere, even her Mum had admitted when she'd come home from Paris for a weekend, that she was slightly mystified at the way Grace had ended the relationship.

'It just wasn't doing anything for me,' Grace had told her. 'Gavin is, well, sometimes I found him *too* nice.'

'I don't think there's any such thing as being too much of a good guy,' her mother had said, her voice tentative as though she was afraid of what Grace might say or do. 'We need plenty of good manners to help us get through the ups and downs of everyday life. More so than ever in this day and age. I thought you and Gavin were all set for the altar rails.' Her mother had given Grace a studied look which Grace interpreted as there being something lacking in her, and that she hadn't fully appreciated Gavin's finer points or her good luck in landing a man like him. Not like her clever older sister Lucia, who'd only ever had a serious relationship with one man, the equally clever and successful Robert, and had dutifully married him in a blaze of perfect wedding glory.

Looking at Gavin across the table, Grace knew that far from missing him, she'd been utterly relieved to be on her own in the apartment without feeling like she was running out of air, not to mention her guilt for failing to muster up the requisite feelings of love and devotion.

'I haven't changed my mind,' Grace said softly, feeling guilty again because Gavin was staring at her as though he'd hoped for a different answer. 'I think we both needed to spread our wings.'

Something dulled in his eyes.

She clenched her hand, her fingernails digging into her palm. 'How's everything in the world of accountancy?' she asked. 'Still keeping them on their toes?' She forced herself to sound cheerful, knowing he liked talking about his career and his climb up the ladder. McCabe Corrigan had big-name clients on their list.

'I've just finished the latest round of exams and we've big stuff coming up in the New Year.'

'Partner here we come,' she said

'That's the plan. Hopefully, that one won't misfire,' he said pointedly.

She ignored his reference to broken plans. She knew they could trust Gavin to be diligent about every aspect of his casework. It helped that he had a kind of eager-to-please face. Sometimes in those last few weeks together that face had begun to irritate her immensely.

'And how's your cousin?' she asked.

'My cousin?'

'Yes, Trevor. You told me you were moving in with him.'

Gavin, in his astute wisdom and perfect timing, had entered the property ladder and bought a house as an investment when prices had plummeted at the lowest point of the recession, but it was on the outer edge of the commuter belt, so he'd it let out when he'd moved in to Grace's more convenient south Dublin apartment. He'd been unable to return there after the split with Grace, moving instead into the spare room in his cousin's apartment.

'Yep, it worked out handy enough,' he said. 'But it's just temporary until I find somewhere else. Are you still on your own?' he asked.

'Of course I am,' Grace said. 'Why?'

'Once or twice …' he gave her a half smile, and began to move the salt and pepper mills around the wooden tabletop as though he were shifting pieces on a chess board. 'I wondered, Grace, if you'd finished with me because you'd met someone new.'

He plonked down the salt cellar right in front of her as though he was declaring 'checkmate'.

'I don't know why you thought that,' she said.

'So you haven't, then ...'

'Hey, give me a chance,' she laughed, feeling hot and embarrassed. He was so intense, he could have been searching for irregularities in a revenue return. 'It's only been a few weeks. And who says I want anyone else in my life?'

'So even though there's no one else, we are *over*, over.'

'I guess we are ...' she spoke softly and looked as regretful as she could, given the fact that she knew she'd made the right decision. 'I hope you meet someone if that's what you want. Someone lovely. And I hope she'll really appreciate you and all your good qualities and make you feel amazing. You're on the way to the top of your career, you're a brilliant person – you deserve someone really special.' Was she really trotting all this out? Grace wanted to kick herself for sounding so sanctimonious.

'But you won't be my someone special.' He smiled crookedly. 'No more Gav 'n' Grace ...'

Gav 'n' Grace; it had been their pet name, their signature. He'd made it up, thinking it sounded cool. She'd begun to hate it.

'No, I think you and I ... just kind of fizzled out.' She twirled her silver bracelet round and round. Then she remembered that he'd given it to her for her twenty-ninth birthday in September, and she allowed her sleeve to drop down and cover it in case he thought it was significant that she was wearing it tonight.

'And here was I hoping you might have changed your mind and realised we were in it for the long haul.' He gave her a soft, lop-sided smile. 'Before the split, I'd started to look at some rings so I could pop the question. I thought Christmas would be the perfect time.'

Her stomach tightened at the mention of engagement rings. There was a burst of laughter and loud whoops from the adjacent table, all the more off-putting in its total variance with what was happening at theirs.

'Just as well we found out before we made any big commitment,' Grace said, feeling sad and hollow.

'Found out what?'

She was suddenly at a loss. 'Found out … that we weren't meant to be,' she said lamely.

She'd known that ending the romance wasn't going to be easy, but she wished he hadn't mentioned marriage, reminding her of the extent to which she'd let him down. It had been the first real relationship for both of them and now there was nothing much to show for it.

'Weren't we?' He took her hand in his. It felt a little sweaty and she swallowed hard. She would have preferred that he not touch her and she hoped it didn't show in her face. 'No worries, Grace. I hope you'll have a good Christmas,' he said, squeezing her hand. 'And I hope you have a great rest-of-your-life, you deserve the best. Obviously I'm sorry it won't be me, but no hard feelings, okay?'

'Okay,' she said. 'Thanks.'

'So this is it, our final goodbye then.'

'Seems as if it is.'

'Still friends?'

'Still friends,' she said.

'Good. Do you mind if I run now? I'm a little worse for wear after last night and I need to get out of here.'

'Sure.' She was relieved to have a legitimate reason to slide her hand out of his. She picked up her bag but he stalled her.

'No, you stay and finish the wine. I feel like shite – sorry – and I need some fresh air so I'm going to make a dash for it.' He was already up on his feet and shrugging into his coat. He filled her glass with the last of the wine, and he came around to give her a kiss on the cheek. She thought he murmured something about always loving her, but it was lost in the laughter coming from the next table and then he was gone, sidling through gaps in the too-packed tables towards the door.

She was left alone, left high and dry at Christmas-party central, his final, sad little smile searing through her brain.

I'd started to look at some rings.

For a long moment, Grace couldn't breathe; everything swam around her, a sea of curious faces throwing her sidelong glances, a jumble of silly party hats and mistletoe being tossed around the adjacent table, overhead strands of fairy lights blinking in her face and competing with the blaze from the laneway outside. Everything was embellished even further with a backing track of a maudlin Christmas song about being lonely at Christmas.

She saw her reflection in the plate glass window, her face pale, her short blonde hair gleaming. She took a gulp of her wine, her lips feeling rubbery. She'd done the right thing, she was sure of it, so why did she feel so crap? Gavin had looked so sad, that's why. She'd dashed all his hopes, his expectations, his dreams, with her rejection. She'd seen right through his attempts this evening to make it sound like he was having the time of his life, with parties stacking up around him. He'd probably forced himself to go out with the gang of accountants last night. She was to blame for the greeny-grey look of him. She was also to blame for him being lonely at Christmas – but a ring around her finger would have felt like a noose around her neck.

She took more gulps of her wine. Under the table, she clenched her knees together to stop them from knocking wildly. She should never have agreed to meet him. She'd forgotten how much courage it had taken to start the splitting-up process and finally say goodbye, and now she felt weak and dazed.

Her glass was almost empty. Then as she was sitting there, too shaky to move, Danny appeared, whirling into her life like a gulp of sparkling fresh air.

Chapter Two

'Are you okay?'

Grace blinked, looked up and slowly let out her breath. The man gradually came into focus. Thirtyish, or near enough, same as her. Friendly green eyes, a wide, generous mouth, a black leather jacket, and narrow, jean-clad hips; best of all, no party hat cocked at an angle on his unruly muddy-brown hair, and no sign of any mistletoe. She tried to speak, but her mouth was dry so she took the last sip of wine.

'I'm fine, thanks,' she said, smoothing her hair behind her ears, realising that her fingers were trembling and she wasn't fine after all. She knew if she tried to get up, her legs would buckle from under her.

'I thought you looked a bit shaken,' he said, his eyes warm with concern. 'That guy, he wasn't giving you any grief was he? He shouldn't have walked out and left you like this.'

'No, it's fine. We were just having a Christmas drink. Ex-boyfriend.'

'*Ex*-boyfriend?'

'Yeah, we split up recently ... hey, why am I telling you this?' Timing, that was why. Plus, he had the kind of empathetic face that made her feel he was safe to talk to.

'You don't have to tell me anything at all,' he said, in a lilting, west-of-Ireland voice, the warm tone of which matched his face. 'Will I wait here for a few minutes to make sure you're all right? Can't have you sitting there, crying all alone.'

'Am I crying?' she asked, giving a shaky laugh. She put her hand up to her face and felt the tears on her cheek. She rummaged for a tissue and swiftly dabbed them away. 'You must be Fireman Sam coming to the rescue,' she said. He was someone you wouldn't mind giving you a fireman's lift. On the contrary.

He grinned a charismatic grin. 'So you do need to be rescued. I don't know who Fireman Sam is and I'm not sure how good my rescuing skills are but Danny McBride is willing to give it a go.'

'Well Danny, it's very convenient that you're standing there right now,' she said, her voice still a little trembly, 'because you're blocking the view.'

'Blocking the view?'

'Yeah, the view that gang at the next table is getting – the ones who can't seem to stop staring at me.'

'Glad I'm useful for something.'

She leaned back and scrutinised him properly. 'Where did you come from? Haven't you anything better to do with your time? Some party to go to?'

He said, with a perfectly straight face, 'I'm due in the North Pole shortly. I need to help an important guy assemble a few teddy bears. Other than that, no.'

'Okay, you can sit down,' she said, making up her mind swiftly, even though he didn't answer the first part of her question. After the strain and tension of talking to Gavin, Danny and his friendly manner made for a welcome distraction. Sitting in the chair just vacated by Gavin, he blocked her from the view of the women at the next table, like some kind of personal bodyguard.

He poured her a glass of water. 'Get this into you,' he said. 'All of it.'

'Thanks. You're a friend in need. And Grace Bailey could use a friendly face right now.'

He made a funny face. 'Is this friendly enough, Grace?'

'Mmm, sort of.'

He caught the waitress's attention and ordered a fresh carafe of water. It appeared almost instantly, even though the gastropub was jammed, because a guy like him had no problem getting service. Danny McBride's green eyes were fringed with thick dark lashes. When he slid off his jacket and scarf, he was wearing a black jumper underneath. He had nice hands. He poured more water, taking a glass for himself, and he was so easy to talk to compared with edgy Gavin that she found herself unwinding little by little.

'So, you've split from your boyfriend.'

'Yes. A few weeks ago.'

'Ah … did he … or did you …?'

She hesitated.

'It's good to talk to someone neutral, you know,' he said. 'Like a stranger on a plane. No strings. Honest. I'd forget whatever you said as soon as I walk out of here.'

How come she felt so at ease? And so comfortable with him? As though she'd known him forever? 'It was me,' she said, relieved to unburden herself. 'I suggested a break and it snowballed from there to a total split. I felt so bad about it the day he moved out that I suggested a Christmas drink for old times' sake, but now I know that wasn't a good idea. We'd parted on good terms,' Grace went on, 'so I was quite happy to meet him tonight for a Christmas drink, only it was harder than I realised. I thought it was just a drink for old times' sake, that he'd become as … bored with me as I was with him. But I was wrong.'

'Bored?' his eyes twinkled. 'Don't you know life's far too precious to waste one single minute feeling bored?'

'Yes, but he's so nice, really, Gavin, and I know I hurt him. He told me tonight that he'd planned on asking me to marry him.'

Danny gave her a thoughtful look. 'And what would you have said?'

She shrugged, forced a half-smile and took a refreshing mouthful of water. 'Unfortunately I would have wanted to say "no".'

'Well then. Isn't it just as well you didn't let it get that far and ended it when you did?'

'I felt sad and kind of crappy. And guilty in a way because I know I hurt him.'

'And if you'd agreed to marry him, to save him that hurt, then what?'

She didn't answer.

'What would your life have been like in five years' time?' he asked.

She looked up at the festive bunting, at the strands of Christmassy garlands and outside to the procession of people passing along the laneway under the rainbow of lights. She turned back to him. 'Don't ask …' she sighed. 'I haven't a clue other than it wouldn't have been me. Still, it's probably the worst time of the year to remind someone that you don't want them anymore,' she finished up, horrified to hear a slight break in her voice.

He smiled. 'Grace, if there's one thing I've learned it's that the loneliest people in the world are those who are trying to be someone they shouldn't be.'

'And when did you learn that?'

It was his turn to be silent for a moment. Behind his friendly banter, she sensed something deep and thoughtful about him. He topped up their water and gave her a wry grin. 'When I learned to stop following the pack. Eventually.'

'I see,' she said, wondering what pack he'd been following, knowing intuitively not to ask.

'If you didn't feel the right kind of stuff for Gavin, it would have been crazy to pretend, for both your sakes. God knows what you would have been like in a few years' time.'

'Cracking up, most likely. Or living a half life, like a kind of shadow.'

'So what made you decide to end things?'

She felt a smile rippling across her face. 'I was stuck in a lift one day, a couple of months ago,' she said. 'I began to think what life without Gavin would be like ... and I knew then that I had to make the break.' There was a pause, Grace only half aware of the laughter coming from the adjoining table.

Danny asked, 'Well then ... you were right. Apart from tonight, were you doing okay?'

'I was doing fine.'

'That's great, but I don't think we can sit here much longer dragging out a jug of water,' Danny said, pushing the carafe away. 'Would you like some food? Or a drink?'

'No, thanks, I'd rather leave,' she said, knowing she could go on talking to him all night, but needing to get away from where she'd finally said goodbye to Gavin.

'How about we take a walk up to the Christmas markets on the Green?'

'I hardly know you, Danny McBride,' she smiled, because it scarcely mattered.

'I'm twenty-nine next birthday, originally from Mayo, that beautiful great footballing legend of a county ... I love my motorbike, and music, and holidays by the sea – preferably in Mayo – and home cooking ... I've been working for myself since I was made redundant – tell you about it sometime – but if all that sounds too scary, I promise I won't abduct you, scouts' honour.'

'Were you in the scouts?' She was playing for time. She'd already felt, like a sense of fate, that from the moment he'd stopped at her table and the instant connection between them, it would lead to a long conversation they were just getting started on.

'I was, a lifetime ago,' he said, the ghost of something passing across his features, like a hint of regret. It made him seem all the more human and vulnerable, and it clicked with her. His face cleared as he smiled at her. 'Your turn …'

'Mmm, thirty next birthday, work in home insurance, love books and music, can't really cook, drive my mother's car … and you might see this as a heinous crime, but I've never been to Mayo …' she pulled a face.

He grinned. 'I'll try not to hold it against you.'

Outside, they walked down the laneway and came out onto a teeming Grafton Street where they had to battle crowds of shoppers and groups of carol singers, and she'd no choice but to cling to his hand in case they were separated. He tucked their linked hands into his jacket pocket. It felt good. Too good. He stood directly under a big, sparkling chain of Christmas lights and told her to look straight up.

It was like looking up into a million shining, white stars.

'If a guy asks you to marry him, that's how you should be feeling on the inside,' he says. 'Beautiful, glittering and absolutely amazing.'

'When you put it like that …' she shook her head, unable to remember ever feeling so exuberant about Gavin. Secure, yes; settled, very much; and then had come the creeping suffocation and edgy irritation, for which she'd blamed herself. Something warm washed over her at the way Danny's face appeared, superimposed on the lights. This was crazy. It was *mad*. But it was *nice* mad. Happy mad.

They walked up to the Christmas markets on St Stephen's Green, and strolled along the festively decorated huts, inhaling the medley of cooking aromas, chatting about what Christmas meant to them. Danny ordered hot dogs and they munched them as they walked along, carried with the crowd, Grace beginning to feel more like herself. She looked up at the necklaces of lights strung between the huts.

'I love the way the way the city centre is lit up,' she said, 'and everywhere else, all the houses and apartments have Christmas shining through their windows. I think it's my favourite part of the season. What's yours?'

'I love the movies. It's hard to watch *Home Alone* or *Miracle on 34th Street* without feeling like a kid again …' He stopped to shoot his hot dog wrapper into a bin. Grace finished hers, wiped her mouth and tossed her napkin and wrapper.

'What are you doing for Christmas?' she asked.

'I'm off home to the family in Mayo,' he said.

'Who's family for you?' she asked. Finding out about him gave her a warm glow inside, like unwrapping a birthday gift you knew you were going to enjoy.

'My parents and two sisters.'

'I bet you're the apple of their eye.'

It was there again, a hint of regret. 'Not quite,' he said.

'I'm spending Christmas with family too,' she said, deciding to steer away from his family.

'Where's that? I could have sworn you're from Dublin.'

'I am. I rent an apartment in Rathbrook Hall. It's in south county Dublin, at the far end of the Luas. I meant I'll be with my family for the day, my parents, my sister and her husband. My parents are working in Paris at the moment but they're coming home for a few days and we're spending Christmas day in my sister Lucia's house.'

'Nice one.'

'It will be, except she's determined to make it an ultra-perfect day and I think she's already been to Christmas cookery lessons and table-arranging classes. I'll be the one turning up with the bubbly and shop-bought dessert, trying to pass it off as my own.'

'Nothing wrong with passing off shop-bought dessert to impress the family,' he grinned. 'We all have a few skeletons in the cupboard.'

'Even you?'

'Yeah, sure. And I'd say my skeletons are far grimier than yours.' He stared at her thoughtfully but she sensed he was seeing something else instead of her.

'So it is safe to be out with you like this?' she teased.

'Probably not,' he said. 'What do you think?' Then he laughed, his green eyes warm with amusement. He caught her hand, brought it to his mouth and kissed it. She was charged with something that crackled through her veins like a shot of electricity. His mouth was surprisingly warm or else her hand was cold. Either way, he didn't let go of it and she loved how comfortable and snug it felt tucked up in his. And she didn't want to say goodbye to him after tonight. She wanted more of Danny McBride in her life.

'I like you, Grace Bailey,' he said. 'What are you doing New Year's Eve?'

Giddiness rose up inside her. She didn't know this guy, yet on another level, she did. It was something that began thrumming in her heart when he had stopped at the table; a recognition, a familiarity, as though it was part of a grand, orchestrated plan that he arrive just then, and she had been waiting for him to come along and infuse her with a new kind of vitality.

'I've lots of invitations but I haven't decided yet,' she said, laughing at the blatant lie.

'How about spending it with me?'

'I'll add your invitation to my list,' she said.

'Make sure you put it right on top. I need to talk to you about your New Year's resolutions. And mine.'

'*Your* resolutions?'

'Yes, I have a bucket list of things I want to do that I might need some help with.'

'A bucket list?' she felt a sudden chill. 'Isn't that something …?'

'Nah …' he shook his head easily. 'It's a life-affirming list of things I want to do before I'm thirty.'

'Oh.' She smiled at him and squeezed his hand. 'I'll think about it.'

By then Christmas, along with the after-effects of Gavin and the thought of him being lonely without her, would have passed. What better time for a new beginning than New Year's Eve? And who better than with this man and the nice mad – happy mad – way he made her feel?

Chapter Three

They couldn't wait until New Year's Eve.

They met up several times before Christmas Eve, laughing and joking and making the city their playground, like kids determined to soak up every ounce of the Christmas atmosphere; Grace allowing herself to be swept up in the fun moments, with nothing else on her mind. One afternoon they caught a matinee viewing of *Miracle on 34th Street*, Grace wiping surreptitious tears away, then another day they went ice skating, and Grace loved the feel of clinging to Danny as they whirled around. They had a Saturday stroll through a wintry Phoenix Park up to the wonderfully festive Farmleigh. The day before Christmas Eve, they even joined in on some carol singing on O'Connell Street, right outside the GPO, snuggled in scarves and gloves.

They filled each other in on their lives, and she told Danny that Gavin had been her first serious relationship. On leaving secondary school she'd studied for a business degree. By the time she'd graduated from college, Ireland was on the brink of a recession, but a university qualification had opened a door for her into a job in the claims adjustment section of Arcadia Insurances, and she was lucky she hadn't had to emigrate for a job like a lot of her friends. She often found she was the one who was delegated to break the bad news to unfortunate customers about the shortfall in their insurances.

'According to my manager,' she told him, 'I'm good at listening to sob stories and handing out virtual Kleenex over the phone lines.'

'I can guess the rest … because you have the human touch and persuasive communication skills?' Danny said. 'But is this really what you want to do? How you want to spend your life? It's the only one you have, you know.'

'Let me think about that.'

'Well do. Too many people just drift into things without thinking about them.'

'Says the voice of experience,' she joked.

'Unfortunately so,' he said, looking unusually serious. She sensed there was a lot more behind his answer, but she didn't push.

Danny told her he'd gone to college in Galway. He'd recently been made redundant from a website design company that had been struggling, but he was turning it into an opportunity. He was using his redundancy package to help set up his own business, and he was currently working from home – in his case, a bedsit in Harold's Cross, where he sometimes needed ear plugs to drown out the sound of the other occupants, mostly singletons from Mayo like himself.

Grace got through Christmas with her family, a little embarrassed that her parents and Lucia were extra kind to her, fussing around and thinking she was still getting over Gavin. Instead, she was quietly hugging thoughts of Danny to herself, like a shiny secret. But on New Year's Eve, as she walked towards Trinity College where they'd agreed to meet, she wondered if the spark between them would still be there. Maybe she'd been too caught up in a festive whirlwind beforehand to see Danny properly. She could have been painting him in a rosy light, and might be wrong to start imagining a new kind of future with him. After all, she'd only just extricated herself from a long relationship that had been fraught near the end, and the last thing she'd expected was to be seeing someone else so soon. Then again, she'd laughed more with Danny over a handful of dates than she'd laughed with Gavin over the past year.

But she needn't have worried. Danny was waiting for her; she saw him before he saw her. Her heart lifted and she could no more turn back the tide than slow down her footsteps as she walked towards him, feeling she was stepping onto some kind of magic ground.

'I wasn't sure if you'd come,' he said, looking at her with undisguised happiness. 'I was wondering if it had all been a dream.'

'What kind of dream?' she asked.

'The best kind that you never want to wake up from.'

* * *

They sat in a small, quaint pub, tucked away from the busy city streets and noisy crowds, where the curtains were closed across the windows and heat radiated from a cosy log fire. Most of the clientele seemed to be inner city locals, content to have a relaxing night seeing in the New Year. Danny went up to the bar and came back with a pint for himself and a glass of wine for Grace.

'How was your Christmas?' he asked.

'It was the perfect Christmas Day,' Grace said. 'Lucia surpassed even her own high standards, and everything ran like clockwork. There was even the colour-coordinated toilet roll in the guest bathroom, so I felt a bit of a fraud with my Marks and Spencer's dessert. There are five years between me and Lucia, but it might as well be five centuries, we're so different.'

'Isn't that what puts the fun into life?' he said.

'How was Christmas with your family?' she asked, remembering the reference he'd made to having grimy skeletons in the closet and the hint of regret in his eyes. But whatever had happened, if anything had happened, he wasn't about to say.

'It was fine,' he said. 'Quiet enough. I came back to Dublin a little earlier than expected.'

'Are you close to your sisters – or like them at all?'

'We're all totally different. Great fun altogether. How did we get on to families?' he said. 'There are other things I'm more interested in finding out about you.'

They chatted for a while about their favourite books and movies and music, Danny admitting that it was all *Lord of the Rings* for him and that his childhood holidays running wild on Achill Island were his most memorable. Grace told him about her J1 experiences waitressing in Boston and Cape Cod with her friend Karen and her cousin, trying to sleep on wafer-thin mattresses and finding ten different ways to eat pot noodles.

After a while Danny said, 'So how does Grace Bailey, all grown up, intend to make the most and the very best of the next twelve months?'

'I don't have a bucket list like you,' Grace said.

'You must have a few ideas of what you'd like to do.'

'I feel as though I've hit the pause button after the last few months. Actually,' she went on, sitting back against the banquette, feeling relaxed enough to tell him, 'I think everything has been on hold inside me for a long time. For three years it was all about Gavin, and now I'm just getting used to having my own space back, so I haven't yet figured out what I really want …' her voice trailed away. 'Apart from, well I enjoyed the times we went out before Christmas, it was the most fun I've had in ages,' she admitted shyly.

'Good. You could start by asking yourself what was the most important day in your life so far.'

She burst out laughing. 'I knew you'd make it easy somehow.'

'Well go on.'

Grace stared into the heart of the crackling log fire, and ran through a number of milestone days. 'Mmm, the best day of my life …' she hesitated. 'I think it has to be the day of my college graduation,' she said, smiling at the memory of the crisp, clear

November day and the sense of celebration, the excited buzz in the university grounds, her feeling of accomplishment and pride.

'Why?' he asked.

'That should be obvious.'

'Not to me. Tell me.'

'It was the culmination of all my school years and it was a success. I did well. I got my degree. My parents were happy. They were proud of me. Even Lucia was delighted.'

'So you think the most important day in your life so far was linked to making your parents proud of you and Lucia happy on account of your academic achievement?'

When he put it like that, it made her think. 'What's wrong with that? I worked hard to get there.'

'There's nothing wrong with that, but was your college course what you wanted to do with your heart and soul?'

'It wasn't medicine or dentistry,' she said. 'And it wasn't a first in economics, like my brainbox sister ...' her voice trailed away.

'Forget about Lucia – what did you really want to do?'

'My heart said English, but my head said otherwise. Even at that,' she admitted, 'there's a world of a difference between Lucia's big job and my job in Arcadia. She's senior manager in sales and marketing in the Dublin HQ of Izobel, the multinational health and beauty group. She's clever – very clever. On top of her Masters qualification, she's now studying something called behavioural economics, whatever that's supposed to be. She's an expert on behaviour – excellent behaviour. She could probably give the lectures on it.'

'You're still talking about your sister and not you,' Danny said.

'I suppose that's telling me something.'

'Only if you're listening,' Danny said. 'Education is important because it opens doors and gives you more opportunities in life. But I think the most important day in your life is the day you're born.'

She felt a smile play around her lips. 'I had a feeling you'd have something deep and meaningful to offer.'

'It's all very simple. From before conception to the actual birth, have you any idea what the odds are on not being born?'

'No, I can't even guess.'

'The odds of not even being born are stupendous, so you owe it to yourself to have the best life you can, and the one you really want to be living, whatever it is.'

She laughed. 'Hold on, Danny, it's not always that straightforward.'

'It all comes down to your choices. Just think … if there were no obstacles in your way, what would you really and truly love to do with your life?'

'I need to think about that …' she said.

'Do that, and report back to me. What did you love doing as a child? What makes your heart beat faster? If you knew you had six months to live, what would you do with that time? If you weren't here with me tonight, how best would you be celebrating the New Year?'

'That last bit is easy. I'd be out clubbing with Karen and Suz, my friends in Arcadia.'

'The same Karen as in Boston with the pot noodles?'

'Yeah, we met in college and we were lucky enough to get jobs in Arcadia, almost the last to be taken on before a recruitment freeze, and we started the same day as Suz.'

Her friends had already texted her, in case she wasn't coming out with them on account of feeling nostalgic because it was her first New Year since breaking up with Gavin. Tonight they planned to be out downing cocktails and wine and getting happily woozy before the clock struck midnight.

Instead, Grace waltzed with Danny across the Rosie Hackett Bridge at midnight, where the dark velvety Liffey flowed underneath, to the strains of music coming from the party down on College Green and the distant peal of bells from Christchurch. They stopped and looked at each other, and Grace felt a big grin breaking across her face as he threw his arms around her and pulled her close. His face was cold against hers but his kiss was warm and tender. Then it became deep and searching, and she didn't want it to end or him to let go. They broke away eventually and she was trembling.

'Happy New Year, Grace,' he said into the side of her neck.

'Happy New Year, Danny.'

'I hope this year brings you everything you wish for.'

'And I hope all your dreams come true this year.'

'It's getting off to a brilliant start,' he said.

'It is, isn't it?'

'I'm glad you feel like that too. This is the best New Year's Eve ever.'

'Absolutely.'

They stood entwined, looking at each other in the glow of a street lamp, enclosed in a world of their own, the sound of the city and clamour of nearby festive crowds floating away on the air. Danny lifted her off her feet as he held her even tighter against him in a great big bear hug. Grace knew there were more brilliant fireworks going off in her heart than those lighting up the city streets.

* * *

When Grace woke up on New Year's Day she felt lighter somehow. Happier. At ease. Then her mobile rang, Danny's name popped up on the screen and a surge of joy rippled all the way through her.

'Where are you?' he asked.

'Why, where am I supposed to be?'

'Down here, ready and waiting.'

Elation made her dizzy. 'Down where, exactly?'

'I'm down in the car park. Rathbrook Hall. This is where you live, isn't it?'

'Yes, but–' she was out of bed. She ran to the window, pulled back the curtains. Outside it was a calm, sunnyish morning, kind of quiet and peaceful, like the world was waking up slowly to the brand new year after the partying of the night before. Everything inside her was whirling around like a child's spinning top. Last night, Danny had said he'd call and they'd go somewhere on his bike, but she hadn't been expecting him this early.

'Give me ten minutes,' she said, feverishly calculating how quickly she could shower and dress. 'Do you mind waiting fifteen?' Maybe she should ask him up. Offer him some coffee. Then again she hardly knew him and she didn't want him witnessing her tearing around the apartment like a crazed maniac while she threw herself together.

'Fifteen minutes,' he said. 'Then I'm coming looking for you.'

She laughed. What did you wear on a motorbike? What would it be like with Danny today? She paused; breathed in and out; closed her eyes. *Focus,* Grace. Shower, dress, makeup, bag, boots, jacket. Could you eat a banana and put on mascara at the same time?

Down in the basement car park, he was leaning against a shiny black motorbike, dressed in leathers. Arms folded. Waiting for her. There were two crash helmets balanced on the seat of the bike. Coming down in the lift she'd felt overcome with a tidal wave of shyness, but now it dissolved as he smiled at her with those gorgeous eyes. Ten minutes later she was leaning into his back as the bike surged up the ramp and out into the cold, clear January day, where he took the motorway for Bray. It was the most unusual New Year's Day that Grace had ever experienced. They climbed Bray Head, taking their time, Grace laughing in between pants and puffs at the effort involved in getting to the top.

'Good job I don't have a hangover,' she said.

'It'll be worth it,' he said, taking her hand and helping her up through a forest trail, where the tops of the trees met overhead, blotting out the sun, and the floor was a thick carpet of pine needles.

'Why do I get the feeling you might be right?'

Up on Bray Head, the folds and valleys of Wicklow fell away behind them, spreading like a vivid carpet under the pristine morning light, encircled by a looping chain of hazy blue mountain peaks. Far beneath them, the shimmering sweep of the sea appeared to be motionless. Grace filled her lungs with slow breaths of the cool air.

'Being here now is as good as it gets,' Danny said.

'I'm glad you dragged me up here,' she said. 'It's a brilliant way to say hello to the New Year, and it's blowing the last of the cobwebs away.'

'What kind of cobwebs?' Danny asked, his eyes crinkling.

'Oh, this and that,' she said, smiling at him, as a warm glow spread through her. 'New year, new me.'

'Good. That's the whole idea of today.'

He took her by the hand and walked her around the summit, pointing out some landmarks. Thanks to this man, Grace felt everything that had held her trapped slipping away from her and being picked up by the fluttering breeze and lifted far away from her, all the way out to sea, until they vanished, way beyond the hazy blue line of the horizon.

Chapter Four

It was a breezy Saturday afternoon, unexpectedly bright for the middle of January, and they were muffled up in jackets, boots, scarves and gloves, laughing like excited children, bumping into each other as they chased a butterfly-shaped kite and watched it swooping and soaring, billowed by the wind currents, a splodge of bright, cheerful colour against the grey-blue sky.

Grace tried to run down the field, to force the kite higher against the capricious breeze, but Danny stopped her.

'Just relax and let the wind do the work,' he said, showing her how to stand with her back to the wind and spool out her string. The breeze ruffled his hair and his eyes were warm and interested whenever his gaze rested on her. She wanted to take a selfie but he gently put her off, saying other people's phones, even Grace's, were better off without his mug shot. And why miss the best of the moment looking for the perfect angle?

Had it been an afternoon in her previous life, before the new Grace, she might have spent it in a shopping centre, with or without Gavin, stopping for a drink if she were with him, or a coffee without him, or else they might have relaxed in front of the television or gone for a pizza or to an early evening movie show.

But that was all over now and this was different. There was

something calming about being out, moving around under the high January sky, with the colourful kite soaring gracefully on the breeze. It filled her with a peace as well as a playfulness that she hadn't experienced in a long time. Even the park itself was full of a stark wintry allure. There was something beautiful in the pattern of denuded trees and the life-affirming sight of pools of snowdrops pushing up through the ground along the path. And whatever it was, whatever was happening in the course of this happy, carefree afternoon, her heightened awareness of Danny by her side, loping around the park with her, sent something magical imploding in her chest every time their eyes met in a laugh.

* * *

Something more magical again left her breathless with desire when he came up to her apartment afterwards for coffee.

He'd been here a couple of times already; they'd sat talking into the late hours, chatting about anything and everything. In his attempts to help Grace to see what she was most passionate about, and what her New Year's resolutions should include, Danny now knew exactly what she loved as a child (reading and playing in the school yard), what delighted her most as a teenager (joining the adult library; passing out Lucia in height until she realised that she felt like a clodhopper around her petite, elegant sister), the events that most shaped her school years (discovering she would only ever be average at school, Lucia always being more mature, brighter and cleverer; her brilliant English teacher; wanting to make her lovely parents proud of her). She didn't know as much about Danny, apart from the things on his bucket list, as he'd been the one posing the questions and had gone home after a few hugs and kisses.

That afternoon though, Grace felt different. Something passed between them, out in the January park, a deep-down connection and a certainty that hit her with all the power of a cosmic force field and made her want to leap for joy. She sensed it humming between them as they went up in the lift together, Grace fidgeting with the tail of her red and yellow kite as a form of distraction.

'So that's number one off your bucket list,' she said to Danny. 'Kite-flying.'

'Only a half a dozen more to go,' he said. 'And I might add on one or two more,' he went on, the look in his eyes making her weak.

'I'm going to hang this up,' she said, when they were in her apartment. 'It's a shame to leave it lying somewhere.' She decided to hang it off the side of the tall kitchen press that housed the fridge-freezer, but she needed Danny's help. He found it easy to reach up, anchoring the head of the kite to the top of the side panel and letting it stream downwards in a blaze of yellow and red. She was standing close to him as he did this and when he pivoted back round he was just inches from her, his mouth directly at the level of her eyes. There was a moment when everything went blank, as though she was stunned, and in the next moment everything shifted around like a colourful Ferris wheel, and she bit her lip and placed her index finger on his full mouth and traced the outline.

'Danny,' she whispered, all her nerve endings suddenly alive, straining for his touch.

'Grace,' he murmured, taking her finger away. But he didn't let it go; he caught her hand and held it so that it nestled between both of his. Coming from him, it felt like a warm and intimate gesture. He held her gaze and the way he was looking at her almost made her forget to breathe. His eyes darkened and she couldn't help leaning into him, and tilting her head, her lips millimetres from his.

He drew back slightly. 'Grace ... are you sure?'

'Yes,' she whispered, her skin a quivering mass of nerve endings.

His gaze scanned her face, taking in every curve and dip from her forehead to her chin. For an infinitesimal moment she saw a flicker of uncertainty in Danny's face.

Uncertainty? Danny? It seemed strange for someone so at ease in their own skin. Then he kissed her at last, a slow, deep and very thorough kiss, his lips teasing, his hands anchoring her to him. Although she was afraid she might dissolve with the sensations he was arousing in her, something pure and bright and beautiful flashed through her body, and she knew it was the best moment of her life so far. Until they moved into her bedroom and she realised his kisses were only a very pale shadow of what it was like to go to bed with Danny McBride and have him slowly and teasingly take off her clothes, and inch down her pants, and kiss every part of her aching skin, telling her she was beautiful, making her *feel* beautiful, stroking and soothing her as she tingled in places where she'd never tingled before, especially savouring the long drawn out moment he finally, slowly, sensually, filled her up … again and again.

Afterwards it rained, drumming down against Grace's bedroom window. They listened to it as they lay together cuddled under the duvet.

'I think that maybe you should stay the night,' she said, curled into his chest, enjoying the touch of his hot skin against hers. A fresh spatter of rain hurled itself against the window. Snuggled together, the bed was a warm and cosy cocoon. She was still floating on some kind of high. No way was she sending him home.

Danny ran his fingers through her hair, sending delicious shivers around her head. She wanted to stay in this perfect moment forever.

'Funny, I was thinking the same myself,' he said. 'I'd like to kiss you awake in the morning.'

He did.

He ended up staying until Sunday evening, and two weeks later, he moved in.

But first, there was the little matter of Grace telling her family.

Chapter Five

'So come on, Grace, spit it out,' Karen said, breaking her blueberry muffin into bite-sized pieces.

'Spit what out?' Grace looked innocently at Karen while she made up her mind. Maybe telling her friends about Danny could be a trial run for breaking the news to Lucia.

'Your new man,' Karen grinned.

'Yeah,' Suz joined in, dipping her finger into flakes of her croissant. 'It's not fair on us to be keeping him a secret.'

'Who says I'm keeping any secrets?' Grace asked.

'We do,' Suz said. 'It didn't take us long to figure it out.'

'One: this is the third weekend in a row you haven't come out with us, including New Year's Eve,' Karen said. 'Two: you're going around with the kind of grin on your face that spells out good, lusty sex, so three: there's definitely a new guy in your life.'

'Maybe I just want to stay in and chill,' Grace said.

Karen shook her head. 'Uh huh, no way. You might be staying in, but I'd guess it's more like hot and steamy.'

Grace hesitated and looked around the Arcadia canteen, her hands cradling a mug of coffee. The canteen was noisy with the usual Monday morning hubbub, where catching up with weekend gossip was the order of the day. They were up on the fifth floor with a view of city-centre rooftops, and the January sky outside was a cold, pale grey. She had a sudden longing to be outside in the fresh air, rather than being stuck in here with the rest of the day to get through and four more days until the weekend. Four more days after today, during which she'd be the bearer of bad news to plenty of customers who found themselves underinsured.

'Life's too short to waste a single minute feeling bored,' Danny had said. She wondered what she could be doing with her life if she wasn't in this job. Then her thoughts turned like a magnet to Danny and she wondered what he was doing right now.

'See? You have that dreamy look on your face, the kind that says you're thinking about it,' Suz said wickedly.

'Hey!'

'Is he good in bed?'

'Never mind,' Grace said, feeling the skin on her face heating up.

Suz and Karen exchanged conspiratorial nods. 'I think she's answered that question,' Karen said.

'Okay, okay …' Grace relented.

Karen and Suz were delighted she'd moved on so quickly after Gavin. And Danny sounded wonderful. He could only be good for Grace, they said, if he was putting that glinty light in her eyes.

Lucia was something else.

* * *

Sitting in the café in Harvey Nichols in Dundrum Town Centre, Grace watched Lucia approach.

Lucia was all-over lovely – there was no other way to describe her. From the top of her sleek, shiny dark hair, down to her elegant feet clad in patent leather pumps, she was perfectly groomed. She was a petite five-foot-two, compared to Grace's five-foot-seven. Today she was wearing a cream woollen jacket with a collar of feathery cream fur that softly framed her heart-shaped face, her hair was caught back in a sexy chignon, and she could, as usual, have just stepped out of a beauty parlour. Or with much the same ease, stepped onto a podium.

Lucia often gave marketing and sales talks at industry seminars on the latest innovations in health and beauty. It was part of her high-flying career. Grace was terribly proud of her, and she envied Lucia's ability to stand up fearlessly in front of large audiences. Lucia said it all sounded far grander than it was in reality. Still, she had a stylish wardrobe to match her corporate image and a state-of-the-art office just north of the docklands. Although she did work long, sometimes unsociable hours, these included glamorous receptions mingling with other bright, talented people and standing around sipping wine and exchanging clever ideas.

Even her house was a fitting backdrop to Lucia's successful lifestyle. Sometimes when she visited her sister, Grace found it easy to imagine she was moving around in a photo shoot for a *Better Homes* catalogue. Lucia's house had lots of glass and shiny white surfaces. It was tucked into a cul-de-sac in Mount Lismore, a leafy enclave surrounded by perimeter railings and mature landscaping close to Clonsilla, a north Dublin village. Occasionally Grace had wondered if Lucia felt the need to tick all the must-have mod con boxes as though to prove to herself and the world at large that she deserved full marks for having the perfect, A+ home, until she reminded herself that the brilliant Lucia of all people, with her high powered job in Izobel Group, certainly didn't need to prove anything to anybody, unlike far-less-brilliant Grace.

Lucia's big, expressive brown eyes were full of warmth as she greeted Grace, kissing her on the cheek, and she slid off her jacket to reveal a navy knit dress that would have been totally unforgiving on Grace but sat perfectly on Lucia's slim frame.

No surprises that Lucia opted for a skinny latte, while Grace ordered a cappuccino and custard pastry. She needed some bolstering, calorific comfort while she broke her news to Lucia. Her older sister, who had always accomplished everything perfectly and according to the golden rules, would never understand her whirlwind romance. Then again, from childhood, Lucia had always looked out for Grace, almost to the point of making it her business to oversee aspects of her sister's life. Lucia had even introduced Grace to Gavin, and had wholeheartedly approved of and cheered on their romance from the sidelines, taking a personal interest in it. She'd been unable to comprehend why Grace had called off such a promising romance, and said very little at the time, but her silence and furrowed brow spoke volumes.

'You're *seeing* someone? Already?' Lucia's jaw dropped.

'I've been seeing Danny since before Christmas,' Grace said. 'We are now officially an item.'

"Officially'? After three or four *weeks*? In other words, you're sleeping with him.' It was almost an accusation.

Grace lifted her chin. 'I am and it's special. Very much so.'

Lucia raised a perfectly curved eyebrow. 'This Danny must be very special to follow Gavin.'

'He is.' But not in the way you might think, Grace wanted to add. Lucia would find out in time that Danny had none of Gavin's secure, gilt-edged prospects.

'So there's no chance you and Gavin–' she asked, lifting her coffee cup with beautifully manicured hands.

'Absolutely not.'

'I'd half hoped you'd arranged to meet me to tell me you two were getting back together,' Lucia said with a small smile. 'I still harboured visions of being your matron of honour. You know he wanted to marry you.'

Grace shook her head. 'That won't ever be happening. In fact, Lucia, you might as well know that Danny's moving in with me next weekend.' She heard her sister draw breath but barely gave Lucia a chance to comment before she went on, 'Aren't you glad for me?'

'Moving *in*?' Lucia leaned forward in her seat and looked at her worriedly. 'Oh Grace, it's not just … on the rebound, is it? Are you sure you know what you're doing?'

'Lucia, I'm not five or six anymore, I'll be thirty this year.'

Lucia sighed and spread her hands. 'I know, and of course I'm happy if you're happy again, but look, please don't rush into anything. You're bound to be raw and emotional after your first Christmas without Gavin. It's only been a couple of months since you broke up and you were with him a long time.'

'Right now, honestly Lucia, the only emotion I feel is amazing happiness.'

Lucia studied her for a while, and then seemingly satisfied she said, 'Well, come on then, don't leave me in suspense, tell me more about this … amazing person. What's he like? What's his background? Where did you two meet?'

Grace glossed over the finer points, explaining that Danny was from Mayo and she'd met him over Christmas drinks. There was no need for Lucia to know that Danny had been made redundant the previous November. The word 'redundant' didn't compute for Lucia in any shape or form. Even Robert, her executive husband, had high-tailed it off to a job in London before the company where he'd held a very senior position was taken over, in order to avoid the ignominy of becoming surplus to requirements after 'a rigorous cost-cutting exercise following an amalgamation'.

'Danny's an up-and-coming entrepreneur,' Grace said. 'He's involved in his own start-up company in web design.'

There was a spark of interest in Lucia's eyes. 'I should be able to google him.'

'Yes, probably,' Grace said. Let Lucia go ahead. There was little or nothing to find on the internet about Danny. He'd already told

Grace that he wasn't signed up to LinkedIn, and it would be weeks before his own business website was live, as everything had to be in place first. He'd closed down his Facebook page a long time ago, and he'd never been on Twitter or any other social media platform. He'd made a joke about needing to keep a lot of space between himself and all his fans, but Grace had sensed there might have been more to it, only he wasn't saying.

'And we'll have to meet him,' Lucia was saying. 'How about the next time Robert is home for the weekend? We could all go out for a meal.'

'Sure,' Grace said. There would be safety in numbers, and better than Lucia coming over to Rathbrook Hall to give Danny her eagle-eyed once-over at close quarters.

'When are you going to tell Mum and Dad?'

'Soon,' Grace said.

'Let me know,' Lucia said. 'I won't mention Danny to them until then.'

'It's not exactly top secret,' Grace said.

'Isn't it? Why didn't you say anything at Christmas?'

'It was early days then.'

'It's gone from early days to letting him move in with you in a very short space of time.'

'Sometimes you just know these things, Lucia.'

'I hope so, Grace. I hope you'll be happy. I'd hate to see you getting hurt in any way.'

'I won't get hurt. Definitely not.'

Chapter Six

It snowed the Friday evening Danny moved in.

Grace was in a fizz of excitement when she heard her buzzer ringing and his voice at the other end telling her he was down in the car park. She buzzed him into the apartment block, and less than five minutes later she threw open the hall door to where he stood on the threshold in his motorcycle gear with a brown and rather battered suitcase plonked beside him. He slid a backpack down off his shoulders.

'Is that all you have?' she said, needing to concentrate on something other than the heart-stopping sight of him stepping into her hallway.

'That's a nice welcome.' His voice, with the slight lilt, was warm.

'How did you manage this with your bike? You've brought that too, haven't you? You know where to park down in the basement, don't you?' Words. She was only gabbling silly words to delay the inevitable moment when he had officially moved in, because she was suddenly overcome with the hugeness of all this. Danny, sleeping beside her every night, kissing her awake each morning, sharing her life, the ordinary ins and outs of her days and weeks to come. Encouraging her to believe in herself, urging her not to waste a minute doing anything that pulled her down.

'I didn't do it all alone. I had help,' he said, without elaborating.

She wondered why he didn't bring his friend up and introduce him to her. It might have been nice to meet one of Danny's mates, seeing as how he was about to move in with her, and it wouldn't have taken a minute, but they had plenty of time for that in the weeks and months ahead. Plenty of time to find out everything there was about each other. Here, tonight, it was just about the two of them.

'So is there any room in this apartment for all my worldly things?'

She laughed when he arranged his meagre assortment of clothes in her wardrobe.

'Is that all?' she said, looking at shelves that were only half full and the unused clothes hangers where Gavin's carefully arranged suits had once hung.

'Yep,' Danny said. 'I have stuff back in Mayo but I travel light. It's the only way.'

He took his laptop out of his backpack and Grace gave him the code for connecting to the Wi-Fi.

'And you're okay with me working here during the day?'

One of the things she liked about Danny was that he wasn't just telling her to follow her dreams, he was doing it himself by becoming his own boss, taking solid steps to get his web design business off the ground.

'You can always throw on a wash or two while you're lounging around eating grapes,' she laughed. 'Maybe do a bit of cooking?'

'It'll be far easier to work in the peace of your kitchen compared with the bedsit in Harold's Cross, where the other Mayo guys were always barging in and out,' he said. 'So it's no big deal to make sure you're fed properly and have clean clothes.'

'And the dishwasher. I hate emptying that.'

'Okay, and the dishwasher,' he said. 'I might even do something with that wall,' he looked at the main wall in the living area where it was marked in places. 'What were you doing, throwing darts?'

'That's where photos of me and Gavin used to hang,' Grace says. 'I took them down as soon as he'd left, but whatever way they were stuck up, some of the paint came away as well. He's gone two and half months now.'

'Can we agree on something?'

'That depends on what it is …'

'No looking back before the time we first met, okay? Actually, no looking back at all.'

'Fine with me.'

'But seeing as you've already made a mess of the wall I could put up some posters instead?' Danny offered. 'You'll like these. Promise. Hey – look,' he said softly, staring over Grace's head and beyond her, all the way across to the big picture window. There was a soft glow from the peach lamp beside the sofa in the living area, and the curtains were open to the darkening evening, reflecting the lamp. Only it wasn't quite dark. The underbelly of the sky had a light grey tinge to it, and whirls of snowflakes were pouring dizzily from the sky and dancing around in front of the window. Feeling like a child on Christmas morning, Grace laughed and half-danced, half-ran across to the glass, looking out into the silent, whirling flakes.

'I don't believe it. You arrived just in time,' she said. 'I'm glad you didn't get caught in that on a motorbike. This has to bring us luck, hasn't it?'

'Only if you're up for making a snowman later on.'

'That's number three on your list, isn't it?' She said with a grin, 'Bet I can make a better one than you.'

'Nah. No way.'

Grace sat back on the sofa, her feet curled under her, alternately watching the snow, then watching Danny moving around, finishing his unpacking, the sight of him sending little ricochets of joy into her chest. He showed her a photo of his parents and two sisters that had been taken at his youngest sister's graduation, and he put it on his bedside table. Grace breathed in slowly and felt she was taking big sips of champagne. No matter that Lucia might have misgivings at the swiftness of it all, Grace was doing the right thing. She brushed aside the tiny niggle that right up to the time Danny had arrived with his suitcase, she wasn't sure if he would actually turn up. In the cold light of day, the critical part of her head was telling her she hardly knew this guy, but her heart was saying otherwise.

Later, after it had stopped snowing and thick drifts covered the courtyard, they wrapped up, took the lift down and went outside. The air was chilly but fresh, the icy edge of it stinging Grace's face. The night had a luminous quality, with the blanket of snow swathing everything, and here and there squares and rectangles of light shone from windows in the apartment blocks. Grace and Danny were the only ones brave or foolish enough to venture out. She saw their moving shadows silhouetted across the surface of the snow as they rolled cold clumps of it into big, round shapes. Their laughter and banter carried in the still air and Grace fancied it shimmered upwards like a stream, drifting up through the space between the apartment blocks, up, up into the watching, starry night sky.

This was happiness.

Chapter Seven

Danny was as good as his word. He helped with the laundry, and in the evenings he put his laptop away before Grace came home from the office, and cooked for both of them. He covered the marks on the wall with his favourite inspirational posters, so instead of empty spaces where Grace and Gavin used to smile down, now when Grace wandered into the living room in the mornings she was met with life-affirming messages that made her feel happy, energised, and glad to be alive.

She bought new cushions and a rug for the sofa, and took out candleholders that had been tidied away when Gavin moved in. This evening, a week after Danny had moved in, the sky in the west had not yet sunk into total darkness, but was still streaked with bands of petrol-blue light as Grace reached Rathbrook Hall. She loved seeing this sign that winter and the dark evenings would soon have passed. Her walk up from the Luas in the chilly February evening had invigorated her so that her hands and feet were tingling inside her warm mittens and furry boots. Danny had offered to collect her on the bike, but she'd laughed and said there was no need, it was only fifteen minutes. After being in the stuffy office all day, she knew she needed fresh air. Besides, he was cooking the dinner.

She let herself into the apartment block and walked across to the lifts. She was still brimming over with the newness and shininess of having Danny living with her that she still wondered if he would really be there when she came home from work. It was so different from the dread she used to feel coming home to Gavin that sometimes it made her giddy and light-headed. How could her life have changed so utterly in a few short months?

Excitement rippled through her as she put her key in the lock and opened the door. She stepped into an apartment where warmth and cosiness enveloped her, along with the succulent aroma of something in the oven.

'Home!' she said, marvelling that she was calling out to him like this. She dropped her bag on the floor. She shrugged out of her thickly padded coat and hung it up on a peg in the narrow hallway, before walking into the living room. The living area was in semi-darkness, lit only by a small disco ball, multi-coloured lights flashing around the walls. It was new. Danny must have bought it. He was down at the kitchen end, busy chopping up peppers. There was a stream of dance music coming from his iPod docking station set up on the counter. He looked around at her and smiled. He pulled off some kitchen towel and wiped his hands, then he walked over to her, put his hands on her shoulders and kissed her. He whirled her into his arms and danced her into the small kitchen, and back down to the living area, and back up to the kitchen, over and over until she was gasping for breath.

'Hey,' she squealed, leaning into him, 'this is a lovely welcome home.'

'This is what every welcome home should be like.'

'I wish.'

'Your wish is my command,' he said, running his fingers through her hair with one hand, cupping her chin with the other, before tilting it towards him and kissing her on the mouth. Her arms slid around him. His kiss deepened. Once again she marvelled at it all, this time at how much could be said without words. She slid her hands up under his fleece, feeling the warm cotton of his T-shirt underneath. He stopped kissing her, drew back, looked at her. His eyes locked on hers.

'Food will be another ten minutes,' he said, drawing her over to the sofa.

'Perfect,' she said.

* * *

'Where did you learn to cook?' she asked later as they sat at the kitchen table. Danny had served up a hearty stir-fry, complete with side salad and chunks of bread. The disco ball was still on, but had been moved to a slower, less frenetic setting. Grace was wearing her velour dressing gown and a pair of fleecy socks, and her gaze idly followed the kaleidoscope patterns glowing across the room. Danny had changed the music, and slow rock anthems swirled around the space where they sat.

'I can't be telling you all my secrets,' Danny said.

'I've kind of noticed that.'

There was a brief silence. Grace waited to see if Danny was about to talk, but he said nothing, merely busying himself with collecting the plates and cutlery.

'I'm very impressed. With your cooking,' Grace went on, deciding not to push things or spoil the moment.

'Didn't you believe me when I said I'd cook for us?' he asked, and she sensed a slight question in his eyes – don't you trust me to carry out my word?

'I wasn't expecting such a feast,' she admitted.

'That was easy stuff.'

'At least let me know who was responsible for domesticating Danny McBride?'

Another brief silence. 'I taught myself,' he said.

'When and how?' She was curious because she hadn't expected culinary expertise to be on Danny's no-time-to-waste, live-every-moment list of priorities. 'You're shy,' she laughed. 'You don't want to tell me. Go on, I dare you to admit that you've been secretly watching *MasterChef*.'

He looked away as though he was making his mind up about something. 'I got fed up with junk food,' he finally said. 'It messes you about. Your energy, your moods, and your ability to do things come directly from everything you eat, so it makes sense to eat the best you can.'

'Oh, wow, so it all comes back to living life to the max. You don't just talk the talk …'

'Yeah, that's it.'

'I'm so impressed that I've a good mind to ask Lucia and Robert over here tomorrow evening, instead of going out with them,' she paused. He didn't look the least bit fazed. 'On second thoughts,' she continued, 'it's probably better to go along with Lucia's carefully laid plans. She has a table reserved since last week in honour of meeting you for the first time – some new bar in Leeson Street I haven't heard of.'

She decided not to forewarn him that Lucia had misgivings about their whirlwind romance, nor to tell him that she had been personally invested in Grace and Gavin's relationship, having introduced them. There was no need. As soon as Lucia got talking to Danny, she would see exactly why he had swept Grace off her feet.

'New place?' he said. 'Does that mean I need to wear a suit in honour of the occasion?'

Grace waved her hand airily, 'No way, come as you are, Danny, you'll be fine.'

'Are you sure? For meeting the brilliant Lucia? And that's a joke, Grace,' he went on. 'I can only be as I am, and so should you. You're just as brilliant as Lucia, no more, no less. Never forget that.'

He'd already figured that Grace used to feel somehow lacking compared with her smart, clever sister, because she never measured up to the gilt-edged standard Lucia had set, and had found it a tough role, trying to follow in her elegant, stiletto-heeled footsteps. It didn't matter anymore, now that she had him in her life, helping her to feel so amazing, so free to be herself and stop doing what she thought everyone else wanted and expected.

'You still haven't told me where you learned to cook so well,' she said, teasing him, partly because she knew there was something he still wasn't telling her.

'If you must know, Ms Nosy, I used to work in a kitchen,' he said. 'So I know my way around pots and pans and gas hobs. I enjoy cooking, putting ingredients together and seeing how good the end result is. If you follow the recipe, you can't go wrong. I find it all very … satisfying in a way.'

'Bring it on,' Grace said. 'It mightn't be my kind of therapy but feel free to have the full run of my pots and pans.'

'Thanks. It's even better when I'm cooking for both of us.'

She was about to ask him what kitchen he'd worked in; was it in a hotel, as a student? She wondered what had messed him up that made him get serious about his diet, and why he wouldn't talk about it, but he had cleared the table and changed the music to Prince's 'Purple Rain', and he wrapped her in his arms and slow danced her around the kitchen once more.

Chapter Eight

Lucia Edwards's gaze darted across to the bar to where her husband Robert was standing, deep in conversation with an ex-colleague of his. A female one. Chloe, from Accounts, in his previous Dublin firm. She felt like dragging him back to their table, even if she had to do it with her fingernails. Not that she didn't trust Robert – although he seemed to be enjoying the chit-chat, and the young woman was laughing rather flirtatiously with him, running her hand through her long blonde hair and angling her lycra-clad body rather provocatively. And they looked well together. Robert would look striking anywhere, with his thick, dark blond hair and bright blue eyes, but it was his modest, unassuming personality and his calm, intelligent face that had snagged Lucia's attention from the time she first met him at a London conference.

Tonight she had other things on her mind. She was finding to her discomfort that too much Danny McBride wasn't good for her.

She'd found herself sitting beside him, sinking back into a squashy sofa drawn up to a low table, while Grace and Robert had sat on the armchairs opposite them, and might as well have been half a mile away. Grace had winked at her from across the chasm, as if she was delighted to see her sister and her new boyfriend getting to know each other, but so far, for Lucia, the night in the new and much fêted

Leeson Street venue had been a disaster of sorts. For some reason or other, this slightly raffish man, with the gleaming green eyes and irreverent approach to everything was managing to pull at the silk-covered walls of the life she'd carefully constructed around herself. He'd plunged right in and asked her soul searching questions about her best childhood dreams, what she saw as her life's purpose, what she was most passionate about, what event had most shaped her life, her favourite ever toy – *I mean, what?* Robert had never even asked her that. He wasn't only content to ask her the kind of books she liked to read but also why. She'd given him only half answers that conveyed nothing about the real Lucia Edwards.

He hadn't been the least bit impressed that she knew her way around the extensive wine list, or that she'd gone to wine tasting classes. 'Isn't that where you go to spit it out?' he'd said. 'What a waste of good wine.'

He hadn't been the least bit sarky or sceptical or trying to get at her, he'd been just puppy-dog friendly and humorous as though it were all great fun. She'd almost found herself *laughing*. Now Grace had disappeared to the bathroom, Robert was stuck at the bar, and Lucia had been alone with Danny for a whole ten minutes.

And he still wasn't finished with her.

'What would you say you're most proud of, in your life to date, Lucia?' he asked, sitting back against the cushiony sofa.

'My work ethic,' she said. 'I hold down an extremely busy and successful job.'

'Have you any regrets?'

'No.'

'So you won't be looking back in twenty years' time, thinking about the things you should have done?'

'Absolutely not.'

'Do you ever pause long enough to taste the breeze? Or feel the sun on your face? Or breathe in the scent after the rain? And I don't mean in the Seychelles. Your back garden would do just fine.'

'What is this, Danny? Mastermind? Or is this your ingenuous way of filling in time until Grace comes back?'

'I'm hoping to get to know Grace's sister.'

Get to know? Lucia was caught up in her busy life, the fast-moving treadmill that repeated itself every week, and Danny was asking questions that she had never taken time out to ask herself. Everything he asked was put to her in a light-hearted, non-threatening fashion, as though he were genuinely interested in what made her tick, and it wasn't just some clever game. He was like a long, cool, refreshing drink of sparkling water that seeped into all the rigid corners of her life. She visualised him and Grace having this scary kind of late-night, finding-yourself conversation on a one-to-one basis in the quiet of Grace's apartment or maybe in her bed, and to her annoyance, she felt a spike of jealousy.

'Know this about me – Grace is very special to me,' she said. 'I love her to bits and if so much as a hair on her head is harmed in any way, you'll have me to answer to.' She saw Grace coming down the stairs from the first floor bathroom, but to Lucia's irritation, she paused by a table and began chatting to the women sitting there. Robert's ex-colleague had finally gone and he was now ordering fresh drinks.

'Good,' Danny said. 'Grace is very special to me also. You're exactly the kind of sister she deserves. Loving and caring. Ready to be at her back if anything goes wrong.'

Lucia stared at him. 'Absolutely. And what could possibly go wrong?'

'We don't always know what fate has in store, do we?'

'We're each in charge of our own lives, Danny.'

'To a large degree, yes. But you and Robert: Dublin and London. What's that all about?'

'Exactly what it is. Robert works in London and we see each other every weekend. Either I go to London or he comes home.'

He shook his head. 'It must be a long week without Robert, and vice versa. Don't you miss each other?'

'We're both far too busy with our day-to-day schedules to think of cuddles during the week, but we plan the weekend to include everything we could possibly want.'

'It sounds like a lot of your life is planned out in convenient little boxes. It doesn't give you much time to smell the roses.'

Coming from anyone else, the words would have stung. But Danny seemed to be on her side and his tone was one of friendly concern more than anything else. 'And what's wrong with that?' she asked.

Danny shrugged, his eyes filled with guilelessness. 'Absolutely nothing, Lucia, if it's what floats your well-organised boat.'

'Happens it is,' she said airily, smoothing her hair and wishing Robert would hurry up. It did float her boat. Very much. She had money and security and her life was in her total control, the weeks and months ahead mapped out accordingly. Exactly as she wanted. There were no surprises in Lucia's life, certainly no unpleasant ones. But Danny was reminding her that with Robert working in London and living in a bachelor pad, and only seeing his wife most weekends, there were many days and nights when he was mixing with colleagues and friends, with no Lucia by his side, no Lucia to come home to and no Lucia in his bed. Robert was an attractive man – in his career and socially he was meeting equally intelligent and attractive women.

'And what happens when the patter of tiny feet comes along?' Danny asked, so softly she wasn't sure if she'd heard correctly.

He was the first person ever to have asked Lucia that question. Neither Grace nor her parents, or even any of her friends or colleagues, had ever alluded to the lack of children in Lucia's life. Lucia fixed him with what she hoped was her sweetest smile and found herself telling him something she'd never told even her mother or Grace. 'That won't be happening.'

'Not part of your well organised plan?'

'Absolutely not.'

* * *

Later, in their grey and ivory bedroom as they got ready for bed, Lucia said to Robert, 'What did you think of Danny?' To her own ears her voice sounded strained. Then again, she found it impossible to sound nonchalant about a young man who'd managed to peel back some of the tightly knit layers of her life with his total insouciance. She took off her jewellery and placed it on the velvet mat on her dressing table. She saw Robert's reflection grinning at her in the mirror as he undid his shirt buttons and shrugged it off.

'He's a little outrageous. Fun, though. Grace seems happy.'

'Yes, she does. He wouldn't be my type, though.'

'Really, Lucia? I thought you pair were having a great chat when I was over at the bar.' She knew by the gleam in Robert's eye that he was teasing her.

'Not as good as the chat you were having with Ms Lycra,' she said, throwing a cushion at him.

Robert laughed and threw it back at her. 'I couldn't get away from her. I was hoping you'd come and rescue me, only you were too busy talking to Danny.'

'I couldn't get away from him either. I don't know how on earth Grace kissed goodbye to Gavin and the nice life he was offering her, only to hook up with Danny.'

'She must have had good reason.'

Lucia snorted. 'Good reason? For breaking up with Gavin? Search me.'

Robert pulled back the duvet and got into bed. 'Relax, Lucia. Grace knows her own mind. They're just having some fun if you ask me.'

Lucia went into the en suite, and came out wearing just her lace pants. She saw her pale reflection in the mirrored wardrobes as she padded across the carpeted room, reassured that she was the same neat size ten as she'd been on her wedding day. She slid into bed beside Robert, nuzzling against him, letting her hand drift down to his hips.

'I had some good news today,' Robert said.

'What kind of news?'

'Miranda's had a baby girl. Mother and baby are well.'

Her hand stilled. She slid it away from his hips and turned on her back. 'When did this happen?'

'She texted me this afternoon to say baby Sophie arrived early this morning.'

'Why didn't you tell me before now?' She stared at the ceiling and resisted the urge to prop herself on her elbow and look into his eyes.

Miranda. His London colleague with whom he worked closely. Tall and beautiful, with chocolate-brown eyes and amazing, coffee-coloured skin. Clever and quick-witted – and *thoroughly* professional, which is what she'd told herself sternly when images of Robert debating over a piece of work with the sexy Miranda flashed into her head. Most importantly, she was married to Neil, her equally sexy South African husband. Up to recently, they had socialised with them regularly whenever Lucia was in London. And now they had a baby daughter, Sophie.

'I forgot,' Robert said mildly.

'How could you forget something like that?'

Had he really forgotten until now, when they were in bed? Did lying together, almost naked, somehow help him conjure up Miranda, or was she going completely soft in the head, with her crazy assumption?

'I didn't think you'd be all that interested,' he said.

She didn't bother pointing out the difference between genuinely forgetting and deciding she mightn't be interested. 'I'm very happy for Miranda,' she said. 'That's great news.'

'I suppose it is, for her. She'll be out on leave for a while. We'll miss her in the office.'

There was a short silence.

'Do you miss me during the week?' she asked, surprised that the question popped out so easily, considering she hadn't planned on asking it.

'Of course I do,' Robert said.

'I'd hate to think you were lonely in London.'

'I miss you but I'm usually too busy during the week to be lonely,' Robert said. 'And why are we wasting time talking?' He turned around in bed. He slid down her pants and moved on top of her, bending down to kiss the hollow of her neck, her forehead, her jawbone, her ears, her rose-tipped breasts. They made love, urgently. She deliberately cleared her mind of everything except the sensation of Robert inside her, before she came in a surge of rippling pleasure.

Afterwards Robert cuddled her and kissed the top of her head. 'Good night, darling, love you.' He said, before turning on his side and clicking off the lamp.

'Night, love.' It took Lucia a while to fall asleep. Surprisingly enough, thoughts of Miranda tucked up in a London hospital with a new baby were vaguely unsettling, but they paled alongside thoughts of Robert keeping the news from her until they were lying in bed together.

Chapter Nine

'Danny, what have you done?'

Grace had just arrived in from work and was about to walk down to the bedroom to change out of her work clothes when Danny came out into the hallway and stopped her, putting his hands over her eyes.

'Close your eyes,' he said. He propelled her into the bedroom, walking closely behind her. Inside the bedroom, he shut the door. They stood together, Grace's eyes still closed.

'Just be patient for a minute and don't turn off the light,' he said.

She giggled. 'How can I, when I can't see where the switch is?'

After a couple of minutes she heard him clicking the switch, plunging the room into darkness. He took his hands away from her eyes and told her to look up.

Grace looked up to a ceiling that was transformed with stars of all sizes trailing across her ceiling in big wheeling loops and circles as though they had fallen where a big giant hand had scattered them.

'Oh wow. It's *gorgeous*. Where did you get them? What made you think of this?'

'Too many questions,' he said. He pulled her down on the bed. 'Just lie back and enjoy.'

The two of them lay stretched across the bed, fully clothed, staring at the ceiling. From outside the window came the muted roar of traffic. Inside, all was quiet.

'Have you ever slept under the stars at night?' he asked.

'I will be now.'

'You haven't lived until you've done the real thing.'

'So you've done the real thing?'

'Not just yet. Someone I know did.'

'Who? Not another of your mysterious friends?'

'Never mind … just someone who told me how wonderful it is.'

'I bet that's your next plan for us …'

'Yeah, didn't I tell you? The Kerry night sky is the place to see the stars. The weather will be ideal next weekend, clear skies, and it'll be warmer than normal for this time of year. But much as I love the motorbike, a trip down to Kerry on it is out of the question.'

'Kerry, next weekend,' she said. 'Danny, what's this all about? I know it's on your list of things to do before you're thirty, but you seem in an awful rush. Why not wait until later in the year?'

'Just wait until you're there,' he said persuasively. 'You'll wonder why you waited so long. Could we go in your car?'

'I knew you had an ulterior motive for moving in with me,' she said. 'You were after the car all along.'

'I had three ulterior motives,' Danny said.

'Oh yeah? And what were the others?'

'I want to help Grace Bailey to have a wonderful year, and to work out what she really wants in life rather than drifting through it.'

It was easy to talk like this, staring up at the stars. 'I've always wanted to write,' she said, holding her breath in case he'd find this funny. When she'd plucked up the courage to tell Gavin, one night after a few drinks, he'd looked at her as though she was off the wall and asked her if she realised she'd never earn a living from it.

'That's wonderful, Grace,' Danny said warmly. 'What would you like to write?'

'Stories for children. Fun, fantasy and adventure.'

'Sounds brilliant. Have you anything written so far?'

'Yes, I have lots of stuff started, and notes and things … I have some of it on my laptop but I've a lot printed and it's all in a big carrier bag in the wardrobe. It's been a while since I looked at it … over three years,' she admitted.

'I see,' Danny said meaningfully. 'I won't even ask why your dreams were put on hold for three years, or what your notes are doing hidden away, but Grace Bailey, I expect whatever is in that bag to see the light of day … say before Easter, is that a deal?'

'Deal,' she said happily.

'And you'll have to put aside some time every night to follow your dream. Agreed?'

'Agreed. So … what was your third ulterior motive?'

'I'm just about to show you.'

She made a pretence at rolling away from him but he cupped her face in his hands and she closed her eyes as he began to kiss her, gently at first, soft touches against her lips and the side of her face, along her chin, on top of her nose. She opened her mouth as he finally returned to her lips and kissed her so slowly, deeply and thoroughly that everything dissolved around her and inside her. Without breaking the kiss he took one hand away from her face and pushed it up under her shirt, wriggling around to release the clasp of her bra and allowing her full, soft breast to fall into the palm of his hand. He grazed the nipple with his thumb and she felt a shockwave running through her. His hand slid down under the waistband of her trousers and she thought she was going to faint under the ache of desire. She slowly came out of a daze and murmured that she'd never made love under the stars before. She lifted her hips and slid off her trousers and sank back onto the bed. He began to touch her – *just there, yes, God* – and all her insides turned to liquid gold. The heat, warmth and excitement of it all was everything it should be and could be, and so very much more.

So what if she knew very little about Danny when he'd first moved in. So what if he hardly spoke of his family, or friends, or the guys from Mayo he'd been sharing a house with, and she hadn't met any of them yet. Nor did it bother her if occasionally he took his mobile into the bedroom to take a call. 'Business,' he'd said, making a funny face – he'd already told her he didn't want it seeping into their time together, it was so precious. Right now, they were living in a bubble of their own, in a world of their own, where no one else managed to get a look in.

* * *

The Kerry night sky was stupendous.

They decided to go it alone, rather than check out the stars with an escorted group or an individual guide. They booked accommodation in a guest house close to the sea and were provided with maps of the best viewing areas and directions to parking bays. As advised, they went out earlier in the evening to get their bearings before the light faded from the sky.

After the darkness settled they went back out. The immense breadth of the skyscape arched over them like a midnight-blue tapestry studded with millions of tiny gemstones as ancient and fresh as time immemorial. Grace felt she was looking into the true vault of heaven, at something much grander, far more powerful and deeply tranquil than she could ever imagine. The chilly breeze danced against her face and she could taste the briny sea on her lips. Danny threw his arms out wide and turned round and round, his head tilted to the sparkling sky. He seemed to be floating and she sensed he was aligned effortlessly with this atmosphere of beauty beyond belief, and the way it hummed silently with potent energy.

They went down to where the sea unrolled a restless silvery carpet away into infinity, and Grace felt she was tiptoeing along the edge of the world. When her eyes adjusted to the depths of the night, she saw a startling purity in the wild and wonderful beauty around her and it snagged at her heart. Then Danny caught her, hugging her to him as he waltzed her around, his breath warm on her cheek, and she could have danced with him forever like this under the glittering and watchful stars, filled to the brim with the glorious adventure of life and love, and sharing it with Danny.

Chapter Ten

'How did you find this place?' Grace asked. 'It's so quiet and secluded.'

'Someone told me about it,' Danny said.

They were sitting in the shelter of the sand dunes on a blowy, secluded county Wicklow beach. Danny's bike was parked up on the adjacent laneway. There was a small, crescent-shaped beach in front of them, flanked by two spurs of land running out into the bay. They had to drop down a small incline to get here, but they were completely screened from anyone taking the walking trail along the headland, and the nearest bungalow was some distance away. The temperature had spiked so that it was warmer than normal for this time of the year. Twelve degrees, Danny had said.

Perfect for skinny dipping.

'Is this more of your kind of therapy?' she asked.

He grinned. 'Dunno yet, there's supposed to be nothing quite like emptying your mind and getting back to nature, feeling the sand under your toes, swimming in the open sea with the salty ocean gliding off your bare skin. Makes you really feel alive. Or so I've heard.'

'Where? Who's filling you with the mad ideas on how to squeeze the very most out of life?' she said.

'I think I read it somewhere,' Danny said, so vaguely that she knew he was telling her a fib.

'I should still be snuggled up in my cosy, comfortable bed, in my jim-jams, enjoying my Saturday morning lie-in,' Grace said, deciding to ignore it.

'And look at what you'd be missing,' Danny said, indicating the sweeping panorama. It was an overcast morning but still lovely, Grace had to admit, with the pale disc of the sun visible behind the clouds, looking as though it was floating through the sky. The sea was a vast ripple of gunmetal grey, and here and there the crests of the waves rolling in with the tide sparkled where the sun was peeping through. She took a long, slow breath of cool, refreshing air.

'I'm not sure I'm ready for this,' she said. 'Isn't it a bit on the chilly side?' She was still wearing her thick, padded jacket, the one that was perfect for riding pillion with Danny. Underneath that she was wearing a cream jumper and T-shirt with jeans, as well as thick knee socks under her boots.

'Yes, but it'll only take a minute. Your body will adjust in no time. You'll be out and back and I'll have you wrapped in a big, fat towel before you know it. And when we get home you can jump back in to your cosy, comfortable bed.'

'I dunno.'

'Well okay, then, it's just me.' Danny took off his clothes, laying his jacket flat on the marram grass and piling his clothes on top. Grace couldn't help watching him strip down to his black jocks. He pulled out towels from his sports bag and left them beside the clothes.

'Ready and waiting,' he said, grinning at her. 'Here goes.' With a neat movement, he pushed his jocks down to his ankles and stepped out of them.

'Wow,' Grace couldn't help saying. 'Go you.' Seeing him naked like this, away from the usual confines of the apartment was doing funny things to her insides. The perfection of him standing nude on the beach took her breath away. Bare-assed, he walked down towards the water's edge and she couldn't help thinking how bloody beautiful and totally natural he looked in this moment, as if he was at one with the elements of a shifting, timeless sea and a morning sky where the sun was playing hide and seek with the clouds. He'd almost reached the frilly edge of the water when she heard herself call out.

'Hey, wait!'

He stopped. He turned around and her breath seemed to quiver all the way through her. Excitement made her giddy as she took off her clothes, putting them in a pile beside his, hesitating as she reached her underwear, shearing it off and she stood there, gasping with the cold, yet striking a funny pose, letting him look at her. Then she ran across the cold sand towards him, laughing for joy at the utter and total abandon and the silly insanity of doing this. He laughed and caught her hand and together they ran through the freezing shallows, sending up spray, the shock of cold water robbing her voice. The depth of the water slowed them down as it rose to their waists, and Grace held Danny's hand tightly, feeling the suck and swell of the sea against all of her skin. They paddled through the water, side by side, their slick, wet bodies bumping together. Danny urged her to keep moving. After a while they came together in a tangle of limbs and cold water, Danny kissing her wet face, Grace finding it crazy and exhilarating.

'I am alive,' Danny shouted. 'And I love you, Grace Bailey. Never forget that.'

'I am alive, and I love you, Danny McBride,' she said, as loudly as she could with her chattering teeth.

'Right – out of here, now,' Danny said, and they waded back to the shallows and ran up to the waiting towels, giggling and laughing. Danny enfolded both of them in two huge big towels and they twisted and turned as they dried each other off. Grace pulled on her clothes, feeling euphoric, every pore in her skin tingling and invigorated with the vibrancy of it all.

Afterwards Danny found a stick and went down to where the sand was damp and firm. He wrote, cutting foot-high letters out of the sand with the edge of his stick: 'Danny loves Grace xxx.'

She wondered how long the words would remain before they were obliterated by the oncoming tide. She had a sharp sense of the impermanence of everything, and the capriciousness of life with all its twists and turns, the swiftness of it slipping through their fingers as it inexorably rolled out ahead, like the flickering breeze running down the beach – here one minute, teasing her hair, and gone the next. The sun slid behind a cloud. She needed to remember all this, she thought, fixing the image, colour and scent of that carefree morning forever in her mind.

* * *

The following evening Lucia felt a bit like a pretender as she took the stairs up to Grace's apartment. Grace thought she needed to borrow her hair straighteners, but she was really curious to see what her sister's boyfriend was like, away from the frenzy of a showy nightclub. One night hadn't been enough to get a handle on Danny McBride, even if he had got up her nose.

As she stood outside the hall door, she heard the thumping beat of a rock anthem resonating from the living room, which was quietened as soon as she knocked. Both Grace and Danny were very welcoming, ushering her in as though she was a much wanted guest, but there was something about the closeness of the two of them, the barely suppressed effervescence that surrounded them, and the way they moved around the apartment, that made her feel she was interrupting a special honeymoon.

Then there was the apartment itself – during the days of Gavin, it had been tidy and uncluttered, neat and orderly. All that had changed. There was a relaxing aroma of bergamot and geranium coming from a jumbled assortment of mismatched candles and tea-light holders, which flickered across the mantelpiece. The arrangement was interspersed with pretty shells and pebbles. They could hardly have been to the beach, could they? In February? Then again, where the mercurial Danny was concerned, nothing would surprise her.

The sofa was dotted with a scatter of colourful cushions, which were new. A cobalt-blue velour rug, also new, was draped over an arm of the sofa. She tried not to visualise Danny and Grace cuddling under this. Then she tried to figure out the significance of the kite stuck to the press, but that was impossible. On the wall, in place of framed photographs of Gavin and Grace, taken at various nights out, there were three large posters she was unable to resist examining.

One was an image of the sun rising over Dublin Bay, bearing a message exhorting her to think what a privilege it was to be alive, to breathe, to think, to enjoy, to love; it was attributed to Marcus Aurelius. Another one depicted a vibrant firework display and urged her not to be afraid to stand in her sparkle and dream big; a third showed a quirky image of a colourful weed sprouting up on the roof of a Dublin bus shelter – the caption reminded her that she was alive, and to avail of this once-in-a-lifetime opportunity. She couldn't make out the scrawl at the bottom to see whose words of wisdom they were.

'I take it the posters are yours, Danny,' she said to him, when Grace was in the bedroom searching for the hair straighteners.

'Which one strikes you the most?' he asked, sitting back on the sofa, one leg balanced at an angle on top of the other. 'Don't think about it for too long and don't give me an answer you think I want to hear ...'

She decided not to answer him at all. She said, 'Since when did you swallow the Zen instruction booklet for life?'

'You don't need any instructions,' he said, not the least bit fazed by her question. 'Whatever you need is inside you.'

'Oh. Right. Now you're going to tell me I have to sit crossed legged in a trance-like state for three hours before dawn to discover whatever that is.'

'No, Lucia.' He lifted a finger and poked himself in the chest, his green eyes smiling. 'It's simpler than that. You stop the everyday crap long enough to listen to whatever's in here.'

'Right. So are we all supposed to give ourselves permission to walk out of our jobs and dance through life on a wing and a prayer?'

'I didn't say that. You need to be able to pay your way. It sends out the message that you deserve a life free from the worry of paying bills. That's important, too. I thought you loved your busy job. I hope you're doing something you enjoy, that you feel matters.'

'Do you know something, Danny? I don't get you at all.' She felt cross with him. She felt even crosser with herself for allowing him to get under her skin. She was sorry she'd called in and she couldn't wait for Grace to emerge from the bedroom.

She wasn't allowed home without coffee and a slice of the apple tart, which, naturally enough, Danny had baked. Grace talked about their recent trip to Kerry and told her they'd been to the beach.

'In February?' Lucia said.

'It wasn't all that cold,' Grace said.

'We even went swimming,' Danny told her. She saw him gaze at Grace and something in the way their eyes met and held made her feel she'd gate-crashed a very private party. Later, when she arrived home to the elegant house in Mount Lismore, the empty night ahead echoed with silence.

* * *

'I think Lucia was here to check you out,' Grace said, after her sister had left.

'I don't blame her,' Danny said. 'She cares about you.'

'I know,' Grace said softly. 'I have Lucia to thank for wanting to write. She sowed the seeds. When I was young, she used to read to me a lot. All kinds of stories. It gave me such a wonderful, warm feeling inside that it's something I'd love to recreate for others.'

'Tell me what you'd most like to write about,' Danny said, drawing her over to the sofa where they snuggled together under the velour rug.

She spoke to Danny about the kind of stories she imagined writing, what she had done so far, and after a while she made a ceremony of pulling the carrier bag out from the wardrobe, showing him her notes and folders and some of her writing. Now and again her thoughts plunged back to her childhood days, recalling the evenings her parents had lots of friends and relatives dropping in to their old family home, and instead of being tucked up in bed, she and Lucia would sit in their pyjamas at the top of the stairs, laughing and giggling and wondering what was happening downstairs. Lucia used to read her stories to distract her from the talk and chatter, until Grace was ready to fall asleep. They'd even shared midnight feasts, Lucia making a party out of next to nothing.

Then things had changed. Lucia, too, had changed.

They'd moved house when Grace was still young enough to notice that the new house didn't have the big, flower-filled gardens that their old house had had, but was old enough to think her parents were silly when they said they no longer needed a car. The biggest change for Grace had been Lucia. Lucia continued to read to Grace most nights while they settled into the new house, but then Grace had learned to read and adolescence had changed her sister. A gap had opened up between them far wider than the five years that separated them. Lucia had knuckled down to her school books and had emerged from secondary school determined to do well in college. Which she had, following it up with her swift ascent of the career ladder and by marrying the very eligible and equally high-flying Robert Edwards.

She didn't tell Danny that the only time Grace had ever come close to following in Lucia's footsteps was when she'd been in a relationship with Gavin. She'd met him through friends of Robert's, when Lucia had invited her along to a charity fundraiser. Apart from Lucia's delight that they'd hooked up, Grace felt sure that her parents were relieved that their younger, less successful daughter had managed to land such an eligible man. Even Grace had felt some kind of inner validation. After all, she must have been doing something right to have the successful, kind and very thoughtful Gavin in her life, sending her flowers, lavishing her with unexpected gifts and proclaiming undying love for her.

Until that had all gone wrong.

Chapter Eleven

'When are we going to meet this amazing man?' Karen asked, stirring her penne pasta with her fork. 'I'm running out of patience.'

'I think you just want to keep him all to yourself,' Suz teased. 'We'll never get a look in.'

Grace took a sip of water and ran the knife across her pizza. The three of them had passed on the canteen, the spring-like day tempting them outside, and they were having lunch at a small Italian around the corner from Arcadia. Grace couldn't help thinking of Danny and what he might be doing. She knew he wanted to design a selection of websites, so he'd have some examples to show before the customers came calling, and the two of them had some fun imagining the kind he might put together.

'A gardening site,' Grace had suggested. 'And a home improvements one – I'm sure Lucia won't mind you taking some stock photos of her house, just to make it more authentic. Although they'd only be the "after" photos, not the "before".'

'And how about you?' he'd asked.

'Me?'

'Yes, "Grace Bailey, children's author". How does that sound? Correction: "bestselling, award winning, children's author".'

'Hey, come on …'

'You'll need an online presence. I could construct the frame, have it ready to be filled in ...'

'Jesus, Danny, for real?'

* * *

'There she goes,' Karen's voice broke into her thoughts. 'We can't mention the D word but you're off into another world.'

Grace blinked. 'Sorry. I was just imagining my resignation letter.'

'What?'

Grace shook her head and tore off some pizza. 'Joke, joke. I wish. Anyhow, I'll try and arrange something soon so you can meet Danny,' she said, even though she'd no idea what that something might be.

She'd very tentatively suggested to Danny that they have friends around for a few drinks sometime soon, but nothing that would involve too much effort. She didn't have that many friends to ask in the first place, mainly Karen and Suz, as three years with Gavin had prevented her from widening her social circle much. He hadn't liked big parties or noisy get-togethers, or Grace going out on girlie nights. But Danny had put her off, joking that the last people he wanted to see thumping around Grace's lovely apartment were his Mayo mates.

'How about your sisters?' she'd asked. 'Are they ever in Dublin?'

'Rarely,' he'd said. 'Cara's working in Galway and Amy's at home in Mayo. We'll organise something,' he'd said. 'But not yet, okay?'

She was happy with that, it was early days, and they were still living in a bubble of their own. But she couldn't help wondering if there was another reason why Danny didn't want her to meet his family or friends. Since he'd moved in, he didn't seem to have seen any of his mates, unless he'd met them during the day while Grace was in work. If so, he'd never told her. He'd no problem with Grace going out with the gang after work, which she'd done a couple of times, celebrating a birthday and engagement. And the previous night she'd arrived home from work to find two pretty storage boxes on the kitchen table.

'What are these?' she'd asked, admiring the floral design.

'They're for you,' he'd said. 'Open them.'

She took the lid off the top box to find it contained a selection of refill pads, spiral notebooks, a packet of felt tipped pens and highlighters, and a copy of Stephen King's book *On Writing*.

'Danny,' she'd said, feeling suddenly emotional, wrapping her arms around him.

'You need something better than a supermarket carrier bag to hold your dreams,' he'd said.

* * *

The following afternoon, quite unexpectedly, Karen and Suz had their patience rewarded.

Just as Grace was sitting at her desk in Arcadia, wrestling with a report, the call came up from the lobby. A Mr Danny McBride had arrived with an urgent and personal message for Grace. Was it okay to allow him up? It was usually against regulations but he was very insistent …

'Sure,' Grace said. 'Send him up.'

She was flustered when he appeared, dressed in his leathers with his helmet under his arm. In the muted, silvery greys of the rarefied office environment he resembled a particularly attractive alien warrior. He caused such a stir as he marched right up to Grace that, all across the floor, work was suspended.

He murmured in her ear. 'Do exactly as you're told. Tell your manager you're urgently needed elsewhere.'

'What?'

'Go on. It's far too nice a day to be stuck in here.'

Grace's eyes drifted to the window where fresh spring sunshine was glinting across the city-centre streets. It was such an unexpected novelty after the long, grey winter that something inside her broke free of its moorings and bubbled to the surface, tasting like sparkling champagne on her tongue. Grace darted a glance at Myra, her manager, who was sitting in her glass cubicle further down the floor, taking it all in. She stood up and smoothed her hair, feeling everyone's eyes on her as she walked down the floor.

Karen's eyes were like saucers as she mouthed, 'He's hot.'

Myra looked at Grace with surprise but nodded her head when Grace asked for permission to leave as she was needed urgently elsewhere. 'Just one thing,' Myra said.

'Yes, Myra?'

Myra gave her a half smile. 'I hope everything's okay, but the next time Mr Diet Coke arrives in, ask him to make sure it's tea-break time. The productivity in this office has dropped to zilch, and all concentration levels are gone out the window.'

* * *

'I'm needed for what exactly, Danny,' Grace asked him, shrugging into her coat as she followed his stalking figure down the corridor, conscious of the rows of eyes staring after them. He grinned but said nothing, striding out to the sunlit afternoon where his bike was parked on a double yellow line. Then he took a scarf, gloves and a crash helmet out of the carrier and handed them to her. 'Have you seen the baby elephants in the zoo?'

'The *what*?' Nonplussed, she thought she'd misheard.

'We'll get to see them this afternoon.'

'You're daft. I'm supposed to be helping to write up a monthly report. I can't just walk out of the office.'

'You just have. No problem.'

'You sound like you're used to skiving off work. Have you done this before?'

He ignored her question by asking her one of his own. 'What's more important, Grace? How much will the report matter in three months' time? It's a glorious day with a touch of spring in the air. You'll never get this day back again. How do you want to remember it? Being stuck in a concrete bunker? I thought you'd like the zoo.'

She laughed and shook her head. 'I don't believe this. I don't believe I'm going along with it either. Who said you could get away with this kind of thing?'

He shrugged.

'Besides, this wasn't on your list.'

'*Our* list. It is now. What are you waiting for?' He pulled on his helmet and swung onto the saddle, easing the bike off its stand.

She locked her bag in the carrier and jumped on behind him, laughing for the sheer joy of it. She'd never played truant before and it was heady and ridiculous and invigorating as he pressed the throttle and gently manoeuvred the motorcycle down over the kerb. Grace felt a giddiness rising inside her and the coolness of the air streaming by her face as Danny joined the traffic and headed north of the city towards the Phoenix Park and the zoo.

The afternoon was incandescent, the sky pale and soft, the sun sending long, slanting slices of glimmering light through the parklands. They sipped takeout coffee as they watched the elephants, and Grace loved the tiny baby elephant who spent most of the time tucked under his mummy. She was enthralled by the flamingos, their plumage a splodge of bright, glorious colour against the early spring foliage. But she was mostly enthralled by Danny, laughing and joking as they strolled around, stopping occasionally to kiss and cuddle – Danny at his best, his worst, and his most beguiling.

She knew there were still large parts of Danny she didn't yet understand, and couldn't get a handle on, but here and now, being in the moment with him, that didn't seem to matter at all.

Chapter Twelve

The March morning was still dark when he pulled her out of bed despite her laughing protests. Grace giggled at the sight of their reflection in the mirrored wall of the lift. She was tall, and Danny was slightly taller than her; together they were muffled in jackets and scarves and gloves, just a slick of cream on her pale face and balm on her lips, her short, bright blonde hair still tossed from the night before – she could still make out the grooves where Danny had scored his fingers through it last night in bed.

In the chilly basement where his motorbike was parked, they put on their crash helmets and she locked her bag in the carrier. She swung easily onto the saddle behind him, curving her arms around his waist and cuddling into his broad back as he started the motor. The bike swayed beneath her as it surged up the ramp and roared out into the street.

Danny drove through the hushed, sleepy suburbs and up into the mountains, Grace clinging to him, as far below, rows of glittering streetlights shimmered through the ghostly grey, early morning mist. When they left the city behind there was only the light of the motorbike cutting through the dark mountainous road and they were in a world of their own.

He knew where he was going, eventually parking the bike in a clearing close to some woods. The darkness had been thinning out, and guiding the way with the help of a torch, he led her by the hand as they hiked up through a scree-covered trail until they arrived at a good viewing spot high above Glendalough, the site of an ancient monastic settlement in a glacial valley in County Wicklow.

'You've been here before,' she said.

'I might have been.'

If he knew he was at the perfect spot to see the sunrise, then of course he'd been here before. She was curious to know more, but not curious enough to spoil the mood by asking questions. Danny had a habit of neatly side-stepping questions he didn't want to answer. It was all part of the package; the intriguing, sparkling, yet sometimes childlike Danny McBride she had come to love in a few short weeks.

She swung her long legs back and forth over the shadowy abyss. She lowered her voice to a whisper on account of the sense of occasion and said, 'No one has ever made me feel like this before.' The pre-dawn air over the ancient monastic settlement was so calm and still her words seemed to float across it like a soft, perfect bubble.

'Like what?' Danny asked.

'The way you make me feel … absolutely amazing. Free, like the breeze. Wonderful. Powerful.'

'You're kidding.'

Grace laughed softly. 'Although right now it's mixed up with being terrified to death at sitting up here *and* exhausted after getting up at an ungodly hour of the morning,' she said. She peeled off her gloves long enough to secure her woollen scarf a little tighter around her neck. Far below, beyond knots of darkly shadowed woods, and the soft rise of valleys slumbering under a blanket of dawn mist, she saw the glimmer of a lake. From this vantage point it was a long, narrow pool of silvery water caught in the grip of rugged, indigo mountains.

He didn't answer her question. 'Ssh. Just relax. It'll be worth it.'

'I hope so.' She turned and gave him a big grin, to show she was teasing him.

'You're not really frightened to death, are you?' he asked.

'Not quite, but I am hundreds of feet up in the air.' Grace's voice was even softer now as the stillness of the morning and sense of ancient grandeur wrapped round her chest. Sounds of the world around them waking up to a new day, the rustling of the birds and the first, tentative early morning trills, gradually encroached on her consciousness.

'Don't move,' he said, getting up.

'I'm not moving anywhere.'

He sat down behind her and she felt him shoring her up with his body as he stretched his legs on either side of hers, so that they dangled over the edge together. His arms curved round her waist and he caught her tightly against his chest, and told her to forget everything and just breathe very slowly. Together they watched the early morning light sweep up from the horizon in a burst of gold and crimson until the wild, ancient beauty of the panorama around them swam into clearer focus as it flooded with light, and the tender blue sky above them was dotted with fiery clouds.

'Wow. *Wowee*. I feel far more amazed than terrified,' Grace said, leaning back and snuggling into the security of his chest.

'Good. Are you glad I dragged you out of bed?'

'And made me skive off work? Yes, absolutely. Thrilled to bits.'

'I knew the weather would be perfect this morning, you can catch up with work tomorrow.' He dropped a kiss on the top of her head.

'Sure. Once I think up a good reason for not showing up at the office, I think today is going to be a great day.'

'It'll be the best day yet. Wait til you see.'

She wanted to stay in this moment. Her and Danny, having the best day yet.

* * *

When they came home from Glendalough, they raced each other to get through the door, because last one in had to make the lunch. They had breakfasted on coffee and rolls in a motorway service station, so first it was time to catch up on some sleep.

'Race you into bed ...' Danny said, stripping off his jacket and boots in the hall.

'You're on,' Grace said, doing likewise.

Danny was quicker than she was and in the half-light of their curtained bedroom she saw his pale skin gleaming as, naked, he dived under the rumpled duvet they'd abandoned before dawn. She dove in beside him, cuddling under the duvet, and Danny's hands did delicious things to her body before they fell asleep, spooned together.

They woke up around lunchtime, and Grace didn't know where she was for a moment. It was warm. She felt languorous. She turned on the pillow to see Danny propped on his elbow, smiling at her, and it all came flooding back.

'I love watching you sleep,' he said. 'Still the best day so far?'

She loved watching his face as he slept too. Restful. Trusting. Innocent. Sometimes she wondered what secrets he could be hiding. She moved up in the bed, arched her body against his, and kissed the side of his jaw. 'Let's make it even better,' she said.

She couldn't get enough of lovemaking with Danny. He was infinitely tender and wildly exciting in turns; he made her laugh, and then he made her gasp and catch her breath, he filled her up with the wonderful sensation of him, and the spirals of pleasure he gave her pulsed all the way to the tips of her toes.

* * *

Later that afternoon, they were having coffee in the kitchen and Danny was working on his laptop when Grace's mobile rang.

'Grace,' Lucia said, in her best Izobel voice, 'I tried your office but you're not there.'

'No, I'm off today.'

'*Off?* What's wrong? You're not sick are you?'

Trust Lucia to find out she wasn't in work that day. 'Not exactly,' Grace hedged, feeling she'd been caught misbehaving. According to Lucia's code of practice you should only be off work if it wasn't physically possible to put your feet to the floor and get out of bed due to a rare and most serious disorder. Grace smiled at Danny and waggled her fingers at him, then she pointed to the bedroom, indicating she would take the call in there. She didn't want to distract him while he was working or have him overhear her side of the conversation.

'Not exactly?' Lucia's voice rose. 'Don't tell me it was another trip to the zoo!'

Grace was glad she was sitting on the bed, out of Danny's earshot. 'How did you know about that?'

'Robert's sister, Ruth, told me she saw you, complete with your new man, cavorting around the zoo in the middle of the afternoon like a pair of love-struck teenagers.'

Grace's mind filled with the image of Danny and her strolling around the zoo arm-in-arm on that carefree afternoon, stopping every so often to kiss and cuddle, Danny's hands sliding under her coat and around her waist to pull her close. 'You sound jealous.' She couldn't resist it.

'Don't be ridiculous,' Lucia hissed. 'Where are you now?'

'I'm at home.'

'Is Danny there too?' Lucia's voice was tight.

Grace felt her defences rising. 'Danny's working this afternoon,' she said, grateful for the half-truth.

'Really? Did he not take the day off as well?'

Grace stayed silent. There was no need to supply the finer details that Danny was sitting at her kitchen table while he worked on his start-up plan for his business, which he still had to get off the ground. 'Is everything all right?' she eventually asked.

Lucia didn't normally call her during working hours, being far too committed to her career to waste time in frivolous conversation. 'I'd a phone call from Mum,' Lucia said. 'She and Dad will be in Dublin for the rugby match in three weeks' time. It would be a good occasion for us all to get together. I can book a table for the six of us in Blu Grass.'

Grace's gut instinctively rebelled at the thoughts of a night in Blu Grass – rivalled only in the pretentiousness stakes by the Leeson Street venue where Lucia had dragged the four of them the last time – never mind the prospect of Danny coming face to face with her parents over minuscule designer starters and absurdly marked-up wine. Of course she wanted them to meet Danny, but not just yet. The world she and Danny inhabited was still too new and tender to put under parental inspection. 'I'm not sure this is a good idea—' she began.

'What do you mean, you're not sure?'

'Danny and I could be … away that weekend.' She knew she sounded unconvincing.

'I have to go,' Lucia said abruptly. 'I'm needed in a conference call. I'll include you and Danny in the booking. I hope you'll change your mind. It's nice to have the family all together, it doesn't happen that often.'

'Wait—' Grace said, but Lucia had ended the call. Grace put her phone on silent and left it on her bedside locker, hoping she wouldn't call back.

'Hey Danny,' she said, going into the kitchen, 'Give me a big hug.'

He looked up. 'Are you okay? What did Lucia want?' he asked, getting to his feet.

'Nothing much,' she said, walking into his arms. 'Family stuff.'
'Families. Uh huh.'

'What's with the "uh-huh"?' she asked. 'You get on with yours, don't you?'

Once again, he neatly side-stepped her question. 'Sometime, when we run out of things to do, I'll tell you all about mine.' He looked down at her and smiled and she saw a shadow of regret in that smile. Regret? Danny? Then again, all families had issues of some kind or another, didn't they?

'But Lucia – she's cool,' he said. 'I like her.'

He was trying to be nice. He knew Lucia hadn't exactly hit it off with him. Grace privately believed that Lucia looked down her nose slightly at Danny, his relaxed attitude totally at odds with her precise approach to life. She leaned her head on his shoulder, catching the scent of his freshly washed jumper. It didn't matter if Lucia found him annoying, or if Grace thought her parents might find his carefree attitude to life a little ingenuous. Once she found him wonderful and sparky, as well as kind and funny, it was all that mattered.

'We'll do something cosy this evening,' he said, his hand sifting through her hair. 'I'll go out for some wine and your favourite Indian, and then we'll watch happy movies. In bed.' He held her at arm's length and smiled down at her.

'Perfect,' she said, smiling.

At seven o'clock he phoned in the order to the Indian and got ready to leave, fastening his boots, putting on his biker jacket over his leather trousers. He picked up his gloves and crash helmet and came back into the kitchen for his phone. On impulse she went over to him as he stood framed in the doorway of the kitchen, and he leaned down and kissed her forehead, and said he wouldn't be long.

Chapter Thirteen

'Still here, Lucia? Planning on staying the night? Only I don't think the Izobel group will pay for overnights no matter how devoted you are.'

Lucia looked up from her mobile. Aiden Burke, her colleague, stood lounging against the doorjamb of her office, his dark hair flopping across his forehead, a look of amusement on his face. It would have to be him, she wept silently, catching her at a moment when her world had just rocked sideways.

Aiden was also an Izobel senior manager, in finance, although from the way he strutted around he clearly saw himself as the CEO. Occasionally Lucia and he had crossed swords at various meetings and brainstorming sessions, but they both had a professional respect for each other's opinions and knew how to pick their battles.

'I thought I was the last in the building,' he said. 'And I only stayed this late because I'm meeting someone for a few drinks – nothing to do with my expenditure report being days overdue,' he grinned. 'Honest.'

Lucia continued to stare at him in stilled silence. She watched his smile fading and his face registering concern as he stepped into her office.

'Lucia? Are you okay?'

She was still incapable of speech. She sat motionless, watching him advance across the grey carpeted floor and right up to her desk as if in slow motion. She felt him tip her on her shoulder, saw his hand waggling in front of her face.

'Hey, what's up?' he asked.

'I don't know,' she said, her voice sounding peculiar to her own ears. 'I was about to head home when I got this call …' She stared down at her mobile, still caught in her clenched hand.

Aiden perched on the edge of her desk. She sat like an obedient child as he gently peeled her fingers away from her phone, took it out of her hold and placed it on the desk. 'What kind of call? Any funny business?'

It took a huge effort to shake her head. 'No, not that at all. There's been an accident of some kind. My sister's boyfriend...' She felt a tremor run though her and her mouth was strangely stiff.

'Was it bad …?'

She held up her hands in supplication. 'Bad? That's the strange part … the police called me … I thought it was Grace. He's dead. Danny's dead.'

'Oh, God, I'm so sorry.'

Lucia pushed back her leather swivel chair and, gripping the edge of the desk for support, stood up. 'I have to go to her.'

'Of course you do.'

From far away she saw herself picking up her briefcase and stowing her laptop and mobile inside. She took her car keys out of the side pocket.

'You're not going to drive,' Aiden said.

'I'll be fine,' Lucia said, attempting the Herculean task of pulling herself together and psyching herself into survivor mode as she tried to figure out the quickest route to Rathbrook Hall with a brain that felt like it had seized up.

'I'll drive you,' Aiden offered.

'Not at all, you have plans for tonight,' she objected.

'Nothing I can't put back,' he said.

'I can't let you do that. Anyway, I'll need my car.'

'Lucia Edwards, I'm driving you to your sister's, no arguments,' Aiden said. 'You're in no fit state. I'll arrange to have your car brought wherever you want it first thing in the morning. But you're not getting behind the wheel tonight.'

'I'm fine,' she repeated, coming around by the front of her desk. But even this simple act was like staggering around in a bad dream, and she was so unsteady on her feet that when he held out his hand for her car keys she relinquished them.

'Good girl,' he said, but his words slid past her without making any impression. 'Let me know wherever you want your car tomorrow and I'll have it there first thing.'

'Thanks, I appreciate it, but I'll get a taxi out to my sister's. I don't want to impose on you.' She wondered how come she could still talk, considering her chest felt as if it had been thumped by a sledgehammer.

'You're not imposing on me. Let me do my good deed for the day and help a friend in need. Now shut up with your silly objections and give me your sister's address. I'll have you there in no time.'

He ushered her out of the office, stopping to turn off the lights at the door. She looked back into the darkened room. Her desk was silhouetted against the window, which framed a night-time business park lit up by rows of intermittent lights blazing out from other office blocks. She wondered who the shirt-sleeved, faceless people were, working late tonight in anonymous offices. She wished she were one of them.

Aiden drove her out to Rathbrook in his Audi, his voice so kind as he told her to have her phone handy just in case she got another call that she had the sudden urge to close her eyes and rest her head on his shoulder, just for comfort. He offered to pull into a petrol station or supermarket to get her water, or coffee, or something stronger.

'No, thanks,' she said.

He must have noticed she was still shaking because he reached into the back seat, picked up a striped travel rug and passed it over to her. 'Tuck this around you,' he said. She wondered oddly what he was doing with a travel rug in the back seat of his luxuriously upholstered car. It should be Robert who was with her now, she realised with a pang, Robert taking her out to Grace, Robert who would take charge, Robert who would hold her tight later in bed tonight. She hadn't even told him the news yet. Needing to hear his voice, she called his mobile when they were stopped at the traffic lights, but it went straight to voicemail. The part of her that wasn't frozen in shock wondered what he was doing tonight in London that he couldn't take her call. For a moment she couldn't figure out whose turn it was to travel that weekend, then she remembered she was supposed to be packing her overnight case that evening, ready for the Friday evening flight to London.

Aiden pulled up outside the main entrance to Rathbrook Hall.

'I don't think I'll be in tomorrow,' Lucia said, in a flat voice.

'We won't be expecting you. I'll tell Diane and the rest of the team what's happened.'

'I'm supposed to be giving a presentation to the board in the afternoon, on the latest methodology in their marketing initiatives ...' Why was she concerned about work at a time like this? 'Diane could probably cover it,' she said. 'I have all the material in a folder on my desk.'

'I'm sure she'll have no problem finding that.'

She was glad there was no sign of any amusement in his voice, because it was a standing joke in Izobel that although the two women worked in adjacent rooms, and had similar responsibilities, both offices were vastly different. Compared with Diane's office, where children's crayoned drawings were scattered across the whiteboard and an odd assortment of their craft attempts took pride of place on her desk, Lucia's office, with its tidy, leather-topped desk, her 'To do' list clearly itemised on a whiteboard, and her 'Pending' in-tray, was almost far too neat and pristine. Diane would have no problem finding Lucia's notes. Instead of feeling relieved, Lucia took no crumb of comfort whatsoever from this. 'I'll need a couple of days off next week as well,' she said, thinking ahead.

'Lucia, take all the time you need. I'll tell William what's happened,' he said, referring to the Izobel Group CEO.

Suddenly she felt overcome as anxiety gripped her. She dropped her head into her hands. 'Dear God, why am I bothered about the office? My sister is in there and her boyfriend has just died. Danny is gone. *Gone!* This is a bloody nightmare. What can I say to my sister? How will I talk to her? How can I make it better for her?'

She felt Aiden's hand on her shoulder. 'You'll be fine Lucia, you just have to be there for her. Do you want me to come in with you? Can I do anything at all?'

She took out a tissue but she was dry-eyed. 'No, thanks Aiden, you've got me here in one piece, which is great.'

She was grateful to have Aiden by her side as he saw her up to Grace's apartment. He waited until the door was opened by a sympathetic-looking policewoman. He squeezed her arm and said, 'Chat tomorrow, and please give Grace my sympathies. And let me know if you need me for anything.'

She felt suddenly vulnerable and very alone when he was gone. The policewoman smiled at her and said, 'You must be Lucia.'

'Yes, I am, that's right,' Lucia said, squaring her shoulders as she stepped into the apartment, preparing to be there for Grace.

Chapter Fourteen

Grace stared at her sister as if she was a stranger. She couldn't understand why Lucia was looking immaculate, in a beautiful taupe-shaded trouser suit, clutching a patent briefcase that matched her stiletto pumps, her dark hair caught in a loose chignon at the nape of her neck as though she was dressed for the office. Then she realised that Lucia had probably come from a late night at Izobel. Her sister's usual air of brisk capability and supreme competence was overlaid with warm concern. Lucia had to reach up to throw her arms around Grace, holding her in a long, tight, fragrant embrace.

'Dear God, I don't believe this. What's happened?'

'That's the thing,' Grace said, her voice feeling and sounding wooden. 'I don't know. It's some kind of crazy mistake. Danny went out to the takeaway and off-licence and he still hasn't come home. I'm sorry the police dragged you over here, but I told them it couldn't have been Danny in that accident. They even made tea for me,' Grace said. 'But he's still not back …'

Grace saw the policewoman exchange a sympathetic glance with Lucia. Over in a corner of her small kitchen, taking up lots of space, a policeman was on his mobile. She still couldn't grasp what they were doing here or why she'd let them in.

It hadn't bothered her unduly when an hour had gone by and

Danny hadn't come home. Sometimes there was a long queue in the takeaway or a delay in the off-licence. She'd looked in vain for her mobile in case Danny had been calling. After a while she'd remembered she'd silenced it and thrown it onto her bedside locker after talking to Lucia. But there were no messages. She'd been just about to call him when the intercom buzzed, but it was the police who were knocking on her door, shattering the calm silence with words that had crashed like alien missiles.

Collision … Instant … Fatality … Next of kin …

They'd asked if they could call someone for her, and the only person she could think of, the only person she wanted apart from Danny himself, was Lucia.

'I've told them it wasn't Danny,' Grace said, her head swimming so much that the floor was wavering in front of her. 'They said the accident happened close to the M50, but Danny couldn't have been on that road, he was going in the opposite direction, to the Indian and the off-licence in the village. It doesn't make sense.' It was somebody else who had slammed into a wall, somebody else whose bike was a mess of twisted metal. Somebody else who hadn't felt anything.

Somebody else who was dead.

Wasn't it?

The policewoman looked at her with such compassion that Grace felt all the warm familiarities of her life harden and change forever.

The policewoman turned to Lucia. 'We've explained to Grace that the motorbike involved in the collision was registered to this address, in the name of Danny McBride, when the motor tax was renewed last month. He also had a Public Services card on his person, in that name. We need to ask Grace a few more questions, it's vital that we contact his next of kin, so it's good that you're here.'

Grace felt her face crumple. 'Oh, Lucia! How is this happening?' None of this made sense in the context of freewheeling, joyful, larger-than-life, fun-loving, beautiful Danny. She made fists of her hands, her nails digging into her palms. Her apartment had turned into a parallel universe, possessed by something dark that swirled around, resonating against the walls and pouring down her throat like invisible black mist. She'd already told the police that strictly speaking she wasn't Danny's next of kin but she'd been too shocked to talk further.

'Grace,' Lucia said gently. 'You'll have to help the police.'

'I am, I will,' she said.

Lucia drew her across to the sofa, and sat down beside her, wrapping her arms around her.

'We need to contact Danny's next of kin as soon as possible,' the policewoman said in a gentle voice.

'Danny and I … we're not together all that long,' Grace said.

'Has he family?'

'He has, in Mayo, parents … and sisters. I don't have their details.' In spite of her numbing shock, she felt ridiculously stupid at this lack of basic knowledge. 'They're probably on his mobile phone … aren't they?'

There was a tense silence.

'Did Danny have his phone with him?' the policewoman asked.

'Yes, I'm sure he had.' Grace saw him picking up his wallet and zipping it into his jacket pocket. She couldn't remember what he'd done with his phone, but he didn't go very far without it.

'We don't seem to have recovered that just yet,' the policeman said in a very kindly voice.

Grace felt breathless as the full horror of what the policewoman was saying began to spread through her body like cold, thick mud. Two hours ago, in an earlier, sweetly innocent life, Danny had stood in her doorway, broad-shouldered and vibrant, and she'd closed her eyes as he'd kissed her on the forehead; a kiss so soft it was like the touch of a butterfly, alighting there for a brief but perfect moment.

Now, according to the police, somewhere in a windowless part of the hospital, people Danny had never met before were looking at his lifeless body and going through his things. Somewhere in Mayo, Danny's family was going about their business this evening, totally innocent of the devastation that was about to be unleashed on them.

'His parents ... they live in Castlebar.'

'The previous address we have on our motor tax records for Danny is Phibsboro,' the policewoman said.

'Phibsboro? I thought ...' Grace faltered.

'You thought what?'

Instinct made her shake her head. 'Nothing.' She tried to hide her confusion. She could have sworn Danny had told her he used to live in Harold's Cross, house-sharing with some guys from Mayo.

It's much easier to work in your kitchen, Grace, than the rented house in Harold's Cross ....'

Wasn't that what he'd said? Or was it, though? Her head felt too foggy to recall.

The questions went on.

'Do you know if any of Danny's family or close friends live in Phibsboro?'

'No.'

'So they didn't?'

'No, I don't know.'

'Just how long was Danny living here?' the policewoman's voice was marshmallow soft.

Grace tried to pull herself together. It was as impossible as trying to pick up water with her hands and even her bones felt as though they were sliding apart. 'Six weeks,' she said, her teeth beginning to chatter.

Six weeks. Suddenly all that wonderful, amazing time was reduced; shrunk to a swift, six-second time-lapse video in Grace's head, beginning with the snowy January evening she'd thrown open both the door and her life to him and his battered brown case and his warm eyes; they'd both laughed at this great new adventure and he'd stepped over the threshold and wrapped his arms around her, and had held her there in the centre of his embrace – in every way – until he'd walked out earlier tonight.

The police went on to talk about formal identification of the body. The body? *No.*

'I can't do that,' she whispered. It was unimaginable. Surely Danny would walk back in through the door any minute with a big silly grin on his face telling her it had all been a huge misunderstanding. Or else she was in the middle of a nightmare and she'd wake up soon.

The policewoman looked at her sympathetically and said it might be best left to the family. 'We'll call to the address in Phibsboro, but do you have any idea at all of Danny's parents' address?'

'No, but it was close to Castlebar, just outside the town ...' Or had she misunderstood, like with the house in Harold's Cross? She was conscious of Lucia hearing her hesitant answers, and in a ridiculous way she thought her uncertainty took some of the shine off the whole wonderful package she shared with Danny McBride. As though she hadn't known the real Danny, and somehow that reduced the wonder of their amazing relationship and the happiness they'd enjoyed.

'Danny and I ...' her voice was hoarse and painful, but she had to say it, 'you see, it was just about us, me and him, and no one else got much of a look in. I never met his family, but I heard about his parents and two sisters. We didn't know each other all that long, but in that time we were ... everything to each other. It was just us ... nothing else mattered. Anything outside of us didn't come into the picture.'

Lucia came to her rescue. 'I don't think Grace can help you any more for now,' she said, tightening her hold around her sister.

'We understand,' the policewoman said. 'We should have enough to go on, but we'll take your details because we will be talking to you again.'

'She'll be staying with me,' Lucia said, in a brisk, efficient tone that told Grace there was no point in arguing with her. Lucia gave the police her address and both their mobile numbers, sensing correctly that Grace was incapable of thinking straight.

When the police left, everything including the space inside her and all around her seemed horribly stripped bare to Grace, as though a plug had been pulled, and all the joy and happiness and the very essence of life itself had drained right out of her and flowed down into a gaping dark hole. She turned to Lucia, her limbs stiff, 'I'm not going anywhere.'

She didn't want Danny to be gone. She didn't want to be someone who needed the help of her ultra-organised, micro-managing, rising-star older sister because her boyfriend had just – according to the police – died in a motorcycle accident. She wanted it to be a normal evening. She shook her head and blinked, wondering how soon she could get out of this nightmare and get back to where they were supposed to be: she and Danny cuddled together in bed watching the television.

'Yes you are,' Lucia said. 'I'm not leaving you here on your own.'

'Why are you doing this? You didn't even like Danny.'

'Grace, darling, you're in shock. What does it matter whether or not I liked Danny? You're my sister. I want to help you, that's what sisters do.'

'Are you doing this because you want to or because you feel you should?' That's what Danny used to say if Grace was dithering about something. He'd ask her to check her gut reaction to see how it felt. Then she'd know whether it was right or wrong for her.

Lucia shook her head. 'No way am I leaving you here on your own. Gather whatever things you need for a couple of days. I'll help if you point me in the right direction.'

'I don't know …' Leaving now with Lucia was like walking away and leaving the imprint of Danny behind, the shadow of him standing in the doorway. She still hoped he'd come breezing through it in his biker jacket and trousers, juggling his crash helmet along with the food and wine, bending to kiss her on his way to the kitchen counter.

Lucia took both her hands in hers and spoke to her in a gentle, motherly way, like you would to a small child. 'Listen to me,' Lucia said gently. 'The next few days are going to be tough. The police will need to talk to you again. They'll contact Danny's parents who will certainly want to talk to you.' In a far corner of her mind, Grace was surprised to see a different side to her dynamo sister and it brought flickering memories of an earlier time in her life when she and Lucia had been much younger.

'There'll be a funeral,' Lucia was saying. 'Oh darling, you can't deal with this on your own. I'll be here for you all the way.'

A funeral. She hadn't even thought of that. *No*. Dear God, not Danny. Sweat broke out on her forehead, a sour taste filled her mouth, and then she was running to the bathroom, where she was violently sick.

Lucia cleaned her face, and Grace watched through the fog as Lucia packed enough essentials for a couple of days, and organised a taxi as her car was still in the office. In Lucia's house, Grace's feet didn't seem to be connecting with the floor; she hovered around feeling weird. She saw her disembodied head reflecting faintly off white glossy presses and couldn't grasp what she was doing here. She sat on the edge of a long cream sofa in the timeless elegance of Lucia's sitting room, and she sipped large brandies that Lucia insisted on pressing into her hand with her neat, slender fingers, saying something about the brandy being good for shock and helping her sleep. Grace wanted to laugh; she would never sleep soundly again. Instead she clutched the crystal brandy balloon as though it was the most important thing in her life right then, thankful that Lucia pretended not to hear the sound of Grace's chattering teeth bashing against the expensive glass. Later, Grace floated upstairs into Lucia's beautiful guest bedroom. Even though the central heating was on, it had the cold, flat ambience of a room that was rarely used, and it seemed in perfect tune with the cold, flat feeling that was engulfing Grace. Lucia followed her up, bearing her bag that contained a change of clothes and some toiletries. She offered to stay with her, but Grace refused.

She lay sleepless on top of the ivory coverlet, conscious that only a thin film of numbness held at bay the most frightening pain imaginable, and she wondered why Danny had been travelling in the opposite direction to the village that evening, because it didn't make any kind of sense, any more than Danny crashing headlong into a wall made sense.

Chapter Fifteen

When Lucia saw Grace coming into her kitchen the following morning, the sight of her white face sent panic fluttering around her. She stood frozen, and searched for appropriate words to say.

'What are you doing?' Grace asked.

Lucia dropped the cutlery and place mat she'd been laying out, and gave Grace a big hug. 'I'm getting some breakfast for you,' she said, wishing there was something she could do or say to take that dazed look off Grace's face.

'I don't want breakfast,' Grace said stubbornly. 'I want to go back to the apartment in case Danny comes home. Why aren't you in work? I'm sure you're up to your tonsils as usual.'

Lucia wished there was a simple step-by-step guide to tell her how to best soothe and care for a suddenly bereaved loved one. Problem was, she was so used to keeping control of everything in her life, and keeping an eye out for Grace – especially keeping an eye out for her younger, more easy-going sister, because with five years between them she'd been very much in the role of big sister – that she was finding it impossible to cope with the helplessness swamping her while her sister was numbed with grief. Her chest was aching and she seemed to be sliding around her own house as if everything was slippy underneath, from the pale oak floors to the limestone tiles.

But even if she wanted to weep silently for the tragic and untimely loss of Danny McBride, she had to put that to one side and hold it all together for Grace. Then again, she'd held it all together for Grace years ago, when the '80s recession had stalked their childhoods.

'Grace, darling, you don't realise it, but you're in shock,' she said. 'I've arranged a few days off work. They're not expecting me in.'

'That's a first. I thought you hated your staff pulling the family emergency card.'

'Not when it's genuine,' Lucia said, striving to keep her voice calm. 'I've called your office as well, but told them you weren't taking any calls just yet.'

'Amn't I?'

'You hardly feel up to talking to them, do you?'

'I might want to talk to Karen and Suz … but, yeah, not just yet.'

'And I called Robert this morning. He's shocked too, and sends his love. He'll be home on the early flight tomorrow.' She didn't want him here first thing in the morning. She wanted him now. Even a reassuring kiss and a hug from him would have settled her panic a little.

'What day is it?'

'It's Friday. I've spoken to Mum and Dad too.'

'You must have been up early.'

'I was. Mum wants to talk to you as soon as you feel up to it and I'm to let her know the funeral arrangements.'

'Mum?' Grace said, her soft blue eyes ringed with dark hollows. 'What's the funeral got to do with her? She never met Danny.'

'Oh, Grace, it's *you*. Mum wants to be here for you.'

Grace gave a half laugh. 'Maybe she thinks it serves me right, after splitting with Gavin.'

Jesus. 'I know you don't mean that,' Lucia said. 'No one thinks that, least of all Mum.'

This wasn't the time to admit that they'd all loved Gavin. He was mannerly, unassuming, had been mad about Grace and already seemed like part of the family. Mum had even been looking at hats, following broad hints from Gavin the last time he'd met Dad, when Grace had dropped the bombshell that they were over. Then Grace had met Danny, who seemed to have possessed some kind of magic that had turned Grace's head completely. And now he was gone, in the most horrendous way imaginable.

Lucia blanked all this out, as she couldn't afford to think about his sad end. 'Sit down, Grace,' she urged. 'Please. You need to eat.' She took orange juice out of the fridge and poured a glass, handing it to her. 'Here, sip this for starters.'

'I don't want anything. It wasn't just a bad nightmare, was it?' Grace said, in a thin, wavery voice. 'That did really happen last night, didn't it?'

'I'm afraid it did, love.' She braced herself for Grace's hysterical grief, but instead Grace's face seemed to close down on itself, so that it looked like a pale mask with slits of red-rimmed eyes. When Lucia hugged her again, she might as well have been hugging a marble statue.

Aiden Burke arrived soon after ten o'clock with her car while Grace was up in the shower, and Lucia insisted he come in for coffee before he got a taxi back to the office. Even though it was strange to see him there, having him in her kitchen passing on the sympathies and best wishes of the Izobel staff filled her with a funny kind of comfort. Somewhere outside of this nightmare, life went on as normal in Izobel and Aiden was her link to that.

'And Diane is okay with the presentation?' she asked.

'It's all sorted Lucia, no worries on that score. You've enough to cope with right now.'

'Grace … she's still in denial and Jesus …' Lucia shrugged, 'I don't know what to do for the best.'

'Whatever you do, look after yourself,' he said. 'I didn't know what to do for the best last night, you were in shock. I'm not used to seeing you so, if you don't mind me saying, human and vulnerable.'

She managed to smile at him, even though his keen gaze was a little unsettling, as if he was looking at her afresh. 'You did exactly the right thing. You gave me some practical help.'

'There you are then, that's what you can do for Grace.'

When the company taxi arrived she went to the hall door with him, conscious of her jeans, soft cream jumper and make-up free face, compared to his perfect professional appearance in his sharp suit and ice-white shirt.

'Thanks, Aiden,' she said, suddenly at a loss and struggling for words.

'You're more than welcome,' he said. 'Take care of yourself.' This time as well as squeezing her lightly on the shoulder, he bent down and kissed her cheek, and she caught a whiff of his aftershave.

And if she'd felt at a loss before, now she felt completely cut adrift when she watched Aiden wave through the window as the taxi did a U-turn before heading back into Izobel and a normal Friday morning.

* * *

She was glad she was useful for something when the police phoned later to say that Danny's parents had arrived from Mayo and had formally identified Danny.

'There's going to be a post mortem to find out the exact cause of—' Lucia swallowed, '… Danny's death. But they don't need to talk to you for now, and they're not looking for anyone else in connection with the incident.'

'What do you mean, anyone else?'

'The collision forensics examined the scene this morning. It doesn't seem to be anything other than a motorcycle accident.'

'This whole thing is a load of crap,' Grace said. 'It's like the world had gone mad.'

'I know,' Lucia soothed. 'Of course it is. The police said they'd put you in touch with a liaison officer.'

'No.'

'It might help, Grace.' *Better than I can*, she thought.

'I said no. Please, Lucia. I'll talk to Mum later.'

'Good. She asked me to call her again to let her know how you are. She's worried about you and hates being away at a time like this.'

But not as much as she hated Robert being in London right now.

He arrived home on Saturday morning and as soon as he took her into his arms, Lucia felt shored up, as though some frayed parts of her body and soul were being glued together again. Then she took a call from Holly, the police liaison officer. Danny's parents, Tess and Joseph McBride, wanted to meet Grace. They were staying in Joseph's sister's house in Dun Laoghaire, pending the release of Danny's body.

Later that afternoon, Robert drove them to Dun Laoghaire, pulling up outside an attractive red-bricked Victorian house, where spring sunshine glinted off the windows and drifts of daffodils swayed prettily in the garden.

'I can't do this,' Grace said in a flat, monotone voice. 'How can I face Danny's family? They're probably blaming me for what happened. He went out that night because of me.'

Lucia gripped her hands. 'Grace, it was a senseless accident. These things happen.'

'But was it an accident?' Grace said. 'I don't understand why Danny was going away from the village. And he was so careful on the bike that I can't accept he went into a wall. It's *mad*. How can I talk to his parents?'

'Just take it nice and slow. How ever you feel, Grace, they'll be feeling a whole lot worse. He was their son. It might do you good to talk to them.'

A net curtain twitched at an upstairs window and Lucia knew they were being watched as they got out of the car and walked up the garden path. She deliberately linked Grace's arm, knowing that this was going to be difficult for her sister. However, it turned out to be difficult for her sister in a way that Lucia hadn't been expecting.

Danny's family hadn't known anything at all about Grace.

Chapter Sixteen

At first Grace was relieved that she was far too numb to absorb Tess McBride's words. She knew it would come back to hurt her later – the disappointment that he'd never mentioned her to his family. She stared at the slim woman whose lovely face was pale and pinched with shock, and whose eyes were glassy with pain.

'We thought Danny was staying in a bedsit in Phibsboro, didn't we, Joseph?' Tess threw a worried glance at her husband as though, Grace thought, to confirm it was okay to admit this. Joseph McBride was distraught, removing his glasses every so often so he could stem the tears is his eyes. Danny most resembled his father, Grace realised, forgetting for a long, heart-stopping moment that he was gone. His parents' grief was thick and palpable, surrounding them like a six-foot wall. Holly, the police liaison officer, was there, her face full of warm sympathy.

'The police told us about you and where Danny had been staying,' Tess said. 'We were … quite surprised, to say the least. How long had Danny been with you?'

'About six weeks,' Grace said.

'We hadn't seen him since Christmas,' Tess said. 'I'd spoken to him, on the phone, a few times since then. I'm sure he was going to tell us about you the next time he came to visit.'

There was a tense silence.

'How did Danny … seem?' Tess asked.

'Great,' Grace told her. 'We were happy. Danny was a great one for making the most of every day.'

'Oh, gosh.' Tess was fidgeting with the collar of her blouse. 'How did he seem that evening? Before he went out? The police told us you said he was supposed to have been going to the village. What happened?'

'I don't know. He just went out to get some wine and a takeaway.'

'We were wondering if anything had gone wrong … that evening …' Tess said hesitantly.

'Like what?' Grace asked.

His mother shrugged. His father seemed to be miles away.

'Danny was perfectly happy going out the door,' Grace said. 'There was nothing unusual in the way he left. We'd had a lovely day.' There was something in his mother's sad, resigned face that made Grace continue, even though it hurt like hell to say the words, 'Danny was the most sparkling person I've ever known,' she said. 'We had a wonderful few weeks together.'

'Really?' Tess said, her voice a little faint.

Danny's father stared at her silently as though he didn't quite believe what he was hearing.

'He was so full of life it was infectious,' Grace went on, her voice choking. 'He was great fun to be with. He knew how to make the smallest, simplest thing feel like something special.' Surely they knew what their own son was like? Obviously not, because Tess looked stunned and Joseph McBride made a gasping sound.

'Are we talking about the same Danny?' he spluttered.

'Joseph!' His wife reached towards him, and patted his arm. She smiled faintly at Grace as tears filmed her eyes. 'You must have brought out the best in Danny. We didn't always …' she hesitated, her face shadowed. She dabbed her tears with a hanky.

'We didn't always have such a great relationship,' Joseph said, exchanging glances with his wife.

'Danny never had anything bad to say about his family, or either of you,' Grace said. It was the truth, mainly because he'd rarely spoken about them. 'He kept a photograph of his sister's graduation – he seemed very proud of it.' A white lie. Even in her own distress Grace knew there was no harm in using it to help ease the lifetime of devastation and regrets Danny's parents were facing. He must have been proud of that photograph, she reckoned. Danny wasn't the kind of person to have kept it unless it meant something to him.

'Amy's graduation,' Tess said. 'Did he really?' she smiled, but her eyes still held that hard glassy look and Grace wondered if anything would ever soften that pain.

'He did,' Grace told her.

'His sisters are here with us, Cara and Amy, but they preferred to stay upstairs as they're too upset to talk.'

'I have … the photo …' Grace stopped for a breath, her heart squeezing, 'I have other things … Danny's stuff … in my apartment. Not much,' she went on, gulping a little, 'clothes, some books, the most valuable thing I have is his laptop.' She didn't know what had happened to his motorbike or the clothes he'd been wearing the night of the accident, but she couldn't bear to think about that.

'I'd be grateful it you kept them to one side until we can pick them up,' Tess said, 'and if it's okay with you I'd like to see where he spent the last few weeks, and where he seems to have been so happy. But not just yet.'

'Any time,' Grace said. She zoned out as Danny's parents began to talk of the funeral arrangements – she couldn't take this in. She threw a 'rescue me' glance at Lucia and Robert who discussed the arrangements with the McBrides, had a few words with the liaison officer Holly, and then signalled it was time for them to go. 'I'm sure you've enough to be doing,' Lucia said sympathetically, ushering Grace out into the hall.

They were standing rather awkwardly in the hallway when a young woman came up out of the kitchen and Grace recognised her as the blonde girl in Danny's photograph – his sister Cara. Tess McBride made a half-hearted attempt to introduce them, but Cara brushed past, crying anew, her red-rimmed eyes darting a resentful glance at Grace before she hurried up the stairs.

'The girls …' Tess flapped her hands and shook her head sorrowfully. 'They're taking it very badly. Danny was their …' Her eyes filled with tears.

Grace heard Lucia talking as if from far away. 'Of course they are,' Lucia said smoothly. 'It's very sad, and words are absolutely useless at a time like this.'

'Thanks for calling,' Tess said, seeing them to the door. 'We'll see you soon.'

* * *

The next few days were a series of blurry, disjointed images for Grace.

Lucia brought her to Dundrum Town Centre early on Sunday morning, helping her to choose an appropriate funeral outfit speedily and efficiently and in the time it would have taken Grace to order a cup of coffee. Her parents arrived in from Paris on Sunday afternoon and Grace was bombarded with every ounce of their warm compassion.

'I'm sorry I never had the chance to meet Danny,' her father said, enfolding her in a bear-like hug. 'He must have been special.'

'He was, very,' Grace said, without elaborating, still finding it ridiculous that this had happened at all, wanting to stay muffled in his jumper.

'Have you any photographs of him?' her mother asked, her face wreathed with sorrow.

Grace shook her head. 'Another time, Mum.'

'Of course, darling. I just thought you'd like to talk about him. Sometimes it helps.'

'Not yet.' Besides, she'd hardly any photographs of him.

All her energy was gone, Grace realised, as though someone had pulled out her plug. She zoned out and let the chit-chat between Lucia, Robert and her parents flow over her head.

On Tuesday morning she zoned out at Danny's funeral too – hard to believe it was happening. Fresh shock pierced her when she saw a framed photograph of the Danny she had known and loved sitting on the coffin. His sisters brought up gifts to the altar to represent his life: a basketball and a Mayo football jersey.

Had Danny played basketball? Grace hadn't known that about him. Then again there was so much she hadn't known. Like why he'd made out that he'd been living in Harold's Cross, instead of Phibsboro, on the other side of town. Like the way she'd never met any of his mates.

Outside in the churchyard, where people mingled after the ceremony, his parents gave her a cursory hug, and accepted her parents' condolences, but after that, their glances slid over her as though they were wary of her. His sisters seemed to be huddled tightly with their friends, and Grace caught occasional pained looks in her direction, while Danny's shiny coffin, covered by a large spray of lilies, took centre stage.

After the burial, the family invited everyone back to a local hotel for refreshments.

'I'd rather we went somewhere ourselves,' Grace said.

'Don't you want to stay and talk to Danny's family?' her mother said.

'Not really,' Grace shrugged, freezing cold although it was a bright spring afternoon. 'I just want to get away from here.' She wanted to get far away from the nightmare sight of his coffin being lowered into the gash of freshly opened earth to the sound of his sisters' sobbing. Neither could she bear to look at Danny's family anymore, or notice the way they were keeping her at arm's length. And she didn't want to risk overhearing a conversation that might show a different side to Danny, the one who hadn't had a good relationship with his parents. The Danny she'd laughed and danced with and made love to had gone. Vanished in the space between a kiss on her forehead and a knock on her door.

How or why she still couldn't understand.

Chapter Seventeen

Back in Rathbrook Hall, in the first couple of weeks after his death, the ghost of Danny flitted between the rooms, bouncing off the walls and shadowing all the surfaces. When Grace called his name, he never answered. When she found herself picking up his favourite chocolate in the supermarket her heart rushed up into her mouth and she thought she was going to vomit. When she turned around in bed at night, the space where he'd lain was flat and vacant and she wanted to scream with the longing for him.

Occasionally in the dead of those quiet hours after midnight, she counted her breaths, amazed that they kept on coming without any effort on her part. Sometimes when she lay awake she heard the roar of a motorbike out on the main road. It seemed to be going up and down the road as though the rider were doing a continuous circuit – she'd hear it coming up the perimeter road towards Rathbrook Hall, the roar of the engine gearing down and receding as it sped past the apartment complex towards the retail park and the M50. Then a few minutes later she'd hear it coming back up past the apartment and on up to the village of Rathbrook. On nights like these, she thought she was going mad, because it was far too easy to imagine there was someone out there who was deliberately taunting her, reminding her of Danny.

She thought it was bad enough to imagine she heard it at night, until she began seeing it during the day. Whenever she felt the walls of the apartment crowding in on top of her, or felt Danny's absence like a hard physical pain all over her body, she put on her trainers and went out for a long, brisk walk, down through the park adjacent to the apartment complex, across the bridge over the river, and up to Rathbrook village. Problem was, she had to get used to seeing other bikers out and about on the roads; she wanted to stop each and every one and urge them to take care. And sometimes she seemed to be seeing the same bike over and over again. A bike that reminded her of Danny's. Twice, coming back from the village, as she'd waited to cross the road, it had come up from behind her and stopped at the traffic lights and she'd deliberately studied it, troubled by a strange feeling in her gut. She could have sworn the bike was identical to Danny's, and the rider was wearing a thick black jacket and a full-face helmet, just as Danny had worn. The only difference was that this biker's helmet had a tinted shield, so Grace couldn't see his face.

Lucia came over to Grace's apartment two or three times a week, bringing glossy magazines, a bottle of wine, or expensive cosmetics along with tempting cakes, as though Grace were some kind of invalid in need of cheering up. Grace was glad to see her, and touched by Lucia's thoughtfulness, especially as it was probably anathema to her sister to gorge on the calorific creations she brought over, but she was equally determined that Lucia wasn't going to waltz in and take over organising her life with her characteristic efficiency, or see Grace's recovery as her next project.

'It's bound to take you a while to come to terms with what has happened,' Lucia said when Danny was gone two weeks and Grace still hadn't returned to work. Although Karen and Suz had called to see her, pledging their support, she knew she was incapable of functioning in an office environment where she had constant dealings with demanding customers and often complicated insurance adjustments to make.

'In a way I can't come to terms with anything, that's the problem,' Grace admitted. 'I don't understand what happened to Danny that night. Sometimes I blame myself. Sometimes I think Danny's family blames me. You heard the way his mother asked if anything had gone wrong that night, as if we had a row or something before he left and it made him careless.'

'Grace, please don't do this to yourself. How could the accident have been your fault?'

Grace gripped her hands until her nails were digging into the palms. 'If it hadn't been for me, Danny wouldn't have been going out that evening. Why didn't I say I'd cook and we'd just sit in? Or that I'd love another of his stir-fries? He was a great cook, you know. Why did I let him go out the door?' She felt panicky because the memory of his last kiss on her forehead was already becoming a little fainter every day, overlaid by the nightmare of everything that had crashed into her life after it.

'Why didn't you hide his motorbike keys so he'd never find them again?' Lucia asked. 'Why didn't you both hibernate in your apartment and do all the shopping online so you'd never have to venture out again? Or stop the whole business of living? Anything can happen to anyone, at any time. You could go on forever with a list of what-ifs and what-might-have-beens. It's not going to change a single thing. So put all those mad thoughts out of your mind. Danny's accident had nothing to do with you.'

'Other times I wonder … what if it hadn't been an accident?'

'Of course it was an accident. How could it not have been?'

'I don't know,' Grace said, feeling helpless. 'I haven't got a reason. It's a gut feeling, a kind of uneasiness about the whole thing.'

'What kind of uneasiness?'

'I keep seeing a bike, just like Danny's, when I go out for a walk.

As though I'm being followed. I often hear it at night.'

'There are lots of bikes like Danny's out there,' Lucia said. 'And lots of traffic going by the front of Rathbrook on the way to the M50.'

'I can't understand why Danny was going in the wrong direction that night. He said he'd only be a short while.'

Lucia came over to her and put her hands on her shoulders. All the angles on her face were taut, so that her beautiful cheekbones were even more pronounced. Her brilliant eyes were dark and smoky and full of love. 'Look, sis, this kind of thinking isn't helping you at all. It's keeping you stuck, and it's upsetting you. I'm so sorry for what happened, Danny didn't deserve it, *you* didn't deserve it, but you're going to have to start learning to let it go. Sometimes there are no explanations for the rotten things that can happen in life, no matter how much you search for clues or try to figure out what went wrong.'

Grace wondered why Lucia was setting herself up as an expert on the rotten things in life, considering her life had always flowed seamlessly from one success to another, right from the get-go.

Her sister continued, 'If you start analysing it too much you'll end up driving yourself crazy, which is a natural enough state after the shock you got. Why don't you talk to Holly?'

'Holly?'

'The liaison officer. I'm sure she'll go through the case files with you, if you want, and answer any questions you have about what happened. She said she'd be there for a call any time.'

I know what happened, Grace wanted to say. *For some reason Danny's bike mounted the pavement and went into a wall. But I don't understand how or why such a ridiculous thing happened.*

'Don't forget I'm here for you and I'll help you as much as I can,' Lucia said. 'We'll get through this.'

'Thanks.' Grace stepped back out of Lucia's reach and busied herself making tea to have with the chocolate éclairs Lucia had brought over, reluctant to voice the questions that slithered constantly through her mind and added to her general uneasiness.

Why hadn't Danny told his mother about her? Or even let her know his new address? He hadn't been planning a trip down home in the foreseeable future, as far as she knew. Then again, impulsive being his middle name, Danny had rarely planned things much in advance. Had he had any particular reason not to tell his parents about Grace? How come his parents seemed to think she was talking about a different Danny, someone they didn't know?

Then there were the questions he'd skilfully evaded, ordinary questions about ordinary things he'd chosen not to answer. All of these added up to make her realise that her main problem was she hadn't known enough about Danny to fill in the missing pieces, or to figure out what might have been perfectly innocent – or not.

* * *

Three weeks after Danny died, at almost the same time as the police had called that fateful evening, her buzzer sounded. Grace tensed. She hadn't been expecting anyone. Lucia was in Galway at a conference. Holly, the liaison officer, had phoned Grace to see how she was and offer support, but she didn't want to meet her. Her friends Karen and Suz were calling over the following evening. She'd been in the apartment all day, as it had rained heavily and now she was surfing through the television channels unable to settle on anything.

'Who is it?' she asked.

'The Green Coriander restaurant, here with your order.'

The Green Coriander. The village takeaway Danny had supposedly been heading to when he'd left here that night. The walls of the room slanted in on top of her before receding away like a sucked-out tide.

'What order?' she asked, alarm slithering up and down her spine.

'The order for Grace Bailey, apartment 2D, eh … Chicken biryani.'

Danny's favourite. Her heart lurched. Who could have done this? Exactly three weeks after he'd died? 'I didn't order anything.'

A short silence. 'This is your name and address? And is this your mobile number?' The delivery guy proceeded to called out her mobile number.

'Yes, but I told you I didn't order anything. When was this order called in?'

'I dunno, maybe half an hour ago, I just deliver the stuff. Boss is going to go crazy if I go back with this. Would you not just take it anyway?'

'I didn't order it. I don't want it,' Grace said, feeling sickened at this crass joke. She hadn't been near the Indian restaurant since Danny's accident. She never wanted to set foot in it again.

'I'll not charge for delivery. That's on the house.'

'I don't *want* it. Go away. If you don't stop pestering me I'll call the police.'

'Okay, okay, chill, lady. But don't be surprised if the Coriander refuses to take another order off you.'

'I can live with that,' Grace said, almost weeping.

What she felt she couldn't live with was life without Danny. It was impossible to think she'd never, ever hear him tell her he loved her in his warm voice. She'd never feel his touch on her skin again or hear his soft laughter in her ear. Or have him kissing her awake in the mornings or dancing her around the kitchen. Problem was, given everything that had happened, and the questions now flooding her mind, she was wondering how perfect it had really been between her and Danny.

Whatever about imagining she was being taunted by a motorbike, she hadn't imagined his favourite takeaway being delivered on the three-week anniversary of his death.

Chapter Eighteen

'Grace, it's just a thought, but if it helps I could store Danny's stuff in my house,' Lucia said, her face shadowed with concern.

'No thanks,' Grace said.

'I thought seeing his things still around might be upsetting for you.'

Grace shook her head. 'I appreciate the offer but it's fine.' She did appreciate Lucia's generosity. Her sister had come straight from the Izobel office. She looked classy and elegant in a softly tailored, slim-fitting, petite, charcoal-grey suit with black patent shoes and a designer bag, especially compared with Grace's skinny jeans and white cotton top. She looked far too polished to be carting off the remnants of Danny's belongings. Besides, between her Monday-morning cleaner and Lucia's mid-week efforts, Lucia's house was forensically tidied and deep-cleaned to within an inch of its life, with nothing superfluous allowed to lurk in any corners, so Lucia offering to store Danny's possessions was a big gesture.

'Don't you think …?' Lucia's voice trailed away. Her gaze roved across the room to where the posters were pinned to the wall and her pale brow creased a little.

'Think what?' Grace asked belligerently.

'It's been six weeks now, surely it's time to start letting go ... even a tiny bit?' Lucia looked at her, her eyes wide with sympathy.

Six weeks. Grace felt a stab in her stomach. Six weeks since Danny had kissed her goodbye – the same length of time that he'd lived with her. One had almost cancelled out the other. Easter had come and gone, spring had well and truly arrived, the trees were budding and releasing frilly new leaves Danny would never see. Even the clocks had moved on into summer time, bringing long, bright evenings, heralding a summer Danny wouldn't be around for.

'I'm not taking down his posters,' Grace said.

'I didn't mean them,' Lucia said, her worried glance flicking up to them again. 'It's everything else.'

Apart from moving Danny's laptop from the kitchen table to a shelf under the television, everything else was as it had been that night, even down to his toothbrush sticking out of the holder in the bathroom and his toiletries on the shelf. So it was easy to believe he might pop back through the door at any moment.

'I don't have a problem with Danny's stuff,' she said.

'I'd like to see you picking up your life again. Getting out a bit more. I hate to think of you being here on your own so much.'

'I've gone back to work, haven't I?' Grace pointed out. After three weeks of hibernation, she'd somehow managed to drag herself back to Arcadia Insurances. The first few days had been another nightmare of sorts, trying to hold it together. She'd never have managed without the support of Karen and Suz.

'It must have been tough but it was the right thing to do.' Naturally Lucia would think that. Her career was the be-all and end-all. Grace had told Lucia about the takeaway arriving out of the blue and while Lucia agreed it had been a fairly crap thing to happen, she'd thought there was a simple explanation, an order mix-up, or an old docket still on their books somewhere.

'What do you think Danny would want you to be doing? Right

now?' Lucia asked gently. 'You don't have to answer that,' she went on. 'Just think about it yourself.'

Her words echoed in Grace's head long after she'd left. As the dusk fell, she slotted her mobile into the docking station and selected 'Purple Rain', blasting up the volume. She lit rows of tea lights, leaving the curtains back so that the flickering candlelight was mirrored in the windows. She spent time moving around the apartment looking at Danny's things, laughing and crying over them, reminding herself that he'd never again pick up his John Connolly paperback that was still sitting on the window sill, or his tablet that was on the coffee table with its charger. He'd never put on his navy fleece that was hanging over the back of a kitchen chair, exactly where he'd left it. He'd never make her coffee in the special mug he'd bought Grace as a moving-in pressie, which was still upturned on the kitchen drainer after the very last time he'd made her coffee. It was bright pink and it bore a legend in silvery writing, exhorting her not to let anyone steal her sparkle. His sports shoes and spare boots were still lying in the hall. His leather jacket was hanging on a peg. She'd begun to wear it to help her feel close to him. Lucia's eyes had widened a little when she had first noticed her wearing it, but wisely, she'd said nothing.

What would Danny want you to be doing?

Grace poured a glass of wine and sat looking at his posters for a while. Later she lay sleepless in bed and looked at the soft glow of the stars in the ceiling until they faded away.

The following evening, on her way home from work, she went into the retail park and picked up a small plastic crate. Without thinking about it too much, she put most of Danny's things away, packing what she could into his brown suitcase, his backpack, and the rest into the crate, except for a few keepsakes: she left his posters on the wall, the kite flaring against the press, a small bottle of his aftershave in the bathroom and his leather jacket in the hall.

She opened the wardrobe door. Her carrier bag with all her

writing materials was still there where she'd left it after showing it to Danny, alongside the pretty storage boxes he'd bought her. She took it all out to the kitchen table, making space in the wardrobe for his packed-up belongings. She put the kettle on and washed out her pink mug. She made tea, filled her mug, and brought it over to the table. Then she took a deep breath, emptied the carrier bag, opened the boxes, and dusted off her dreams.

She'd forgotten how much she loved this, Grace realised an hour later. Why had she neglected this essential part of herself? As she went through her notes and old material, she realised that something was happening to her. The dark cloud that had shadowed her since Danny's death was lifting a little, enough for her to see a sliver of light opening up in front of her.

* * *

Two weeks later, Grace had some post in her post box in the ground-floor foyer, along with a mobile phone advertisement. It was a small padded envelope, buff coloured, addressed to her in block capitals. Up in her apartment, she slit the envelope open and looked inside.

At first she didn't know what to make of the small pieces of coloured paper that were tucked inside. She poked them out with her finger and spread them across the table, turning the coloured side up. Then from one of the pieces, his eyes looked up at her, from another, his mouth. Another one showed the top of his head. And a fourth piece was a segment of his hips. She sifted through the fragments, turning them this way and that, piecing them together.

It was a photograph of Danny, torn into a dozen or so pieces.

Chapter Nineteen

Outside the staff entrance gates to a south county Dublin police station, Matt Slattery pressed the fob for the steel gates, and swung the steering wheel with one hand. The car turned in off the road and slid smoothly through the gap in the opening gates. He didn't need to check the time to know he was late for work. The traffic had been shite on account of the rain and he'd been delayed collecting Abbie and dropping her to the crèche.

He'd done Abbie's drop-off as a favour to Janet. She had had to fly to Birmingham for a meeting that day and needed to be in the airport before nine o'clock. Calling to Janet's door in the early morning had not been a good idea. He'd found himself unable to take his eyes off her, with her shiny auburn hair and trim, navy suit, and he'd found himself envious of the people she'd meet and share her day with. Then the roads were busier than he'd expected. It seemed every child in the neighbourhood had a personal escort to school or crèche. Roll on the school holidays. It was early May, which meant they couldn't be too far away now.

The gates clanged shut behind him. As he'd guessed, there were no spaces left in the police station yard, so rather than go back out and shunt around the block to the supermarket's underground car park, he flung his car into a spot where he was blocking in the

Superintendent's car. He could come and get him if he needed him to move.

Matt turned off the wipers and shut down the engine. Rain drummed off the roof and slid in thick zig-zag trails across the windows, obscuring his view of the yard and enclosing him in a murky space of his own. He flipped down the visor and tried to grin at his reflection in the small mirror, but with the dark shadows underlining his blank-looking eyes, it seemed more of a grimace. Taking a deep breath, he prepared to put on his face for the day.

He pulled up his jacket collar, and opening the car door, he made a dash for it, running around and opening the boot, reaching in hurriedly to grab his backpack. Then everything stood still when he spotted the flash of something pink in among the jumble of his gym bag, track suits and sports shoes. Abbie's lunchbox. He paused in the act of slamming down the boot, standing motionless while the rain veiled his face and cold beads of moisture slid down the back of his neck.

It was just a pink, innocuous looking, plastic lunchbox, but it might as well have been a landmine about to go off, exploding in the mess of his already debris-strewn life. He saw Janet walking up the hallway in the house they'd once shared, her face set in those tense, unhappy lines it always seemed to be cast in nowadays; the face that she kept especially for him, or else the kind of face he provoked in her. 'Whatever you do, Matt, make sure Abbie takes her lunchbox … she doesn't always like the lunches in the crèche, and at least this way I know …'

Yes, yes, yes, rub it in, he'd wanted to say, *you* know what she likes, *you'll* make sure she gets fed; remind me that you're her brilliant, capable, omnipotent mother and I'm just her good-for-nothing pseudo-father. He couldn't wait to get away from Janet's face, even though he didn't want to leave. He wanted to be able to stay, to have the power to kiss it all better, to bring the light back into her eyes, to hear her laugh and cuddle her in bed at night. Especially cuddle her in bed at night, and go to sleep wrapped around her curvy body, and feel warm little Abbie wriggling in between them at an ungodly hour of the morning, her baby-soft hair tickling his nose, her monkey teddy wedged under his neck. The memory of it all rushed at him like a golden bubble, exploding into nothingness on his face. He rubbed his wet-slicked cheeks and sighed heavily. It was his fault that he wasn't in that bed anymore. Totally his fault that Janet had shown him the door, after both of them being best friends, soul mates, lovers, as well as mummy and daddy to Abbie.

In the five months since Janet had thrown him out, he'd learned nothing, Matt berated himself. He couldn't even drop a three-year-old child to the crèche and get into work on time, let alone manage the basics of ensuring her health and welfare were taken care of. Going back to the crèche with her lunchbox was out of the question. The round trip would take an hour and a half in this morning's traffic. He slammed down the boot and hurried to the staff entrance, keyed in the code and stepped into station, securing the door behind him.

Detective Matt Slattery reporting for duty.

He was engulfed with the ambient scents of damp linoleum, old dusty files, disinfectant and strong coffee, all underpinned with a faint residue of desperation and weighed down with a futile kind of despondency. Police stations were not always inspirational places. The nature of their work meant they were dealing with problems and crises and general shite, never mind crimes of varying seriousness, all on a nonstop, twenty-four-hour carousel.

Still, maybe it was him who was the desperate and despondent one, and it was filtering through all his senses, colouring everything in his life with a heaviness that seemed to hang around him like a cloud.

He made a call he hated having to make.

'Janet – um, I forgot to give Abbie her lunch,' he said, speaking hurriedly. 'Is there anything special in it that she needs? I could try to get up there at lunchtime …' he fibbed. He knew he couldn't. Not when he had case files including witness statements to prepare for a court appearance. He knew this would take the best part of the day and he had to get out on time that evening to collect Abbie.

'I do not want to hear this,' Janet said. He heard a tannoy in the background and it drowned out her next words. After a while he heard her say, 'My flight has been called, get on to the crèche and let them know they'll have one extra to feed.'

* * *

He was passing through the police station lobby that afternoon when he saw her at the end of the queue. The rain had stopped but the skies were low and the early summer afternoon still held the taste of dampness in the air. Except for the young woman bringing up the rear, the queue looked the same as most days, a mix of customers from all walks of life. They trudged through the station with a variety of problems: needing to present their insurance and driving licence; asking for passport photographs to be stamped; reporting a break-in, a stolen car; looking for a bed for the night; some were just plain drunk or drugged up to the eyeballs; and a few honest citizens were handing in lost property.

'Good luck with the Cameron Diaz lookalike,' he muttered to Kevin, the uniformed guard manning the desk.

Kevin threw his gaze down the length of the queue.

'Right at the end,' Matt said, glancing down again before going through the security door.

Not quite Cameron Diaz, maybe her much younger sister. Or Cameron Diaz as she had been in *Something About Mary*. Only this babe was wearing a blank, kind of numbed look in her big blue eyes. Her hair was like a blonde cap circling her head and she was wearing a black leather biker jacket that was too big for her.

Passport photos, he guessed. What was the betting she'd realised too late her passport was out of date and now she needed it sorted pronto. Her boyfriend was going ballistic because their holiday in the sun was on the line. Or else she'd been stopped at a road traffic checkpoint and had been unable to produce her licence. Or maybe she'd lost her pet kitten. Did she look like the type who'd have a kitten? Whatever it was, she stood out like a bright, shining beacon in the shuffling, nondescript queue, and something in her eyes reminded him of Abbie.

Matt was back at his desk working on his reports when Kevin looked for him.

'What's up?'

'That girl you were talking about – she's looking for Holly. She called Holly's mobile but was directed here.'

'Feck.' Matt threw down his pen. He leaned back in his chair and stretched his arms. Holly had been taken ill yesterday, with a suspected miscarriage at four months, and was now lying flat on her back in a maternity hospital, too terrified to move, hoping her baby would make it. God only knew how long she'd be out of action. 'What's up with her?'

'Something to do with her boyfriend's accident. Holly's the liaison. This lady's not sure if it was an accident after all and she wants to talk to Holly.'

'What does she mean, "not an accident after all"?'

'I could hardly get the words out of her, she's too scared to talk to me. After all, it's not very private out there. That's what she wants to talk to Holly about.'

'She can't talk to Holly. Is there anyone else?'

'I don't know who's going to cover for Holly and she's so pale I'm afraid she's going to faint on me or something. I can't do fainting blondes.'

'I'll talk to her.'

'Thanks Matt. I knew I could depend on you.'

'I can't do fainting blondes either.' Matt glared at his sprawling mountains of paperwork before pushing them away, then he got to his feet and went into a small interview room.

Chapter Twenty

She sat down at the table, looking out of place in the dingy room, fidgeting with the strap of her bag. She looked around the shabby walls, not really seeing them, her expression telling him she was seeing something else. Up close, her face was very pale, almost translucent, with faint shadows under her eyes. It was the smudges under her eyes that struck a chord with Matt. He poured them both some water from the cooler, putting two plastic cups on the table.

He explained that Holly wasn't available, but that in light of her concerns, he'd talk to her.

'I'm Detective Matt Slattery,' he said. 'And you are?'

'Grace Bailey.' She glanced down at his pad, where he was noting the date, the time, and her name. 'I have my driver's licence, in case you need to confirm my identity.' Her fingers trembled as she extracted a pink document from her bag. She passed it across the table. He opened it and glanced at the details; her licence was four years old, and even in the passport picture she looked far younger and a lot more innocent than she did now. Her date of birth told him she was four months short of her thirtieth birthday, two years younger than Janet and four years younger than him.

That reminded him: Janet's birthday would be coming up soon.

'Is this your current address?' he asked.

'Yes,' she said.

He made a note of it. Rathbrook Hall. Three miles away as the crow flies and not too far from him. A Celtic Tiger apartment complex, constructed in a hurry, and almost all units rented out, just over a mile from the village of Rathbrook, which had once been a sleepy south county Dublin village in the middle of nowhere. As well as Rathbrook Hall plonked on the edge of the village, the picturesque village now had a large retail park in the vicinity, a supermarket, a fast food outlet and a petrol station – thanks to being close to the M50 and within walking distance of the Luas. The whole shebang was linked together by parklands – the fancy-sounding Rathbrook Demesne – through which a gurgling stream ran. There was a small lake, too, man-made, with ducks on it, in a half-hearted nod to the young kids who lived in the complex. The cops had had to search the lake a couple of times recently for murder weapons. Typically, the station in the village had been closed down due to cutbacks just as business in the area began to pick up. That was why Grace had had to come here, where they were ridiculously busy and short staffed.

'So, Grace, you have concerns about your boyfriend's accident.'

She took a deep breath. 'I don't know how to put it … I know it sounds …' she paused, and visibly composed herself. 'My boyfriend, Danny McBride. He was killed in a motorbike accident in early March. Only I'm not sure it was an accident.'

A different slant on bereavement, he guessed. Denial in its most extreme form. Where was Holly when he needed her? He could give this lady ten minutes max, then refer her to another liaison officer in the District, who'd undoubtedly recommend bereavement counselling. *Danny McBride.* He wrote down the name, thinking it was vaguely familiar.

'It seemed like one, on the face of it,' she said. 'But I have a gut feeling that … that something else went wrong.'

'What do you think went wrong?'

'I think it might have been made to happen.'

'*Made* to happen?'

'Yes, as in … he was … killed.'

Matt felt disappointed. She looked far too nice to be one of the crazy people who regularly haunted the station, claiming to have killed someone, just looking for attention, or one of the lonely ones who were desperate for someone to talk to. Because she'd presented herself with such a serious claim, he'd have to take some kind of statement.

'Tell me about the … what happened,' he said, summoning his most sympathetic voice, and feeling so out of his depth that he wished Holly was around. He was useless in the face of women's emotions. He knew that already, judging by the way he'd left Janet high and dry.

'It was strange,' she said, in a thin kind of voice that told him she was back there. 'Danny—' she swallowed, and threw him a nervous glance that he would have found endearing in different circumstances. 'He said he was popping out to get some wine and a takeaway. I didn't expect him to be more than forty minutes or so. We were going to have a cosy night in...' she paused. A spark of something flashed across her face as she recalled whatever they had planned to do that evening, and he felt a ridiculous stab of sadness mixed with envy for the departed Danny McBride, that he'd had the power to make a woman's face illuminate in such a soft, golden way. She seemed to have completely forgotten where she was.

'You said you were going to have a relaxing night in,' he prompted, jolting her out of her reverie. Her face closed over as she looked at him.

'The next thing I knew the police were in the apartment, telling me there had been a fatal accident. After that,' she smiled sadly, 'everything went a little … haywire.'

From the sound of it, everything was still going haywire if Grace really believed that Danny had been murdered. Still, there would be no harm in checking out the case notes. He wasn't a grief counsellor, but he knew it might be beneficial to give this lady a chance to talk, to say the words aloud and help her come to terms with it.

'They told me it happened on a straight stretch of the road. He went up off into the verge and hit a wall. You must have it all on your system?' she said, raising her blue eyes to his. 'Danny was far too good a driver to have a silly accident like that.'

He'd been right. Some kind of misplaced denial. He pushed a plastic cup of water towards her and wondered if Janet would be as cut up were he to meet with an unfortunate accident or if she'd be dancing on his grave. Matt hadn't the heart to tell Grace that most accidents occurred as a result of a split second of silliness. The roads were unforgiving and only a hair's breadth lapse of judgement was needed to shatter whole lives. Sometimes people were pure unlucky and simply in the wrong place at the wrong time.

'As well as that,' she said, 'Danny was nowhere near the Indian, or the wine shop.'

'Sorry, could you explain that?'

'Danny was going to the village,' she said. 'But the road where he crashed was in the opposite direction.'

'I see.' He made a note on his pad. There could have been any reason for Danny's diversion, most of them perfectly innocent.

'I know you don't believe me,' she said in a flat voice. 'You think it was a genuine accident, they happen every day, and I can't accept that and I've lost the plot.'

It was so exactly what he thought that he was too embarrassed to look at her.

'I know it's what my sister thinks, so no surprises there ...' her voice trailed away.

He came at it from another angle, forcing a neutral expression onto his features before he made eye contact, but her face was so honest it caused a stabbing sensation in his stomach. 'Grace … it's not up to me to think anything at the moment. I'll have a look at the case files and go back over the accident report. I need to ask you if there's any specific reason why you think someone would want to end Danny's life. Had he any enemies? Was he in any kind of trouble? Did he owe money? Had anyone ever threatened him? There would have to be a motive of some kind.'

She didn't look like the kind of girl who'd be involved with a waster or a druggie or someone who 'had form'. He'd find out soon enough when he keyed Danny's name into the system if he'd been 'known' to the police in any way – the politically correct way of saying he might have had some brush with the law. He realised that instead of answering his questions or providing some background information, she was sitting there silently, staring into space.

'Well?' he asked, his pen poised.

'I don't know,' she said, her voice a little shaky. 'That's the problem. I don't know the finer details of Danny's life. He could have had an enemy or two, he could have had someone threatening him, but if he had, he kept it well hidden. I don't know why Danny was heading in the wrong direction that night. I find it very odd.'

'Maybe he took it into his head to go someplace else for your takeout.'

She shook her head. 'He'd already called ahead and ordered it. He told me he'd be back in a jiffy. I certainly don't get it that he crashed into a wall. We went everywhere on his bike; he was a safe and careful driver. Someone could have made him crash, couldn't they?'

'They?' he asked.

'That's what I don't know yet …'

'The accident scene would have been forensically examined at the time,' he said. 'Witnesses would have been asked to come forward. The bike itself would have been examined. Anything untoward would have been thoroughly checked.' At least that was what he hoped. The bike might have been too mangled for a comprehensive examination.

'I know I sound mad,' she said, 'but Danny was so brilliant to be around, so shiny and full of life, enthusiastic about everyday things that it was contagious. My gut instinct is telling me it's impossible that a silly accident could have ended all that.'

Something deep inside him unfurled at the sound of her words: *so shiny and full of life, a silly accident.* It was a tiny grain of memory stirring in a place where he never went, feather-light and soft as it nudged his subconscious, and just as softly he nudged it back into place before it flickered into life. *Don't go there ...*

He told himself to be careful with this lady, as she was clearly upset. 'You do realise the gravity of your allegations, don't you? Murder is a very serious crime, not something to be tossed around lightly. Do you seriously think someone had it in for your boyfriend? Badly enough to make sure he had an accident of sorts?'

There was silence.

'Look, Grace,' he leaned forward across the desk a little, trying to connect with her in a less formal manner. 'I'll pull up the full report and read it,' he said gently, 'but I don't see that anything you have said is a basis for further investigation. So if there are any other details you're holding back, now is the time to tell me.'

She seemed to be trying to think hard, to put her words in the correct order. 'I keep seeing a motorbike, just like Danny's.'

'Whereabouts?'

'When I'm out for walks, or coming up from the Luas. Not all the time,' she added hastily. 'Just often enough to upset me. I feel it's kind of following me. I even hear it at night, as though it's going around in a loop between the M50 and Rathbrook village.'

Christ. 'I see,' he said, making a note. Definitely a case for bereavement counselling.

'And then there was the takeaway ... as though someone was trying to spook me.'

'Tell me about that,' he said.

She gave him the details. 'My sister thinks it was just a genuine mistake.'

He couldn't help agreeing with the sister. This happened all the time in takeaways, particularly on busy evenings.

'And then there was the photo …'

'What photo?'

'I got a photo in the post, one of Danny, only it was all torn up.'

This was different. Intimidation. Harassment. The kind of thing a jealous ex-girlfriend might do.

'Did you bring it with you?'

'No, I dumped it immediately.'

'Had Danny any old girlfriends that you know of?'

'We were only living together six weeks,' she said. 'I didn't know … everything about him. See, there were times when Danny avoided answering my questions. So there could have been something going on that I didn't know about. That's also why I feel uneasy about everything.'

'What kind of questions?'

'Just ordinary stuff.'

'Ordinary stuff?' He couldn't help raising an eyebrow. So the guy didn't want her to know all his business. Nothing he was hearing gave him any grounds for believing Danny's death could have been anything but an accident. Grace seemed to be struggling. Eventually she took a deep breath.

'I sensed Danny was … holding things back.'

He looked at her without speaking, waiting for her to elaborate.

Grace twisted her handbag straps between her fingers. 'Now and then he was a little guarded with his phone calls. Like, he ended a call when I came into the room, or he went outside to talk. But then, you see, I did that too, whenever I spoke to my sister.'

She fell silent, and again he waited.

'I didn't particularly want Danny to overhear what my sister was saying, or second-guess the conversation from listening to me.'

Ditto, he almost said, thinking of Janet and her sister, and the phone calls he'd witnessed them exchanging before the split, Janet disappearing into another room to take the call and sometimes reappearing teary-eyed. His gut clenched at the memory of it. He tried to compartmentalise the mess and upset of it all, dragging his thoughts back to the present.

'Why didn't you want Danny to overhear?' he asked.

'My sister wasn't … what you'd call overly fond of Danny.'

Ditto again. He had something in common with the sadly departed Danny. There was no love lost between him and Janet's sister. Some nights when he'd tossed around in the bed in the dark depths of the night, missing the warm feel of Janet beside him, the clean fresh scent of her after a shower, the sound of her breathing, he'd wondered if he might have managed to mend fences with Janet but for the insidious, righteous voice of her sister in her ear. He knew in his desperation he'd been grasping at straws. Janet's sister hadn't been in the least to blame for him behaving like a childish monster. His grip tightened on his pen.

'I've even asked myself if Danny sensed something,' she said.

'Like what?'

'When I look back, he was always going on about life being too short, about making the most of every moment and seizing the day. Danny was—' she gulped, 'like no one I've ever known before. He had this kind of sparkling energy, he squeezed every drop he could out of ordinary things, fun things. Now, when I think of it, it was like he was afraid … well, that he wasn't going to have gallons of time left …'

Once again that look was back in her eyes, a kind of raw honesty that shone out of her and told him she fully believed every word she said. It was amazing the way people could interpret things to suit their beliefs. He felt as helpless and useless as he did when Abbie asked him in a wistful voice why he wasn't sleeping in mammy's bed anymore. He wondered how much longer he had to wait before he could relax in his apartment with a cold beer. Hours. He had to finish his reports and get out of here in time for Abbie, who had to be collected and then brought home as soon as Janet arrived in from London.

Janet. He would certainly need a beer or two after that. He bit back a flicker of annoyance at himself. Listening to Grace's heartfelt words, added to what she'd already said about the circumstances of the accident, he was coming to the slim but sad possibility that perhaps the sparkling Danny McBride had burnt himself out and brought about his own unfortunate end. Maybe deep down she knew that too, but was finding it impossible to face.

'Had there been anything different about the day of the accident?' he asked gently. 'Anything out of the ordinary?' Anything to indicate, he meant, that Danny might have been depressed or out of sorts. Instead, her face lit up and glowed with the memory.

'Yes, it was a brilliant day. A five-star day.' She was lost in thought. When she spoke next her voice had changed, softened. 'Lots of days with Danny were brilliant. But he'd said, only that morning, that this would be the best day yet. It was the best and ...' she gulped, 'and then it turned out to be by far the very worst.'

'How was it different – the brilliant day, you said?'

'I took the day off work.'

'Was that out of the ordinary?'

'Oh, yes, very much, except I'd done it a couple of times before for Danny.'

He raised an eyebrow but said nothing.

Grace said, by way of explanation, 'So we could do things together. On the spur of the moment. Danny was spontaneous like that. We got up early that morning and went to Glendalough to see the sunrise. I'd never done that before, even though it's on our doorstep.'

Sounded like they were having a good time together. It was a long time since he and Janet had had a good time together.

'And what happened after Glendalough?'

'We went for breakfast and then back to my apartment, and—' she paused, something rippling across her face that made her look beautiful, before she lowered her eyes. She was lost in thought for a moment, then she sat up straighter and went on, 'that was it really. We were both at home, Danny did some work on his laptop and then he went out … and never came back.'

'So, although it was different, there was nothing unusual about the day that would have given you any reason to be concerned?'

'No, nothing.'

'Your relationship with Danny – how long had you been together?'

'I met him …' she paused for a while. Then she swallowed and went on, 'Before Christmas. He moved in with me a few weeks later. We were living together for just six weeks, when …' her voice trailed away.

He must have been a fast worker, this Danny guy. Pity that they just had six weeks together. They'd still been in the middle of that wild, passionate, eyes-only-for-each-other honeymoon phase when he'd died. They hadn't started to have silly rows over the rubbish being taken out or the cap left off the toothpaste or whose turn it was to empty the dishwasher. They hadn't started to have questions or jealousies about previous loves that could have wrenched them apart. No wonder her face lit up when she thought of him, and looked so lost and woebegone when she went on to speak of his accident.

'Thanks, Grace. I think that covers everything, unless you've something to add?'

She looked at him for a long moment before she shook her head.

'I'll be in touch with you, when I read up the report,' he said. 'Can I have your mobile number?'

She gave him her number in a resigned kind of voice that told him she didn't really expect to hear from him. He decided to make a point of talking to her again, even if it was just to find out more about Danny McBride and in particular discover how he'd managed to put that luminous light into her eyes. It was a helluva long time since he'd seen Janet looking at him like that. He ushered her outside and went to the desk, tore off a piece of notepaper, scribbled down his name and mobile, and handed it to her.

'If there's anything I can do, or if you think of anything else, call me.' He didn't have to do this, but what the hell, she looked like she needed the reassurance. She looked like she needed to be tucked up in a cosy bed with the comfort of a hot water bottle and a fairy tale story with a happy ending.

Besides, it made him feel like Mr Nice Guy for a few minutes, which was a very pleasant change.

Chapter Twenty-one

Grace glanced in the rear view mirror. It was there again. The motorbike. The same one she'd seen before. Or was it?

It was four or five cars behind her, weaving between lanes, veering out from the inside lane to the middle and back again, edging closer before dropping back. As if it wanted her to spot it. As if it were playing hide and seek. *Look out, I'm behind you. Now you see me, now you don't.* Something about it reminded her of Danny's bike.

She'd taken a half day off work to reorganise her health insurance and some direct debits on her bank account, jobs that had been left in limbo since Christmas, and it had seemed good timing to drop into the police station to voice her fears.

He'd seemed nice and approachable, that detective, Matt. He was tall and lean with dark hair and grey eyes. She wondered if he was married or had a girlfriend. It had been difficult to go through it all, but she knew it had to be done if he was to take her seriously. As she'd talked, he'd kind of softened a little and she'd sensed something empathetic about him. He'd looked at her as though he was seeing a real person and not just another statistic or a file. He hadn't dismissed her or referred her on to a counselling expert, like a problem case.

After she'd left the police station, she'd gone back to Rathbrook Hall and now she was heading over to Lucia, who was home early to get ready for a conference dinner that evening. The late afternoon traffic on the M50 was light, so the journey from Rathbrook Hall to Lucia's house off the Clonsilla exit wouldn't take much more than fifteen minutes or so. She kept her eyes on the road in front, kept pace with the traffic and tried to figure out when she'd first spotted the motorbike. Then it was right behind her. Almost tailgating her. She couldn't see the cyclist's head in the rear view mirror – her view was just of the gleaming head lamp and gloved hands on the handlebars. It could have been a man or a woman. Her hands clenched the steering wheel and she felt a trickle of sweat run down her back. Suddenly it pulled out from behind her and roared into the fast lane, overtaking a line of traffic and disappearing from her sight. Relief poured through her veins as she passed the exit for Knocklyon.

She was approaching the exit for Clondalkin when her heart seized. There was a motorbike behind her again. Was it the same one? Cutting in and out of the lanes of traffic, as before? It came right up behind her before accelerating off into the distance. All she saw was a blur of shiny black machine and black leathers, with the glint of a black helmet. It could have been anyone. She held her breath as she drove along, passing the exit for Liffey Valley, driving over the high bridge that spanned the River Liffey with the Strawberry Beds far below. The next exit, less than five minutes away, was thankfully hers.

By the time she parked outside Lucia's house in Mount Lismore, she was weak with relief.

* * *

'All you have to do is sit and watch telly,' Lucia said, her black high heels clicking on the tiled kitchen floor as she marched around, organising her keys, her mobile, picking up a sheaf of papers off the island counter and folding them into a slim leather briefcase. 'And help yourself to whatever you feel like.'

'It's the first time I've ever had to house sit,' Grace said.

'Thanks Grace, I really appreciate it. It's a bloody nuisance that the appointment clashes with the conference but I need to get the boiler fixed ASAP. It's leaking all over the place, and I'm in London this weekend, so I won't be around. Hey, I like the bag,' she said, indicating Grace's canvas tote bag. 'Is that new?'

Grace nodded. She'd picked up the cream tote bag in a shop in Drury Street because it bore the same silvery logo about not letting anyone steal her sparkle that was on the pink mug Danny had bought for her. It had seemed like a talisman to her. She wasn't ready to tell Lucia about the contents of the bag yet.

Lucia went into her utility room where the boiler was housed and brought out a flowering plant, putting it on the kitchen table. She went back in and took out a small pile of laundry, leaving it on a chair. 'Please ignore the mess. I need to get these out of the repair guy's way. He promised to be here for six o'clock, and it'll take an hour or so. After that, feel free to leave.' She pointed to a small rack containing remote controls. 'You know how to work the telly, don't you?'

Grace looked at Lucia's wall-mounted, state-of-the-art television set in her seating area and the array of remotes, some with millions of different shaped buttons, others pencil slim. They promised the ultimate television viewing experience.

'I'm sure I can manage,' Grace said. Something made her add, 'If not, I can always call you.'

Lucia flashed her a sharp glance, which softened as she realised Grace was joking. 'Yes, do that at your peril. This is an important evening and I'll have my mobile on silent. The Chinese delegation wouldn't appreciate disturbances. Neither would my colleagues. I'll be speaking around half-past seven.'

'So it's not just a drink fest.'

'No way. I have to give a talk on – wait for it –' Lucia grinned, 'our top-down, bottom-up analysis of the proposed penetration of Izobel Group into the Chinese market.'

Grace smiled. 'Don't worry, I won't call. And you look great. You'll knock 'em dead.'

Lucia was wearing a black and cream block-colour dress which skimmed her trim figure, and her dark glossy hair had been professionally blow dried so that it waved gently about her face. She went across to the island counter where she'd left her briefcase, and checked the contents one more time.

'I went to the police this afternoon,' Grace said. She hadn't meant to say it now, with Lucia on the way out, but she was unsettled after the motorbike experience. 'Holly, the liaison, wasn't around so I got talking to a detective. I told him about the concerns I had.'

Lucia said nothing for a moment, but the rigid tension of her back told Grace she wasn't pleased. She'd already talked to Lucia again about her misgivings, one night when Lucia had called over to the apartment and Grace had had a glass of wine too many, but Lucia had just looked at her with indulgent sympathy. Even when Grace had told her about the torn photograph, she'd rationalised the incident by saying there was bound to be a jealous girlfriend somewhere in Danny's background, who was crazily upset that he'd died. For all Grace knew, she could have been at the funeral, chatting to Danny's sisters, finding out all about Grace and where she lived.

'The detective said he'd look into everything,' Grace went on.

Lucia sighed and turned to face her. 'Look, I really feel for you, I know you must be missing Danny out of your life, and I'd do anything possible to help, but you'll have to accept the fact that what happened to him was an accident, pure and simple. They happen, unfortunately.'

Grace stayed silent.

'I know it's hard to believe that Danny's life ended so abruptly …' Lucia paused and frowned, as though she, too, was finding great difficulty with this.

'You never really took to him,' Grace found herself saying.

'That has nothing to do with it. I might have thought your relationship was a bit sudden – especially so soon after finishing with Gavin.'

'Gavin.' Grace's stomach lurched at the sound of his name. 'So now we're coming to the truth of it.'

'There is no truth as such,' Lucia said. 'I was ... surprised, I suppose, that you finished with Gavin in the first place, you seemed so settled together. He even—'

'He even what?' Grace asked quietly.

'You might as well know that he called me a couple of times around Christmas, wondering how you were. He asked had you broken up with him because ...' Lucia hesitated.

'Because what?' Grace felt sick at the idea of Gavin speaking to Lucia like this, enquiring about her.

'Because he thought you might have met someone new.'

There was a moment of silence. 'And what did you say?'

'I said of course not,' Lucia looked at her thoughtfully. 'It was the truth, wasn't it? Even though there were only a few weeks between Gavin and Danny.'

'It was long enough to put the right space between them.'

'Were you still upset after the break up? Even Mum and I,' Lucia swallowed, 'we thought Danny ... well, that you might have been on the rebound. She was as concerned as I was when you let a guy you only knew a few weeks move in with you. Having said that ...'

'I told you, Danny was ... different to anyone I ever met before. He changed my life around completely. We just – clicked, or something. He made me feel amazingly alive.'

Lucia's mobile bleeped. 'Blast. I have to go. The taxi's outside. I was going to say that having said that, I can see you were very happy with Danny. Happier than I'd ever seen you with Gavin. Look, sis, please come to London with me this weekend? It would be good for you to get away. We can shop or just relax or go to a spa. There's a spare room in Robert's apartment. You and Gavin never managed to make the trip over, but there's nothing to stop you from coming with me. I'm not heading over until Saturday morning.'

'No, it's fine,' Grace said. She couldn't face going over to London this weekend, to be beholden to Lucia's munificence.

'Think about it. I'd love you to come,' Lucia kissed her on the cheek.

Grace sat on Lucia's comfy sofa in a corner of the kitchen while she waited. She'd no intention of thinking about London, because she wasn't going to go. Neither did she need to figure her way around the maze of remote controls, because she wasn't going to turn on the television. Instead she silenced her mobile, dipped into her tote bag and took out a spiral-bound notebook with an attractive swirly cover that Danny had bought her and a packet of felt pens.

Chapter Twenty-two

As he took the shortest route possible from the police station to Abbie's crèche through the south county Dublin suburbs, Matt knew he was already late for pick-up time. Janet was so well organised that she never had a problem getting to the crèche before the critical closing time. But he, cast in the role of errant dad, barely made it to the crèche before he got a call from them.

'Here's your Daddy now,' Moira said as she opened the door to him after he'd pressed the intercom. He didn't bother to correct her.

Abbie's squeal of happiness as she saw him and bounded up the hall was worth having to grovel to the sanctimonious sounding Moira.

'Traffic,' he said, making a face, knowing Moira wasn't impressed. Traffic or no traffic, the crèche closed at six o'clock and all the children had to be collected by then, no matter what kind of delays parents had to contend with. What a total pain in the ass.

'Are you minding me instead of Mummy?' Abbie asked as she skipped alongside him, over to where his car was parked at the kerb, the pink bag on her back bouncing up and down in time to her skips.

'I am, is that okay?' He opened the rear door, and Abbie wriggled her tiny shoulders so that her backpack slid down to the ground. She picked it up and handed it to him before she climbed into the car and sat in her booster seat. He belted her in and tucked her backpack in beside her. That part was easy peasy. It was the rest of it he felt useless at.

'Am I going home with you?'

'First we're going for some food.' McDonald's. His usual haunt when it came to feeding Abbie.

'McDonald's?' she asked.

'Yes.'

'*Again*? Is there no food in your parparment?' Her tiny forehead wrinkled and her eyes – so like Janet's – were almost accusatory as they stared at him.

Matt thought of what was lurking in the fridge of his apartment in Stepaside: a few bottles of beer, a hunk of cheese, an opened jar of Mexican sauce he hadn't the energy to dump and a half pint of milk, the other half of which he'd drunk directly from the carton that morning.

'I don't have enough nice things for you to eat, Abbie,' he said, hating her to think he was somehow lacking in some way.

'You have to come back and live in our house, Daddy,' she said, giving a loud sigh. 'We have lots of things to eat.'

'Then you wouldn't be able to come to me on your holidays.'

'Aww.'

'What did you do today?' he asked.

'I played with my friends, but they wouldn't share their toys with me.'

'That's too bad.'

She surprised him by saying, 'What did you do today, Daddy?'

'I was in work.'

He could almost hear the synapses in her brain whirling around looking for connections to something he might have said before. After a while she said, 'Daddy, what do you do in work?'

They'd had chats before about his job, Abbie wondering what his job was about, but Matt wasn't sure how much she'd understood. 'I help people when things have gone wrong in their lives,' he said. 'People who have lost things … people who are hurt.' And people who are lost, people who hurt others, he wanted to add.

There was another silence from the back seat as Abbie absorbed his words.

Matt drew to a halt behind a long queue of red tail lights at the traffic lights. Who did he think he was? Mr All-Powerful? Superman? No way. The job was a protection of sorts, for him. The rank shielded the real, shaky Matt Slattery that no one got to see. Sometimes it was like he was acting a part in a play, his lines already rehearsed. Thanks to the nature of his job, there were procedures to be followed, parameters within which he worked and boxes to be ticked, all of which were a safeguard for him.

An image of Grace Bailey and her soft eyes flashed into his head. He hadn't had a chance to bring up the report into her boyfriend's accident that afternoon. He'd been hard pressed to complete his paperwork for the upcoming court case on a drugs bust.

Abbie's voice piped up from the back seat, just as the traffic in front began to move. 'Then why don't you help Mummy?'

'What makes you think I don't help her?'

'Mummy's hurt 'cos sometimes she cries.'

Oh, brilliant. Bloody brilliant. How come a three-and-a-half-year-old had the power to make him feel like the biggest jerk of all time?

'When does she cry, Abbie?' he asked softly, taking his eyes off the road long enough to glance at her in the rear view mirror. Mistake. The innocence in her eyes clawed at his chest.

'When she's looking at the telly.'

The telly! She was too soft for her own good, Janet was. *One Born Every Minute* often had her in floods. Sometimes she used to hide her face from his, embarrassed by her tears in front of his cynical ridicule. She cried at the drop of a hat over a wide repertoire of programmes, weepy movies or sad news features, or reality types, where family members were reunited after thirty or forty years.

'You can't believe all that shite,' he heard himself say. 'Of course they knew their long-lost sister was hiding in the next room. They've come prepared. They all look like they've just stepped out of the beauty parlour.'

He'd never want her to be any different, though. If he was back there again he'd say nothing and let Janet have her cry in peace. If he was back there again he'd never slag off her soft, sensitive feelings. Instead he'd reach out and give her a big, warm cuddle. He even imagined himself kissing away her tears, and a bolt of longing swept over him.

Hah! The futility of it all washed over him like a sour aftertaste. He was as bad as Grace, refusing to accept reality. He'd never be back there again unless he came up with a decent plan to help mend things with Janet. A plan that would help to convince her how much he loved her. He wanted her to see him in a whole new light. He wanted her face to glow when she thought of him, like the way Grace's face had glowed when she spoke of Danny.

It felt like he had a mountain to climb.

* * *

At half-past seven Janet texted to say her flight had landed and she was in a taxi on the way home from the airport. All was calm in Matt's apartment in Stepaside. Abbie was happily watching a *Peppa Pig* DVD that Matt kept especially for her, and the room was tidy. The cartons from their McDonald's takeaway had been cleared up, and Abbie's hands and face were clean, all traces of tomato ketchup gone. He got ten out of ten for now, he said to himself.

'Right, Abbie, home to mammy in five minutes, okay?'

'Can I just watch to the end?' she wheedled.

'Of course,' he said, feeling generous, knowing there were only about five minutes left.

As soon as the episode was over, he gathered Abbie's things, trying to help her with her jacket even though she was determined to do it herself. It was the same with her car seat. She clambered into Matt's car, announcing regally she could do it by herself. He waited patiently until eventually she allowed him to secure her in.

'It's Daddy's job to help people,' he said, trying not to let the delay chafe. He wanted the opportunity to see Janet, yet conversely, to get it over with as soon as possible. He always found it awkward whenever he dropped Abbie home; he didn't quite know where to look, or what to say, standing awkwardly in the porch, feeling like a plonker as she said her goodbyes to him, knowing the house was off limits, even though he'd lived there with Janet for almost two years.

Janet lived in a quiet, residential area of Dundrum. It had been her parents' home, but they had both died within a year of each other, before Matt had met Janet. The rain earlier in the day had given way to bright evening sunshine and it glinted off the hall door as Abbie ran up the path. Last summer, on evenings like this, Janet and he would sit out on the patio at the back of the house, where they had a view of the rim of the mountains in the near distance, sipping chilled beer or wine, chatting cosily about their days before going up to bed together and making long, slow love, the kind that filled him with utter peace. The warm memory lingered for a minute, before fading away. This summer he didn't even step into the hallway. Since Janet had shown him the door before Christmas, he hadn't attempted to cross the threshold.

Janet's car was parked in the garden. Through the glass in the door, he saw her coming up the hall. His insides squeezed as she opened the door. She hadn't yet changed out of her work suit and she looked gorgeous, with her expressive dark eyes and auburn hair he wanted to trail his fingers through. Remembering how easily Grace Bailey had lost her loved one, he had a huge longing to squeeze Janet tight. Abbie scrambled into the house and hugged her mother's hips before running down the hall.

'Hi Abbie, did you have a good day?' Janet called after her.

'Yeah. What have you got for me?'

'Hang on a minute, come back here and say thanks to Matt for minding you.'

She had started to address him as Matt when she spoke of him to Abbie, and it hurt.

There was a shout from the kitchen. '*Thanks, Daddeee!*' Matt felt a tiny victory. He saw Abbie waving at him before disappearing behind the kitchen door.

'Well.' His hands felt awkward by his sides.

'Well, what?' Janet asked coolly.

'How did it go today?'

She shrugged as if to say it was none of his business, seeing as how he didn't share her life anymore. 'Fine,' she said. 'How did you manage?'

'Great. Ten out of ten.'

She stood there silently.

'Hang on, I forgot something,' Matt said, mentally kicking himself. He hadn't got ten out of ten after all. He went out to the boot of his car and rummaged in it until he found Abbie's pink lunchbox. He came back up the path and handed it to Janet. 'Sorry about that.'

'It looks like Abbie survived anyhow,' she said wryly.

'Give me a shout if you need any help with her,' he said. 'Otherwise I'll pick Abbie up on Saturday week, take her out for a couple of hours.'

Janet looked at him steadily. 'Saturday week … no, I don't think so,' she shook her head.

'Huh?' She was hardly stopping him from seeing Abbie, was she? Although he had no official rights to see her. But it was the one and only thing they had agreed on before the split. Abbie was used to Matt being a big part of her little world, and he was mad about her, loving her as though she was his own, so rather than wrenching that apart, he could continue to see her, taking her out for a couple of hours at the weekends, or looking after her if Janet needed to be someplace else and her sister wasn't around to babysit. It had worked in a funny kind of way, and gave Matt a good reason to continue to see Janet, even though their encounters were often bittersweet to say the least.

'Simon will be here then,' Janet said coolly.

'Simon.' He tried to keep a calm expression on his face, even though mention of the name was anathema to him. Simon. Abbie's biological father, with all the rights that Matt didn't have. Whatever way Janet organised Matt's outings with Abbie, she made sure that Matt and Simon stayed well apart.

'Yes, he'll be back from holidays so he wants to call in for a while to see Abbie,' Janet said, emphasising the second half of her sentence.

'Well … see you … sometime.'

He was halfway down the path when she called after him. 'Matt?'

He wheeled around. 'Yes?'

'How about Sunday?'

Sunday. He felt a slight reprieve. He tried to recall his roster. 'Yeah. I could do the morning, say at ten o'clock for an hour or so? Bring her to the playground if it's fine …'

'Great. Text you beforehand.'

This is the way it was going to be, he told himself. He got into his car and accelerated off. He'd have to learn to share Abbie with Simon, because if he didn't, he'd find himself being shut out, having no more contact with either the child or Janet. And bittersweet as it was for now, he couldn't bear the thoughts of having no contact at all.

Back in his apartment, Matt took a cold beer out of the fridge and sat by the window as the May evening sank into a purple twilight. The apartment complex was built at the foothills of the Dublin mountains and from this vantage point, framed in the large picture window, the city looked pretty, lights twinkling in the veiled dusk. No matter how serene it appeared from this perspective, down on the ground it was different; he knew it would be a busy night in the station, with the usual melee of drunks and public order offences, never mind road accidents and other unfortunate incidents all the way up to drug and sex offences, domestic violence and murders. He'd had to learn to distance himself from the everyday upsets of the job, to put it to one side when he was off duty – and Janet had had a particularly effective way of helping him switch off that he sorely missed – otherwise he would have driven himself nuts

Despite that, he couldn't help thinking of Grace Bailey, and that odd moment when something had unfurled inside him as she'd spoken of a Danny who was shiny, sparkling, full of life; it was the sense of a memory he'd buried immediately before it saw the light of day. Forget it for now. He had other things to think about. He was going to get his act together and take charge of himself. Rise above his ridiculous, childish jealousy and petty resentment of Simon. Find a way back into Janet's heart somehow, so that he, Janet and Abbie could be together again, like a happy family.

Simples.

Chapter Twenty-three

The doors hissed closed and the Tube rattled out of the station at Heathrow and gathered speed. Amid the press of bodies and luggage, Lucia sat composed in her seat, clutching her bag on her lap, her overnight case wedged between her knees. It was her turn to visit Robert in London this weekend but she'd put off travelling until Saturday morning as she'd been out to dinner with the Chinese delegation the night before.

She changed at Earls Court and eventually came out into the May morning at Putney, the dazzling sunlight prompting her to put on her sunglasses, the slight breeze welcome after the dry air on the Tube. The apartment complex where Robert lived was just a ten-minute walk. She took her time crossing the wide bridge over the Thames, soaking up the flickers of light on the river and the warm sunshine on her face, wanting with every step she took to put space between her life back in Dublin and this weekend with Robert.

Since Danny's unfortunate accident her life had been on hold, in a kind of limbo, because all her energies had been taken up with supporting Grace. But now, two months after the accident, in the same way that she'd encouraged Grace to start moving forward again, it seemed high time for her to begin reclaiming some of her old life. This weekend would just be about her and Robert.

* * *

Lucia had never thought she'd be lucky enough to meet a man like Robert. She knew a lot of these things were down to luck; a chance encounter of two similarly minded people who just happened to be in the right place at just the right time. Eight years ago, coming up to her twenty-seventh birthday, she wasn't looking for love, having already endured the anxiety of two half-hearted, failed relationships in her early twenties. She'd more or less decided that she preferred her own company, that way she'd know exactly where she stood in the great assault course of life – and it most certainly was an assault course. She was going to concentrate on making her career the best it could be, and making her newly acquired, mortgaged apartment a backdrop for her busy lifestyle. Besides her career, there were her further studies, her weekly Pilates class and her French language lessons.

She had few friends; she'd kept none from her schooldays and never socialised with work colleagues unless it was an event connected with the job, but she went out occasionally with a group of college friends she still kept in loose contact with since her university days. Although she sometimes felt more like a hanger-on, she usually enjoyed it and knew it was important to be part of the group of like-minded women, even if she was merely clinging to the edges.

She had been attending a two-day conference in Canary Wharf when she met Robert. Over the course of the conference, when the delegates had broken into workshops for further discussion around the safe use of marketing data and new advances in analytical software, they'd been in the same group time and time again. Thrown together in the face of hypothetical problems to solve, Lucia found herself drawn to the neatly dressed, reserved man who was also Dublin-based working in financial data management, and who was thorough and clever with the assignments they'd been given.

He was clearly intelligent – it was in his eyes – yet it was his air of gentleness that most intrigued her. She didn't think such men existed anymore; quick off the mark with everything that was current, but too authentic to feel the need to be anything other than quiet and modest. She sensed he was a bit of a loner, like herself, and liked his own company.

She wasn't the flirty type, but that first evening, when a group of delegates were having a post-dinner drink in the nearby hotel bar, something made her gravitate towards him and say, 'I've been to lots of these sessions, but I don't think I've ever met anyone quite as … conscientious as you before.' Immediately, she was mortified. What had made her say that? And *conscientious*! How could she say she found it sexy, in a still, calm, kind of way?

'Haven't you?' He looked at her inquisitively, as though he wasn't sure whether she'd meant it as a compliment or not. He'd changed out of his beautiful suit and was wearing chinos and a crisp white shirt. 'I've been called lots of things but never that.'

'I haven't finished,' she said. 'I was going to say except for … maybe myself.'

'Ah,' his face cleared. 'So it's good?'

'Of course.' She tipped her glass against his. 'It means everything is taken care of and there are no horrible surprises.'

'You don't like surprises?' He looked at her afresh, as though she'd piqued his interest.

'I like things being taken care of properly. I like to know where I stand. I don't like shocks or surprises or the rug being pulled from under me,' she gave him a half smile, wondering what he'd say to that. She sensed she could talk to him, knowing somehow, that he was on the same wavelength.

'You remind me of someone I know,' he said.

'I do?'

'Yes. Me.'

'That's good. Isn't it?'

They lingered at the bar chatting easily as the other delegates gradually dispersed. They didn't need to try to impress each other. They seemed to both understand exactly where the other was coming from without having to search for words. Lucia felt a warm peaceful glow envelop her, a sense of completeness, as though she'd found not exactly the other half of herself, but someone she knew would give her life a whole new meaning. The following day, she was filled with a warm kind of thrill and a sense of fate unfolding as she noticed him quietly watching her while they went through the programme. Later that afternoon as the delegates were breaking up, clustering in groups and exchanging contact details, Robert came over to the table where Lucia was packing her briefcase and asked if they could continue their chat over dinner in Dublin some time.

Her heart raced. She'd been a little concerned in the cold light of the daytime conference room that she'd been so open with this man the previous evening. Then again, it had seemed as though he read her with consummate ease, and she didn't have it in her to play hard-to-get. 'I'd like that, thanks,' she said, facing him squarely. She knew instinctively it wasn't in his nature to issue dinner invitations unless it meant something to him.

'I'll call you … next week?'

She smiled. 'Perfect.'

A couple of female delegates edged over towards Robert, flaunting their business cards, and she busied herself filing the last few notes into her briefcase, hiding a tiny smile.

Later that summer, she found, to her delight, that Robert was just as thorough and conscientious in bed, and good at taking all-round care of her, both in and out of bed. A year after they met, Lucia rented out her apartment and moved in to Robert's, and over the next couple of years they got engaged, bought a house together and had a wonderful wedding day that Lucia still looked back on with pleasure. Now, almost five years married, with Robert working in London for the past two years, they fell in together at the weekends as seamlessly as if they'd never been separated during the week, and the separation even helped to keep things fresh between them. Lucia didn't have to listen to Robert getting up before his early morning alarm, and forgetting to switch it off; she didn't hear him venting about unexpected delays in his commute, the lack of variety in the office canteen, the shirt that came back from the dry cleaners still marked with a stain. He didn't have to listen to the petty annoyances of her daily life either. Since he'd moved to London to work, their marriage was like a long, continuous weekend; full of date nights and relaxing, enjoyable activities. Life was great.

And, she sometimes reminded herself with a deep and unwavering gratitude, it was a far cry from the hellish time her parents had lived through when her father's business had gone bust at the tail-end of the '80s recession. That had been a scary thing to witness as a child, and a nightmare she was determined that she and Robert would never find themselves in.

Chapter Twenty-four

Just as Lucia reached the door to Robert's apartment, he opened it.

'Good timing,' she said, wheeling her case into the hall and kissing him on the cheek. He was still wearing his bathrobe, and his hair was slightly damp from the shower and scented with coconut gel.

'Excellent timing,' he said, barring her way and catching her to him.

'Just out of the shower?' she asked.

'Yes, and I missed you in it. Pity you couldn't have come over last night.'

Their time together was precious. Usually on Saturday mornings they had a lie-in and made love before showering together.

'Sorry about that. I needed to be around for the Chinese delegation wrap-up.'

Lucia was moving out of his embrace into the bright living area when he caught her hand and pulled her back against him.

'Hey, not so fast.'

She stopped, 'What?'

He nodded towards the bedroom. Then he held her close once more, sliding his free hand inside the front of her shirt, tracing the outline of her breasts. 'I needed you here as well. I missed you in bed last night, but we can fix that right now.' He nibbled her ear lobe.

She was caught by surprise. Her surprise. She hadn't expected this so immediately and to her acute discomfort she didn't feel like it. In her head she'd visualised them having coffee and a chat before going out for a leisurely brunch, and maybe having a stroll by the river bank before they went to a show that evening.

He drew her into the bedroom, taking her silence for agreement. The white drapes of the wide picture window were open, but it was okay, they were looking out at the tops of trees and the silver gleam of the river flashing through the greenery. She tried to relax and get into the mood as he slid off her shirt and opened the button on her jeans, drawing them down off of her before grinning at her as he let his bathrobe slide to the floor.

'Hey, look at you,' she said, admiring the naked sight of him and the way he was ready to make love, hoping to coax herself into feeling sexy. To fill up the evenings when she wasn't around, Robert spent time in the gym in the basement of the complex and went for jogs along the river path, and his body was lithe and trim.

She was a little removed as he began to kiss her and edge both of them across to the bed. It was still unmade from the night before, the duvet askew, pillows lobbed against the tall leather headboard. She couldn't help the thought sparking – had he had a restless sleep? Alone? She felt she was watching from a distance and going through the motions as she and Robert fell across it and he slowly slid off her underwear. It wasn't Robert's fault if she didn't feel ready for sex. Besides, their weekends were too special to be marred by any disagreement so she did her best to make sure he enjoyed it, knowing that Robert was giving it everything, making sure to satisfy her. She arched her body against his, trying to lose herself in the moment. She wrapped her legs around him, drawing him in deeper, focusing on the taste of Robert's skin, the sound of his quickened breath, the slick heat of his body against hers, how much she loved this man. How much she trusted him, despite her ridiculous imaginings. She met his pace as Robert shifted up to a faster rhythm, but she had the strange sense of not being engaged.

'You ok?' he smiled at her afterwards, tucking the sheet around her.

'Yes, great,' she lied, glad she was lying down in bed because she was a little light-headed after faking an orgasm, something she rarely had to do. If she was supposed to be getting her old life back, she thought weakly, then that had been a hopeless start.

He smoothed her hair. 'Good, I have another treat in store for tonight.'

'Have you?' *More sex?*

'Yes, I managed to nab a table for us in Soul.'

'You didn't.'

'I did.' He bent his head to kiss the tip of her nose.

Soul – it was the latest and newest west-end London restaurant, a dining experience that had opened in a blaze of publicity and to glowing reviews, where bookings were already filled well in advance.

'How did you manage that?' she asked.

'Miranda had a table booked for herself and her husband for their wedding anniversary, but their baby is sick so she offered it to me. They're like gold dust, so ...' he played with her nipples, 'lucky us.'

Miranda. Sophie was two months old now and Miranda was still on maternity leave. How and when – and why – had she offered Robert this table if they were like gold dust?

'Yes, lucky us,' she echoed his words, feeling somehow empty inside.

She watched as the husband who had given her everything she had ever needed leapt off the bed and padded into the bathroom.

Come on, Lucia, she urged herself. It was more than time she got a firm grip of her life after the upset of the last few weeks.

* * *

'Pity about Miranda and Neil,' Robert said. 'They don't know what they're missing.' He took a photo of his starter with his mobile and sent it to them.

Soul was living up to its reputation. Situated on the top floor of the Piccadilly building, it had fantastic views of the London evening skyline. While the decor was relaxed, the front-of-house service was keenly attentive and the price list reflected the luxury status Soul conferred on itself. Most of the clientele were professionals. The soft, seductive music throbbing in the background made Lucia imagine a sultry, continental night club beside a twilight beach somewhere. She wished the image was real somehow and that she was there, miles from everywhere she knew, slow dancing cheek-to-cheek with Robert, connecting with him for the first time.

A short while later, Robert's mobile pinged. He laughed at the reply before reading it out to Lucia. 'Miranda says "Enjoy! Sophie just puked up all over the new cream sofa. Bleurgh!" Rather them than us,' he went on. He took a photo of the champagne bottle in the cooler. 'I'll send her a virtual glass of bubbly,' he said. 'That reminds me, I must get them a bottle to say thanks. They must be kicking themselves that they're stuck at home tonight.'

'I'd say they're far more worried about little Sophie than a missed night out,' Lucia said.

Robert looked at her as though she'd stuck a pin in his big shiny bubble. 'Missed night out? Hello, Lucia, there's a two-month waiting list to get in here. Bad timing for them that Sophie had to get sick now but bully for us,' he said. He smiled at the waiter who was topping up their champagne before touching his glass to Lucia's. 'At least we don't have that kind of problem.'

They didn't have that problem because, Lucia carefully reminded herself, before they'd even become engaged, they'd made a firm, non-negotiable agreement, both of them together, in the cold, clear light of day: no kids.

'How's Grace?' Robert asked her, when the remains of their starters were taken away.

Lucia took a sip of her champagne before answering. She wished Robert hadn't mentioned her sister. She was trying to be here in the moment with Robert and not anywhere else. 'Grace is ... I don't know what to say.' Lucia sighed and twisted the stem of her glass. 'She seemed to be doing okay, then next I hear she's actually gone to the police with her idea that what happened to Danny wasn't just an accident.'

'You're joking.'

'I wish I were.'

'She hardly still thinks someone bumped him off.'

Lucia winced. 'Bumped him off' in terms of ending Danny's life seemed sacrilegious. What had happened to him was tragic enough without entertaining the appalling thought that it had been done to him on purpose.

'She seems to think that all right.'

'Maybe going to the police is the best thing she could have done. I'm sure they'll sort her out quickly enough. They can't afford to waste police time on imagined crimes.'

'I hope for her sake it's over soon and we can all get back to normal. It's actually ... Robert, I feel totally helpless because there's nothing I can do for Grace.'

'I can see it's upsetting you,' he said, a little contrite, reaching across the table to squeeze her hand. 'I'm sorry now I brought it up.'

'I'll get there,' Lucia said. 'I want to. And so will Grace, in time.

I told myself coming over that this weekend is about us and no one else. We work hard enough during the week. Goodness knows I put in enough twelve-hour days, as do you.' She waved her now empty glass of champagne. 'Here's to us.'

'Hey … wait til it's full before we make a toast.' He picked up the wine list. 'What do you fancy with your fish course? Chardonnay or Chablis?'

'I'll leave it up to you,' she said. She wanted to ask for the one with the highest alcoholic content, because she had the sudden need to get comfortably woozy as quickly as possible. But she didn't say that out loud because Robert would want to know why, and she didn't want to know the answer to that herself.

Chapter Twenty-five

Grace strolled through the plaza of the retail park, dodging children and buggies and Sunday afternoon shoppers. Staying in Dublin meant that she didn't even have to make the effort to talk to anyone, and she could spend as much uninterrupted time as she liked going through her writing notes, throwing down ideas, and creating an outline story board for the characters that were starting to take shape in her head.

She was amazed how much support there was on the Internet. There was a whole community of writers out there that she was now giving herself permission to join. In a short space of time she'd found some great writing blogs, and she was following writers on Twitter and Facebook. It made her feel less alone in her big ambitions, and there was a huge range of articles available on all genres of writing, which she was now devouring.

It was giving her a new lease of life, a sense of purpose, but more than that, it was some kind of affirmation that Danny had been there in her life, giving her back the confidence she'd needed to do something that was special and important to her. She'd had to coax herself to come out for fresh air, just to break up the day and get some exercise.

'Grace! Stop! Wait!'

She stopped, turned around and stared at the man in the business suit. Her mind whirled and went blank and then she recognised him. 'Gavin? What are you doing here?'

He was slightly out of breath as he neared her. He lifted his briefcase. 'I had some business to do, in one of the outlets.'

'On a Sunday?'

'You know me,' he smiled. 'Diligent to the end. I thought I recognised you ahead of me. How've you been?'

She shrugged. 'I'm okay.' Gavin had texted her on and off in the last few weeks, suggesting coffee, but she hadn't seen him or spoken to him since the night they'd met for a drink before Christmas, and she was a million miles away from that person now. As well as that, in the aftermath of Danny's death, things that had aggravated or annoyed her beforehand were now completely below her radar. So it was quite easy to face Gavin now and feel absolutely nothing at all; no irritation of any kind, no feelings of being suffocated or stifled, and no regrets whatsoever.

'I was sorry to hear about – about Danny,' he went on. 'It must have been a terrible shock.'

'It was. Thanks for the texts,' she said. 'I got so many from different people that I couldn't reply to them all.'

'Of course you couldn't. I'm sure you got hundreds. And on top of that you were probably feeling gutted.'

She winced at the expression, but let it pass, knowing that he couldn't have the slightest clue about how she felt.

'Would you like to go for that cup of coffee?' he asked.

She hesitated.

'Hey, it's me, Gavin, remember? The guy you used to …' he hesitated, 'hang out with.'

The guy I used to sleep with, she thought, surprised that a dart of panic showed up on her radar.

'I know I left you in the lurch the last time we met,' he said.

She stared at him, not comprehending for a moment.

'Christmas? For the drink?' he said. He touched her arm lightly and she jumped. 'I'd no right to walk out like that and I apologise,' he went on smoothly. 'At least give me a chance to make it up to you by buying you a coffee, even if it is five months late.'

'How did you know about Danny?' she asked, playing for time while she made up her mind about the coffee.

He shrugged. 'Word gets around,' he said.

'So you knew we were together?'

'Yes, a friend of a friend,' he said, without elaborating.

'Robert's friend?'

'Huh?'

'Robert – that's how we met. You were at the charity bash with his friends.'

'Yes, that's right. I like the way you remember that, our first meeting,' he said, smiling. 'Then I heard about the accident …' he fell silent.

Grace was used to this by now, awkward conversations peppered with uncomfortable, silent moments as a sort of mark of respect for Danny. It had happened with almost everyone she'd met in Arcadia when she'd gone back to work. She knew he'd be laughing from beyond the grave at these intervals filled with nothing but a sombre hush.

She hated the thought of Danny being in a grave. She'd rather have scattered his ashes somewhere, like sending them fluttering off the ledge in Glendalough. Still, if Danny was to be remembered in any way, she knew he'd far prefer to be remembered by people *doing* something: enjoying a burst of laughter over a joke, indulging in a moment of mischief, Grace deciding to follow her dreams. Or surely in her case right now, Grace having a cup of coffee with an old boyfriend instead of returning to a silent apartment where no matter how much she'd picked up her life again, in quiet moments she still saw Danny's smile around every doorway and heard his voice echoing through the walls.

* * *

The café in the retail park was the perfect place for a casual meet-up. Industrial-sized, busy with families and shoppers, noisy with clamouring children and loads of distraction, it wasn't the place for serious conversation.

Gavin put his briefcase under the table. He took his mobile out of his pocket and left it on the table. Then he went up to the counter, returning with a laden tray. He was no sooner seated, having organised the tea, coffee and chocolate brownies, when a small child at the next table flung her bottle, so that it rolled under their table. Gavin bent down and picked it up, handing it back to the mother with a big, indulgent smile on his face. Grace watched all this, studying him objectively, as though he were a stranger. Gavin stood out in his beautiful suit amongst the Sunday afternoon casually dressed customers. He was quite an attractive man, with his neatly groomed dark hair and pleasant face. A good catch. The kind of gentlemanly man your granny would have loved and heartily approved of. As had her parents and Lucia.

'It's good to chat to you Grace, you're looking well, considering ...' he broke off, clearly unsure of how to continue for fear of hurting her.

'It's been tough,' she said, realising there was no point in pretending otherwise, but keeping her voice devoid of emotion. 'All I can do is get on with it. Which I am.'

'You're very brave.'

'Brave? Huh, there's nothing brave about it. I've no choice but to get up every morning and go to work to earn money to pay the bills. You think—' she paused.

'What do you think? You can talk to me, Grace,' he said gently. 'We go back a long way and I'm happy to listen. I've never lost someone I've loved – well I mean they haven't actually died – so I can't even imagine it.'

Grace had said little or nothing to her friends and colleagues in Arcadia about the nightmare of living in the immediate aftermath of Danny's death, knowing they were already ill at ease about what had happened, skirting around her awkwardly. It had even been awkward at times talking to Lucia. Grace had been wary of dropping her defences long enough to open up to Lucia to any big extent, because that would have had her rushing to Grace's rescue, trying to fix the impossible. But Gavin … they'd shared so much and he'd seen the best and the worst of Grace.

'It must have been a dreadful shock,' he said. 'I don't know how you managed to cope with it.'

'I had to learn to cope with it,' she said. 'I have learned, but when it happens at first, a shock like that, you think you're going to seize up yourself, fade away into nothing.'

He nodded encouragingly.

'You want to disappear into a dot, you feel you're going mad, but the business of living goes on. Your breath comes in and out, you get hungry and need to eat even if you don't taste the food. You need sleep so eventually your eyes close and you nod off, and even if you wake up again an hour later, you fall asleep again. But, thankfully, I'm coming out the other side now.'

'You don't need to put on a brave face for me,' he said. 'How did it happen, the accident?'

She shrugged and picked at her napkin, tearing pieces off it. 'I don't know. Danny just went out to get … a message, and he never came back. It's a total mystery to me.' She didn't mention the wine and the takeaway, as she didn't want to paint a picture for Gavin of the kind of laid-back evening they'd intended to have.

'What did the police say?'

'They're looking into it, but it seems to be straightforward, insofar as any of these tragic things can be. I still can't understand how it happened.' She stopped short of telling him that she wasn't convinced it had been just a straightforward accident, but he seemed to guess what she was thinking.

'Knowing you, Grace, you were probably thinking all sorts of things, weird scenarios as to how it might have happened.'

She nodded her head.

'I bet you were even asking yourself if it really was an accident.'

She nodded again.

'I'm sure that's perfectly normal, in the circumstances,' he said. 'Your imagination is bound to be firing all over the place, driving you mad, wondering what happened to Danny, or if he knew anything about it. I wish I could do something, anything, to help.' He gave her a smile that was so soft and kind she felt herself wavering a little.

'I'm getting there, Gavin,' she said, pulling herself together. 'Life goes on.'

'There's no need to pretend, I can see this has hit you really hard,' he said. 'I'm still your friend, don't forget that. I haven't … there hasn't really been anyone else since you, I guess it's still early days. But any time you want to talk or chat, or go to the cinema, or even have some company for a walk in the park, feel free to give me a shout – I'm not stupid enough to expect anything from you, and I know our romance is …' he hesitated and grinned at her, '… long over and out, but that doesn't mean we can't be friends, or that I can't help you to heal a little, especially at a time like this.'

'Thanks, that's very kind of you, considering everything …'

Considering the way she'd broken his heart, considering the way he'd expected marriage to be the next step. He reached across the table and held her hand. She thought of all the times those hands had made love to her, and a sudden vision of him looming over her in bed made her feel a little hysterical. She made a show of looking for a fresh napkin, using it as an excuse to slide her hand out of his hold.

'Sorry, didn't mean to bother you.'

'You didn't bother me,' she said, embarrassed that he realised what she'd been up to.

'Could I ask you something? And don't get annoyed.'

'I can't promise not to get annoyed if I don't know what it is.'

'Was there any one thing about me – any one thing I did or didn't do that made you call a halt to us? I'd like to know for my own sake.'

'Don't think like that,' she said, playing for time. 'You're perfect the way you are. And please don't think you have to change yourself or your personality. You're brilliant husband material.' Perfectly kind, courteous, dependable; most women would grab Gavin Molloy with both hands and hang on to him for dear life.

'All the same, I must have lacked something for you to reject me.'

Grace sat back. How had the conversation changed? She didn't like the probing expression on his face, the one that said he'd be scrutinising her answer carefully. It made her feel uncomfortable and it reminded her of one of the reasons she'd parted with him.

'Oh shit, I'm sorry, strike that,' Gavin said. He smacked the side of his head in a pretence of annoyance. 'Don't answer. I didn't mean it to sound the way it did.'

'Whatever was missing was on my side,' Grace said, pushing her empty teacup away. 'I didn't appreciate you enough.' It was partly true, she hadn't valued Gavin enough, he was perfect husband material, solid and dependable. Pity she couldn't have settled for that.

'*Don't ever settle for anything less than you deserve …*' It was one of the first things Danny had said to her, and now, his voice seemed so close, he could have been standing over her shoulder.

Gavin's face was a mixture of emotions. She saw them flashing across his face until it resumed its usual composed expression. 'That's very good of you, thanks. And don't worry, I'm not for one minute expecting we can go back to the way—'

She shook her head.

'But I'd like to think we can be friends,' Gavin said. 'Just that. Friends.'

'Friends. Okay.'

'Come on, I'll drive you back.'

'That's okay, I'll walk,' Grace said. 'I need some fresh air.'

He looked at her with a slight frown on his face that made her think she'd said something wrong. 'It's just that I've been cooped up all day,' she said, feeling the need to explain herself. 'I could do with the exercise.'

'Then I'll walk you back,' he said, pulling his briefcase out from under the table.

She hadn't wanted that either, her face was already aching from the effort of talking to him but it would have been churlish to refuse. They walked back out to the plaza, across the pedestrian walkway and out onto the path by the main road. The sun had finally broken through the clouds and it was a beautiful May afternoon. The breeze came in little gusts, and any remaining clouds were small patches of cotton wool high in the soft sapphire sky. She tried to concentrate on that rather than the man by her side, relieved all the same when they reached the side gate of the Rathbrook apartment complex.

'Seems a shame to be stuck in on such a lovely evening,' Gavin said, swinging his briefcase. 'It's the kind of evening for a walk along Dun Laoghaire pier.' He smiled at her with a question on his face.

Grace's chest tightened with panic in case he invited her along. She couldn't think of a reasonable excuse to refuse him. A walk along Dun Laoghaire seemed a perfectly normal thing for friends to do on an evening like this.

'I'm seeing Lucia later,' she said, hoping her face didn't give away the fib.

'Later? So Robert's in Dublin this weekend?'

Why did she feel he was invading her space when he obviously remembered Lucia's well-regulated domestic arrangements? She was uncomfortable and guilty that he'd almost caught her out in the lie. 'No,' she said, making it worse for herself, but needing to back up what she'd said, 'I'm calling over to see Lucia later, after she's back from London.' Too much information.

'Never mind, Grace,' he smiled indulgently. 'Don't look so worried. I wasn't asking you to come out to Dun Laoghaire. I know you're still all over the place after Danny.'

She wished suddenly he wouldn't talk about Danny or mention his name. She didn't like the familiar sound of it on his lips. He didn't know Danny at all, she wanted to scream, nor was he similar to him in any way.

'Any time you want a shoulder to cry on, or just want to talk about it, don't feel you have to be alone, please call me. We can just chat or whatever. No strings whatsoever. Just friends.'

'Thanks Gavin,' she said. 'I appreciate that.'

The problem was, she didn't. Neither did she want Gavin to see her as a victim and drag her back to the dark place she'd been in after Danny. He leaned in towards her and she struggled to keep her face neutral as he kissed her on the cheek. Some of the purposeful, feel-good humour that had got her through the day vanished, and standing there in the gorgeous afternoon she felt a moment of terrible rage that Danny was dead and Gavin was still alive, going about his day much as usual, even taking the liberty to kiss her. She couldn't believe the wave of pure relief that washed over her when he turned to go back to the retail park and his car. It wasn't far off the sense of liberation she'd felt on New Year's Day when she'd finally given herself permission to forget all about him.

Chapter Twenty-six

On Monday morning Lucia felt totally disconnected as she walked into the foyer of Izobel Group and took the lift to her fourth-floor office. London and Robert hadn't been the relaxing weekend she'd hoped for. Even the gourmet dinner in the much-rated Soul had failed to lift her spirits in any meaningful way, despite her best intentions to slot back into the familiar contours of her life.

When she got out of the lift, Aiden Burke was strutting up the corridor.

Whereas before Aiden would have passed her by with a nod and a quip, since Lucia had come back to work after Danny's death, he seemed kinder to her, almost as though he had taken on the role of watching out for her. On her first day back he'd insisted on bringing her out to lunch, and since then they'd gone out to lunch three or four times. It was purely a friendly gesture and they usually had a light-hearted chat about work, but she'd caught herself wondering if Robert brought his female colleagues out for coffee or lunch and how much he enjoyed their company.

Now Aiden paused, and looked at her as though he had all the time in the world to stop and chat. 'Hi Lucia! Did you have a good weekend?'

'Hi Aiden, it was lovely thanks,' she said smoothly. 'And you?'

'Not as good as it might have been,' he said, making a funny face.

'It wasn't long enough?' she guessed.

'That too, besides other things.'

Lucia lifted an eyebrow.

Aiden smiled self-deprecatingly as he leaned a little closer to Lucia. 'She doesn't want me anymore.'

Lucia was surprised at the admittance. She hadn't a clue who he was referring to, but from what she gathered from the office gossip there was no shortage of women fighting to get into Aiden's bed.

'What a pity,' she said chattily. 'Her loss.'

'Thank you Lucia, good to have you on my side,' he said, giving her a wink. He began to walk down to his office, and then he wheeled back around suddenly, 'Coffee, later?'

'I can't, not today, Aiden,' she said automatically.

'Get you again,' he said, raising his hand in a friendly salute.

Was this how it started? A perfectly innocuous friendship, an innocent lunch here, a quick cup of coffee there, then a conversation about a failed relationship, perhaps getting more personal … Lucia pulled herself together. She was making a song and dance about nothing. As she sat at her desk, held meetings with staff, put the final touches to reports, spoke to Diane about the running order for an afternoon conference on the autumn promotion programme – noting Diane's whiteboard was jammed with several more adorable drawings of misshapen hearts and kisses – she was conscious that in a weird kind of way, running under the surface of her carefully organised day was the fear that her life was equivalent to a car tyre getting a very slow puncture; a puncture invisible to the naked eye, but it meant everything wasn't operating on its usual full power. Problem was, she didn't know how to find the cause of the puncture, let alone fix it. And if she didn't fix it soon, the tyre might flatten completely and send everything careening off the road, out of control.

And the one thing Lucia feared was the thought of not being in control. It had happened to her before, as a child, and was something that had left a lingering imprint. She'd vowed, when she'd been old enough to fully understand what had happened, that her life would never be pulled apart again.

* * *

Her parents tried to keep the worst of it from her. She was eight years of age when she first realised something was wrong. One day her mummy laughed light-heartedly at something three-year-old Grace said and Lucia realised, with a slight sense of shock, that it seemed a long time since her mummy had laughed like that.

Her mummy used to always laugh like that.

As though someone had peeled away a layer of cotton wool that had been holding together the innocent fabric of her childhood, she began to notice other things. Her parents were different from the way they had been. They didn't smile as much, and when they moved around the house they seemed stiff and jerky instead of flowing and soft.

They hadn't gone on holidays to the seaside for two years. They used to go every year, as far back as Lucia could remember, even the year Mummy's tummy was fat with Grace. Mummy had stopped buying any treats and when she went to the supermarket, she brought a small list, sticking to it even if Grace kicked up looking for something nice. Lucia would walk by the ice cream cabinets, longing for an ice cream, but Mummy would hurry past and she knew not to ask for it. She couldn't remember the last time there had been sweets or biscuits put into the trolley. One day Mummy went bright red at the checkout when she didn't have enough money and she had to put some cereal back. The lady at the counter made a fuss over calling the supervisor to fix the till and Lucia thought she was going to vomit when she saw her mother's hand shaking as she counted out the coins. Then there was the day Grace threw her bowl of rice on the floor, because they'd had it for dinner three days in a row and she hated it. Mummy looked like she was going to cry and Lucia felt scared.

After a while it was like a dark cloud had settled on top of the house. Some days Mummy didn't answer the door, asking her and Grace to stay really quiet in the kitchen, that she was playing a great game. There were no more pretty clothes. Neither she nor Grace got new shoes for a while, and when she went back to school after the summer break she was wearing the same jumpers and shoes as the previous year even though they barely fitted her.

There were lots of letters coming through the door but Daddy didn't seem to want to open any of them. Lucia was well able to read by now, and lots of them had *Urgent* or *Final Reminder* on the envelopes. She didn't like the look of the thick black lettering and Daddy's face got cross when he saw them and he shoved them out of sight behind the toaster in the kitchen, where Mummy picked them up with shaky hands and a very white face.

Some nights she sat on the stairs after she was supposed to be in bed, trying to hear what her parents were talking about downstairs, trying to understand what was going on. Other evenings her aunts and uncles dropped in, their voices hushed. Sometimes she even heard Mummy crying. Often Grace crept out of bed and joined her, giggling and laughing and looking like a little fairy in a pink nightdress with her halo of white-blonde hair all fluffed up from the pillow. Lucia distracted Grace by reading her stories and pretending this was a great game. The visitors sometimes brought treats or biscuits and she would share some with Grace, having a 'midnight' feast, even if it was long before that hour.

The worst was when her father stopped going to work the following year. He didn't seem as tall as the daddy who had happily gone out to work each morning asking Mummy to look after his princesses. His clothes seemed too loose for his body. His face was like a thin mask of the daddy she'd once known and it frightened Lucia. Mummy started going out in the afternoons, to clean offices somewhere. They got rid of the car because they didn't really need it anymore, they told Lucia. Often now, she heard Mummy crying when she thought no one could hear her, so she continued to read to Grace, finding it a distraction for both of them.

It got far, far worse when Mummy told them they were moving into a lovely new house. Her voice was bright and thin and so full of pretend happiness that it almost cracked. Lucia felt like vomiting lots of days. The new house was much smaller and older, it smelled strange and seemed darker, and there was no front garden full of beautiful flowers, or long back garden with a swing or a slide, there was just a tiny back yard.

But the new school was a much bigger, far noisier school, where the playground was huge and children ran around very fast. Lucia's voice was different to everyone else's, and they laughed at it and pulled her hair and called her 'posh'. She was glad Grace was only starting out in Junior Infants when this happened. At five years of age it was a great new adventure, like the stories Lucia read her at night.

But at ten years of age it was something else entirely.

Chapter Twenty-seven

The rain that had been threatening all day in the shape of dark, big-bellied clouds decided to pour down from the skies and spread huge puddles on the pavement just as Grace came out of the supermarket at the corner of the retail park on Monday evening. Had she gone straight home from work, she would have avoided a soaking, but instead she'd gone to an early evening reader's event in a large city-centre bookstore, where two young adult authors were in discussion with David Walliams. She'd seen it advertised on Twitter and had booked a place.

At first Grace had felt a little awkward taking a seat. There was a mixed audience, she'd come alone and so many others had come with friends or seemed to know each other from book clubs or literary events. However, her awkwardness didn't last long. Two middle-aged women sat down beside her and they included her in their chit-chat, introducing themselves as Gemma and Sally.

'Are you a reader or a writer?' Gemma asked her.

'Both,' she said, glad she'd had the guts to admit it, feeling as if she was stepping out of a closet.

'What do you write?' Sally asked with interest.

'Children's stories,' she said. 'I'm just getting started, actually.'

'Keep it up,' Sally said. 'Perseverance wins out.'

She was delighted to find out they were both published authors of commercial fiction, and by the end of the event she had their Twitter contact details and lots of suggestions as to other events and websites she'd find useful. She'd also relaxed and enjoyed the discussion, feeling she was in her groove, and lots of the comments and pieces of advice resonated with her.

She was so charged with enthusiasm when she got back to Rathbrook that the rain didn't bother her. Nor did she mind making the short detour to pick up some milk and eggs. Now she stood inside the supermarket door trying to arrange herself and her belongings against the torrential rain before she braved the dash to Rathbrook Hall.

Her phone was tucked into the inside pocket of her tote bag along with her purse. She took out her door keys and put them in the zipped pocket of her jacket to have them ready. She clutched her bag to her chest, making sure the side with her phone and purse was tucked against her for maximum shelter against the deluge. And then she ran, head bent, hopping over puddles, taking the shortest route possible to the apartment complex, already saturated to the skin by the time she reached the pedestrian gate to the side of the main road. She ran through the landscaped courtyard just as the rain stopped for a moment. She shoved her wet hair back off her face. It would only be a short breathing space, to judge by the lowering clouds.

Already in the shade thanks to the height of the apartment blocks, the courtyard seemed more sombre than ever on this darkening evening. Something about the heavy atmosphere pressed down on her and sent a chill down her spine. She glanced up at the tiers of apartments, and she fancied she was the only person left in the world, as there was no sign of life anywhere. Nobody was out on a balcony in this downpour, there were no faces at the windows, but she had the odd feeling of being watched as she took the flagstone path between the raised beds of greenery towards the back door to the south block.

Her imagination was working overtime.

She tried to shake away the brooding atmosphere as she rummaged for her key, her wet hands cold and white after the rain. Eventually she let herself into the hall, breathing hard after her dash from the shops, relieved to be out of the elements, and she took the short passage around to the bank of lifts. Her shoes were squelching and her jacket was stuck to her as well as her clothes as she walked down the corridor to her apartment.

Her immediate thought, as she unlocked the door, pushed it open and stepped inside, was that someone had been here. And could still be here. There was a shift of some kind in the atmosphere. A miniscule waft of a different kind of scent. The apartment didn't seem as static as it usually did, when it had been unoccupied for hours during the day.

'Danny?' she said his name lightly, almost a whisper. Nothing stirred. There was only an eerie silence and even the air seemed to be holding its breath as she moved into the room. She mocked herself. No way had she expected to see him getting up from the table or turning around from the cooker, and the thoughts of his absence sent a knife twisting through her guts, but the feeling that someone had been there, flitting through her rooms, still persisted as she peeled off her wet jacket and hung it on a chair.

And then she turned around and saw the posters.

Something thudded into her chest. Two of them had come away from the adhesive that had been holding the top of them to the wall, and they were secured only along the bottom, so that they were hanging upside down, the backs of them facing out blankly. It gave her such a start that her chest heaved and tears prickled her eyes. It was nothing to worry about, she told herself. All she had to do was get some heavier tack and stick them back up again.

She went around the apartment to see if she had left a window open, because a sudden draught of wind might have caused this, as well as giving her the feeling that the air had been disturbed. But all was fine. She went over to the kitchen window and looked out, but down below, the courtyard was empty, and as she watched, the rain started to fall again. She pulled down the blind against the dismal evening. Then she headed into the bathroom where she peeled off her damp clothes and stood under the shower, closing her eyes and keeping her mind deliberately blank.

Suddenly she opened her eyes again. The kite. Had it been it its usual spot? Or had that, too, floated off its moorings? She thought she'd never get out of the shower quickly enough to check that it was still where Danny had put it. If that had fallen down, too …

She grabbed her towelling bathrobe and wrapped it around her wet body as she left the bathroom, crossed the narrow hallway and went through to the kitchen.

She let out her breath.

It was there, still, exactly where Danny had put it, during that memorable afternoon two weeks before he'd moved in.

Chapter Twenty-eight

'You shouldn't have,' Janet said, taking the bouquet of flowers from Matt and burying her nose in the scented blooms.

'It was the least I could do. Happy Birthday.' Standing in the porch, hands in his pocket, Matt felt awkward. Janet wasn't asking him in and she seemed to be keeping the door as closed over as far as possible without shutting it in his face. He'd known immediately by the uncomfortable look in her eyes that she was slightly embarrassed at this display of friendship. Still, he'd wanted to mark the occasion of Janet's birthday somehow. He hadn't sent a card. This time last year he'd got her a lovey-dovey card with hearts and kisses and butterflies on the front and a romantic verse on the inside, he'd bought her jewellery and a sexy, gossamer-thin negligee set that he'd ordered online – how did you follow that? Flowers were the safest option. Not roses, though; a summer bouquet, the girl in the shop had said. Suitable for anyone aged eight to eighty.

As he stood there, he noticed something else – Janet was all dressed up as though she was going out. Well of course she was, it was her birthday, only she wasn't spending it with him, like she had the last few birthdays. This year she was most likely spending it with her sister. He wondered who was babysitting Abbie. He hoped it wasn't Simon. He would have looked after Abbie for her, if she wanted to go out with her sister, only he hadn't been asked.

'Going out?' he raised an eyebrow, trying to look nonchalant.

'Yes, any minute now, we—' that was as far as Janet got before Abbie ran up the hall and began to dance on the spot just inside the door.

'Daddy,' she squealed. 'Guess what, it's Mammy's birthday.'

He bent down and hugged her, wishing he had the freedom to give Janet a hug like this. Then he realised that Abbie, too, seemed to be all dressed up in some sparkly white top with a pair of blue embroidered jeans and a glittery band in her hair.

'*More* flowers,' Abbie said. 'The house will be bursting with flowers.'

Matt straightened up. Janet was slightly pink. She remained silent.

'Your Mammy's a good person,' Matt said to Abbie. 'That's why she gets lot of nice flowers on her birthday.'

'Yes, but Simon's flowers are huge, *this* big,' Abbie went on, stretching her arms as wide as she could. 'They came in a special van and all. A very special flower van. Did your flowers not need a special van?' Without waiting for an answer, she flung back the hall door so Matt could see the enormous arrangement of pink and white blooms taking over the hall table.

Matt eyes flicked to Janet.

'Well …' she said, looking embarrassed, 'it is my birthday.'

'Can I see your flowers Mummy?' Abbie stood up on tiptoe to see Matt's flowers as Janet lowered the bouquet. 'Simon's flowers are much bigger, they're gi*normous,*' she went on.

Matt couldn't stop his gaze from boring into Janet's eyes. She stared back at him defiantly.

'Mummy told him he must have sent the whole shop. Is that why we're going out with him tonight Mummy? Because of the flowers? Can Daddy come too?'

Matt raised his eyebrows and looked at Janet. 'Out? All of you?'

'Just for a couple of hours,' Janet said. 'We won't be staying out late with Abbie.'

No, thought Matt bleakly. *We. We'll* be home to read her a story and put her to bed; both of you together tucking her up, then downstairs to relax in the garden with a bottle of wine like Matt and Janet used to, in the good old days. The ordinary yet brilliant everyday pleasures that he sometimes took for granted, which he'd give the whole wide world to have back.

'Can Daddy come please, Mammy?' Abbie wheedled.

Matt didn't wait to see how Janet would react. 'I can't Abbie,' he said. 'Not tonight.'

And not any night that Simon was around.

Abbie's face fell. He wasn't sure if Janet was slightly relieved or if he was imagining it.

'We'll go out a different night,' he said. 'I have some work on this evening.' Which he had, sort of.

'Okaaaay. Mummy can we keep Daddy some cake? Simon is bringing a big cake,' she said, her eyes lighting up. 'A *huge* cake. It'll be nearly as big as the flowers. Will he have enough room in his car for it? Or do you get a special van for a cake?'

'I'll leave you to it,' Matt said. 'Enjoy your evening.'

'The flowers are lovely, Matt,' Janet said. 'You didn't have to.'

Oh, but I did, even if they don't compete with Simon's, at least they're a reminder of me and that I exist. And that I'm someone who once knew you intimately enough to be able to give you an intimate gift for your birthday, one that both of us enjoyed. He blanked out an image of her coming towards him in the softly lit bedroom.

He backed down the garden path. Even though Janet was actually smiling at him as though she meant it, he felt a lump in his throat as he saw them there, standing in the porch, both his girls, all dressed up for going out with another man. Only it wasn't just any other man.

* * *

Simon was Abbie's biological father, who'd run to Australia so fast when he'd discovered Janet was pregnant after a brief fling that he'd left nothing but a trail of dust in his wake.

Matt had been there for Abbie since she'd been six months old, when he'd first met Janet at a house party. The minute he'd noticed the brown-eyed girl with the soft voice and gentle laughter, his heart had flipped over and something had clicked. He felt as though he knew her already. When they got together in a corner of the kitchen, both of them knowing they both felt a little giddy at how seamless their conversation flowed, both of them sensing this could be more than a shared beer, she'd shown him a picture of Abbie on her mobile and told him they came as a package. That, too, had been perfect. Nine months later he'd moved in with Janet. Since then he'd been Abbie's father in every other way.

Abbie began to call him daddy as soon as she could talk. Matt had tried to dissuade Abbie from using the title, but to no avail. As far as Abbie was concerned he was living in the house with her and mummy, therefore he was daddy. Boys were the daddies and girls were the mummies. Like Peppa Pig, only she hadn't got a baby brudder. Yet. This had been delivered in a calm voice, Abbie's eyes looking at him with perfect trust as though he was going to deliver on the 'brudder' sooner rather than later.

Then most conveniently for himself, Simon had reappeared on the scene last August, when Matt had been living with Janet for about eighteen months and Abbie was a couple of months short of her third birthday.

The title didn't bother Simon when Matt and Janet explained the situation to him. He was only too glad to let Matt have that title. 'I don't deserve to be called her daddy, after the way I bolted,' Simon said, giving Matt and Janet a sorrowful look, a look that Matt itched to slap off his face. 'But now that I'm back in Dublin, and she is my daughter, I'd like to see her from time to time, see how she's getting on, maybe I could be her uncle, or something ...'

It had been the first crack in the relationship between Janet and Matt.

'I don't trust him,' Matt had said. 'He's after something.'

'Don't be ridiculous, what could he be after?'

'Your lovely body? A decent roof over his head? I'd love to know what brought him home from Australia now.'

'Matt, leave it. And he's not after my body.'

'How do you know? Maybe he wants to enjoy it all over again,' Matt said, unable to push away images of Janet and Simon, together, in the bedroom upstairs. As they had been before. He was disgusted to find himself wondering how good Simon had been, in bed.

'You sound jealous.'

'I'm not.'

'You are. You have nothing to be jealous of. Are you really that lacking in self-confidence that you see Simon as a threat? He's no threat at all – he doesn't feature anywhere on the scale of you and me.'

He said nothing.

'We agreed to draw a line under our past relationships, didn't we? I never asked about your stream of girlfriends, did I?'

'There weren't that many. And nothing serious enough to have any mini-Matts out there.'

Janet gave him a long look. 'Simon and I ...' she paused. 'I'm reminding you for the last time that it was just a quick fling. I *told* you. I was down in the dumps after Mum died and he ... just happened to be there, that's all. I'm sure you've had convenient sex at least once,' she raised her eyebrows. 'Only I was careless one night – although it was the best kind of carelessness,' she smiled. 'I knew Simon was planning to go to Australia. He hadn't worked here for six months and he'd a job lined up in Sydney. I found out I was pregnant a week before he was due to fly out.'

'So you knew you were pregnant but still he ran?' Matt wondered why he was being so mean. He'd always prided himself on being non-judgemental, especially in his job, where things weren't often what they seemed.

'That's your version of events. I told him to go, right? His visa was organised, flights booked and paid for. We weren't in a relationship, we were never going to be and I didn't once try to persuade him to stay. I didn't want him to change his plans.'

No, because you're too soft and gentle and you let people take advantage of you.

The cracks had widened in the next few months, Matt finding it hard to tolerate Simon's occasional presence, wishing heartily he'd take a long, running jump out of Janet's life.

'I don't know why you're so resentful of Simon,' Janet said, after another episode when Matt had slagged him off for bringing Abbie a rake of toys. 'He hasn't done anything wrong to you. All he does is come to visit Abbie, he doesn't even take her out.'

Matt spluttered. 'He's practically a stranger to her. You can't let him take her out.'

'I won't. Unless I went with them,' Janet said.

'See? That'll be the next step. The happy little family, all out together.'

'Is that what this is about? Your not being Abbie's biological father?'

'No.' He could cope with that. He couldn't cope with the interloper Simon having any claim on what Matt saw as his precious little family.

'Don't you trust me?'

'I do trust you, of course I do …'

'It's as though you're looking for an excuse to break us up.'

'Don't be ridiculous.'

'It's true, Matt, I can't help feeling you're using Simon as a reason to sabotage us.'

'And why would I do that?'

'That's what I'm trying to figure out. I can't understand why you have trust issues.'

Another night he came home from a late shift to find Simon having a glass of wine with Janet, when Abbie was tucked up in bed.

'What was that all about?' he demanded after Simon had left, beating a hasty retreat thanks to Matt's glowering face and the sudden, sub-zero temperature in the room.

'We were relaxing our inhibitions before we went upstairs to have fantastic sex,' Janet said.

'*What?*'

'No way, you big eejit. I was showing him some baby photos of Abbie. That job is crossed off the list. It won't be happening again. And a lot of the photos included you.'

Still, later that night when she turned to him in bed, he'd been mortified to find he couldn't sustain an erection. *What the fuck?*

'Is he really getting to you that much?' Janet had asked softly, trailing her hands lightly down along his thighs.

'Why should he be?' Matt had countered, furious with himself. Why should he be indeed? What had Simon got that he hadn't? Still, a little voice whispered, he'd given Janet the wonderful and precious Abbie. So in a way he did have one up on Matt.

'There's absolutely no reason in the world,' Janet had said, kissing his cheek and pressing her body against his.

But when she began to talk about the possibility of Simon visiting on Christmas Day, it was the last straw.

'Just hear me out,' Janet said.

'No.'

'Matt – listen – a visit, on Christmas Day. It won't kill either of us to share a small part of the day with him.'

'No. It's *our* day, our family day. I want it to be special for us, without Mr Interloper.'

'Don't talk about Simon like that. He is Abbie's father, after all.'

'Remind me of that all-important fact, why don't you.'

'I didn't mean it to come out like that. I meant her biological father. He does have rights.'

'He gave them up the day he left for Australia.'

'He wouldn't have gone, he said, if he'd known how beautiful she was going to be.'

'Oh, so he's had a change of heart? How convenient. He's definitely after something. I'm back on duty on Stephen's Day, let him call around then.'

'So you're allowing him to call here when you won't be around?'

'Don't worry, I'll set up a surveillance camera,' he said flippantly.

There was a silence. 'You would too, wouldn't you? Why? Why are you being so nasty? Why don't you trust me?'

The rows went on.

'It was a mistake for me to allow Abbie call you "Dad".'

'Thank you.'

'I don't mean that in the way you think. What can I say to her when she's older? I need to explain who Simon is and tell her the truth. She needs to know who her real father is. Thing is, I thought you and I were in it for good, and Simon was gone for good. I kind of visualised sitting her down when she was about ten or so, and you and me might have been … married or something, and that would have given her security of sorts. Now it's all messed up.'

'I didn't mess it up.'

'You're not helping …'

'I'm torn in two,' Janet said. 'I love you, Matt, but I don't like this part of you.'

'It comes with the package.'

'What's got into you? If you're going to be like this …' she paused.

'Well, go on, if I'm going to be like this, what? I can't help being distrustful of a man who abandoned you so easily, skived off for a few years and thinks he can pick up where he left off.'

'Jesus, how many times do I have to tell you? He's not picking up where he left off? I'm not putting up with this crap, Matt,' she said. 'If you can't trust me, then I don't see a future for us.'

'Fine.' Deep down, he knew it was himself he didn't trust, not Janet. But the reasons why he didn't trust himself, and why he allowed Simon to get in under his skin and make him feel resentful sat like a dark cave inside him that he didn't want to enter, and he couldn't find a way of articulating that. His head told him he was thirty-four years old; he should be in charge of his own life now, and not letting someone else dictate the way he felt, certainly not someone like Simon. From her upstairs bedroom, where he'd just tucked her up a half an hour ago and read her a story, Abbie began to cry. And that was it, really. Janet might be as soft as they come, but behind that, right back at the very essence of her, she had a core of steel.

'I'm not having Abbie witness this kind of carry on ever again,' she said, after she'd settled her again. 'If you can't promise to behave yourself, I'd prefer that you leave.'

By now, he was far more furious with himself and his own lack of control and general childishness than with Janet or the interloper, Simon. 'Fine then. Throw me out.'

'You're throwing yourself out,' she said.

It didn't help that he knew deep down inside she was right.

Chapter Twenty-nine

There was no need for Grace to know he was officially off duty, or that this wasn't exactly protocol, Matt decided as he drove down the ramp and slid into a parking spot under Rathbrook Hall. He pressed the keypad by the underground entrance and announced himself through the intercom. Grace unlocked the door. It was almost two weeks since she'd dropped into the station, but work had been crazy and he hadn't found time to see her until now. He hoped she didn't think he had any answer for her. He'd gone through the file and reports but he hadn't come across anything whatsoever to suggest that what had happened to Danny McBride had been anything but an accident. Now the case was in limbo until the inquest.

Her apartment was last on the right as he came out of the lift.

'Hello, Matt.'

She was wearing black jeans and a loose cream top, her blonde hair a little messy as though she'd washed it and run a towel through it hastily. There were mauve shadows under her eyes. They reminded him a little of when Abbie had been sick and up all night with a pain in her tummy.

'Thanks for seeing me now,' he went on.

A faint lift of her eyebrows. 'It's me who should be thanking you for coming along and ...' she seemed momentarily lost for words,

'Well, come in ...'

He stepped into a long, narrow hallway. Two doors on the right led into a bathroom and bedroom. The door on the left brought him into a kitchen-cum-living room. The galley kitchen had a small window looking out to the side of another apartment block. At the other end of the room, a large picture window faced out onto the main road in front of the complex. On the wall in the living area there were three posters pinned up that looked interesting, but he didn't want to stare at them too much. He had to remind himself he was off duty and there was no need for him to case this apartment.

'Will you have tea or coffee?' she asked.

'I'd love a cup of coffee, thanks,' he said. He thought it might relax her a bit and give her something else to focus on besides him.

'I just have instant, is that okay?'

'Yeah, fine. Milk, no sugar,' he added. 'Nice kite, by the way,' he said, looking at the vibrant splash of colour against the anaemic-shaded press.

'Danny put that up after the day we went kite-flying.'

'Kite-flying.'

'Yeah.' Her face softened with memory. 'Please, sit down,' she said, waving her fingers at the sofa drawn up at right angles to the picture window.

He checked out the posters, wondering if they'd belonged to Danny or Grace, or if they'd chosen them together. He liked the one of the firework display, telling him not to be afraid to dream big. Grace came over then, pulling out a small table and putting down the mug of coffee. She remained standing, hugging herself.

'Have you any – did you get a chance ...'

'Sit down, Grace, and we'll talk.'

She perched on the opposite end of the sofa, staring at him as she clasped and unclasped her hands.

'I checked out the accident report and ...' he looked away from her as he tried to think how best to put it. Communication skills were not his strong point. Especially imparting unfavourable news to women. How much detail did she want? She hardly wanted to hear that the autopsy showed that Danny had died of a broken neck, and that he'd had multiple injuries to his internal organs, consistent with a motorbike crash into a wall. It didn't appear that speed had been a factor; there were no apparent skid marks but the front half of the motorbike had been so badly damaged that it had been impossible to extract anything significant out of the examination.

He wasn't going to tell Grace, but the mangled remains of Danny's motorbike were still in a corner of a shed behind the station. After the inquest, it would most likely go to the breaker's yard as there was little there for family to take home.

Grace put up her hand. 'Please – I don't want to hear the details,' she said, filling him with relief. 'I couldn't bear that. I just need to know if you found anything at all that would …' she swallowed. 'Anything unusual.'

'I didn't,' he said quietly. 'Everything in the report files seems to be very straightforward.'

'Straightforward,' she echoed, looking at him with hurt in her eyes as though to say how could he label her boyfriend's accidental death as straightforward? How could it be just another file in a press?

'But that doesn't mean … look, there could be a slim possibility that something might have been overlooked.' He found himself saying words he shouldn't really be saying, to let her down gently, although it was wrong of him. He shouldn't be suggesting the hugely improbable idea that something had been missed. Still, as he'd gone through the file, he couldn't help wondering himself how a perfectly able-bodied man, on a night when the roads were dry and adequately lit, had mounted the verge and gone into a wall. He'd even passed down by the scene where it had happened; it was a feeder road with two lanes of traffic and boundary walls set back from narrow grass verges. It wasn't a particularly busy road outside of rush-hour traffic, and had no dangerous bends, just a gradual curve. The speed limit was 80 kilometres an hour, enough to do major damage if Danny had been distracted in any way.

There had been no witnesses to the actual crash. The van driver who was first on the scene recalled a motorbike overtaking him some distance back, then another one overtaking him less than a minute later, which had been involved in the accident. He had come upon the scene within minutes of it occurring. Despite requests for witnesses to members of the public, no one had come forward, not even the first motorcyclist to have passed out the van driver, but if he or she had been doing the maximum speed, they would have been a mile out from the accident when it occurred.

'So what happens now?' she asked.

'Have you anything at all, any other information that would suggest it hadn't been an accident?

'Not one big thing, no,' she said. 'It's just a combination of everything, and an overall gut feeling.'

The gut feeling didn't wash with him. He could only deal with hard facts. He tried to recall other details she'd given the day she'd called to the station and he remembered the gut feeling he'd got, that somewhere in her account of things, Grace wasn't telling him the full truth.

Maybe there was something she knew that she hadn't yet faced up to, something that was causing her to think there was more to Danny McBride's motorcycle accident than there appeared to be. She looked like an intelligent woman, not the kind to be given to fantasy.

He shouldn't even be here. Grace obviously needed help to get her to move out of the denial phase. She was looking at him as Abbie had countless times when she wanted him to fix her Lego. The best thing he could do was give Grace the name of the liaison officer, who'd shortly be covering for Holly.

'I wish I could help,' he found himself saying. Great. Where had that come from?

'Thanks,' she said softly.

He hated walking out and leaving her on her own. Deep down, way, way beneath the protective shield of his police identity card, he knew he was too soft himself. Which was why he'd gravitated towards Janet, sensing a kindred spirit. Which was why he was still here, sitting in this young woman's apartment instead of getting up to leave.

He astounded himself by saying, 'Why don't you start at the beginning, when you first met Danny, tell me everything that happened. I might pick up on something that could be checked out further.'

Her forehead creased. 'Have you got time for this?'

He hadn't. Not really. There were cases stacking up in the station and every phone call brought something different. Another crime, another assault, more victims, tons of paperwork, and he'd be on a night shift for the next few nights. 'Don't worry about that,' he said. 'Just tell me, in your own words, how you met Danny.'

'You want to know how I met Danny?' It was clear she hadn't expected this. She looked like the proverbial deer, caught in the glare of headlights.

'Yeah, didn't you say it was just before Christmas?'

He could have sworn a flicker of relief ran across her face. After years in the force, it chimed an odd note. He had the feeling that she was telling him a fib again.

'That's right,' she said. 'Christmas. I was meeting up with my ex-boyfriend for a drink when things went kind of sour and Danny came to the rescue ...'

There was a short silence after Grace was finished recounting the events of the night. 'That was it,' she said, looking at Matt. 'Danny and I spent Christmas with our respective families, but after that, we were hardly apart.' He heard her voice quivering a little, and his instincts told him he was missing something.

'This guy Gavin,' Matt eventually said. 'Was he real upset?'

'Not really. He'd had too much to drink the night before and he was actually more sick than anything else.'

'Do you think he might have been sour that you took up with Danny? Would he have had a problem with it, like, was he a jealous kind of guy?'

'God, no,' Grace said immediately. 'Gavin is a proper gentleman, kind and caring. One of the good guys.'

Matt smiled faintly. 'One of the good guys? Yet you let him go?'

'I did. Gavin and I … it had all gone rather flat. Being with him … I knew it wasn't something I wanted to do for the rest of my life. When we broke up, it was amicable enough, all very low key, no big drama.'

'Okay. So Gavin wouldn't have been out for Danny's blood?'

'Gavin wouldn't hurt a fly. I met him recently and we had a friendly, civilised coffee. He said to give him a call if I ever wanted a shoulder to cry on. That's the kind of thoughtful person he is.'

'Right. If you remember anything important or you just feel like talking, leave a message on my mobile and I'll get back to you as soon as I can.' Maybe the next time she talked to him she might be more open to being referred on to the officer liaison.

'Why are you doing this?' she asked on impulse. 'Calling in, sounding as if you believe me? No one else does.'

'It's part of my job – you made a statement to say you have concerns about a death so it has to be followed up.'

'Yes, but …' she said. 'So you're following things up even if you don't believe me?'

'Grace,' he ran a hand through his hair, 'I'm not saying what I think one way or another, it's nothing to do with whether I believe you or not, right? I'm just doing a job, but I want to do it in the best way possible.' He got to his feet and nodded to the posters on the wall, 'Yours or Danny's?'

She smiled that luminous smile again. 'Danny's. They're helping, believe it or not.'

'Good.' He looked at the one encouraging him to dream big and wondered how he could apply it to himself and Janet.

Chapter Thirty

Lucia held her mobile in her hand, chatting to Grace as she click-clacked around the kitchen, giving a final, unnecessary wipe-down to the work surfaces.

'You'll be glad to hear that the police went through the accident report and found nothing. It was as straightforward as can be,' Grace said.

'I *am* glad to hear that,' Lucia said. 'Maybe you can start putting your worries behind you now.'

'I am putting it behind me, but now and then I still feel something isn't right,' Grace said. 'Especially after getting that photograph.'

'Definitely a jealous ex,' Lucia said. 'Ignore it.'

'Sometimes I still see a motorbike that reminds me of Danny's,' Grace said, 'I seem to see it a lot, when I'm out and about, going for a walk in the evenings.'

'Of course you do, that's natural,' Lucia said gently. 'There are probably hundreds of bikes just like Danny's on the road, it's just you're paying more attention to them now. It's perfectly normal, Grace. You were madly in love with Danny, you were on a high after he moved in with you, carrying on like you've never carried on before, as though he was some kind of …' Lucia paused momentarily, '… enchanting wizard. But Danny wasn't a superhero who was above and beyond the normal crap that life can throw at us. He was an ordinary guy who just happened to, I dunno, lose concentration for a split second because something caught his attention, or maybe there was a problem with his bike and the brakes went, he could have swerved to avoid a dog or a cat and the bike went out of control …' Lucia gulped.

'Hey, you've really thought about this, haven't you?'

'Of course I have, but darling it's the obvious answer.'

'We'll never know for sure.'

'I have to head out soon, but will we go for a drink tomorrow night? Meet me in town after work. I'll leave the car at home and we'll have a good chat.'

'Yeah, thanks. Where did you say you were going tonight?'

Lucia gave a short laugh. 'I didn't. It's a school reunion, of all things. St Anne's.'

'God. That's going back. You'd have to drag me kicking and screaming considering my track record. I bet you'll fly it, though.'

'Not too sure about that. I'll text you tomorrow.'

* * *

Lucia put the key into the ignition and sat in her car for a while before switching on the engine. Grace thought she was off for a night of fun; little did she know that Lucia would have given anything to swop places with Grace and stay at home instead of heading off for the school reunion.

What had possessed her to agree to this? Then again, it had seemed like a good idea at the time. The invitation had arrived to her email address on LinkedIn; it had been sent to as many of the past pupils of the class of '98 in St Anne's secondary school as the two ringleaders could trace on social media. They'd asked everyone to forward on the email to whoever they were still in contact with and share it on Facebook to make sure as many as possible knew about the reunion.

Lucia had no contacts to pass it on to. It was seventeen years since they'd all sat their final state exams and cast off their wine uniforms – seventeen years since Lucia had pulled off her Head Girl badge and dropped it with huge relief into the bin – not exactly a milestone celebration, but three of the class who had emigrated to the Far East were all home for a holiday at the same time, so it seemed like an opportune moment to have a get-together, the organisers said, just low key and a practice run for a bigger celebration in three years' time. Lucia had agreed to go in the heat of the moment, caught with her defences down, not thinking straight in the aftermath of being whisked up into Grace's grief over Danny.

She rested her head against the leather steering wheel. It had been a difficult time, but she thought she'd handled it as best she could, glad to follow Aiden's advice to focus on the practical. Problem was, no matter what Lucia did, all those weird feelings she'd had lately, about her life flattening out and careering away from her, hadn't gone away, and she was slowly realising it wasn't only Grace's grief – but also hers. Maybe at a slight remove, but far too keenly felt and enriched with a generous slice of guilt and a niggling resentment she couldn't comprehend.

She was finding it more and more difficult to hear Grace talking about Danny, because it reminded Lucia of his sparkling vitality, his irreverent approach to life and his free-spirited fun. Apart from the ache that someone so vital had lost his life so young, it held a mirror up to her own life, and to her great consternation she didn't like what she saw.

As time went on, she'd found herself mulling over some of the things Danny had said; things about stopping to take a breath now and then, smelling the roses, feeling the wind in your hair, searching for the stars in the dark night sky – about finding your life's unique purpose and feeling excited about it.

About not looking back in twenty years' time and having regrets.

She wondered what indeed did scare her the most. She'd found herself wanting to talk to him again and had even dropped into Grace's apartment on the pretext of borrowing her hair straighteners, but that hadn't satisfied her. She'd even hoped Grace might arrange another night out, yet she was scared of what else he might say to cause her to question the meaning of her life, but sadly, that hadn't happened.

All those sound bites he'd uttered, all the things he'd said that gave her a reason to pause, that had opened a chink in the smooth fabric of her life, seemed more precious, more poignant and more meaningful than ever, even if they confused and disturbed her tightly scheduled, well-ordered existence. Then just when she thought Grace might be adjusting to life without him, and that Danny's unsettling philosophy might fade away in time and her life thankfully settle back to normal, Grace had decided that Danny hadn't just died, he'd been killed.

Agreeing to go to the school reunion offered her an opportunity to get a stamp of approval on her life, to affirm that it was a good life, worthy to be held up to examination in front of curious eyes and not found wanting – particularly to the schoolgirls with whom she'd had a less-than-friendly relationship. They would all see that Lucia Edwards was a success, with all the trappings that went with it. If she backed out of the reunion at the last minute they'd all think she'd had cold feet or that her life was far less perfect than others', and not up to scrutiny. She ran through phrases in her head suitable to be taken out and aired, ones that showed everything in the most positive light possible. But no booze, no matter how much she was tempted to settle her nerves with a cool glass of Sauvignon Blanc. Better to keep a crystal-clear head.

* * *

'And this has to be Lucia,' she heard someone say.

Maisie Byrne. Older, with a new polish, but instantly recognisable. Her voice plunged Lucia back to the classroom and the ribbing she'd often got for being a swot.

'Hi, all,' Lucia said. She slid off her jacket and looked around at the semi-circle of upturned faces.

'Do you remember us all?' Maisie asked.

'Of course I do,' she said. Belinda, Anne, Hayley, Fiona, Jennifer … She was surprised to find that seventeen years on, it was easy to put a name to most of the faces.

'You're all looking great,' she added. 'Maybe there was something to be said for the nuns in St Anne's after all.'

'Are you having a drink Lucia?' Hayley asked. 'We're all putting thirty euro in the kitty, it's the easiest.'

'Sure, but I'm driving, so I'm sticking to water,' she said.

'You haven't changed a bit,' Maisie said.

'Haven't I?' She'd thought the gloss of marriage and corporate success would have given her an extra coat of veneer.

'Still as perfectly behaved as ever,' Maisie said.

Lucia let that pass.

'So what's everybody up to?' she said, plastering a bright smile on her face. 'Kids? Partners? Spouses?'

'You must have well made your first million by now,' Belinda said.

'Oh, several,' Lucia said, laughing as she waved her hand. 'Then I lost it all in the recession.'

'Who didn't! I think if we'd had this get-together a few years ago,' Fiona said, 'we'd all have had different tales to tell.'

'I was surprised by how many of the class has emigrated,' Anne said.

'I wasn't,' Belinda said. 'We were almost taking that journey ourselves, until I got a job in a new techie company and things started picking up for Cian.'

'You've obviously done all right, Lucia, millions or no millions,' Fiona said. 'Let's be honest, most of us are here tonight because we're doing okay. From what I gather, there have been a few marriage break-ups and bankruptcies already.'

'And a couple of girls aren't here tonight because they didn't make it this far,' Anne said soberly.

'Who?' Lucia asked.

'Erin and Aoife. Cancer and car crash, respectively.'

'I'm sorry to hear that,' Lucia felt a cold tremor.

As the night progressed, they sat in small groups, circulating and mingling. Lucia was quite happy to keep her distance from Maisie Byrne, finding most of her old school mates easy to chat to as they brought each other up to date, condensing large chunks of their lives into a couple of sentences. She heard herself uttering her prepared sound bites, the ones designed to show her life in a good light. A life with no room for regrets.

'Yes, my husband, Robert, works in London. For a multinational finance company.'

'Don't ask … ha ha … something to do with data intelligence.'

'We take it in turns to commute back and forth every weekend.'

'It works for us.'

Then when she was sitting next to Jennifer, after she'd admired Jennifer's photos of her twin baby boys, Jennifer said, 'That was a terrible tragedy with Danny McBride.'

'Danny?' Lucia's mind went blank for a nanosecond.

'Yes, Danny McBride, he died recently, a motorbike crash.'

'Of course, yes.' Hearing his name unexpectedly caused a twist of pain. She couldn't believe how sore it was. God help Grace, who must be feeling ten times worse.

'My sister, Emer, was at the funeral and she recognised you in the crowd. When she went to talk to you afterwards, you were gone.'

'I was there with Grace, my sister. She knew Danny. My parents were there as well, but we didn't hang around too long. I didn't see Emer at all.'

Jennifer smiled. 'Even if you did, you wouldn't have recognised her, she's gone blonde now and all glam compared to her schooldays. Emer recognised you immediately. But Danny – that was an awful tragedy. Especially in the circumstances.' Jennifer paused.

'What circumstances?'

Jennifer made a funny face. 'I'm not exactly sure of the finer details. Emer was in college in Galway with Danny's sister Cara. She knew Danny as well, he was a year behind. She'd only seen Cara on and off since she graduated but she got the feeling from what she picked up the day of the funeral that Danny had been in some kind of trouble or other, but seemed to have been turning his life around when everything fell apart. I thought you might know more.'

Lucia shook her head. 'I don't. He'd been living with Grace at the time of the accident, they only got together after Christmas, so it was all very short. It was a terrible shock for her, but we didn't hear anything like that …'

'It was just something Emer picked up from his sisters when she spoke to them. They're all gutted, especially his youngest sister Amy, and an old girlfriend of his, Stacy.'

'A girlfriend?'

'Well, sort of. The poor girl was always hanging around Danny, Emer said. She gave Stacy a lift back to Dublin afterwards. Stacy could hardly talk, she was so upset. She'd phoned him the night of the accident but got no answer.'

'Grace was all over the place too. It must be horrendous for the family. She only met Danny before Christmas, but he made a huge impression on her.'

'Really? I didn't think he was the kind to make that much of an impression on anyone from what Emer remembered of him.'

'Like what?'

'He was just …' Jennifer shrugged, 'kind of immature, only interested in having fun. According to Emer he either dropped out of college, or else barely scraped through. It seems like he was the black sheep of the family. Oh look, forget it. I feel terribly guilty talking about him like this, especially after what happened. No one deserved his fate.'

Lucia sighed. 'No.'

She was relieved when they were interrupted as the group shifted around again, and Fiona sat down between them, asking Lucia where exactly she'd got her bag.

'London,' she said.

'Shopping spree? I fitted in a few shopping sprees in New York before my job bit the dust. When I think of the money I wasted now, it was crazy.'

'My husband brought it home from London after I reserved it. He works over there during the week.'

'That's handy. You've somewhere to go if you fancy a weekend away.'

'We take it in turns to go back and forth.'

'Best of both worlds.'

'I think so too.'

Lucia was the first to leave, making the excuse of an early start in the morning as she stood up and slipped on her jacket.

'We won't leave it as long again,' someone joked.

'I'll circulate all the email addresses I have,' Maisie said. 'It'll be easier for us all to keep in some form of contact.'

Lucia smiled agreeably, just wanting to be home.

'Tell Grace I was asking for her,' Jennifer said, walking out to the foyer with her.

'I will.'

'If she ever feels like talking to Danny's sisters, maybe in a few weeks' time when things have settled down a bit, I'm sure I could arrange it. Although maybe she shouldn't talk to Stacy.'

'Stacy?' Lucia hadn't forgotten who she was, but she was curious to see if Jennifer would elaborate.

'Danny's girlfriend-in-waiting. She wasn't happy that it never took off for them. And now it never will.'

'Get you, right,' Lucia said, pulling her car keys out of her bag, deciding there and then not to tell Grace that Danny's name had even cropped up in conversation, let alone that he seemed to have turned his life around from something-or-other. Whatever he'd been up to beforehand, it didn't sound too savoury. There was no point in upsetting Grace either, with talk of a girlfriend-in-waiting. Better that she knew nothing at all and learned to move on from Danny.

She pulled out of the hotel car park, deciding to forget whatever she'd heard about Danny's less-than-scintillating past.

Chapter Thirty-one

'Matt, I'm sorry about this but would it be okay if you didn't take Abbie out this Sunday after all?' Janet said.

Matt's hand clenched around his mobile. It was Thursday evening. He was sitting at the kitchen table finishing up a meal that had gone straight from the M&S food hall into his microwave, which he'd washed down with a beer. The television, tuned to a football match, was on in the background and he had the sports page of the newspaper spread out in front of him.

'What's up?' He knew instinctively that Simon was behind this somehow. He told himself he had a choice as to how he was going to react: instead of allowing the blood rush to his head, he could take it easy. More importantly, he could prevent the feeling of not quite measuring up from getting a grip on him. He was getting his act together, wasn't he? He could have been like the poor unfortunate Gavin, banished from Grace's life – he'd found himself feeling sorry for 'nice guy' Gavin being rejected like that – but thanks to Abbie, he still had a foot in the door of Janet's life. If he wanted to mend some fences, he badly needed to soften his attitude.

'She's been invited to a birthday party,' Janet said, her voice carefully neutral.

'A party.'

'Yes, Simon's niece is six and he'd like to bring Abbie along. There'll be a bouncy castle and a clown and face-painting. He'd already told her about it before I had a chance to say she was going out with you. She's all excited.'

Was there a hint of apology somewhere in Janet's rushed words? 'I don't blame her,' he said. 'It sounds more exciting than something from Hamleys in Dundrum followed by a Happy Meal. I can't compete with that.'

'I told you before,' Janet said calmly, 'it's not a competition. It never was.'

'Oh yeah?' For fuck's sake. He should have bitten his tongue. It had just slipped out, but sarky remarks like that wouldn't help his cause in the slightest. Janet was in no doubt about how he felt about Simon. He had to ignore his twinges of jealousy, put them to one side and focus instead on making things better. He had to at least make Janet feel good, if he couldn't make her feel amazing. Listening, hearing what she had to say instead of jumping in or going on the defensive. Attempting the almost impossible task of making her fall in love with him again.

'Sorry, I didn't mean that to sound the way it did,' he apologised.

'Before you say anything else, I was invited along as well but I'm not going,' Janet said, surprising him with her honesty.

Oh. 'Why not?'

'I don't need to explain myself to you, Matt. I've already made my position clear,' again the neutral tone of voice. 'But I'm reminding you about it, just so you're in the picture in case Abbie ever asks you …' a pause.

'In case Abbie ever asks what?'

Another pause. 'In case she says anything to you about Simon moving in and becoming her new daddy.' Janet's voice was low and subdued as if she knew he wouldn't like it.

His heart sank. 'Has she asked that already?'

'No, but apparently one of the kids in the crèche asked her when she was telling the playgroup about Simon coming out with us on my birthday.'

'Balls,' he said.

'Yeah,' she said, heartening him with her agreement. 'I'm not happy about it, but you know kids, they get all sorts of ideas. I wouldn't mind, but I didn't give Abbie any reason to think that. Simon went straight home after the meal that evening.'

Whoop! He had the feeling she hadn't just dropped that in by accident. He fist-bumped the air, inadvertently connecting with his bottle of beer. There was a clatter as it rolled across the table, spewed out the contents, soaked his newspaper, and crashed onto the tile floor.

'What was that?' Janet asked.

'Nothing,' Matt said, deciding to ignore it for now. 'You were saying …?'

'I just want to let you know that no matter what Abbie might say, there is no "me and Simon",' Janet went on. 'As in, we're not an item, and as far as I'm concerned we never will be. Simon knows that. You know that. Full stop and end of story.'

It was different when he ignored his baggage and just listened to Janet. For the first time they were having an actual conversation instead of fencing around each other. Instead of him trying to score points off an invisible Simon, Matt found he was enjoying the sound of her soft voice right in his ear as it washed over him like a blessing. And now that he was giving Janet his undivided attention, he could hear the truth in her voice.

She was still talking. 'But she is his biological daughter, and by extension his family are technically hers, her aunts and uncles, grandparents and cousins … they know she's his daughter, but Simon has explained to them that Abbie doesn't know this yet.'

'It could be a bit of a minefield,' he said after a while.

'It sure is. I'm just feeling my way through this for now,' she said. 'Abbie's still very young, but I don't want to complicate things any more than I have to. The main thing is that she feels secure and loved no matter what happens.'

'If there's anything I can do …' he found himself saying.

'Thanks, Matt.'

Thanks, Matt. He couldn't remember the last time Janet had said those words to him in such a pleasant tone of voice. The simple words were a balm to him. Far, far better than a row. If he dug deep below his ego, he knew that of course Simon had to have access to Abbie, it wouldn't be fair otherwise. The most important thing was how everything was handled for Abbie. Only Matt Slattery, the big eejit, had gone off at half cock, with a pistols-at-dawn mentality that didn't help anyone, least of all Janet.

'I mean it,' he said.

'We just have to go with the flow for now. Take it nice and easy. I wanted to warn you in case Abbie said anything to you about Simon. If she does, just distract her or change the subject, okay?'

'I'll be the soul of discretion,' Matt said. 'I don't want to complicate Abbie's little life any further either. Or yours,' he added.

'Oh?'

'I mean it, Janet,' he paused for a moment, and stared out to where the city was shimmering under a blue-grey hazy blanket that made it hard to pick out the horizon. He was suddenly conscious of life in all its glory and troubles teeming away beneath that neutral-looking facade. Bad things, happy things, unexplained tragedies, loves lost and found. The likes of Grace Bailey, with a wonderful, sparkling boyfriend, until his life was so sadly cut short.

He found himself saying, 'No matter what happens or doesn't happen, Janet, I just want you and Abbie to be happy, right?'

A long pause. 'Seriously?'

'Yes.' He meant it. Even if it was Simon that made her happy. It was worth more to him than a bruised ego.

'And you're okay about Sunday?'

'Yeah, no worries, I'll catch up with Abbie sometime soon.'

'Any time, Matt. And thank you.'

That had been easier than he'd thought, he decided, as he ended the call and began to clear up the beer-soaked newspaper. He felt winded, as though he'd climbed a steep hill.

The first of many such hills, but it was a start.

Chapter Thirty-two

Lucia lifted her head from the pillow and her bad dream dissipated slowly. She wasn't sitting in a crowded exam hall looking blankly at an answer book. She was in bed, nestling in the warmth of lavender-scented cotton sheets under a cream duvet. A long dart of sunshine sliced through a gap in the buttercup-coloured curtains. The white bedside locker held her mobile phone, some jewellery, a small vase of flowers and an antique lamp. Close by, two fluffy bath towels were folded over the back of a wicker chair.

She let her head sink back into the soft embrace of the pillow. She slowly exhaled as her brain cleared itself of a horrible dark fug and her stomach relaxed. She was in Paris. She was safe. It was Saturday morning and she was here for the weekend, visiting her parents. Normally she would have been in London, but Robert was going to be tied up in the office all weekend. A new IT system was going live and he had to be on hand in case he was needed to fix any bugs. On the spur of the moment, Lucia had booked a Friday night flight to Paris, deciding it was the perfect opportunity to catch up with her parents.

As well as being the perfect opportunity to put some space between herself and a life that was beginning to feel unsettled.

Lucia pushed back the duvet and got out of bed. She slid her feet into her mules and went across to the window. She opened the curtains and parted the voile panels. She had a view of a small courtyard park where children were playing. She took a minute to absorb it all, breathing slowly to get rid of the tail end of her bad dream. It had been a long time since she'd dreamt of doing her final school exams.

She'd never liked her schooldays, but she'd pretended otherwise to her parents. She knew they had enough worries to contend with in making ends meet as the recession kept grinding along and eventually came to an end. And Grace – funny, loveable, tall-for-her-age Grace – seemed to be made of sterner stuff. She was managing fine, standing up to any playground bullies and not being too bothered if her school reports bordered on the average. Lucia had kept her head down and put her nose to the grindstone, determined to do the very best she could.

In the final two years, most of the St Anne's teachers were determined to get them over the finish line in style, and Lucia went all out to succeed: good results in her Leaving Certificate meant a place in university, and results in university meant a job that would lead to a rewarding career, enabling her to have a good, secure lifestyle, with more than enough money to pay her bills and keep a decent roof over her head. A simple equation.

It had all worked out according to plan, Lucia reminded herself as she picked up a fluffy towel and went into the en suite.

* * *

Sarah Bailey had a delicious breakfast ready for her. The table was pulled up to the windows, which were open to the sparkling morning, and Lucia listened to the sound of church bells and children playing as she enjoyed freshly squeezed pineapple juice, creamy natural yogurt, and melt-in-the-mouth croissants with raspberry jam from the farmer's market in the nearby square.

'This is gorgeous, Mum, and so very relaxing,' she said.

'You picked a good weekend to come over,' Mum said. 'I managed to swop my hours today and your dad's on the early shift so he's around tonight. We'd already made dinner reservations for later, along with friends of ours who are over for a few days, but it was no problem to add an extra place for you. And now we're going shopping and after that I'm taking you to lunch.'

Lucia sat back and smiled.

Her parents had survived the horrible '80s recession, which seemed to go on forever, and had risen from the ashes, eventually. Her father had turned his back on his construction business and had taken work wherever he could, eventually settling into a reinvention of sorts by working as a barman in various Dublin bars and hotels, remaining in that trade even during the Celtic Tiger days. Then two years ago he'd been offered a job managing an Irish-themed pub in Paris, and both her parents had jumped at the opportunity of working abroad for a while. Her mother had also held down a series of jobs helping to make ends meet, and now she was working part-time in a chic Paris boutique and loving every minute of it.

Danny would have heartily approved, she realised with a pang.

'What is it?' her mum asked.

'Nothing,' Lucia waggled her hand.

* * *

Later they mingled with Saturday shoppers strolling around the Galeries Lafayette, where Lucia admired a couple of silk scarves and exquisite soaps that her mother instantly bought for her. They stopped for lunch in a pretty patisserie, where her mother brandished the lunch menu and insisted it would be her treat.

'You're spoiling me,' Lucia said. They were sitting inside out of the warmth of the day, while the tourists paid extra to bake outside on the sun dazzled terrace.

'I so seldom get the opportunity to spoil you that it's a pleasure,' her mother smiled.

At fifty-eight years of age, Sarah Bailey was trim, petite and dark-haired like Lucia, although nowadays she had help from her hairdresser to keep her colour. Whatever hardships she might have gone through in those grey days, they didn't show on her face or in her warm, dark eyes.

'Do you know, Mum, sometimes you look more continental than the continental women themselves,' Lucia commented.

'Would you go away,' her mother smiled. 'You mightn't say that if you saw me at three in the morning, dragging myself out of bed to take a trip to the loo. Anyway, I'm ordering us a glass of bubbly, even if it is only one o'clock. And I want to hear all about you and Robert and what you've been up to. Phone calls or emails aren't the same. And I hate Skype.'

'And I want to hear all about you and Dad and what you've been up to,' Lucia said. She sat back and listened to her mother chatting about her part-time job, her father's latest Irish-themed drinks promotion. Sarah went on to chat about the books she'd read recently and movies and plays they'd been to, then the weekend they'd spent in a castle in Provence, France, visiting the wineries.

'A real-life castle?' Lucia playfully tut-tutted.

Her mother laughed. 'Didn't you know? One must stay in a French castle if one is touring the vineyards.'

Lucia looked out at the Paris square, where tourists and shoppers were milling around the pavements whitened under the glare of the sun. 'I bet you never thought in a million years that you and Dad would end up here in Paris.'

'Yes, it's an awful place to end up in,' her mother joked. 'Seriously, though Lucia, when I look back now, there have been so many twists and turns in our lives that it's been mad. It's been hectic and mad, but a really thrilling roller-coaster ride.' Her mother's voice was proud and boasting. Lucia couldn't believe that she felt a twinge of jealousy. Her life and Robert's could never be described as hectic and mad, let alone a thrilling roller-coaster ride.

'Even the bad times?' Lucia couldn't stop the words from slipping out.

There was a beat of silence.

After a short while her mother gave her a puzzled look. 'What bad times?'

'The time when Dad's business collapsed and he lost his job and we had to move house.'

Her mother sighed and a slight frown settled itself between her eyes. 'Of course I know what you're referring to Lucia, I'm not that stupid. They were hard years, but not necessarily *bad* years. We went through a very difficult time financially, it was tough, but outside of that, everything else was great.'

'Great? Are you serious?' Something sparked inside Lucia at her mother's words – anger, hurt. It didn't help that her mother looked at her as though she were surprised by her sharp tone of voice.

'Yes, apart from the money aspect, everything else was fine,' her mother said. 'I loved your father and he loved me, we always had each other, we worked together to get ourselves out of a financial mess, which we did eventually. And we had you and Grace, which was brilliant.'

Lucia stayed silent.

'Okay, it was hard work keeping the show on the road,' her mother went on, speaking slowly as though she was back there briefly, recalling it all. 'And it was very tough when we lost the car, and the house in Rosetree Gardens and had to scale back completely, but Michael and I always knew we were blessed with other things that were more important – each other, our wonderful girls, and all in good health.'

'I would have thought it might have been easier on you had we not been around. Less to worry about,' Lucia tried to sound flippant, but it came out wrong. Irreverence didn't suit her, unlike Grace. Grace could be funny at times, but sometimes when Lucia tried to be jokey she almost sounded belligerent.

Her mother put down the menu and gave Lucia her full attention. 'I'm very surprised that this has come up now. Has anything happened, Lucia?' When Lucia stayed silent she continued, 'I'd hate you to think that being short of money made any difference to the love we felt for you both or to the joy you brought us.' She took a sip of water before continuing, her eyes clouded with concern. 'We were so in love with you that we went ahead and planned another baby to love and cherish even though the writing was on the wall with your father. Naturally I would have preferred more money for treats and nice clothes and holidays, sometimes I felt very angry and frustrated that I couldn't give you those things, but I found out that if I became too fixated on the stress of our financial situation, I'd miss out on all the other good, everyday things that were happening with you and Grace. And while we're on the subject, Lucia …'

Her mother poured more water into her glass and Lucia braced herself. On the subject of what? Babies? Was her mother going to cross an invisible boundary and ask the unaskable of Lucia?

'When I look back on your childhood, I only remember the good times,' her mother said. 'I don't care if I sound corny but your father and I are still so grateful and thankful *and* appreciative that we have both you and Grace in our lives. You mean the world to us. Never forget that. Now, no more talk about me or money or days gone past. Back to the present.' Her mother looked at her keenly, head tilted to one side. 'If you're certain you're okay and there's nothing wrong, tell me, how is Grace? Her phone calls and emails are telling me nothing.'

Lucia swallowed. The sudden change of topic disorientated her and she dragged her scattered thoughts together. It felt like she was trying to sweep up dry leaves in the breeze. 'Grace is – kind of okay, but she still has the idea Danny's death was no accident.'

'Oh, dear.' Her mother looked worried.

'She's getting on with things, but it's the first time someone so close to her has died.'

'It would have done her good to come over with you for the weekend.'

'I asked her, but she wanted to stay put,' Lucia said, remembering the relief that had darted through her when Grace refused. Much as she loved her sister, Lucia wasn't in the mood for putting up with her this weekend if it meant listening to what she had to say about Danny.

'I asked her too,' Mum said. 'But she made a silly excuse or other. Do you know if she's taking any time off work for holidays?'

'No, she said she doesn't want to think of them yet.'

'It's sad and it's horrible, but it's life unfortunately. I'll try harder to get her over here for a break. Better again, I'll go over to visit her as soon as Michael and I can arrange time off, but don't tell her. It'll be a surprise. What are you and Robert doing? Any plans?'

'We're going to the south of France as usual,' Lucia said.

A sudden memory sparked of the time she'd talked to Danny about holidays.

* * *

'I bet your life is so organised you even go on the same holidays every year,' Danny said. 'To the same kind of five-star hotel, at the same time of the year. You like it, so why risk something different or step out of your comfort zone?'

It was so close to the truth she was annoyed with him, even though she'd dropped into Grace's apartment secretly hoping to talk to him again. Whatever Grace was up to in her bedroom, it was taking her a long time to find her hair straighteners.

'So?' she glared. 'What's wrong with that?'

'Nothing. If you want no surprises, then that's the way to do it. Let me see ...' he looked at her thoughtfully for several moments and said, 'France.'

'Why France?' She was thrown. How did he know?

'That would appeal to your sense of order and cool reserve. Spain would be too hot and passionate, like an unruly flamenco dancer, and Italy would be too noisy and disorderly for your liking.'

'Disorderly? Italy?'

'Yeah, the graffiti is bright and garish and all over the place ... even alongside the most historic monuments ... you wouldn't like it, you'd find it an eyesore, and totally chaotic, but the food is to die for, the scenery breathtaking and the people are warm and happy.'

'So you've been there?'

'Yes.'

* * *

'Lucia? Are you okay?'

Lucia blinked. She found herself wanting to ask her mother what Italy had really been like; she'd been there a few times with her father. 'I'm grand, Mum,' she said, giving herself a mental shake and snapping back to reality. 'I'll try and have another chat with Grace.'

'It's funny the effect grief can have on different people. No one ever knows how they might react until it happens to them. I wish I were at home at a time like this.'

'Do you?'

'Of course, nothing beats being around for the people you love when they need you most.'

'I'm there for Grace as much as I can be. Although work is hectic as usual. I have a couple of new projects that I'm still finding my way around.'

'Good and bad,' her mother said, smiling. 'It's nice that my ultra-successful daughter is so happily employed but ...' she paused.

'But what, Mum,' Lucia asked, on her guard.

'It would probably be better for you if it were a little less hectic.'

'You know me, I prefer to be busy,' Lucia said. She picked up her bag, signalling she was ready to go. Tonight out in company with her parents' friends there would be no opportunity to indulge in any heart-to-heart chats. She would make sure to steer clear of any emotive topics during lunch tomorrow, and then it would be home to Dublin. Back to her busy, no-time-to-think, safe-as-houses, everything-as-it-should-be life.

As if she could ever go back to that.

Chapter Thirty-three

Grace came out of the LexIcon in Dun Laoghaire on a high. The library workshop on writing for children had filled her with enthusiasm. One of the most important points she'd learned was the need to put herself in a child's frame of mind in order to be able to communicate with them through story; the other was the fundamental need for discipline, to show up at the page regularly, that writing a book of any description was the simple but difficult act of putting one word in front of another. Best of all was the feeling of recognition running through her veins that she was in her element.

She drove home in the dusky evening, putting on some music. She only had to think of the fun she'd had with Danny to put herself in the right frame of mind. As she hit the motorway, she was focussing on the traffic, but thoughts and images were swirling in her subconscious. By the time she pulled up at Rathbrook Hall, the concept of Katie and her adventurous kite had started to come together.

She spent over an hour working on ideas, jotting them down, her enthusiasm spilling over, and reluctantly went to bed.

When a noise shrilled through the darkness of her apartment, disturbing her sleep, she reached out for her mobile, not sure what had woken her. Flicking on the screen, she saw it was two o'clock in the morning. The noise came again and she realised it was her intercom.

Grace froze. The skin on the back of her neck prickled. It buzzed again, but she was incapable of answering it. Someone, surely, was pressing the wrong number.

Then all was silent. She went across to the bedroom window, which looked out onto the front of the block. She opened the curtains a chink but all was quiet in the darkened night save for occasional traffic rumbling past on the road outside. She waited, her heart rising up to her chest, but there was no sign of any movement directly outside. Her senses on full alert, she crept out to the landing and across to the kitchen, glancing out the small window to the courtyard.

There was a person down there, visible in the courtyard lights, idling close to the shrubbery, facing the back entrance to the block; a motorcyclist, wearing dark clothing and a black helmet. Grace shrank back from the window and went back to her bedroom. She didn't know how long she sat in bed, her heart racing, until a short while later, the silence of the night was broken by the sound of a full throttled roar as a bike accelerated up onto the road outside. At two in the morning, it was easy to believe someone was trying to torment her.

If that was the case, she decided crossly, to hell with them.

* * *

When she arrived home from Arcadia the following evening, the apartment seemed cheerful and friendly, the living room full of summer sunshine. Danny's mother was finally coming that evening to collect his belongings. Grace had become used to looking at Danny's things packed into her wardrobe, but now it was time to let them go.

Tess McBride came alone. Her jeans and light peach jumper hung loosely on her frame. Her face was drawn, with dark grey circles under her eyes.

'Is your husband not with you?' Grace asked, her expectations for the evening shifting a little. She'd visualised Danny's parents, coming together.

Tess made an attempt to smile, her skin stretched tightly across her cheekbones. It was so brittle. Grace thought it was about to crack. 'My husband found it too difficult,' Tess said.

'Please …' Grace gestured for her to come in.

Tess hesitated and tightened her grip on her black leather shoulder bag and Grace could have sworn she looked ready to turn and run. Then she visibly straightened her shoulders and stepped through the doorway. She looked around Grace's living room with an air of surprise, as though it was totally different to what she'd expected. 'This is … lovely …' she said. 'It's really nice.'

Why the surprise? What were you expecting? Grace wanted to ask. She reminded herself that Danny's parents hadn't known anything at all about her, hadn't even known where Danny had been living, so God knows what they'd expected. Instead she said, 'Would you like tea or coffee?'

Tess McBride's thin face showed more surprise, looking at Grace as though she'd offered her very expensive champagne. She stood rather stiffly in her living room. 'Are you sure? I don't want to put you out, but tea would be lovely.'

'You're not putting me out,' Grace said, sensing her watching as she went over to the sink and filled the kettle. Some of the tension shooting out from Tess McBride's body was beginning to coil around her chest as she took mugs out of the press, along with a milk jug and a bowl of sugar.

'No sugar, thanks,' Tess said.

Grace replaced the sugar. 'I've sent you on any post that came for Danny,' she said, more for the sake of talking, wanting to fill the strained atmosphere. 'There was very little. I don't think Danny had got around to informing everyone of his change of address ...' Her voice trailed away. Tess was staring at her very oddly as though she couldn't believe what she was hearing. 'What's wrong?' Grace asked, her mind flashing back over what she'd said.

Tess blinked. She shook her head. 'Nothing. Please go on, Grace.'

'That's all I had to say about the post ... there was very little. Whatever there was I sent on.'

'I know you did, and thank you.'

The kettle boiled and Grace made tea for both of them. Tess sat down, and Grace was afraid she was going to snap in two, she appeared to be so fragile.

'I don't have all that much belonging to Danny,' she said. 'There are clothes, a few books, DVDs, his laptop and tablet and an iPod.'

'Had he actually moved in with you?' Tess asked. 'He wasn't just ... coming and going?'

'Yes, he lived here for six weeks.'

'He was happy here, wasn't he?' Tess's ravaged face begged for an affirmative answer.

'We were both very happy,' Grace said, her throat constricting. Suddenly it mattered to her that Tess knew how wonderful Danny had made her feel. 'We had six amazing weeks together. He brought fun and sunshine back into my life.'

'It means a lot to me to hear that,' Tess said. 'Do you work, Grace?'

Grace thought the question strange. How else did Tess think Grace supported herself? 'Yes, I work in Arcadia Insurances, in the city centre.'

'And you were happy to have Danny around?'

'Absolutely, I was. Besides everything else, he was a great help around the place.'

'A great help?' Tess gave a sad smile. 'I've heard my son being called lots of things, but that's the first time anyone has called him a help.'

'He was great,' Grace said. 'He cooked the dinner most evenings, took out the rubbish, and he knew how to manage the dishwasher and washing machine.'

Tess was staring at her again. 'I see,' she said faintly. It was clear by her face that Tess didn't see.

'He even put the posters up on the wall,' Grace went on.

'*Danny* did that?' Tess's gaze was one of shock as it fastened on the posters. There was a long silence. She seemed lost for words as she continued to look, transfixed, at the posters her son had stuck up on Grace's wall. Some of her consternation transferred itself to Grace, who felt a moment of panic. How come it was such a shock? Surely Tess knew the kind of person her son was? Cheerful, warm, generous to a fault, bubbling over with life.

'I was going to ask you if I could keep them, as a memento of him,' she asked. 'Unless you really want them ...'

'No, of course you can hold on to them, Grace,' Tess said, looking as though she was miles away. 'I wouldn't dream of taking them down, and if there is anything else of Danny's you want, feel free to hang on to it.'

'His leather jacket?' She liked wearing it. When she put her arms into it and felt it across her shoulder blades it was like a hug.

'That's no problem, Grace, I'm not here to strip everything of Danny from your life. I came to see where he last stayed, to check out his belongings in case there's anything *I* need and to get rid of anything that's in your way ... I'll take his laptop and such back to Mayo.'

'I've kept it safe for you. I haven't opened it since he ...' Grace blinked. 'Since the night of the accident. I don't know his password, so it's been lying idle. You might need to do something about the business he was setting up. I haven't done anything about that either, as I'm not sure who his contacts were.'

Tess McBride's face changed. It grew tighter and her eyes were suddenly steely.

'What's wrong?' Grace asked.

'What do you *mean* – the business he was setting up, the contacts?' Tess's voice was as steely as her eyes.

'The website business,' Grace said, a wobble in her voice.

'*Web*site business?'

'Yes, since he was made redundant he was using it as an opportunity to set up his own business.'

'Are you having me on?'

'Why would I do that?

'I don't know. You tell me.'

'Sorry, Tess, I don't get this.' Sudden tears pricked Grace's eyes. It seemed Danny had been holding things back from his parents also. They hadn't known about Grace, the fact that he'd lived with her, or his plans to set up his business. For such an effervescent person, he'd kept some things very private. Light and dark, she thought involuntarily; she'd known the bright, sparkling, funny side to Danny, but not the shadowy side. The side where he'd held things back, from Grace, from even his parents.

Why though? She didn't know how well he'd got on with his family, so that could be it. But surely someone like Danny was bound to get on well with his parents and sisters? She took a steadying breath.

'This much I know,' she said. 'As soon as I went to work in the mornings, Danny took out his laptop to work on his business plan and broaden his network of contacts. He also needed to get some sample websites up and running. Before I came home in the evenings, he had the laptop away and had started the dinner. In the six weeks he was here, we hardly saw anyone else. I'm sure that would have happened, eventually. We did lots of fun things, but it was mostly just the two of us, together. So I don't know all that much – hey, I don't know anything about his business or his contacts, apart from he used to talk about the kind of sample websites he'd set up. Landscape gardening was one, stargazing was another and he was considering something about cookery as well.'

'I'm sorry, Grace, for overreacting and talking to you like that, you must think I'm …' Tess closed her eyes as though to shut out what she was seeing, '… an overly fussy mother,' she went on, her voice strained. 'I just can't tell you how hard it's been since Danny …'

'You don't have to tell me,' Grace said, anxious to reassure her. 'It must be very tough for you as well as his father and sisters.'

'His father couldn't come with me this evening,' Tess said. 'He's still cut up about Danny. He blames himself. Not literally, of course. But he feels guilty because the last time they spoke they had an argument.' She paused.

'When was this?' Grace had to ask.

'Just after Christmas. They'd a big row before Danny came back to Dublin. They hadn't spoken since. I kept in touch, of course, but it wasn't easy trying to walk a tightrope and keep the peace between two grown adults, both of whom I love very much. So Joseph has to live with that as well, and it's tearing him apart. It's total bloody shite, to borrow my daughter's phrase.'

'I'm sorry,' Grace said, utterly relieved she hadn't troubled Tess any further with her suspicions or dug a deeper pit for the woman. 'Have you talked to any of Danny's friends?' she asked, hoping Tess might say something about them to help to clear up some of her questions.

'His friends?' Tess looked vague.

'Yes, his friends back in Mayo … or the friends he house-shared with.' Grace made herself sound knowledgeable, hoping Tess might volunteer information; names, perhaps even an address.

'No ... no I haven't,' she said. 'Why?'

'I thought it might be good to talk to his friends. I'd even like to talk to them myself.'

The other Mayo guys ... Danny had said. Talking to them might shed some light on Danny and whatever else might have been going on in his life.

'I can't help you there, Grace. Danny ...' Tess said cagily, 'he didn't have a big circle of friends back in Mayo, a lot of his contemporaries had scattered, and many of them had emigrated. Guys don't keep in touch like women do. I don't know who he hung around with in Dublin. He had a bedsit in a house in Phibsboro ... I'm sure you know that already. I think some of his friends were at the funeral, but I wasn't really talking to anyone that day. I couldn't even tell you who was there. Tell me about ...' Tess tilted her head like a small bird hungry for morsels of food. 'Danny's last evening. His last week or so. What was he like? How did he seem?'

'Happy. Danny ... changed my life around. He showed me how to enjoy the ordinary fun in every day. Sometimes he was like a whirlwind, full of energy and excitement, getting me to burst out of my comfort zone. Then other times he was quiet, and loving and kind.'

Tess's eyes filled with tears. She flapped them away. 'Sorry, I ... it's wonderful to hear this Grace. It means a lot.'

'Why don't I make some fresh tea and we'll talk more? You'd be surprised with all the things we did in a few short weeks. The zoo, kite-flying, stargazing ...'

Tess smiled wanly. 'Thanks. I'd like that. I'd like to hear everything.'

* * *

She brought Tess into the bedroom and showed her the stars on the ceiling, and her heart was heavy as she slid his brown case out of the wardrobe. Tess's face convulsed when she saw it.

'There's also his backpack and a small crate,' Grace said, lifting those out also.

When Tess was ready to leave, Grace helped her down to the car, wheeling the case through the apartment door, feeling as though her life was spooling away backwards to the snowy January evening Danny had first arrived with a big grin on his face. No looking back, she reminded herself.

They stood in the car park and Tess reached forward and they held each other in an awkward hug.

'If there's any more post …'

'Yes, I'll send it on.'

'You're very kind.'

'Not at all. It's the least I can do, considering …' *Considering you've lost your beloved son. I've only lost someone I knew and loved for a long, bright, brilliant moment.*

'I've just realised I probably have keys belonging to your apartment,' Tess said. 'They were in his personal effects that were returned to us. I should have brought them this evening.'

'I'll get them again sometime,' Grace said.

'Take care of yourself, won't you?' Tess said.

'You too,' Grace said.

'It was lovely to meet you and see where Danny was … so happy,' Tess said. 'Thank you.'

Grace watched her drive off and went back up to her apartment. A row with his father. It explained why Danny had been so reticent about his family. The row had upset him far more than he'd let on to Grace. Later, when she went into the bathroom, she realised that Danny's aftershave was still there, as though he was going to come back at any moment and use it. She smiled to herself. Ridiculous though it was, it was like a tiny piece of him had been restored to her.

Chapter Thirty-four

'What on earth have you done with your hair?' Robert said, staring at Lucia.

A tiny bud of insecurity started to bloom inside Lucia, until she deliberately forced it down and replaced it with a tiny bud of victory. It was Saturday afternoon and in the melee of the arrivals hall in Perpignan airport, Robert was looking at her as though he didn't recognise her. He wasn't happy about not recognising her, but for some mysterious reason, Lucia was pleased. She put a hand up to her dark bob. She'd had it cut in a geometric style and the new shape still felt strange. Short and layered at the back and sides, with a full, thick fringe swept dramatically to one side, Lucia hardly recognised herself. Her hair had far more attitude than she'd ever possessed. It was a bold bob and a far cry from the obedient, shoulder-length style Lucia had usually worn – and this made her wince – for about fifteen years. Ever since, in fact, she'd had her long hair trimmed a couple of years into college.

'I felt like a change,' she said.

'A *change?*' His face was an equal mixture of surprise and annoyance. He'd clearly expected his same-old, same-old wife to come through the gates. She couldn't remember the last time she'd provoked such a reaction in Robert, or if she'd ever done anything she half suspected he mightn't like.

'Yes, a reinvention of sorts,' she said, sweeping a hand through it carelessly. 'Don't you like it?' If she'd been hoping he'd say her hair was sexy and sassy and terribly cute – the hairdresser's excited words when she'd uncovered Lucia's new look from under the weight of her straight hair, like Michelangelo finding David in the stone – and he loved his wife's new look, *he loved his wife, full stop,* she was disappointed.

'You never told me you were going to … change your hair so … drastically. What did they say in the office?'

'They haven't seen it yet,' she said. She'd seen the choppy hairstyle in a glossy magazine that someone had left in the office during the week, and known the funky hairstyle would look cool on her. Still, she'd been surprised she'd broken out of her comfort zone so easily. She'd had it restyled after work on Friday evening, deciding that the holiday period was the perfect time to test it out and get used to handling a new style while she had the time to lavish on it, as opposed to her hurried shower and blow dry at seven a.m. on work mornings.

'Oh well, if it's what you wanted …' he said, sounding a little cross, still a little at odds with her and her new hairstyle. 'Now, let's get the hell out of this place.' He took her case and wheeled it through the arrivals concourse.

A great start to their holidays – not, Lucia decided. They were spending the first fortnight in June in their usual villa in the province of Languedoc-Rousillon, France. Robert had flown in from London on an earlier flight.

'I have the car keys,' he said, leading her across to the exit and out into blinding white sunshine.

'Already?'

'Yes, of course already,' he bristled. 'What do you think I was doing while I was waiting for your flight?'

Robert always booked the usual Ford Focus in advance along with the flights during the summer flight sale. She could picture him earlier, finding the best vantage point while he waited impatiently for his case to appear on the luggage carousel so that he could hoist it off as soon as possible and beat the queue to the car rental desk. Robert hated any form of queuing. He considered it a huge waste of time. So did she, she silently admitted.

Lucia rummaged in her bag for her sunglasses and put them on. She wondered if he'd be too distracted by her hair to notice that these were new, a last-minute buy in Dublin airport, the kind of purchase she never usually made. Despite the inflated airport-lounge prices, the sunglasses had been cheaper than the designer ones Robert had bought her in a sale, *and* far more gaudy, with lots of glittery bits glued to the sides. They'd jumped out at Lucia, an embodiment of everything that was tacky and careless, silly and fun, in contrast to the meticulously planned, safe and unadventurous two weeks that lay ahead. Her mind didn't have to search too far to know what had instigated her impulsive purchase. Or more to the point, who.

He was gone almost three months now, so she shouldn't have been imagining the spirit of Danny McBride and his irreverent green eyes laughing and teasing and joking alongside her as she'd gone through the boarding gate for the flight to France, clutching her gaudy sunglasses along with her matched set of luxury cabin baggage.

'What's keeping you?' Robert asked as they arrived at the pedestrian lights just as they flickered from amber to red, too late to risk a sprint across the intersection, which meant they had to wait, Robert glaring at the drivers surging forward as though it was somehow their fault the lights had changed.

'Nothing,' Lucia said. 'Hey relax, we're on holidays.'

'I *am* relaxed,' he said, his exasperated tone of voice saying the exact opposite. She knew she had thrown a spanner in the works with her radically altered appearance. She'd made a statement of sorts, and Robert saw it as a sort of threat. Which it was. After all, Lucia had done something completely out of character.

* * *

'This is the life …' Robert took a sip of his gin and tonic and stretched out his legs as they sat in comfortable rattan chairs on the first floor balcony of their rented villa. 'Home from home.'

Lucia moved her chair in under the shade of the striped canopy. She adjusted the cushions at her back and took a large gulp of her drink. It was the first full day of their holiday. One of the benefits about coming back here year after year was that they did feel at home as soon as they arrived and got into holiday mode straight away. They didn't have to waste time finding their bearings, or searching for the best restaurant or wine shop. They knew exactly where to go for all of life's little luxuries. They loved this beautiful corner of the south of France and all the amenities to hand. They knew exactly what to pack for their fortnight away and what they could pick up locally. The five-star villa with its private swimming pool was part of a secluded enclosure situated in a quiet area just on the edge of a charming, whitewashed, terracotta-roofed village, where the central, picturesque square was shaded by plane trees. The farmhouse-style villa was always spotless, with all mods cons and a deep, claw-footed tub in the bathroom that Lucia loved relaxing in. So all in all, it was a totally stress-free experience. They didn't have to risk going somewhere different only to be disappointed and have their precious down time ruined.

And why was she rationalising all this, Lucia asked herself. Before this holiday was over, they would have next year's booked already, securing the same two weeks with a ten per cent discount for the early booking. Better to be sure than sorry, Robert would say. She lifted the bottle of vodka and topped up her glass. She rarely drank vodka, but for a change, she'd put a bottle into the trolley when they were doing a supermarket shop for some essentials earlier that day. Robert had merely lifted his eyebrows but said nothing.

Now he looked at her glass and asked her if she needed a little more tonic.

'No, it's fine,' she said.

The balcony was off the upstairs living area and had a fabulous view of the surrounding countryside, where fields of purple lavender and sunflowers undulated into the distance and their scents carried on the air. Sometimes during the past year when Lucia had had to put up with stressful days in work, she coped by visualising herself sitting on this balcony, feet up, a glass of chilled wine at her hand and a view that came straight from a Monet painting spread in front of her. She was here now, in the moment, and it was drowning her senses.

Where else would she rather be?

'Did you ever think of going somewhere else on holiday?' she asked Robert.

'Like where?'

She shrugged. 'I dunno, somewhere different. Spain, maybe, or Italy.'

'Why take a chance and end up going home disappointed if it doesn't work out? We have everything we need right here, it's the perfect holiday. I thought you loved it here. It suits us. It's so … graceful and civilised and sophisticated. Like you, Lucia.' He smiled at her in a way that told her he was looking forward to making love that night. 'The traffic in Italy is crazy, you take your life in your hands crossing those choked-up streets in Rome.'

She had a sudden vision of Aiden Burke gripping her hand as he laughingly guided both of them through the snarling, diesel fumed traffic in Rome on a hot afternoon. Where the hell had that come from? Dear God, what was *wrong* with her?

'Hey, are you okay?'

Lucia took another gulp of her vodka and told Robert she was perfectly fine.

Chapter Thirty-five

On Tuesday morning after coffee, Grace came back to her desk in Arcadia to find a small package sitting beside her keyboard.

'What's this?' she asked.

'It must have come in this morning's post,' Karen said, sitting down at the next workstation.

'I can see that,' Grace said, noting the way her address had been typed up on a label. She turned the small package around in her hands, but there was nothing to indicate where it had come from.

'Did you order anything online?' Karen asked.

'Not recently,' Grace said. She gave the package a shake, but that didn't give her any indication as to what was inside.

'Well go on, open it,' Suz said. 'We're all dying to know what's in it.'

'Yes, come on, Grace, put us out of our misery.'

Grace took a scissors out of her drawer and cut open the tape around the outside of the package, lifting the flap. There was something wrapped in tissue paper inside. She pulled back the tissue paper to reveal a small grey elephant, a child's soft toy, with a pink ribbon around its neck. Picking it up, she saw that the label was still attached. There was no card, no note, nothing to say who had sent it. For a long, dizzying moment she thought it must be from Danny until she realised that that was impossible, unless it had been delayed over three months in the post. Which, going by the recent postmark, it hadn't been.

Delighted with the distraction, Karen, Suz and the other girls gathered around.

'Aah, would you look.'

'Isn't it *so* cute?'

'I'd love a friend who was thoughtful enough to send me a cuddly toy.'

'It's not your birthday, is it?'

'Hey, Grace, is this a fun way of telling us you have some *news*?'

'No to all your questions. I haven't a clue who sent this or why.'

Grace sat down, perplexed. It was a cute little toy that any small child would enjoy. She checked the packaging again, turning the elephant around in her hands, taking off the fat pink ribbon in case it was hiding something. Then when she saw what the ribbon was concealing, a cold sense of foreboding ran up her spine.

As soon as she got home to Rathbrook Hall that evening, she called Matt.

He answered immediately. 'Grace – hi. Everything all right?'

'I don't know. You said to call you … if there was anything …' She hesitated. This was going to sound ridiculous.

'I did. What's up?'

'Something weird happened in the office today.'

'How weird?'

'It sounds mad, but someone sent me a soft toy, an elephant. It came in the post and I've no idea who sent it.'

'Does that bother you?'

'Yes, I can't even say it. Danny and I—' all of a sudden her throat closed over. Eventually she managed to pull herself together. 'Sorry, I just lost it there for a minute.'

'Are you okay?'

She blinked hard and stood up straighter. She looked across to her kite and focussed on a spot in the middle of it. 'Yep, I'm fine.'

'I'm busy right now, Grace, but I'll drop in at the end of my shift. It'll be a couple of hours, okay?'

'Thanks.'

It was half-past eight when Grace buzzed Matt into the complex, and she opened the apartment door for him just as he reached it. She brought him in and showed him the package on the table, lifting out the cuddly elephant. 'I have no idea where this came from,' she said. 'I think it's all a bit freaky.'

'Freaky?'

'Yes. It seems fine until you do this. Look.' Grace untied the pink ribbon from around the toy elephant's neck and slowly pulled it away. There was a deep gash in the soft grey material, where the elephant's neck had been slit. 'See?'

'I see what you mean,' Matt said. 'Not very nice. And this was sent to you in work.'

'It came in the post this morning.'

'But what has it got to do with Danny?'

'Maybe nothing, but we spent an afternoon in the zoo, in February. It was a special kind of afternoon.' Her voice caught.

'Any particular reason?'

'I bunked off work,' she said, feeling a smile tilt the corners of her mouth at the memory. 'It was unexpected and against the rules. It made me feel like a child who'd been taken out of bed to go to a glittery carnival. It was fun to be doing something out of the ordinary with Danny on a Tuesday afternoon instead of being stuck in the office.'

'Who else knew you were at the zoo, that afternoon?' Matt asked.

'My sister found out afterwards. I didn't tell her at the time because Lucia would have frowned at such frivolous behaviour and given me a right ticking off …' she paused at the look on Matt's face.

'My sister is a real stickler for doing everything by the book. I love her to bits but she drives me mad at times being Mrs Perfectionist. Ruth, her sister-in-law, saw us strolling around the zoo and passed on the gossip. I don't care what anyone thinks, Danny and I had a brilliant afternoon.'

Matt picked up the elephant by the ear. 'Your sister would hardly have sent this?'

Grace laughed. 'No way. If you met her you'd know she'd be incapable of doing anything like this. I bet she wouldn't even know where to buy a toy elephant, it's so far off her radar.'

'How about the sister-in-law?'

Grace shook her head. 'Ruth? I was surprised she recognised me. Besides, whoever sent this knows where I work and I doubt very much if Ruth does.'

Matt was silent for a while. 'Has anyone ever sent you stuff like this in the post before?'

'Apart from the torn-up photograph, no.'

'Are they from the same person?'

Grace felt something cold slithering down her spine. 'I can't say. The envelope with the photograph was addressed in block capitals in black felt pen. This was typed on an address label. Both postmarks were Dublin.'

'Have you still got it?'

'I dumped it,' Grace shuddered. 'I couldn't bear the thoughts of it lurking in the apartment.'

Matt leaned forward. 'Is there any chance that Danny might have ordered this for you, only it was delayed big time? Supposing the stitching came loose because it was faulty?'

'I thought of that, just for a moment, but the postmark is recent. And if he'd ordered it for me, surely there'd be a note with it? I just think it's weird. That's what I mean about all this … Danny's accident,' Grace said. 'There's nothing big that's jumping out at me, they're all small, silly kind of things, but when you try to add them up … I'm still hearing that stupid motorbike and then a couple of weeks ago in the middle of the night, I thought I saw someone dressed in motorbike gear, down in the courtyard.'

Matt looked at her sympathetically. 'Thing is, Grace, I bet if you do a check of all the apartment blocks you'll find half a dozen or so motorcyclists living here. But if you think you're being deliberately followed at any time, get the registration number of the bike and I'll check it out. I agree the elephant thing is a bit odd, but at the moment I don't see what I can do.'

Grace shook her head. 'I'm not expecting you to do anything, Matt. Or solve the mystery of the fluffy elephant. I wanted to show it to you, that's all.'

'Put it away safely, just in case.'

'In case of what …?'

He shrugged and got to his feet. 'Grace, in my game you just never know. Just look after yourself, okay?'

'Thanks.'

They walked out into the hallway. 'Call me again if you need to,' he said.

'I'm sure you're very busy with all sorts of terrible crimes …'

'Unfortunately, regardless of how hard I work, or how many hours I put in, the terrible crimes will always be there. I don't mind if you need to run anything by me.'

She folded her arms and leaned against the doorjamb. 'But you don't think Danny's death was anything but an accident.'

His eyes held a hint of apology. 'Not from where I'm standing, no.'

'But you just said you never know.'

He smiled. 'That's true too. Keep in touch.'

She locked the door after him, realising she'd forgotten to tell him that Danny's mother also knew she'd been to the zoo with her son. Not that it would make any difference. Sending Grace an unpleasant gift in the post was hardly the kind of thing Tess McBride would have stooped to. Nor would she have any reason to.

Chapter Thirty-six

Lucia and Robert were relaxing in their favourite restaurant, sitting out on the patio as an orangey sunset drifted into a warm, cobalt-blue evening. The waiters greeted them politely and glided around discreetly, settling Lucia into her chair and arranging her napkin, fixing the jug of flowers on the table and lighting the candles. Robert took charge of the wine list, ordering two glasses of champagne as an aperitif, then a small carafe of crisp white for their mackerel starter, and following a discussion with the wine waiter, he ordered a bottle of gutsy red to go with their steaks.

He sat back with a quiet sigh, his face registering utter contentment. 'Good so far, isn't it?'

'It's perfect, Robert, couldn't be better.' It *was* perfect. She was so, so lucky that this was her life, she reminded herself.

'I know what you're saying about somewhere different, but we work very hard, you and I, and our holidays are the only opportunity we have to really chill. Why try to fix something that's not broken?'

'I totally agree,' Lucia said airily. 'It was just a thought that popped into my head, that's all.'

He smiled. 'You look lovely,' he said.

'Thanks.' He must have forgiven her for her hair. But she *did* look lovely. She'd dressed up in a sequinned black top with skinny straps, and a diaphanous maxi-skirt, teamed with jewelled sandals. She'd exaggerated her dark eyes slightly more than usual and her new hair emphasised her shapely cheekbones. White-gold jewellery, gifts from Robert, glinted at her throat and on her hands. This is the real Lucia Edwards, she'd told herself, examining her reflection in the cheval mirror.

They were finished their fish, and sitting in a comfortable, alcohol-induced glow as they awaited the arrival of their steaks – medium for Robert, medium well for Lucia – when the couple with the baby arrived.

Children were welcome at the restaurant, but for the most part, families tended to keep away and dine in one of the more informal, less expensive restaurants further into the village. Lucia could see this couple's air of desperation straight away. They'd been walking by the restaurant at a quick pace when they stopped suddenly as though they had only just registered its existence. They looked at the beautifully crafted menu displayed out front under a spotlight, looked at each other and began to manoeuvre the buggy through to a table on the patio close to Lucia and Robert.

Soon after they ordered, the ominous sounds of a whimpering baby began to float through the air. The couple threw sheepish grins to the diners within earshot. The mother began to jiggle the buggy back and forth to no avail. Robert threw his eyes up to heaven.

The crying increased. Lucia and Robert's bottle of Chateauneuf arrived. He tasted it and announced his satisfaction. The waiter poured, and Robert clinked his glass against Lucia's. The mother gave them an envious glance before hauling the crying baby out of the buggy. Lucia was hopeless at guessing a baby's age but she took him to be about nine months old. However, lifting the baby out of the buggy, giving him a toy, and then a bottle, did nothing to pacify him.

Robert and Lucia's mains arrived. He gave her a smug kind of grin as though to say he was going to enjoy this steak, crying baby or no crying baby. Then the baby's father summoned the waiter and Lucia couldn't help but overhear their discussion.

'Can we just cancel the starters and go straight to the mains?' he said, speaking with a Cork accent.

'Oui, Monsieur.'

'And could you bring them out separately?'

'Separately? I don't understand.'

The Cork man grinned at his wife across the table as though it was a routine known to both of them. 'My wife's order first, as soon as possible, and then mine afterwards, when she is finished. And no dessert.'

Lucia couldn't see the waiter's face, but she could imagine the expression. The father took the crying baby gently out of his wife's arms, then holding him securely against his chest and directing the buggy with his free hand, he manoeuvred it back out to the pavement. He strapped the baby into his seat and, blowing a kiss to his wife, proceeded to push the buggy up towards the town centre, the noise gradually receding into the distance.

'Thank God for that,' Robert said. 'You shouldn't be bringing kids into restaurants if they can't behave.'

'Robert! It's just a baby,' Lucia said, conscious that the mother had probably overheard his sharp comment. She was sitting alone now, her hands fidgeting with the stem of her wine glass. When her meal arrived she ate it hurriedly, putting her hand over her glass and shaking her head when the waiter went to top it up. As soon as she was finished, she picked up her mobile and made a call; her husband, Lucia guessed, because five minutes later he reappeared with the buggy and it was her turn to blow him a kiss and push the baby up the town. He sat down, knocked back a full glass of wine in double-quick time, and ate his meal just as hurriedly as his wife had.

By the time he was finished, his wife had arrived back with the buggy, and the baby had obviously fallen asleep because all was quiet. Nonetheless, they paid the bill and left.

Lucia and Robert were still taking their time over their steak.

'Christ,' Robert said, when the couple were walking back in the direction from which they'd come, 'what kind of a crappy holiday are they going to have?'

Lucia made some kind of non-committal noise. They were going to have a good holiday, she sensed. From where she was sitting she could watch their progress up the street. The husband was pushing the buggy with one hand, and the other arm was encircling his wife's shoulders. She had an arm curved around his waist. They strolled along in perfect time with each other, hips bumping together now and again, and their whole demeanour spoke of a warm familiarity, intimacy, a total unity – happiness.

'Thank God you and I will never have a meal ruined like that,' Robert said.

Lucia smiled and looked at the waiter, who promptly topped up her wine. She wanted to admit to Robert that for a mad impulsive moment she'd been tempted to offer to babysit for the couple, even for a couple of hours, but she was sure he would have choked on his steak. Still, what would have been the harm? Just two or three hours out of her whole fourteen-day holiday, to let the couple out to have a meal together would have been no sacrifice at all, only they didn't know her from Adam and she didn't know them. And as Robert would have accurately pointed out, she hadn't a clue how to handle a baby.

No kids.

Later that night, in the huge comfortable bed, they made love. They'd both had a lot to drink that evening and had lingered over their meal with brandies and coffees, and Lucia felt tired and woozy by the time they reached their bedroom. Robert, however, seemed determined to make it work, undressing her slowly and sensually, stopping every so often to kiss and caress. Eventually he pulled her across the bed into a position they'd never tried before, and her surprise must have shown on her face.

'See, Lucia,' he murmured against her face, 'I can do different as well.' Then with one hand on her hip and the other cradling the back of her neck, he entered her fully with a long, powerful thrust and it felt so good that every part of her melted into a sweet white blur.

The days and nights of their holiday slipped past in a haze of warm sunshine, good food, pricey wines and lazy breakfasts. They took trips to a nearby perfume factory and a vineyard, but mainly Lucia did slow crawls up the length of the swimming pool. She'd turn to float on her back, weightless and free, feeling the sun on her closed eyelids, sufficiently distanced by the two weeks from her normal life that this, now, felt perfectly normal.

This was Lucia Edwards on a much-deserved holiday – sleek and shiny and all pampered out.

Occasionally, she saw the couple with the baby. They didn't return to the restaurant, but she saw them walking through the quaint square in the village, and when she went out for an early morning walk, she saw them when she passed by a nearby apartment complex. They were at the swimming pool, visible through the mesh perimeter fence, obviously out before the day got too warm, the baby covered from head to toe in a blue suit. She heard the baby laugh as his father played with him in the pool and raised him aloft in his arms. It was a pure, joyous, gurgling laugh that streamed out on the air like bubbles. She heard the father laugh in answer, and it was so happy, deep-bellied and spontaneous, that it made her think of Danny. She pushed the thought back. Not here, not now.

Too late. As she walked on, the sunlight shimmered in front of her, bouncing off the bright pavements, mocking in its warm clarity. Danny was all gone, dead, his life over. Nothing of him remained to show he'd passed through, except the spot he'd taken up in other people's hearts. The realisation washed over her like a tsunami; he'd never be here in France like this, eating good food, drinking fine wine, feeling the heat of the sun on his face, diving into the cool blue depths of a swimming pool; never be here like this man playing with his son. Never hold a son in his arms.

Something shifted inside her, like a recalibration of sorts. She recalled what Danny had said to her about regrets, and she felt suddenly cold as she remembered the way she'd been so definite, *so sure,* that she'd never have any.

Chapter Thirty-seven

'Grace. Hi.'

'Gavin.' Grace's head began to thump. It was after eight o'clock on a Thursday night. She'd stopped counting the number of Thursday nights since Danny was gone, as it'd now turned into months. She'd seen Gavin's name coming up on her mobile and her gut reaction had been to ignore the call. She didn't have the headspace or energy to deal with him right now. Still … it was only a phone call. It wouldn't kill her to chat to him.

'I'm in the area so I thought I'd say a quick hello.' From the slightly disjointed sound of his voice he was moving somewhere. She heard a car door clang in the background.

'You must be working overtime,' she said.

'Yep, I needed to talk to people in the retail park, but I'm on the way out now and heading towards the car. Are you at home?'

'Yes, I am, but—'

'Good. I have something for you, to cheer you up, so seeing as I'm close, I might as well just pop up with it.'

Her brain froze. She couldn't think of an excuse to head him off. And she couldn't use Lucia again – besides she was still in France for her usual two weeks and Gavin would probably know that.

'Grace? Are you still there?'

'Yes … um …' Think, Grace, *think*.

'Unless you've moved apartment in the meantime?' he said. 'Sorry, that was a crap joke.'

'No, I haven't.'

'Although maybe you don't want me barging in,' he went on, sounding a little unsure. 'You're probably busy with more important things.'

'You're not interrupting anything,' she said, accepting defeat.

'So it's okay to pop up?'

He sounded so reasonable it would have been churlish to refuse.

Still, the sight of him walking into her narrow hallway a few short minutes later, dressed in his business suit, briefcase in one hand, his other hand proffering a bouquet of white, long-stemmed lilies, filled her with a kind of dread; it plunged her right back to the miserable few weeks she'd endured before she'd finally mustered up the courage to make splitting-up noises.

'Flowers,' she said, plastering a smile on her face.

'Your favourite,' he said.

She didn't recall ever having told him that but she let it pass.

He smiled, showing a dimple in his cheek. 'Seeing as I was in the neighbourhood, as soon as I saw them I couldn't resist.'

'You're very kind,' she said as he put them into her arms, feeling like a fraud of some kind, because if anything, she was finding it irritating to have to accept flowers off Gavin.

'I just wanted to cheer you up, you must be feeling extra lonely with Lucia away.'

The way he knew this gave her a slight start. 'What do you mean?' she asked.

'I guess she and Robert are gone to France as per usual?'

'That's right.'

'First two weeks in June. I remembered,' he said, looking pleased with himself. 'Well don't forget, if you're feeling lonely, I'm here for you. As a friend.'

Somehow they were in her living area. How had he got in this far? She'd allowed him in, that was how. She was cross with herself because he was invading the space that had belonged to her and Danny. The precious space where they'd laughed and danced and made love. Which was ridiculous in a way, as Gavin had lived here for six months. It had been his home. He put down his briefcase. She wondered idly why he hadn't left it in the boot of his car.

'It's even cosier than ever,' he said, his keen gaze scanning her living area. She saw then, by the tilt of his head and shoulders, that he was staring at the posters. He stood stock-still, and remained silent.

And then, after what seemed like ages, 'They're new.'

'Yes.'

'Very nice.'

'Thanks.'

He was still staring at them, so she felt some explanation was needed, some words to fill the sudden tension. 'I put them up … after Danny died. Just to …' she heard herself voicing the words of a blatant lie. She didn't want to admit they had been Danny's. Surely he guessed? He swung around to look at her, a relaxed smile on his face. Maybe she'd been imagining the tension. Like she seemed to be imagining so much else lately.

'Brighten up the place … cheer myself up,' she went on, deciding further explanation was totally unnecessary.

'I suppose it'll be hard to move on until after the inquest.'

'Inquest?' She looked at him sharply.

His face was full of concern. 'That's usually the next step, isn't it?'

'I dunno.'

'So you haven't heard anything about that yet?'

She shook her head and bit her lip; thoughts of an inquest

dragging her back momentarily to the dark place she'd inhabited for a number of weeks. 'No, nothing.'

'Oh dear, you look like you could do with some cheering up,' Gavin said, as though he'd been waiting for this moment. He slid off his tie, and folding it swiftly, he slipped it into the pocket of his jacket. 'I'm glad I thought of the flowers. Tell you what, let's have some coffee if it's not too much trouble. We could both do with it. That appointment I just came from was a bit of a grilling. Some people refuse to face the truth about their finances even when the writing's on the wall. They can be crap to deal with. So I'm feeling a bit bunched myself.'

'Of course,' she said, going across to the compact kitchen area and filling the kettle. She opened the fridge for milk, the movement disturbing her kite so that the tail of it rippled out in a transparent prism of yellow and red light. She caught her breath, seeing it floating up against a blue-grey sky, the sound of Danny's laughter beside her, his warm green eyes smiling into hers.

She turned towards the table, and saw Gavin watching her. She deliberately made her face as blank as possible. In her tense state, she fancied it looked like he was studying her under a microscope, one of his habits that had begun to aggravate her immensely in those last few weeks with him. He took off his jacket and put it neatly over the back of a chair. It was the kind of fluid movement he'd done a hundred times before, yet she found herself feeling irritated with the familiar way he made himself so at home.

'I guess that's something else you've cheered yourself up with,' he said, nodding to her kite.

'That's right,' she said, non-committally, busying herself with mugs. No way was she elaborating. The memory of kite-flying with Danny was far too precious to share with Gavin.

'This is like old times,' he said, when she put the coffee in front of him. Then, 'Don't look so worried, I'll head off after this and get out of your way.'

She should have said, with the best of her good manners, that he wasn't in her way, and he was welcome to stay, but the words stuck in her throat. The suffocation was back again, pressing down on her. Instead of joining him at the table, she deliberately took her time rummaging for a vase, filling it with water and snipping off the ends of the stems before she arranged the flowers. She looked around for somewhere suitable to place them.

'Why not put them right here on the table,' Gavin said, as if reading her mind. 'Then you can see them from every part of the room.'

'Good idea,' she said, finding the scent of them suddenly cloying as she carried the vase to the table. Her eyes met his over the blooms and she had the strange feeling he was judging her.

'Thanks again,' she said. She hoped he'd take the hint that it was time for him to go.

He sat back and folded his arms. 'Is everything else all right, apart from missing Danny of course? Job going okay?'

'Yeah, great,' she said. 'It gives me something to get out of bed for.' She wished she hadn't mentioned the word 'bed'. She could have sworn by the pensive look on his face that he was picturing the sight of her getting up in the mornings, and how towards the end of their relationship, she'd pulled on a robe the minute she'd stepped out of bed.

'That's good,' he said. 'We give out about the daily grind but it's useful in lots of ways. There's a promotion coming up in my job, so I'm keeping my fingers crossed, although there are a few external accountancy heads going after it, including Dean Reilly.'

'Dean Reilly?'

'One of the guys I know from college. He was one of the gang I met for a drink at Christmas. When I ended up staying out until four in the morning. The night before I met you for a drink. He works in that building where you got stuck in the lift that day. Before we broke up.'

'Does he?' A memory ran through her head of the day she'd begun to imagine her life without Gavin. She busied herself picking up the slivers of stems that she'd cut off, and she put them into the bin, leaning back against the counter and folding her arms instead of going back to the table.

'However I don't think he stands much of a chance,' Gavin went on. 'The firm he works for is only a small outfit compared to McCabe Corrigan. He couldn't have the experience I have.'

'The best of luck,' she said. 'I'm sure you'll do great.'

'Sounds like you're sending me home.'

'I've stuff to do before work tomorrow,' she said.

He threw up his hands. 'Sorry, I'm holding you up.' He stood up and picked up his jacket. 'Thanks for the coffee, Grace. Kiss, kiss?'

To her consternation he walked over to her and putting his hands on her upper arms, he held her tightly and bent to kiss her. This time she managed to turn her head at the last moment so that his lips connected with her ear.

He smiled, his blue eyes soft. 'You weren't expecting that.'

'No.'

'No worries. As I said, I'm the shoulder for you to cry on, whenever you feel like it. I mean that in more ways than one. Just good friends.' He reached out and fingered her hair. 'We had some good times, hadn't we? I know we'll never go back to all that, but if you ever want … some company, even at night … if you're feeling lonely and would like me to spend the night with you, I'd be happy to oblige. No strings.'

She stared at him as a muscle moved in his jaw. He was gazing down at her breasts, softly outlined by her T-shirt. Was he really suggesting what she thought? He still had one hand on her arm, within touching distance of her breast, and she stepped back to dislodge it. 'Gavin, thanks ... but ...'

Thanks? Putting it like that it sounded utterly trite. *Thanks for the offer of sex, but no thanks. I don't want you anymore. I don't want to feel your bare skin next to mine.*

'See, we're over you and I ...' she smiled, trying to take the sting out of her rejection.

'I know that,' he said a little impatiently, shaking his head as if clearing his thoughts. 'I'm just saying, if by chance, supposing you can't bear the ... crappy loneliness anymore, you can call on me to kill a few hours, just some comfort, nothing else, promise.'

Something sparked in her head at the way he spoke of being lonely. She knew he was talking from experience, that he'd been suffering from loneliness himself, now that she was out of his life. Only she'd done it to him on purpose, with her cold, clear rejection of him.

It made her soften her voice even more. 'You've been very kind and understanding. However,' she shrugged, 'right now I've things to do and ... a load of ironing waiting for me ...'

'Don't worry, I'll get out of your hair. Hey, what's this?' He nodded to her storage boxes containing her writing materials, which she'd put on a side table in her living area.

Trust Gavin to spot these. 'They're something else that's new,' she said, holding his gaze, daring him to comment.

He flipped open the lid and glanced inside, saying nothing. Then he picked up his briefcase and smiled at her. 'I wouldn't give up the day job just yet,' he said.

'Maybe not just yet,' she said. 'But my time will come, so watch this space.'

As soon as he had left, Grace stripped off and went into the shower, closing her eyes and standing under the stream of cleansing water. She went out for a late evening walk, marching as fast as she could, down to the village and back, stopping for a while on the arched, stone bridge, leaning on the parapet as she watched the stream bubble along over wet pebbles underneath, the gurgling noise fresh and vital to her ears. Walking out in the fresh air helped to put a distance between herself and Gavin. Even when she heard a motorbike roaring past on the perimeter road, she ignored it.

Her calmness lasted until she went back into her apartment and saw the flowers. Their scent was filling the room, but that wasn't a problem. It was the sight of them that turned her stomach. White, long-stemmed lilies; the exact same as the spray that had covered Danny's coffin.

She picked up the vase, poured off the water, and went out to the lift, smiling nonchalantly at the couple in the next apartment to hers who were also getting the lift, as though she carted a vase full of flowers around the complex on a daily basis. Down in the basement, Grace opened the refuse bin and upended the vase so that the blooms toppled into the dark recesses. Back in her apartment, she washed out the vase with hot soapy water, and then she lit a scented candle, put on 'Purple Rain', switched on her laptop and opened her writing box.

Chapter Thirty-eight

It was their last night.

Lucia and Robert were sitting in the same restaurant at the same table when Lucia saw the couple strolling down the street, the father pushing his son in the buggy. They looked happy and relaxed. The mother's hair was soft and loose and she was wearing a spaghetti-strap, floaty maxi-dress in a way that told Lucia she felt special in it and that it was a treat to be able to stroll along like this on a balmy evening in France. Lucia thought she looked romantic and sexy – a woman in love. Having given her man a child. The fruit of their love. This time they passed by the restaurant without even glancing at the menu.

'There go our friends,' she said to Robert.

'What friends?' He'd been checking out the menu and now he looked up, an irritable frown on his face in case the peaceful ambience of his final holiday evening was about to be interrupted.

'Don't worry, they've gone past,' Lucia said, nodding back over her shoulder.

Robert gazed beyond her, and then he spotted them. He laughed shortly and shook his head dismissively before turning back to the menu. 'I think I'll go for broke as it's our last night.'

'Yeah … already. Did you enjoy the holiday?' she asked.

'What do you think? Great food, great weather. Ravishing company,' he smiled easily. 'Total chill-out. Ticked all the right boxes.'

She thought his answer sounded like something he had rehearsed to report back to his colleagues in the office, making sure his comments showed their holiday in the best light possible. For he would never end up on a holiday that was below standard. But where was the spontaneous living in all his box-ticking? The messy, inconvenient, but warm, pure, essentials of life: laughter, fun, love, things going pear-shaped, but being lived to the full. Miles apart from carefully calculated sex positions. And no noisy babies to interrupt their total chill-out, or disturb the perfect ambience of a relaxing restaurant meal. As if his office colleagues would care one whit.

She wondered what he'd be telling Miranda. Would he tell her that Lucia had been ravishing company? Would he be thinking about their warm sultry nights in the big, cosy bed, or the times they'd shared a bath, when Miranda asked how his holidays had been? She wanted to weep. Why was she even thinking like this?

'Didn't you?' he asked, suddenly seeming to realise she was taking a long time to answer.

'Oh yes, I did, it was great. Very relaxing.'

'Then you'll be glad to hear I've already booked us in for next year.'

Lucia felt part of herself escaping out of her body and hovering above where they sat right now, looking down and watching a movie reel of their future holidays on fast forward; the two of them coming here year after year, both of them with a few more laughter lines and slightly thicker waists, gradually moving through their forties. Each holiday exactly a replica of the one before, taking seats at this restaurant, travelling out to the vineyards, and sitting on the balcony of their villa sipping gin and tonics … Lucia even saw herself swimming up and down the same pool, like a hamster going round and round the same wheel, one year indistinguishable from the next.

Was this what she wanted? A lifetime of safe, predictable holidays?

The young couple with the baby would probably go to different places, travelling with their son, who wouldn't be a baby forever. She visualised them in the years ahead; the child would be aged four, five, then ten or twelve, part of their family unit, an expression of their love. Someone to love. A gift. Maybe joined by a sibling in due course. Another gift.

What could be more precious in life, more amazing, and more wonderful than the gift of life itself?

No kids. It had been agreed. It had suited her too. Then.

Then? She caught her breath, feeling she was teetering dizzily on the edge of a mountaintop. What was she most scared of? Really? She'd never been the young and reckless type, every step she had taken had always been considered very carefully and well thought out in advance. She had a dread of making mistakes, of taking a wrong turn, of losing control; a fear of any kind of insecurity. Now she felt out of control. She must be having some sort of panic attack.

'Robert …' she murmured, trying to get a grip on reality, as her stomach flipped over.

Something in her strained tone alerted him. He searched her face. 'Aren't you happy with the same place, same time next year?'

'Absolutely,' she fibbed. 'Are you happy with us?'

'*Us?* What's that supposed to mean?'

She breathed slowly and tried to look nonchalant, as though the outcome of the conversation didn't matter at all. 'You know,' she said airily, waving her hand in a kind of dismissive gesture. 'Our lives, our choices, our decisions …'

'What kind of decisions?'

'Well … big things, like you working in London, for example, and me staying in Dublin. Are you lonely? Do you miss me?'

'You're said this already,' he said. 'Are you missing me during the week?'

Lucia sipped her wine. How could she answer this when she'd been the one encouraging him to take the London job, urging him to grab it with both hands before the spectre of unemployment cast its ugly shadow?

'I thought you were so absorbed in the goings-on in Izobel that you were happy with our set up,' Robert said. 'Is there something you're not telling me?'

She shook her head, recalling the day she'd gone out for lunch with Aiden, just before she'd gone on holidays. It was something she hadn't bothered to tell Robert. And she hadn't told him because it was insignificant. It had meant nothing. She'd hardly be telling him about the details of her lunch with Diane, so it was just the same, even if Aiden was handsome and male and had been looking at her with a different gleam in his eye since the evening he'd caught her sitting shell-shocked at her desk.

'I'm just thinking about you and me, now that we're away from it all and I have time to do that. You're still happy with our decision not to have children?' she asked.

He gave a short laugh. 'Kids! It would be like a bomb going off in our lives.' He stared at her quizzically, as though he didn't recognise her for a moment. 'You're hardly having a change of mind? My super-organised, career-orientated Lucia? The heat of the sun must be getting to you, or else it's a little too much fine wine. Or maybe that vodka you were guzzling has gone to your head.'

'I wasn't guzzling anything, and it was just a passing thought,' she said, forcing a smile, ignoring the way her stomach was still lurching.

'You are in a funny mood,' Robert said. 'I know what it is …' he laughed. 'You're feeling unsettled because you've been away from your usual routine for too long. As soon as you're sitting at your desk, everything will be back to normal.'

Lucia focussed on twirling the stem of her wine glass and tried to ignore the pin-pricks of sweat breaking out across her forehead.

Chapter Thirty-nine

Grace stared down at the padded envelope. She turned it round and round in her hands, reluctant to open it. It was addressed to her in block capitals, in black felt pen, exactly the same way as the package containing Danny's torn-up photograph had been. That had landed in her apartment. This had arrived on her desk in Arcadia exactly two weeks after the toy elephant. Something exploded at the back of her head.

'Ooh, is this another cute package?' Karen said, raising her eyebrows suggestively.

'Yep,' Grace said nonchalantly. 'That's why I'm saving it up for when I go home.'

'Aah, spoilsport. We'd love to know what it is this time, wouldn't we, Suz? There's so little excitement around here we need to grab whatever we can to keep ourselves amused.'

'Sorry,' Grace said, opening her desk drawer and dropping it inside.

She had work to do. She had to call back a customer, with three young children, whose kitchen had gone on fire and break the news that she'd been under-insured. Someone else whose boiler had leaked and ruined the expensive wooden flooring was screaming for her settlement, even though her paperwork hadn't been submitted correctly. But it was impossible to concentrate on her work with the package sitting in her drawer like an unexploded landmine and a feeling of dread running through her veins.

She slid the package into her bag at lunchtime, knowing she couldn't wait until she got home that evening to find out what it contained. Something else designed to upset her, for sure. She opened it out in the toilet cubicle, her breath stopping for a moment as she peeled off the tape and opened the envelope. The contents were wrapped in white tissue. She pulled out the tissue, her fingers trembling. Cardboard stars, like the kind you'd buy in a craft or stationery shop, slid out and fluttered to the floor. But in the same way the toy elephant had been mutilated, the cardboard stars were crushed and broken. Grace felt bile rising in her throat. She sat on the lid of the toilet and put her head in her hands, feeling more alone than she'd ever felt before.

A sick joke, Matt would say. The old-fashioned notion of respect has gone out the door. People could be very cruel and hurtful.

Best to ignore and rise above it, Lucia would say. Sent by a coward, probably a jealous ex of Danny's. Someone who knew the kind of fun things Danny would get up to and had probably guessed he'd done them with Grace. She heard footsteps as someone else came into the ladies, then locked a cubicle door. She couldn't sit here forever even though that was what she felt like doing. She bent down and picked up the cardboard pieces, her fingers shaking as she pushed them back into the envelope. No way were these going to be allowed to invade her apartment. Grace went out to the bin. It was half-full of paper towels and she shoved the envelope and its contents down into it. Then she washed her hands in water as hot as she could bear, needing to get the feel of them off her fingers.

It was only when she reached home that evening that she realised she should have kept the envelope. Just in case. Then in the next breath, she laughed. Matt was hardly going to check it for fingerprints when no crime had been committed. She'd texted him recently with the registration number of the motorbike when she'd spotted it passing her out in the traffic as she drove to Dundrum Town Centre, but he'd replied to say it was in the clear, whatever he'd meant by that.

Maybe it was best to tell no one about this. Lucia was probably right. This was surely the nasty work of a jealous girlfriend of Danny's, who was even more upset that he was gone, and maybe even jealous that Grace had had him all to herself for those last few weeks.

Best to rise above it.

The following evening, the sour taste it had left vanished when an email arrived out of the blue. Grace stared at it, unable to comprehend the words dancing in front of her, let alone make sense of them. Phrases jumped out at her.

> Dear Grace,
> We think your writing shows promise. We understand the material was sent in on your behalf by a Mr Danny McBride. Apologies that this reply has taken so long but due to the high level of submissions, it can take three months to respond. For the same reason, unsolicited material is not returned. We will not be proceeding with this submission; however, we'd like to know if you're working on any other material with a view to seeing that. Please contact us via email ...

The email was signed off by a 'Liz Mulligan of Jigsaw Press: Children's, non-fiction and educational books'.

She didn't care if anyone could see her, up here on the second floor of Rathbrook Hall, as she did a mad, happy dance around the room.

Chapter Forty

Matt drove into the business park in Cherrywood and pulled up outside the recruitment company where Janet worked as a consultant. He switched off the engine and sat for a moment, unaccountably nervous. Maybe this wasn't such a good idea after all.

And where was his spirit of adventure?

He recalled Grace Bailey's face and the glow that had spread across it as she spoke of Danny pulling her out of work, giving her the feeling of being a child whisked away unexpectedly to a glittering carnival. He'd felt a huge pang of sympathy for Grace the night he'd called in, when she'd shown him the damaged toy. Maybe it was just a sick kind of joke – a so-called friend or work colleague, more likely someone who had known Danny. Whoever it had been, they'd stooped pretty low. Then again, some of the cases that came through the station beggared belief, from downright stupid, petty crimes, right up to the most violent incidents. Some of the people he'd come across in the course of his work had been evil personified, adept at fooling themselves and everyone else around them. It had been one of the hardest things he'd had to learn – to distance himself from it all and not let it get him down, to try to keep his soul intact, far away and up beyond the brutality and sheer, sickening crap that went on every other day.

He jiggled his car keys. '*I help people*,' he'd told Abbie, sounding like Mr-All-Powerful. Yeah, sure. He must have been in a really big-headed mood that day. He hadn't been able to make things right with Janet. And he didn't know to what extent he was helping Grace. At least she was talking to him, even if she said she didn't need a liaison officer. If in listening to her, he heard all about the brilliant Danny, he might learn something that would help him reconnect with Janet.

He summoned his spirit of adventure, announced himself at Reception, and took a seat. His first indication that this was not such an amazing idea came when Janet rushed out through a staff door, her face drained of colour.

'Matt? Is it Abbie?' she asked, her voice trembling, her face furrowed with anxiety.

Nonplussed, he said, 'Abbie?'

'Is something wrong?' She put a hand up to her throat in a defensive gesture.

'Abbie's fine, as far as I know,' he said.

He saw Janet breathe out and she sagged down on the other seat. 'Oh, thank God. I thought for a moment ...' she clasped her hands tightly and pressed them into her chest.

'What did you think?'

'I thought the crèche must have called you ... and that something had happened to Abbie.'

He hastened to reassure her. 'No, nothing like that. But why would they call me?'

'Being a cop ... or something,' Janet shrugged. 'Your name is still down as the next contact after me.'

'Is it?' The knowledge filled him with a warm glow.

Janet's face changed and registered annoyance. 'What do you want, Matt? I'm busy this afternoon. Up to my proverbial tonsils and I'm not the better for it after that fright.'

'That's my plan out the window, so.'

'What plan?'

'I thought maybe …' his voice dried up. This was all wrong. Janet didn't look like she needed a bit of distraction, never mind an excuse to bolt from Butler's for the afternoon. If anything she was looking at him as though he was a most inconvenient interruption.

'I was going to ask you to come to the zoo, but I can see it was—'

'*What*? The *zoo*? Are you for real?' she spluttered.

He put his hands up in mock surrender. 'Okay, look, sorry. I can see it was a bad idea.'

'A *bad* idea? Good God, Matt. Are you seriously telling me you barged in here thinking I could drop everything, walk out, and go to the *zoo*?'

'Sorry,' he said. 'I can see it was a ridiculous idea.'

'Ridiculous? It's off the wall.'

'I didn't mean it like that, and I certainly didn't intend to alarm you,' he said, deciding to assert himself a little. 'I thought it might be fun, something different, a forbidden kind of treat on a Thursday afternoon, a mad reason to tempt you to skive off work and give Abbie a surprise when we picked her up from the crèche, but yes, I agree with you, off the wall, and outrageous.'

To his utter relief and it was worth making a total fool of himself just for this – Janet smiled at him warmly. 'Yeah, it was,' she said. 'Ridiculous. Totally outrageous. Thursday's our busiest day with placements for next week. What brought this on?'

'It's such a lovely afternoon … seems a shame not to do something you'd enjoy.'

'I suppose, yeah, and I haven't been there in years … but to think I could play truant and just walk out.' She shook her head. 'I bet you're off duty this afternoon and that you didn't just walk out of the station.'

He hadn't thought of it like that. She had a point. No way could he have just walked. 'I thought the three of us could have had some fun …'

Janet shook her head slowly. So much for sweeping her off her feet and breaking the rules on an impulse. It had all backfired.

'I can see I was mistaken,' he said, getting to his feet. 'Apologies for giving you a fright and disturbing you.' He walked towards the door.

'Matt – wait …'

He spun around.

'How about, the weekend?' Janet said.

'The weekend?'

'Yes, whatever day you're off.'

'You mean all of us?'

'Maybe.'

Maybe. Better than nothing. Her face was neutral. He didn't know what she was thinking, but it was the first time since they'd split that she'd agreed to take part in anything involving the three of them together. It was a start. He wasn't going to mess this up. He was going to be on his very best behaviour. Mr Nice Guy as opposed to Mr Jealous Guy, all insecurities put strictly to one side.

* * *

Janet seemed to be in a similar frame of mind when he called on Saturday at midday. He blinked when she answered the door. Whatever she had done to her face, her skin looked bright and luminous, her eyes were big and dark and sparkly, her lips soft and pink, and her hair was gleaming as it swung around her shoulders. She was wearing a pair of skinny jeans and a white top under a blue striped jacket. The look of her blew him away. He wanted to crush her to himself and drink her in. He wanted to protect her from all harm for all time.

He was jittery as hell when he walked out to his car, Abbie skipping beside him, Janet behind her. He tried to wipe off his silly grin and compose himself to look as though they went out every Saturday as a family unit, but he nearly lost his nerve when Janet got into the car so naturally, as though she did it every day – and not as if it was the first time in six months or so – sitting in the passenger seat, fresh and beautiful, her eyes full of anticipation, her light scent in his nostrils. Their hands brushed as they fastened their seat belts and their eyes locked for a nanosecond, her face so close that it took his breath away.

'Daddy, are we going to see the effelents?' Abbie chirped up from her booster seat in the back. 'All of us?'

His heart squeezed. 'Yes, we are, all of us.'

'Like a daddy and mammy and the little girl, all together?'

'Yes, love.'

Thank God for Abbie. She chatted away excitedly as they drove to the park, her tumble of words filling what would otherwise have been a strained silence. He hadn't realised how anxious he'd feel, thrown together with Janet like this. The queue for the entrance to the zoo straggled around the path outside. Abbie got fed up standing in line and she kept skipping away and skipping back to them. He had to try to talk to Janet, rather than having them both inching their way forwards like two awkward strangers, sticking out like sore thumbs amongst the laughing and chattering family groups. It was the first time in months that they were able to have a face-to-face conversation without it ending in a row, and without either of them trying to score points off the other.

'Everything okay in work?' he asked.

'It's grand,' Janet said. 'How about you?'

'Still the same.' He'd never discussed the details of his working day, gory or otherwise, with Janet. She'd always known by his face if he'd had a particularly bad day, and she'd had the best way in the world of helping him disconnect, which he'd missed immensely after the split. But generally his job stayed in the station and he didn't bring it home.

Except he'd crossed a line of sorts with Grace, he reminded himself. He hadn't updated the file with his visits to her apartment. Bad practice. But Grace was different. He was trying to help, trying to prove he could help, that he was good for something; anyone else would have dismissed her ideas out of hand, and would have dismissed her as a crank of some kind.

'How's Liam?' Janet asked.

Liam was his brother in Canada. Two years younger than Matt, he'd emigrated eight years ago and there was no sign of his moving home to Ireland. Matt missed him. They'd squabbled and play-fought all through their growing-up years, and were just beginning to appreciate each other as adults when Liam had bailed out.

'He's great,' Matt said. 'Still making a small fortune, working hard and playing hard.'

'And your parents?'

'They're fine too. Enjoying their retirement. They left for Canada at the start of May.'

Matt's parents, both schoolteachers, had taken early retirement. They still lived in the roomy home in Kildare where Matt and his brother had been raised, but they spent some time each year in Canada, catching up with Liam. 'I might bring Abbie for a visit when they're back, if that's okay.' he said. 'They'd like to see her.'

'I'm sure we can arrange that,' Janet said. She didn't suggest seeing Matt's parents herself. Matt had been heartened that they'd become very fond of Janet in a short space of time, and equally glad that they had wisely held their counsel after the split. One look at Matt's thunderous face had been enough to reduce them to silence.

At last they were through the entrance and into the grounds of the zoo. Abbie hopped from one foot to another, wanting to see everything at once.

'Hold, on, we've the whole afternoon,' Matt told her. 'Let's take our time.' There was a lake ahead of them and well-tended pathways running round on both sides. 'It's all different from the last time I was here,' he said, unable to get his bearings at first.

'And when was that?' Janet asked. 'Or maybe you don't want to give your age away.'

Was she flirting with him? 'God … twenty years,' he said. Since then, the zoo had undergone a complete redesign along with a big extension programme, aimed to ensure the animals lived in as natural a habitat as possible. Still, elements of it were familiar to him, evoking shadowy images at the back of his mind: the scents and sounds, the very taste of the air on his lips, the very sight of the animals.

Abbie loved the monkeys. Matt soaked up the sight of her laughing at them, enjoying her carefree joy, her giggles, her eyes full of delight. It distracted him and saved him having to face a peculiar ache that was creeping around his heart. As they walked around, taking their time, certain areas struck a chord inside him, like an echo from his childhood vibrating across over twenty years, opening a door to his memory bank that had remained tightly shut until now, bringing him back to a time he'd been in the zoo with—

It was gone, the faint print of an image.

'Matt?' Janet touched him on the arm, and he realised she'd been trying to get his attention. They were outside a café, where an area had been furnished with wooden tables and benches, and he wondered how long they'd been standing there.

'Hey, you're a million miles away,' she said. 'What's up?'

'Nothing.' He didn't know what had happened to him, why he'd had the uncomfortable sensation that the ground had tilted beneath him, but he pulled himself together and snapped out of it. He didn't want to ruin this afternoon.

'Will you have coffee?' she asked, her eyes a little concerned.

'I'd love that, please,' he said.

'And something for Abbie,' Janet went on, smiling at her daughter.

'Why don't we find somewhere to sit down, Abbie,' Matt said, shrugging off the last traces of the sudden cloud that had wafted around him.

'Are we having a picnic?' she asked, jumping up and down beside him as they strolled over to the seating area.

'Yes, sort of.'

'With special treats?'

'Yes, if Mummy says.'

'Mummy!' she yelled at the top of her voice. 'Can I've a special treat?'

At the entrance to the café, Janet turned around and smiled. Silhouetted by the sun, it threw a fizzing halo around her glossy hair. Abbie let out an excited squeal and ran to Matt, burying her face in his legs.

Matt froze the moment in his head and wrapped it carefully in his heart; this was all that mattered right now. If he'd had the strange feeling of something being out of kilter, an old ghost calling him back, he was going to ignore it.

Chapter Forty-one

'Are you feeling good?' Karen asked, with a too-bright smile on her face.

'Yeah, great.' Grace picked up her cocktail and resisted taking a large gulp, satisfying herself with just a sip. She had to pace herself. It could be a long night and she was a little out of practice.

'Good on you,' Karen winked. 'It's great to see you enjoying the party.'

Enjoying the party? She was determined to do her best. In the last three months, she'd been out with Lucia, and Karen and Suz, but that had been to the movies, for a meal or relaxing drinks. Tonight they were having a mad bash to kick-start Karen's thirtieth birthday celebrations, and the gang included Grace and Suz, some of the Arcadia women, and Karen's two sisters.

Suz came back from the bar, laden down with yet more brimming cocktails, which she deposited on the table, miraculously without spilling a drop. 'Sorry about the delay, the queue was a mile long. Hey, drink up Grace, you're falling behind,' she said.

It was too long since she'd been out like this with a group of girls, Grace decided, picking up her glass and putting it down again without taking a sip. She'd forgotten what it was like to be part of a big noisy gang taking over a corner of a pub on Dawson Street;

she'd forgotten the rhythms of it all, and how to blend in with the seamless chit-chat. All she had to do was relax and let the rise and fall of conversation flow around her. In-jokes crackled over her head along with shrieks of laughter and everyone seemed to be talking in shorthand, so that at times she was just grappling for meaning. Danny would never see thirty, she thought, and as she scanned the throngs of lively, happy people, she felt his absence like a gaping wound in her side. He'd come and gone, floating into her life and out just as quickly, and although he'd changed it completely in his too-short visit, to an onlooker, he'd barely left an imprint.

'Listen to this,' Karen began, giving Grace a friendly dig in the ribs before she jiggled the ice in her glass with a plastic stirrer and launched into a silly anecdote about work.

In the burst of laughter that followed, Grace left the table and went out to the bathroom. She needed a few moments alone, to take a few deep breaths and remind herself that she was fine, she could do this, she could live the best life possible, she could live the most amazing life, with Danny always in her heart. She felt herself smile as she remembered some of the things they'd ticked off his bucket list. Nothing would ever dim the memory of those weeks. She felt even prouder of the way she'd begun to follow her dreams, knowing he'd be cheering her on loudly and gustily from the sidelines. She'd emailed Liz in Jigsaw Press a couple of times already, introducing herself and the kind of material she was working on, adventure stories for six- to eight-year-olds, and she had asked for definitive submission guidelines and been cheered by the editor's friendly responses.

She was standing in front of the mirror slicking on some lip gloss when the door of a toilet cubicle crashed back and a blonde woman staggered out. She'd had too much to drink and she weaved across to the sink on very unsteady feet. Grace looked at her vertiginous high heels and held her breath, hoping she'd make it in one piece. The woman finally succeeded in turning on the taps and rinsing her hands, and when she reached across for some paper towels, she saw Grace's reflection in the mirror.

She stared at Grace through unfocussed, bloodshot eyes.

'Holy cow, it's you. Jeez, I would have to be like this when we meet ...' her words were slurred.

'Sorry, do I know you?' Grace said.

'Probably not. I know who you are though.' She gave a short laugh and dried her hands, flinging the paper towel into the waste bin. She opened her bag and took out her perfume, spraying it liberally. Then she stared at Grace in the mirror, her perfume bottle held in her raised hand like a weapon. 'Grace,' she said, clearly triumphant that she'd fished the name out of the foggy corners of her mind. 'You were there with your sister, Lucia.'

Even though the woman was so drunk she was having difficulty pronouncing her words, something cold ran down Grace's spine. She knew instinctively what the woman was about to say, and she wanted to turn and run but it was too late.

'I didn't know at first what hoity-toity Lucia was doing there,' the woman said, making a huge effort to pronounce her vowels. 'Then I found out she was with you.'

'You mean Danny's funeral?' Grace prompted, swallowing hard. She still felt a shock at the juxtaposition of those words – it seemed so incongruous that someone as lively as Danny had already had his funeral.

'Yeah ... and you were Danny's new girlfriend. Big surprise, you know,' she grinned as though it was all a huge joke.

Grace couldn't move. Someone from Danny's past. It was bound to have happened sooner or later, that she'd bump into someone who'd known Danny and had been at his funeral.

The woman dropped her perfume into her bag, fished around, pulled out her mascara and turned back to the mirror, flicking the brush around, hitting and missing her eyelashes. 'I recognised Lucia immediately,' she said, speaking to Grace's reflection. 'That one hasn't changed a bit. She was in St Anne's with my sister Jennifer. Hey, I'm Emer, by the way, but I don't remember you from school ...' her eyes squinted quizzically at Grace.

'I was five years behind Lucia.'

'To think Danny ended up with you ...' Emer turned around from the mirror and looked Grace up and down in a curious way.

'How did you know Danny?' Grace asked.

Emer rolled her eyes. 'I didn't, not really. I'm not his long suffering, wannabe-girlfriend, thank God. I'll leave that job up to Stacy. I went to college in Galway with Danny's sister, Cara. Danny was a year behind us. Although I think he dropped out around the time we graduated anyway.'

Dropped out. The words reverberated through Grace's head. It was something else she hadn't known about him, and another turn in the colourful kaleidoscope that made up different aspects of Danny. It was exactly the kind of thing Danny would have done if he'd lost faith with what he'd been studying.

Emer was still talking as she piled on her blusher. 'I lost touch with Cara, but when I heard what had happened to Danny I had to go to the funeral. It was an awful bloody tragedy. And just when he seemed to be getting his act together at last.'

'What do you mean?' Grace asked, her throat tight.

Emer's face changed and became suddenly guarded, as though she'd said too much. 'I don't know the details, it was something his younger sister said.'

'Like what?' Grace pushed.

Emer flicked a fat brush across her face and shrugged. 'There were problems ...at home. Something serious. That's all I know.'

The air felt suddenly thick around Grace and the scent of the woman's perfume swirled sickeningly in her nostrils.

'What kind of problems?' She forced out the words.

'Don't you know?' Even though she was drunk, Emer was watching her guardedly.

Grace shrugged.

'Just how long were you guys together?' Emer asked.

'Six weeks,' Grace said.

'Six weeks?' Emer laughed. 'Maybe you should talk to his sisters. They're devastated but they seemed to think you might have led him astray … whatever his problem was. Then when you didn't stick around after the funeral … I went looking for Lucia but you'd all left. It looked like you couldn't wait to get out of there.'

Grace stayed silent, transfixed by Emer's words.

Emer sensed she had a captive audience. 'I think you were right to make an escape,' she said. 'And whatever you do, stay away from Stacy – hey, that almost rhymes, easy for you to remember. Stay away from Stacy. You are not her favourite person. At. All.'

'Who's Stacy?'

'Danny never told you?'

Grace shook her head.

Emer's laughter cackled again. 'I'm not surprised, but poor Stacy would be devastated to know that, although she must have driven him bananas, chasing after him. I gave her a lift back to Dublin after the funeral. Worst thing I ever did. She was having a total meltdown in the car. She was friends with Amy, his younger sister, and she'd been crazy about Danny but no matter how hard she tried, he wasn't interested in her in that way. She told me she loved him enough for both of them, that she was sure she'd be able to fix him.'

'*Fix* him?'

Emer shrugged. 'She had his mobile number and she used to call him now and again. She even phoned him the night of the accident, but he didn't answer. She went hysterical when she heard he'd died, because she knew they'd never get together now. Then as if that wasn't bad enough, after he'd died, she found out about you'

'She's probably someone else who feels I led Danny astray,' Grace managed to say, trying to draw Emer out.

'I shouldn't be telling you this … you look nice and normal, and I've had too much to drink, but I've a feeling Danny's sisters are thinking the worst. He never told them about you, they said, and he was with you the night he had the accident, so they half-suspect he might have been in trouble again, after everything his family had done for him.'

Grace's heart began to knock wildly. 'Emer – what are you on about? What trouble?'

'Hey, I don't know the details,' Emer looked at her cagily. 'Maybe you're as innocent as you look. I bet you thought Danny was squeaky clean.'

Grace put out a hand and held the washbasin for support. 'I haven't a clue what you're talking about.'

'No, I'm beginning to think you don't,' Emer propped her bag open and shoved her makeup inside. She closed her bag and turned for the door.

'Wait,' Grace said.

Emer ignored her, and as she pulled at the door it swung back to admit Karen and Suz. Grace watched as Emer staggered through the gap between them and went out to the crowded bar.

'Hey, we were afraid you'd gone home,' Karen said, strolling in, the warmth in her face a welcome sight. 'Instead you're out here beautifying yourself.'

'Is there a more exciting party happening that we don't know about?' Suz grinned.

* * *

Grace's gaze scanned the crowded bar after she left the bathroom with Suz and Karen. There was no sign of Emer. Everything she'd said looped round and round in her head as the gang stayed on, ordering more drinks and then some finger food. Grace tried to nibble some chicken strips but they tasted like sawdust in her mouth. When they left to go to a nightclub, Grace allowed herself to be swept up with the group as they strolled along in high spirits, laughing and chatting and joking, moving up through alternating pools of street light and shadows in the night-time, city-centre streets.

She couldn't make sense of what Emer had said, any more than she couldn't make sense of Danny's accident. The noise in the nightclub hurt her head and faces swam in her field of vision. She was a million miles beyond the Grace Bailey who'd once found the beat of these places exciting. In her mind's eye, she was back in her apartment again, looking at a laughing Danny framed in the doorway just before he walked out of her life on that ill-fated night. She'd a strong suspicion that Stacy, his wannabe-girlfriend was behind the nasty tricks that had been played on her, but she was more upset with the thoughts of Danny being in some sort of trouble, and his sisters seeming to think that Grace might have led him astray. She was determined to get to the bottom of this, even if it meant hearing something she'd rather not know.

Chapter Forty-two

Lucia held the foil strip between her fingers. She pressed a bubble so that the small white tablet it contained fell into the palm of her hand. She studied it for several moments, angling her hand under the light of the bathroom mirror, watching the way it gleamed like a small seed pearl. The difference between taking or not taking this pill was the difference between having a well-structured, comfortable if predictable life, and having the equivalent, as Robert had put it, of a bomb exploding in the middle of everything they'd built up between them.

In the ten days since she'd come home from France, the conversation she'd had with Robert early on in their relationship had been crashing round and round in her head.

* * *

They were enjoying a weekend break in Sligo. They were sitting in the hotel conservatory having pre-dinner drinks. Lucia felt relaxed and happy as she glanced out to the silvery gleam of the sea in the distance, and turned to the man by her side. She had been dating him for several months by now, and it was still very fresh and new. She loved the way she was finding out all about him, discovering how much they had in common and how deeply he was embedding himself in her heart.

'Ruth is pregnant – again,' he said, dropping it casually into the conversation.

'Oh. Was it—' she'd been about to say 'planned' but thought better of it, considering the carefully neutral look on Robert's face. She sensed there was more to his throwaway remark than he was letting on, as though he wanted to sound her out, and see how she reacted. She'd met and liked Robert's sister, Ruth, and got on well with her, sometimes better than he related to her himself, she suspected.

Ruth was the very antithesis of her brother. She didn't appear to have a single-minded bone in her body, any great ambitions, or any order to her life, yet she was obviously doing something right because she held down a job as a part-time lecturer in Carlow University. Her husband worked in an educational supplies firm and she had two children under five. Her house was always in chaos and she lived in the kind of relaxed, haphazard muddle that would have irritated Lucia. Lucia privately felt Ruth could have done with taking her au pair to one side, and insisting on a few ground rules and regulations for the children.

Like, no sneaking into the parents' bed at six in the morning – it was just as well they had a king-sized bed, she'd said to Lucia sounding as if she was boasting. Lucia hadn't thought it was anything to boast about. Like, no television – a bad habit for a small child to get into, and ridiculous to allow them any television at all. That also went for mobile screens of any description.

'She'll have three children under the age of six,' Robert said. He spoke in a perfectly even tone of voice but she knew Robert well enough by now to sense there were weighty questions behind his comments.

What do you think of that, Lucia? Do you think she needs her head examined? Or do you envy her three children under six? The silence stretched between them. So far, there had been no talk yet of any kind of future, no tentative plans, no hints of any kind of commitment, both of them happy where they were right now, working during the week, socialising at the weekends and plenty of good sex to keep them both happy. She sensed that whatever she said would be important to the future of their relationship and would be a line drawn in the sand.

'Good for Ruth if that's what she wants,' Lucia said. 'But ...' she hesitated. Would he think less of her as a woman? Was this a test to see how much she wanted children? Most couples wanted to have a family, after all. Most men wanted a son to follow in their footsteps.

'But?'

She took a deep breath. 'Rather her than me.'

'Oh?'

'I can't see myself in her shoes, ever,' Lucia said, wondering how best to put what she wanted to say.

'Do you mean three children under six, or children full stop?'

'I think children are brilliant and wonderful and all that, and ...' she began. Then she decided that honesty was the only policy here, even if it might end their relationship. This was too important to be fudged. 'Robert, maybe it's just as well we're having this conversation now,' she said. 'Because no matter what happens with us, or doesn't happen, it's only fair to let you know. I don't feel I'm inclined to motherhood at all, and I can't see babies or children featuring in my life.'

'I might as well admit that I don't see them featuring in my life either.'

'Don't you?'

'No. Like you, I think small children are amazing, but it's not for me.'

Something evaporated inside her. A fear she'd had that Robert would finish with her when he found out about her aversion to all things motherhood. She had to be sure. 'You might change your mind when you're forty.'

He laughed. 'I won't.'

'Or even fifty.'

'Definitely not.'

'Not even sixty, when you start to look back on your life? What if you have regrets?'

'Hey, I won't be looking back on my life then, I'll be still going onwards and upwards.'

She had to know why he felt like this, to make sure she understood it. 'Why don't you want children?'

'Lots of reasons. How long have you got?' Robert said. 'Being a parent is a huge, demanding, often thankless responsibility that I don't ever want to take on. Even from a bigger perspective, you just have to look around you. The world is harsh and unfair, cruel at times. God knows what direction this planet is heading in. Seven billion people, the majority living in fear or poverty. Why bring more life onto it? Then there's the messiness of it all, the upheaval in your life. Your weekends, your holidays would never be the same. It's not for me, thank you very much, and I hope that doesn't change anything between us.'

She felt a tiny swell in her heart that they agreed on this major life choice. Then again she'd sensed from the outset that she had lots in common with this man. They both wanted similar things out of life. Security and certainty.

'What you've said ... it doesn't change anything for me,' she reassured him.

'Are you sure, Lucia?'

'Absolutely,' she said, relief and conviction running through her veins in an unwavering straight line. 'I don't think – I *know* – you can't have it all,' Lucia said. 'Motherhood would derail your career.

Your children would have to come first. They'd take over your life. And my career is important to me. I like my job. I like to know where I stand and I don't want to do anything that would put that at risk.'

'Is that the real reason? Your job and career?'

'I'm the kind of person who likes to give one hundred and ten per cent to whatever I do,' she said, smiling at him. 'I want to give my full attention to my career and my relationship, and that means I wouldn't have enough left over for the demands of motherhood.'

'Well then ...' Robert took her hand. 'It looks like we have an agreement of sorts.'

'Yes,' she said, feeling a little faint. She knew there could be no going back on an issue as serious and life changing as this. She knew what she wanted: security and assurance and not the element of uncertainty and instability that having children could bring.

Then on a weekend break in London, to celebrate the two-year anniversary of their first meeting, Robert brought up the subject again, asking her if she'd changed her mind about wanting children. She told him she hadn't. The following afternoon while they were strolling in the palace gardens at Kensington, he stopped by a fountain and asked her to marry him.

'I want this to be romantic,' he said, producing a small box. 'I love you, Lucia, I never thought I'd meet a woman like you and I want to always have you in my life.'

She said yes.

Everything had gone according to plan until the financial company where Robert held a senior position began to make downsizing noises, before they were taken over by a global conglomerate. Robert's CEO quietly called him aside to give him advance warning that heads at the top were about to roll due to the takeover and his job was at risk.

For a few nightmare weeks, Lucia thought her worst fears were being realised. They couldn't survive on her salary, not with their mortgage and car loans. And what about the lifestyle she had come to love? No one really knew how much she appreciated not having to scrimp and save in advance, or how much she valued being able to use her credit card for the occasional luxury without worrying unduly about the bill. Not even Robert understood why she was so gutted at his news. She'd never told him of the nightmarish time in her life when her parents' business had gone under and all the security she'd ever known had disintegrated in front of her. She couldn't go back to that.

However, fate was kind. This time the nightmare was short lived, as before he was even made redundant, Robert was offered a job in London, more prestigious and better salaried than the one he'd had in Dublin.

'It's a choice between hanging on in Dublin where there are hundreds of applicants for every suitable vacancy, and relocating …' he'd left the rest of the sentence hanging in the air.

'There is no real choice,' Lucia had said, her mind already racing ahead, visualising the changes this would bring and trying to rationalise their changed life. 'You could commute, couldn't you? Thousands do it every week.' She'd closed her ears to the word 'relocate'. No way was she giving up the security of her job. Besides, she liked living in Dublin; it was familiar and comfortable to her. She loved London, but only for occasional breaks. Thoughts of living in the huge, buzzy metropolis were one thing, but finding her feet in a new job, and starting out as a small fish in a big pond would fill her with uncertainty.

'Wouldn't you miss me?' he'd asked.

'Of course,' she'd said. 'But we could FaceTime every night, and the weeks would fly by. Think of how much we'd enjoy our weekends. We could take turns going over and back.'

'FaceTime isn't the same as snuggling up in bed with you and feeling your hair tickling my nose,' he'd said.

'Robert! Most week nights I don't even remember falling asleep and neither do you. I think this could be good for us, it will keep our marriage fresh and alive. Anyway, it'll only be for a while, until things pick up in Dublin.'

* * *

Lucia popped her pill, left the bathroom and went downstairs.

'A while' had turned into two years. The economy had started to pick up in Dublin and now there was a fresh optimism and vibrancy in the air, but they were fine as they were. They were *great* as they were. Robert was going from strength to strength in London, and she was doing equally well in Izobel; more-than-respectable salaries were landing into their bank accounts each month, and they were enjoying the good things in life and could continue to do so indefinitely – so why rock the boat? She'd never have to cope with the financial burden of raising a child, or face crèche fees, or worry about being able to give the child everything possible.

Then again she'd never have the sense of fulfilment that having a child of her very own to kiss and cuddle would give her. She'd never have a drawer full of homemade birthday or mother's day cards with stick insect figures and kisses straggling across the page. She'd never know what it felt like to watch a son or daughter grow up. If this was the price she'd have to pay to keep her life on a steady, even keel, she could deal with it, couldn't she?

Lucia poured a glass of wine and switched on the television. She was beginning to wonder if she could deal with the price of Robert being in London. Since the holidays, she'd found herself thinking of him alone in London more and more, wondering what temptations lay in wait. For either of them.

Aiden Burke had done an exaggerated double-take when she'd returned to the office after the holidays. He'd teased her about being the new girl, because he didn't recognise her with that fab hairstyle. Then, unexpectedly contrite for him, he'd asked her to forget what he'd said as he was terrified of not being PC.

She'd felt like replying that it didn't matter what he said or didn't say. It was all in his eyes and the way they'd followed her around that afternoon.

Dangerous.

Chapter Forty-three

The route to Mayo seemed familiar to Grace. The motorway dissected the broad, lake-filled plains of Westmeath and travelled up through the scenic beauty of Roscommon. It was over three months since she'd passed this way, when the countryside had flowed past the window in a blur of pale green fuzz. Lucia had been driving, and Grace had been sitting with a heart like a slab of stone. This time she was driving, and the surrounding countryside sparkled and burst with colour under late June sunshine.

She wondered how often Danny had come this way. He'd probably known every curve in the motorway, every rise and fall of the mountain ranges and every glimmering lake or shiny-slick river like the back of his hand.

It was Saturday morning, a week since she'd been out celebrating Karen's birthday. No one knew she was going out to Mayo. Not Matt, who was such a good listener, nor Lucia, who was doing her utmost to be a supportive sister. She could picture their reactions if she were to tell them she was travelling to Mayo to see Danny's mother as a result of a short conversation in the ladies with a drunken stranger. Danny's mother didn't know she was on the way either, so Grace was taking a chance, hoping the element of surprise would work in her favour.

She pulled into a garage on the outskirts of Castlebar, where she sipped coffee and ate a muffin. All of her instincts told her that this visit could change everything. She'd looked up Danny's parents' address on Google Maps, and half an hour later she drove up a laneway outside the town and pulled into the driveway of an attractive, white-painted bungalow. The front lawns were bordered by neat flowerbeds. The curtains were pulled back, and the windows reflected the sunshine and were open to the fresh morning air, which told her someone was at home. There was a car parked down to the side of the house, in front of a detached garage.

Her legs were shaky as she got out of the car because it hit her forcibly that arriving unexpectedly like this with her questions wasn't fair to Danny's mother.

His sister answered the door, the girl in the graduation photograph – Amy? Her polite, welcoming smile changed to a frown as she recognised Grace. She didn't invite her in, but looked back over her shoulder and called for her mother.

Tess McBride came up the hallway. She was wearing a navy tracksuit that was hanging off her like it would off a clothes hanger.

'Oh,' she said, 'it's you.' Her thin hand fluttered up to her throat.

Grace winced. On a scale of one to ten, this was up there at nine in the league of bad ideas. 'Can I come in?' she asked.

'Yes, of course.' Tess stood back as Grace, her heart quivering, stepped into the hallway of the house where Danny had once lived. Her gaze darted around; Danny had been here – he'd walked up the tiled floor of this hallway hundreds of times, he'd passed by the table holding a vase of flowers, he'd probably stopped to look at his face in the wide, ornate mirror before leaving the house, but there was no imprint of him anywhere. She was the worst kind of intruder – tramping over the eggshells of Danny's home life while he was no longer around.

'Amy, put the kettle on, please,' Tess said.

Amy gave Grace a challenging look before she disappeared down the hall. She, too, seemed to view Grace as some kind of trespasser. Tess showed her into a spacious room that looked out to the front of the house. The room was cosy but elegantly appointed with a cream damask three-piece suite and matching drapes drawn back across the wide window. Occasional tables held framed photographs and a vase of flowers. There were paintings on the wall, and a large photo frame containing a collage of family photographs. Grace thought she recognised a younger Danny in some of them, and she felt a slight catch in her chest.

She shouldn't be here. She'd only known Danny a few short weeks. His family had years of history with him, he'd grown up with them, a beloved son and brother, and theirs was by far the greater loss. What right had she got to be here, upsetting everyone with her questions?

She had the right to clear up the suggestion that she was in any way to blame for Danny's death.

'My husband's not here,' Tess told her. 'He's disappearing more and more into his work,' she explained.

'How are you keeping yourself?' Grace asked her.

'I don't know,' Tess said, smiling faintly. 'The days just keep on coming, one after another, and then they turn into weeks and even more time has gone by. I think I'm still in shock. You wake up at three in the morning and it hits you like a sledgehammer. You don't want to get out of bed ever again, but what else can you do?'

Amy arrived in with a tray containing mugs of coffee, milk, sugar and biscuits which she put down on a side table near her mother.

'Thanks, love,' Tess said. 'We had a lot of visitors, in the beginning,' she went on. 'Amy was run off her feet making tea and coffee, weren't you, Amy? But it's died down a bit now.'

'I'm going into town to meet Jane,' Amy said. 'Can I have the car?'

'Of course, love. Just take care and drive safely, won't you?'

'I will take care.' Her slightly grudging tone of voice told Grace that she'd been told this many times before. Tess was probably wrapping her daughters in cotton wool after what had happened to Danny. Amy must have been sorry for the way she'd spoken, for she bent down and hugged her mother tightly. 'I won't be too long.' She left, ignoring Grace completely.

Tess waited until Grace was sitting back with her coffee before she asked her why she had called. 'You hardly came all the way from Dublin to ask how I'm doing,' she said.

'I want to talk about Danny, if that's okay,' Grace began.

'It all depends on what you want to talk about,' Tess said, her tone neutral.

Grace felt hopelessly out of her depth. Sitting on the edge of her seat, all neat and folded into herself, Danny's mother had an empty look in her eyes. Her hands trembled a little as she raised her cup of coffee to her mouth. And no wonder, for this was her beloved son, and Grace, the last-minute blow in, was trampling all over her grief.

'What he was like, growing up?' Grace said.

Tess didn't immediately reply, staring into space for several moments. Then she turned her gaze to Grace. 'You don't have children, Grace, do you?'

'No.' Grace felt her face flushing.

'Then I can't expect you to have the remotest idea of what it's like when a child of yours dies,' Tess said. 'It's beyond words, it's beyond any pain you can describe, it's a total devastation of everything you once held dear. I feel sorry for my daughters. At least I've had the best part of a life, I don't care if the life I knew is over, but I can't be there for them in the way I used to be, so our family life is shattered and wrenched apart, torn down the middle. No matter what happens in the months and years ahead, we will always feel his loss, like a dark cloud over everything. You want to know what Danny was like growing up? He was a beautiful baby, all nine pounds of him, I wanted to eat him up and keep him safe from all harm forever. He turned into a typical boy, he got into mischief, he got out of mischief, he had fights with his sisters, he loved them to bits, he gave us heartache, he gave us love, but most of all he was alive and breathing, we could touch him and feel him, laugh and joke with him, sometimes have a row. The worst thing is the physical pain, it's in the way your arms ache to hold him, and your ears strain for the sound of his voice, your cheek is sore, waiting for a kiss that never comes. Your eyes see him everywhere, and sometimes you think you see his shadow but when you look again there's just an empty space. There's sadness and anger and sorrow, a whole lot of sorrow and black devastation that I wouldn't wish on my worst enemy.'

Grace was frozen to the spot, gripping her cooling mug of coffee in her hand. The sun had shifted a little and it slanted cheerful columns of light across the carpeted floor. In the hush of the room, she heard a clock ticking somewhere and thought of all the minutes and hours it had ticked away since Danny's heart had stopped beating. She had an urge to smash it up.

'No,' she said eventually, her voice husky. 'I don't comprehend the enormity of what you and your family are going through. I only knew him a few weeks but I miss him very much. I had an amazing time with him, and I was hoping to find out more about him and his life, before he met me.'

'Why?'

'Because …' Grace faltered. Why indeed? Because she was trying to find out why she had the instinctive feeling that his death hadn't been an accident, and why a woman in a pub had said his sisters were blaming her for his death.

'Amazing,' Tess said, repeating Grace's word as though it had particular meaning for her. 'In what way was your time with him amazing?'

'I've kind of told you already,' Grace said.

'You probably have, but it's impossible to take in anything when you're still in a kind of shocked limbo. All I recall is that you told me his last few weeks were happy. '

'We were both happy,' Grace said. 'Things had become … rather stagnant for me. I was at the end of a relationship that was going nowhere … Danny helped me to pull my life around and brighten it up, and make me feel like I wanted to get up in the mornings and make the most of the day.'

'You're not just saying all this to make me feel better?'

'No, of course not. Danny was … as I said, amazing, but in an ordinary kind of way. We didn't do anything extravagant, we didn't spend silly money on going out or enjoying ourselves, we just made the most of the ordinary, simple pleasures in life. The weeks we were together were special. I went out to work, most days, but we were so wrapped up in each other we hardly bothered with anyone else, I never met any of his friends, I'm sure that would have happened in time …' her voice trailed away at the sharp look in Tess McBride's eyes.

'Are you telling me the God's honest truth?'

'Of course I am. What reason would I have for not telling you the truth?'

'And did Danny ever talk to you about anything that happened in his … his past life?'

Something in Tess's tone chilled Grace, like the touch of a cold ice cube sliding down her spine. There was a funny white nose in her head. Just focus on good things, she urged herself, and not what Tess might mean by Danny's 'past life'. 'Not much, no,' she said. 'We lived very much in the present, Danny had a big thing about that, no looking back, no planning too far ahead, we mostly spoke about what was happening that day, that week. We talked about going hot air ballooning for my thirtieth birthday, but that won't happen now.'

'So you don't know ...' Tess said.

'Don't know what?' Grace shivered, a sense of foreboding unsettling her.

'Forgive me, Grace, but this is very difficult for me. I'm not sure if I should be telling you, Danny's father would be completely against it ...'

'Tell me what?'

'Can I just say first that what you are describing about Danny ... the kind of person he was ... it's wonderful ...' she shook her head. 'When we heard about the accident, that was the first we knew that he'd moved out of Phibsboro without telling us, so we feared the worst, but the autopsy came back clear and there were no traces found ...'

By now every nerve in Grace's head was jangling at the alarm bells shrieking inside her.

'Traces of what?' she made herself ask, forcing the words out through her mouth.

Tess gave Grace a smile that was both fragile and heart-rending. 'Traces of drugs,' she said.

'No. Not Danny.'

Tess shook her head. 'Yes, Grace, I'm afraid so.'

Everything Grace knew about Danny rose up into the air and shattered into a million pieces that whirled around like a giddy blizzard of torn ticker-tape. She closed her eyes and dug her nails into the palm of her hand to try and centre herself. After a few moments when she opened them again, Tess McBride was still sitting in the same chair, watching her with the same sad, brittle smile, but everything else had altered beyond recognition.

Chapter Forty-four

'You don't think it will ever happen in your family,' Tess said. 'You read and hear about it in the newspapers and on the media, there are talks in the school, but *your* children are fine. You've raised them from babyhood, and given them every chance in life. You know them, you've given them your blood, sweat and tears, they are part of you from the hairs on the crown of their head down to their toenails. You've cherished them carefully, looked after their every need. You're so happy when they turn out to be confident, able teenagers …' Tess paused and dabbed her eyes with a tissue.

Grace could do nothing but listen, stilled by this awful knowledge that turned everything on its head. The carpeted floor had dulled a little, as the sun had drifted behind a cloud, but then it shone again, the bright columns shifting at slightly different angles across the room. The clock was still ticking and Grace wanted to tell it to shut up; didn't it realise that the time bomb had already gone off? She wanted to go back to the girl who had woken up that morning before she had decided to drive to Mayo. Would she have come? Better again, she wanted to go back to the moment before Danny had left her apartment and somehow make him stay.

Tess pulled herself together, straightening her slim shoulders as if to ready them for taking the burden, and she continued talking, her eyes fixed to a point on the wall, and Grace knew she was seeing it all replay in her mind.

'They study reasonably hard,' Tess said. 'They do well in school and get the points needed in their exams, and oh, the excitement when they get an offer of their top college place and all the years of study have been worthwhile ... And then they go to college and it's all so new and exciting and wonderful, and you don't even realise when they've fallen in with the wrong crowd ... it's small things at first, the odd missed lecture, a late assignment, thinking he could be a little drunk, only there's no smell of alcohol, not turning up for his sister's birthday party ...' Tess was lost in her reverie for a moment and then her gaze turned to Grace. 'They're adults, you have no control anymore. You can't exactly ground them. And everything you've ever done, all the nights you've paced the floor with them as babies, all the times you watched over them as toddlers, the pride you took in their small achievements, all the love you've lavished counts for zilch. Simple, really. The simple but implacable truth.'

Grace swallowed. 'I'm ... in shock. I never knew, never even guessed. I don't know what to say.' She took a long, shaky breath, trying to get oxygen into her chest, which felt compressed with pain.

'What can you say about it all?' Tess said. 'Absolutely nothing. We did everything we could for Danny. We had a few years of him dabbling with drugs on and off; ecstasy, cocaine, mostly ... he wasn't a full-blown addict, but he was on the edges of it all the time and it was enough to disrupt his life. As well as the family life. He never finished college, and the longest he held down a job was for less than a year. It was difficult for all of us, and hard on the girls. Then this time last year everything changed ...' Tess paused.

'What happened?'

'One of his so-called friends overdosed and died,' Tess said. 'I think he had some dodgy cocaine and it was a huge wake-up call for Danny. He was absolutely devastated. I think it really hit home to him that he'd been skittering on the edge of something dangerous and the day of his friend's funeral, he agreed to go into rehab.'

Grace's head was reeling.

Tess continued, speaking the words as though they were a litany she'd gone over and over in her head, trying to make sense of it all, 'We got him into a centre in County Wicklow, and he really seemed to engage in it. Then he left, last November, before the programme was finished. He seemed good. We thought he had recovered. He was home one weekend and apologised for all the hurt he'd caused, all the anxiety he'd brought on us. He said he'd pay back all the money we'd given him, in time. He had a small legacy that his grandmother had left him which we'd been holding for him, and he said he was going to use that to help pay his way while he did a distance-learning college course.'

Grace felt a chasm in the pit of her stomach. 'There was no redundancy or website business, was there?' she asked softy.

Tess shook her head. 'No. That's what I couldn't understand … especially when you talked about contacts. That rang an alarm bell for me. I didn't know what type of contacts you meant. Danny probably didn't want you to know he had begun an online addiction counselling course. He wanted to help others, he said. Unfortunately his father had a different idea. Joseph wanted him to come home and stay here while he studied. He wanted him under our roof so he could keep an eye on him, and that's what they rowed about over Christmas. Joseph told him he'd stand a better chance of making a future for himself and staying on the straight and narrow if he was back living with us. Danny refused. He told us he was completely clean and would be from now on, and he was deeply grateful for our support, but we had to learn to trust him. One word led to another, and there was a terrible row between Danny and his father two days after Christmas, and he headed back to Dublin. He called me occasionally, I called him regularly and he assured me he was fine, he was doing great, not to be worrying about him, he was standing on his own two feet … Joseph was still upset, naturally, so that's the place we were in when we got the phone call that ripped everything apart …' Tess paused and wiped her eyes.

Grace sat, shell-shocked. So much of what Tess said made sense in a way. She only had to look at the way Danny had lived his life, like someone who had valued and appreciated how good it was to be alive and well. He'd been given a fresh start, a chance to begin his life over again and build it from the bottom up.

'When we first heard about the accident, our immediate reaction was that Danny had been careless because he'd fallen off the wagon somehow,' Tess said.

Grace shook her head. She'd have known, wouldn't she? 'No. Definitely not. You hardly think I …?'

'We didn't know what to think,' Tess said. 'Our heads were all over the place. We didn't mention Danny's history to the police who were investigating the accident – Joseph and I had a difference of opinion over that – but it was just as well, because the toxicology reports came back clear. There was no evidence at all of any drug or alcohol use.'

'I could have told you that,' Grace whispered.

'Later we heard that there were signs of damage to some of his organs …' Tess paused.

Grace closed her eyes for a moment. 'No. Please, I can't get my head around this.'

'I know, it's very tough to take in,' Tess said. 'It was only when I called to your apartment that evening that I began to wonder if we'd been mistaken about you,' Tess dabbed at her eyes again. 'From what you've said, Danny *was* telling us the truth, he *was* doing great and standing on his own two feet. Whatever he'd done in rehab, whatever he'd picked up, it seemed to have worked this time out. Maybe he was more mature, maybe something was said that connected with him at the right level … who knows. You must have been doing something right with my son, helping him to sort out his life.'

Even though Grace was in shock, she needed to set this straight with Tess. 'It wasn't me sorting out Danny, or doing something right,' she said. 'It was the other way around. Danny made me think about what I wanted or didn't want out of life, or where I was wasting my time. He made me feel I could … oh, God, do things that really mattered to me, and not because they were things I felt I should be doing.'

Tess was silent for a moment. 'No matter what, I loved my son,' she said. 'I was very unhappy with what he was doing and the way he was wasting his life, but I loved him with every cell in my body, as did his father.'

'I know you did,' Grace said quietly. 'But I don't agree with something you said earlier,' she ventured. 'You spoke about all your love counting for nothing … well maybe Danny lost sight of it for a while but it was there, it was in him, he was all about kindness and tenderness and love, it had to have been there, in his core somewhere. He took pride in showing me your family photo, okay he passed a couple of jokey comments about family ties, in the way most people do, but only people who are secure in that love and who take it for granted can afford to joke about it in that light-hearted way. Does that make sense?'

Tess's face relaxed a fraction. 'Yes, kind of. I'm glad you came today and we had this chat, even if that's selfish of me, because I know I gave you a shock. Joseph and I are hoping to go to Redfern Hill, the centre in Wicklow, as soon as we feel up to it, to talk to John Gordon, his mentor.'

'I can't get my head around what you've told me. I'm just going to remember the Danny I knew,' Grace said. And there was no sense in imagining what could have happened between them in the future. Their future had evaporated in a split second on a Thursday evening.

'Forgive me, Grace, and I know you've already talked to me, but could I hear it again, what the last week, the last few days were like with Danny?'

'I'm quite happy to talk about it, it's all I want to do,' Grace said.

* * *

They were both mopping their eyes by the time Grace was finished talking about her time with Danny. She filled in details she hadn't mentioned before and Tess leapt on them. Afterwards, she showed Grace his bedroom.

'It hasn't changed much from the time he left for college,' she said. 'I've tidied it a bit but I know I'll have to clear it … or something, but not just yet.'

Danny's bedroom had sports posters on the walls, a table with a small television and sound system, shelves full of books and old CDs but few knick-knacks; all neat and tidy. Grace tried to picture him moving around here, but it could have been a stranger's room it seemed so flat, empty and unused, long devoid of the essence of Danny, with nothing there to remind her of him.

Tess brought her into a bright, homely kitchen where Grace had more coffee and a sandwich, sitting at a big pine table. Framed in the picture window was a panoramic view of the peaceful countryside falling away into folds of green and gold. It was easy to connect with Danny's spirit against this landscape, to visualise him taking milk cartons out of the fridge, foraging for cereals in the cupboards, or boiling an egg on the cooker as he assembled his breakfast or a late-night snack. Her heart bled for the silent space he'd left behind.

Amy returned from her shopping trip, acknowledging Grace's presence guardedly, handing back the car keys to her mother with a flourish before disappearing into her room.

'She has taken it very hard,' Tess explained. 'She blames anyone and everyone who had a connection to Danny. I'm leaving her alone for a while because it's still very raw, but I'll talk to her soon.'

'You seem to have everyone else to look out for as well as yourself,' Grace said.

'That helps in a way, because it takes my mind off me, and stops me from going around in a circle,' Tess gave her a faint smile.

It was only when Grace was gathering her bag and car keys and preparing to leave that she realised she'd never voiced her concerns to Tess about the manner of Danny's death. Neither had she spoken of the incidents she'd found intimidating, but after her conversation with Emer she had a strong suspicion that Stacy was behind them. Amy actually came out of her room to say goodbye, and Tess's eyes still held a faint, bittersweet glow in the aftermath of talking about her son. She sensed that neither of them would be very receptive to Grace stirring up suspicions about how Danny had died.

But knowing what she knew now cast a different light on everything, didn't it? She needed to work out how much of Danny's past she was prepared to tell Matt Slattery, without compromising the essence of Danny in any way. Because maybe she'd been right all along about someone wanting to cause Danny harm – hardly Stacy, his devoted admirer, but someone he could have crossed paths with in another menacing life.

Chapter Forty-five

Lucia's Monday morning started badly. Her alarm went off, shrilling obediently across the silence of her bedroom at six forty-five a.m. exactly, as it did every weekday morning. She reached across her bedside table and silenced it. She'd been in the middle of a dream, the details of which were sliding out of her grasp. Then, chasing the last, gauzy remnants of it before it disappeared completely, she turned around in the bed, stretching her legs across the empty space where Robert slept when he was home, and promptly fell back asleep. She woke up almost an hour later. Feeling fuzzy and disorientated, she picked up her mobile, her eyes flying wide open when she registered that it was after half-past seven. She jumped out of bed so galvanised that she became dizzy.

Today of all days, she fumed, leaping into the shower, not even waiting for the warm water to come through as she stood shivering under the blast of cold water. Instant wake-up. She had an important presentation to give at ten o'clock and had wanted to be at her desk by eight at the latest. Now the rush-hour traffic would be far thicker and it would take twice as long to get to the office. She hopped out of the shower, only half-drying herself, so that her tights and blouse clung to her damp skin. Bloody fantastic. She pressed a towel to her hair, mopping up the worst of the wet tendrils before going back into the bedroom and attacking it with the dryer.

She called a taxi to ferry her into the office, figuring it would be faster than driving herself as it could use the bus lanes, and she could go over her presentation notes on the way in. But even this went against her, because her notes were not, after all, in her briefcase. She was flustered and scattered as she finally click-clacked across the tiled foyer of Izobel at five to nine.

She went down to the conference room first to check that all was in order. Her executive team was already there; as she reached the threshold, she heard laughter carrying through the open doorway, which was swiftly muffled as she stepped inside. Sadie was engrossed in setting out paper and pens, Nick was hovering around the podium, ostensibly checking the remote pad for the equipment, and Helen was making a bigger-than-necessary job out of arranging the chairs at equal distance to each other around the big oval table. The studied silence following the suppressed laughter made the hairs rise on the nape of her neck. It was quite obvious that she'd been at the centre of their jollity, and also the butt of it.

She rose to her full height and swept up the room. 'Helen, I think those chairs are fine as they are, we're not having a tea party,' she snapped. 'Sadie, that job should have been delegated, you've more important things to do, and Nick, that equipment should have been checked out thoroughly before you went home on Friday.' She wasn't doing herself any favours by being so snippy with them, Lucia realised, but she felt so thrown off centre that she couldn't gather herself sufficiently to rise above it all.

Back in her office, she searched in vain for her notes, throwing open some presses and rummaging feverishly through the shelves when they were not to be found on her desk.

'Is everything okay, Lucia? Or do you need a hand?'

She turned around. Aiden Burke. Of course, who else? Word had probably reached him already that she'd been barking orders at her staff in the conference room.

'How come you manage to turn up at the wrong moments?' she said crossly. 'And what are you doing in here so early on a Monday anyhow?'

'Ouch. What's the problem?'

She vacillated between telling him to get lost and mind his own business and admitting defeat. In the face of his kind concern, she threw her hands up into the air and said, 'I can't find my notes for the presentation this morning.'

'Does that matter?' he asked. 'I'd say you know every point you want to make off by heart.'

'I do, and you'll probably find this hilarious, but they're a kind of safety net for me, to be sure to be sure.'

'I don't find that hilarious, it's okay to need a safety net, it means that you're just as human as the rest of us behind that power suit. Where did you last have them?'

'I was sure I put them into my briefcase on Friday evening. Hold on …' she lifted her briefcase, opened the zip on the side pocket, and pulled out some papers. 'I don't believe this,' she said.

'If you need a hand with anything at all let me know,' Aiden said. 'Right now I'm getting you some coffee.'

'Thanks a million.' She flashed him a smile, immensely grateful for the takeout coffee he put on her desk ten minutes later. Sometimes the ordinary, little things in life really helped to sweeten a challenging day. She wondered who was looking after Robert when he needed the little things in life at the beginning of a long, busy week.

She lost her train of thought twice during the presentation, using the delaying tactic of taking a few sips of water to give her some valuable thinking time. But that didn't work; each time she glanced at the screen, she felt like weeping, for the words were swimming in front of her.

How important, in the overall scheme of life, was high-quality survey data when it came to measuring cosmetic sampling? Who gave a shit what methodology was used to analyse fragrance sales? It was all just number-crunching. Statistics and research could be slanted and adapted to produce any kind of results. What did all this really matter? She looked around at the dozen or so people sitting around the conference room table, appalled by what she was thinking and how easily she'd framed her thoughts in such coarse language. Someone had pressed the switch to close the blinds to stop the sunlight from interfering with the visuals, but there was a kink in one or two slats and a pencil-thin beam of sunlight streamed through and played across the ceiling like a silvery strobe. It made Lucia think of a magic wand and for a long, contrary, most unlike-Lucia moment, she wished it could magic her out of here right now and transport her to the sunny day outside.

Then she remembered she'd been dreaming about Robert and Miranda before her alarm had shrilled, just as her mobile sounded from her jacket pocket, which she'd hung over a chair to the side of the podium. It was the ring tone reserved for Grace and it echoed round the room. Rather than make an undignified dash for it, she decided to wait until it rang out. Eventually it stopped and just as she drew breath to continue, it beeped twice to tell her she had a message.

'I guess I didn't take enough notice of the housekeeping rules myself,' she attempted a joke. It fell flat, as there was no answering ripple of laughter from her audience, just a big wink from Aiden sitting at the back of the group. 'My apologies for the interruption. Let me resume from point three,' she went on in her formal Izobel voice, using every ounce of energy to drag her scattered thoughts together.

* * *

'I can't say what it is over the phone,' Grace said, sounding subdued, when Lucia called her later. 'But it's about Danny and it's important. I've been speaking to his mother.'

'What made you do that?'

'I bumped into someone who knew Danny, when I was out for Karen's thirtieth. She remembered me from the funeral, her sister Jennifer was in St Anne's with you.' There was a pause that Lucia didn't fill, waiting to see what was coming next. 'And she hinted that Danny had been in some kind of trouble,' Grace continued. 'She also spoke of an ex-girlfriend, Stacy, and I think she could be the one harassing me …'

Stacy. The name Jennifer had mentioned to her at the reunion, that she'd held back from Grace.

'I'll fill you in on everything when I see you,' Grace said. 'Can we meet soon? Either your place or mine?'

Lucia thought rapidly. 'Call over tonight after work,' she said. 'Get a taxi and we'll have wine and … I've some frozen dinners, we can have them.' So what if it was the start of the week? She'd need wine tonight. She'd turned down Aiden's invitation to lunch, deciding that she'd have to nip whatever was fizzing between them in the bud. She'd known by his reaction that he'd got the message and was unhappy with it. Having Grace over would be a good excuse for a large glass of Sauvignon Blanc.

Only that what Grace had to say about Danny caught Lucia totally unprepared.

Chapter Forty-six

'What do you mean, drugs?' Lucia asked. Something hot stained her cheeks as though she'd been slapped. She spilled some wine on the table as she refilled their glasses. She grabbed a paper napkin to mop it up and almost knocked over her glass. Grace shrugged helplessly. 'Just that. Danny, according to his mother, was a recovering addict. He dabbled in cocaine, mostly. Speed. Ecstasy. Not heroin.'

'I don't believe you.'

Grace shook her head. 'I know,' she said. 'I didn't believe it either. It came as a total shock. I've had a couple of days to get used to it but I couldn't get my head around it at first.'

Lucia's heart was starting to pound. 'When did you find out?'

'When I went down to Mayo, to visit his mother last Saturday.' Grace filled her in on the chance meeting with Emer, and what she'd told her about Stacy, who was probably behind the incidents that had unsettled Grace. 'But that was nothing compared to what Danny's mother told me.'

'You had no idea until then?' she asked.

'Absolutely not.'

'And there was no sign of …' Lucia's question trailed away at the look that flashed in Grace's eyes.

'*Are you joking?* Do you even have to ask that?'

'Sorry.'

'All the time Danny was with me, he was fine, I know he was. His mother said he'd been in rehab up to last November and had had a successful spell there,' Grace's voice was quivery. 'He'd left early, though, two weeks before he was supposed to.'

'Jesus, that was close. He was just out a month when he met you.'

It explained a lot, however, Lucia thought, taking a big glug of wine. It explained why Grace's details about Danny's past life were sketchy, and why he'd kept them from her. It explained his almost childish candour, his simplistic way of looking at life like someone with no baggage – because all his baggage had been left behind when he'd walked out of rehab. And it also explained his attitude of not doing anything in life unless it fed your soul. Danny McBride had been a survivor. He'd seen how bad it could get but he'd managed to pull himself back from the brink.

Grace was talking. 'So, you see, there's even more of a reason now, for the way Danny died.'

'Had it something to do with drugs?'

'It could have. That's what I want to talk about.'

'But wouldn't the police have discovered that in the autopsy? There would have been traces in his system.'

'I didn't mean it like that, Lucia. Even his parents feared that, but tests showed that Danny was clean. I could have told them that already. I swear on my life he wasn't using anything all the time he was with me. But I think his past could have come back to bite him and had something to do with his death.'

'In what way?' Lucia asked, suddenly needing more wine for this.

Grace looked at her as though she was failing to grasp the essentials. 'It's obvious. There's a whole different underworld out there that you and I know nothing about. Danny could have made some enemies, people who were unhappy that he was now clean. People who might have been afraid he'd shop them to the police – look at his friend who died from taking something dodgy – or maybe someone who was annoyed that his business with Danny had dried up … Worst-case scenario he owed someone money. I don't know enough about these things but—'

Lucia's heart sank. 'Grace, stop right there. I'm sorry but I'm going to have to be cruel to be kind. How many weeks is Danny gone now?'

'Weeks? It's months now.'

'In all that time, if something was wrong, don't you think it would have come out by now?'

'Not necessarily. Sometimes people get away with murder, don't they?'

The word fell into the silence: *murder*. Their eyes met and held, Grace's open and honest, and Lucia felt choked inside and was unable to look away.

'I'm going to talk to Matt,' Grace said.

'Matt?'

'Yeah, the cop guy I was talking to – remember?'

Lucia had forgotten about Matt. The cop guy. Surely he'd set Grace straight? 'Are you still in contact with him?'

'I am – now and again. He's been very kind and understanding. Danny wasn't even on their radar or else Matt would have picked up on it and told me, so I know he has no police record.'

For a long moment, Lucia wished she was back in the conference room, even if she was in the middle of those agonising seconds when she'd lost her train of thought, or the embarrassing moment when her recalcitrant mobile had bleeped at the wrong time. That she could handle somehow. This was different. She was incapable of helping Grace, with her own emotions firing out of control in all directions at once. She hated hurting her sister, but this had gone too far. She'd no choice other than to bring Grace down to earth. She got up from the table and went around to her, wrapping her arms around her shoulders to hold her steady.

'Grace, please,' she said, 'forget all this talk of Danny, these ideas of foul play. It didn't happen. Nothing happened. Danny had an accident, darling, an *accident*. That's all. It's life, and it can be horrible. Accidents happen all the time, and just when we least expect them to.'

Grace's face was wooden. 'I knew you didn't believe me. I knew you were just humouring me.'

'I wasn't humouring you, I know you've been deeply upset over Danny's death, and I've been helping you through that, I hope, but come on, you hardly still believe that someone killed him on *purpose?*' Lucia hadn't meant her voice to sound so shrill.

'You never liked him, did you?' Grace said, sticking out her chin.

'I did like him, but at the start, I was concerned, as your sister, about the influence he seemed to have over you.'

'Oh yeah, like what?'

'You hardly knew him when you let him move in …'

'Sometimes you just sense these things.'

'Sense what? From what I can see you didn't know all that much about him, did you?'

Grace remained silent.

'You hardly saw your friends in those few weeks,' Lucia went on.

'So? We were in the middle of our honeymoon period, well sort of. And we did go out with you and Robert, and I had you over.'

'He persuaded you to bunk off work. Is that the behaviour of a responsible adult?'

'And you never felt like bunking off work?' There was a beat of silence before Grace continued. 'I'm leaving. I'm sorry if I interrupted your evening but I can't take any more of your perfect logic for now.' She pushed back her chair and stood up.

'Grace, please, I'm sorry if that came out all wrong, but I'm just trying to help. You've put Danny up on a pedestal, but he wasn't supercharged, he was a normal human being with faults, like the rest of us. I did like him, when I got to know him better.'

Grace shook her head. 'Don't pretend, it doesn't suit you. Hey, maybe you knew something I didn't,' Grace said, laughing and crying at the same time. 'You're so squeaky clean that maybe you sensed it about him – that he had a shady past. You must have thought he was a bad influence on me.'

'Maybe in the beginning I compared him to Gavin—'

'Gavin! I always knew you and Mum preferred the up-and-coming, nice and respectable Gavin. Well guess what Lucia, I was only ever with Gavin because of you.'

'*Me?*'

'I felt I could never live up to your trail-blazing glory and then I met him, and in some way I felt he put the seal of approval on my life.'

'*What?* What are you talking about?'

Grace's face was white as she leaned back against the counter. 'I was always in your shadow, Lucia. You might be dainty and petite, but you cast a long, glittering, shadow. Big, clumpy me with only half your brains was always in that shadow. When I met Gavin and he was interested in me, I felt I was doing something right; he tallied with all conventional ideas of success. What could be better than an accountant, the ultimate in professional respectability? On top of that, someone like Gavin, dependable and trustworthy, who would never take a silly risk or put his neck out, but conform to everything politely and obediently, and tick all the boxes that signify a comfortable, middle-class existence.'

'I don't know where you're coming from …' Lucia had started to clear the table, but now she paused by the island counter, taken aback by Grace's words.

'Harum-scarum me never thought I could live up to your trailblazing example. You were always ahead of me at every turn, good as gold, a model student, compared with me. I was the one who got into school-yard scraps, letting down the family name sometimes, and nowhere near as clever. You had the brilliant job and the brilliant husband. I knew I'd never have the high-flying career that you had, but at least I'd have a boyfriend that scored almost on the scale of success as Robert did. It was a kind of validation for me that I measured up after all.'

Lucia blinked. She felt faint. 'This is all ... news to me, Grace. I'd no idea you felt like this. Believe it or not, sometimes I hated the way I was as "good as gold" in school.'

'Really? That's news to me too. Going out with Gavin was fine, I was finally living up to the family's expectations ...'

Lucia shook her head. 'You should never have felt like that, and you never let the family name down, you mad thing. I was jealous of you being feisty and lively, dashing about the school yard, compared with dull me.'

Grace smiled. 'Dull you? You're a brilliant, glittering star, Lucia. But Gavin – after a while of living with him, things changed.'

'How do you mean?'

'It's hard to explain ... the way he watched me ... and he did watch me, hovering around me, taking note of everything I did ... I found it almost obsessive. I began to feel I was drowning, trapped in some kind of quicksand.'

'With gentleman Gavin?'

'That's the thing, he was polite and extremely kind, he still is, he always looked out for me, but it was too much, almost overkill. If I was late home from anything or anywhere I'd get a phone call or a text, wondering what had happened. He wanted a blow-by-blow account of what exactly had delayed me. Talk about twenty questions! He seemed to notice every time I bought something new, no matter how small, even a pair of plain knickers, or a new lipstick or a different magazine. Oh, he was very complimentary, but it made me feel stifled. He even opened my bank statement one time and said he'd been in a rush and hadn't looked at the name properly.'

'What? That's a bit sneaky ...'

Grace was still talking, her words tumbling out. 'He fell all over himself apologising, and bought me a huge bunch of flowers. Said he'd give me some tips on the best way to manage my credit card bill. But only if I wanted him to. See? How could I find fault with that? It just made me feel sick inside. If my mobile rang and he was nearer, he'd pick it up and check to see who the call or text was from before handing it to me.'

'You called it overkill.' Lucia said. 'I think I'd call that possessive.'

'He said he was just trying to be helpful. He didn't want me to miss a call or a message if it was important. He'd watch me putting in my pin code as if he were trying to suss it out. After a while I began to feel smothered. I found even his presence heavy and oppressive, and it was as if there was a brooding atmosphere in the apartment. I began to hate coming home from work in the evenings, knowing he'd be arriving in later.'

'I'd no idea you were that unhappy,' Lucia said. How had she missed this?

'Unhappy? It was more feeling hugely irritated, always on edge ... uneasy. I can't blame Gavin, we just weren't good at living together. He rubbed me up the wrong way. Someone else might enjoy all that intense, microscopic attention. I began to hate it. It made me nervous. Whereas Danny ... it was the total opposite with Danny. He made me feel free, happy, joyful. And sometimes, Lucia ...' Grace hesitated.

'Tell me ...'

'I know this is wrong, but sometimes, oh, God,' Grace said in a shaky voice, 'even though I'm getting on with things – and Danny wouldn't want it any other way – I feel an insane rage that Gavin is still going around and Danny is the one who's gone. It doesn't seem fair.'

'No, it doesn't. And that's a perfectly normal reaction.' Lucia dared to go over to Grace and rub her arm.

'I even feel angry that Gavin has taken it on himself to keep in touch, in case I need a shoulder to cry on.'

'I suppose he's trying to help. But still … if you found him that annoying …'

'I did, but it's hard to know where the boundaries lie … I want to tell him to leave me in peace, but knowing how devastated I was after Danny, I know he must have been feeling something like that when we broke up, so in a funny kind of way I'm trying to make amends …' Grace lifted her chin. 'Anyway, I'm off now, having landed that bombshell on you. Just one thing, Lucia, please don't mention a word about Danny's past to Robert, or even Mum or Dad. I need to get my own head around it first.'

'Sure, I've forgotten it already.' Some hope.

'Thanks.' Grace began to gather her bag and her mobile.

'Do you want me to talk to Jennifer about Stacy and see if I can find out anything for definite?' Lucia asked. 'She was at the school reunion and I have her email address.' There was no point in admitting now that Jennifer had already mentioned Stacy to her, but the least she could do was to follow it up.

'No, leave it,' Grace shrugged. 'I'm not wasting any energy on her.'

When the taxi driver called to say he was outside Grace went out into the hall, Lucia trailed behind her, hugging herself with her arms, feeling inexplicably sad. 'What are you doing this weekend?'

'Oh, lots,' Grace said.

'Robert will be over,' Lucia said. 'Why don't you come out with us on Saturday night? We're going out for food and a few drinks. Nothing too special.'

Grace shrugged. 'I could be busy.'

'Busy with what?'

Grace smiled. 'I'll tell you again. It's something I want to keep to myself for now, something positive. Besides you don't want me tagging along like a gooseberry.'

'You wouldn't be tagging along, and I'm glad there's something positive you're busy with. I'll call you on Saturday,' Lucia said, feeling the need to stay connected with Grace somehow. She leaned over to kiss her cheek. Grace waggled her hands in farewell as she went out the hall door, and the house seemed so silent and empty as it settled around Lucia that she went upstairs as if to inject some sliver of life into the empty spaces. On impulse she stood in the doorway of the main guest bedroom. It was decorated in cool creams and soft yellow, with designer cushions that matched the duvet carefully arranged across the double bed. There was a vase of dried lavender in a pottery jug on the bedside cabinet along with a scented candle and a cream lamp. Two buttercup-yellow guest towels were folded over the chest at the end of the bed.

Very few people had used this room, she realised with a pang. Grace had stayed here for a few nights after Danny's accident, but she could count on the fingers of one hand the number of times it had been occupied. In another life this could have been a child's room, a bedroom for a little son or daughter, Lucia could be tip-toeing in now, watching her child sleep, tucking bedclothes around a small warm body, kissing a velvet-soft cheek, maybe getting an answering murmur, or the clutch of a tiny hand reaching out to her.

But she wasn't. And she never would be, thanks to the agreement she'd made with Robert before they'd got married. Now there was no ignoring the ache that filled her chest, an ache that had begun to steal through her in the aftermath of Danny's death. An ache for a child of their own. New life, coming from the love she felt for Robert. What could be more precious, more infinitely perfect? As she stood there on the threshold of the room, she could suppress it no longer and it washed over her with a cold, startling shock, like diving into a river of icy water.

She felt so cold inside that she needed a big, comforting hug, Lucia realised. A hug from Robert. The warmth of him in her bed that night. A softly murmured conversation after making love. A kiss before she left for the office in the morning.

But that wouldn't be happening either.

Chapter Forty-seven

Matt pushed the treadmill up a notch, moving a little faster than Kevin, who was working on the adjoining machine.

'Hey, Matt, do you remember that girl – the blonde who walked into the station and cried murder?' Kevin asked.

Matt took a long slug from his water bottle and winced at the casual description. 'Who are you on about?' he said, knowing immediately who Kevin meant, but playing for time. He hadn't logged details of his house call to Grace. There was just a brief note on file of his interview the day she came into the station and his observations that Grace was in denial, he'd suggested counselling, and there were no new details or evidence to warrant opening the case again.

'The girl who called in a few weeks ago,' Kevin said. 'Remember, she spoke to you in private? You can't have forgotten her, she was a looker, all blonde hair and leggy with it.'

Her face swam in front of Matt. 'You mean Grace Bailey? Nah, it was nothing. She found it hard to accept the truth that her boyfriend died in a motorcycle crash. She seemed to have been crazy about him, and had this notion that there could have been foul play involved.'

There had been no foul play, Matt was convinced. No matter that someone had targeted her in a nasty attempt to harass her. From what he gathered, Grace had led an innocent kind of life up to now, innocent of the dark underbelly of the city, but he had learned over the past few years just how many twisted and dysfunctional people were out there, from those who were only too happy to take a pop at you when you were down, to others who lived on the margins of society and who were abusive as though it was their right. Somebody had set Grace in their sights for the sake of a cheap, vitriolic thrill.

'Why do you ask?' Matt asked Kevin. 'She hasn't popped in again, has she?"

'Nah, I saw her out the weekend before last.'

'Where?'

'I'm sure it was her, in a pub with some friends.'

'Good. Glad she's moving on.'

He pushed on, moving up another notch, a thin layer of sweat forming across his chest. As if going any faster on the treadmill would put distance between himself and Grace Bailey and all her ideas. She hadn't been in touch with him since the night he'd called over. He hadn't bothered to contact her. He hoped she'd forgotten all about her notions and had put them behind her. She was too nice to be spending time fretting about imaginary murders. And he didn't want to be hearing too much about Danny McBride and the attitude he'd had towards life, amazing or otherwise, or the fun things he'd got up to with Grace, when for some reason it made him feel inadequate.

The zoo had been great, after the nonsensical way he'd tried to coax Janet out of work. He'd felt it had been wrong of him in a way to take some inspiration from Danny's shortened life to do something light-hearted and fun and childish with Janet and Abbie. Yet it had turned out to be a fab afternoon, and even Janet seemed to be looking at him in a new light, except for the time he'd been thrown off-kilter by a memory that had sucked him under the surface until the fine day had darkened around the edges and momentarily disappeared.

But the rest of the afternoon had been great. All he needed to do was figure out what else he could do to bring fun and sparkle into Janet's life.

He set the treadmill to running speed. He found the repetitive exercise a great way of distancing himself from everything and working out problems, letting his thoughts flow through him without taking too much notice of them. If he could just fathom why he allowed Simon to push his buttons and make him feel so second rate.

The following day, when he was having a break in the canteen after showing a drunk and disorderly off the premises, and just when he thought he'd heard the last of her, Grace texted him.

'Can I see u, I need to talk pls?'

He was tempted to tell her there was nothing left to investigate and he was wasting her time and his. His good manners prevailed, however, or else it was the over-riding need to earn some brownie points and be Mr Nice Guy.

'Thursday night?' he suggested.

'Tks. I'll be at home unless u want me to come to the station.'

Come to the station? Why did Grace think she needed to come to the station? He texted back immediately. 'No need, I'll call after 8.'

'Thank you.'

* * *

'What makes you think this changes anything?' Matt asked on Thursday evening, after Grace had finished telling him about her visit with Danny's mother, and the chance encounter with Emer. 'I'm not saying it doesn't,' he qualified swiftly. 'I'd like to know your thoughts on it. You knew Danny, I didn't. You're the best person to know if anything was bothering him. Maybe you're aware of something but you don't realise it.'

Grace shook her head. 'I thought it might have given you a lead,' she said. 'Something else to check for on the police files, or helped you with your enquiries. Isn't that what you say?'

'I checked out the reports after your visit to the station,' he said, 'Danny McBride came up clean as a whistle. I didn't find anything at all on him, not even a penalty point.'

'Couldn't you do another search? Maybe narrow it down by looking at a Mayo angle? There have to be others who hung around with Danny and are still …'

He knew she couldn't bring herself to say it. She was a babe in the woods, so she was.

'Addicts?' he finished for her.

She nodded.

'Grace, you'd be amazed at how many people operate just below the radar, those who dabble in drugs for recreational purposes and who don't put their heads above the parapet in any way. Even if we had records on anyone in Mayo, which we're bound to have, there's no way of linking any of the names to Danny.'

Not in this case, there wasn't. If it had been an official murder enquiry, linked to drugs, no stone would be unturned. But it was far from an official enquiry and it had nothing to do with murder of any description. The only gut feeling Grace was correct about was that Danny had indeed been hiding something from her: his drug habit. While all drug habits were messy and caused endless damage for those involved, it sounded as though Danny's had been at the lower end of the scale. Whether he'd been fully rid of it after his spell in rehab had ended was debatable, but he'd never once come to the attention of the police.

'I really thought …' Grace sighed. 'Forget it, so. At least I've a good idea now that it was Stacy who was harassing me, so at least that's solved.'

'Do you want to take that any further?'

'No, Matt, I'm not bothered. It's nothing compared with the shock I got about Danny's past.'

'I can imagine how difficult it's been,' Matt said, doing his best to sound empathetic. 'I don't blame you for having doubts about Danny's death, you loved him to bits and it seems ridiculous that he's gone.'

'It does, doesn't it?' She fell silent for a moment, and then she asked, 'By the way, what happened about the registration number I gave you? In what way was it in the clear?'

Matt had been hoping she wouldn't ask this. 'I hate to say this Grace, but the number you gave me was the same number as Danny's bike.'

She looked at him blankly. 'Was it? That's strange. I couldn't even tell you what Danny's motorbike reg was because I don't remember it.'

'Well you must have it stored in your head somewhere. Maybe this bike's number is very similar to Danny's, so that you thought it was his, and that's why the bike seemed familiar to you.'

'And maybe you're right and I'm just imagining everything. Even some of the stars have fallen down and I …'

'The stars?'

'Yes, the stars on the ceiling. Danny put them up before we went to Kerry. Now some of them have fallen down.' She gave a half laugh. 'Sorry I can see by your face … I'm not making sense. Look …' She rose to her feet and went across to the door to the bedroom, throwing it open. 'See?'

Matt got up and walked across to the doorway. At first he didn't know what she meant, and then he saw them; two dozen or so cream-coloured star shapes scattered on top of the deep-blue duvet cover. When he looked closely at the bedroom ceiling he saw more of the same stuck up there.

'They glow in the dark,' Grace said. 'I know they're only silly kids' things but they were special to me because Danny put them up. We'd lie in bed and look up at them, but when I came home from work today I saw that half of them fell down sometime today. You'd swear ...' she hesitated, then she shook her head as if to clear it, and walked out of the bedroom.

'Swear what?' he asked.

'You'd swear that Danny's ghost was up to some tricks, trying to tell me to forget all about him by getting rid of the signs that he lived here. I came home another evening and two of his posters had come away from the wall and were hanging upside down.' Grace moved across to the wall, pressing her thumbs to the corners of the poster, securing them firmly. 'They were only stuck up with blue tack, but still ... at least the kite is still exactly where he left it ...'

The kite. Matt looked at the cheap and cheerful blaze of yellow and red against the kitchen press and didn't know what to say.

'Thing is, I am getting my act together, if anything the ridiculousness of Danny's death is making me want to grab the life I have and make the very best of it; who knows what's around the corner.' She spoke with a hard-earned conviction when she said, 'I'm not going to have any regrets,' she urged. 'Life is far too short. Don't waste time, just go for it, my new motto. Do you have a partner, Matt?'

'I'm not with anybody right now. Well, problem is, I wish I was, but she ...' he paused. What did he think he was up to? He was here on police business of sorts. Talking about his private life was off the wall.

Grace must have sensed his discomfort because she looked concerned. 'But you wish you were? With someone, I mean. Sorry, forget what I said, I didn't mean to intrude into your private life.'

'If anyone put their foot in it, I did, with my stupid behaviour,' he said, alarmed that he seemed to be crossing a boundary. He'd no right to bring anything about his love life into the conversation. His problems with Janet had no place here.

'Do you love her?' she asked.

'I do,' he said without hesitation, giving her a half grin. He could answer that easily enough.

'Then don't waste a minute in telling her. I mean it, Matt,' Grace said. All of a sudden, she seemed to be the one in charge, the expression in her eyes making her seem older than her years. 'I'll never forget the first time Danny told me he loved me.'

'How come I have a feeling you're going to tell me?'

'This is strictly off the record as I don't want to be arrested.'

'Arrested? You?'

'Yeah,' she grinned. 'We were skinny-dipping, me and Danny.'

'I didn't hear that,' he said, grinning back, deciding it wasn't something he intended to copy with Janet. The kite looked interesting, though.

He paused in the doorway, suddenly aware of how alone she seemed.

'Thanks, Matt. You've been very patient with me, but I won't be annoying you anymore. Go patch things up with your girlfriend.'

'You're not annoying me. I wish patching it up was that easy.' Shut up, Matt, this is not her problem.

'Nothing is impossible, if you put your mind to it. You know the saying, while there's life …' she lifted a rueful eyebrow.

'Yeah.' In spite of his sombre mood, he felt an embarrassed smile on his face. She was right. He was alive and well and in charge of his own destiny. 'Seriously though Grace, call me any time you need to, or if you have any more concerns ….'

'Thanks, Matt,' she said with a finality that told him she probably wouldn't call.

On impulse he gave her a quick hug, telling her it was off the record, and wished her all the best. He walked down the corridor, hearing sounds of life from other apartments drifting through the thin walls; television sets, music, a baby crying, a heated exchange, and it all made Grace's apartment seem all the lonelier.

Skinny-dipping; it must have been the most absurd, hilarious fun.

His car was parked further away than normal, under the block adjacent to Grace's. He was driving slowly towards the exit ramp when he saw it out of the corner of his eye at the last minute; a shiny black motorbike parked up to the side. The owner obviously lived in one of the apartment blocks. No surprises then that Grace was seeing it around the vicinity. And no surprises either that the only registration number she saw in her mind's eye was Danny's.

He'd have one last glance over the accident reports before he filed them away until the inquest. Not that he expected to find anything.

The following morning, he was in the station good and early, and feeling like Mr Nice Guy, he pulled up all the reports before he got caught up in the hectic day, as Fridays were usually bedlam. He double-checked the toxicology reports, which were clear, but something else he came across caused his coffee to go cold as he read it twice, three times, before he made a couple of phone calls. Then he sat ignoring his mountain of paperwork as he absorbed the full implications of what it could mean.

Chapter Forty-eight

'Do you feel like doing something different today?' Lucia asked
Robert on Saturday morning. There was something in the calm new
morning and high, pale blue skies overhead that gave Lucia the urge
to break free from the normal routine.

Robert looked up from his iPad. He'd propped it up in front
of him to allow him scroll through the newspaper online editions
as he tucked into a bowl of yogurt, fruit and muesli. 'Something
different?' he asked. 'Like what?'

Lucia paused, thinking how stupidly ridiculous it was to be
nervous of Robert's reaction.

Almost, without fail, they went out for drinks and a meal on a
Saturday night, whether in Dublin or London, while on Saturday
afternoons when in Dublin, Robert sometimes went golfing or
watched football on the television. Occasionally they went to an
early evening movie showing, or went shopping together. Lucia did
her main grocery shopping online every fortnight, popping into the
supermarket on Saturday mornings for fresh bread and last minute
items the weekends Robert was home.

'What were you thinking of?' Robert asked, an irritable frown on
his face.

'How would you feel – it's such a nice day, and to do something completely different and make the most of the day, it might be fun to go to the zoo,' she finished up hurriedly.

He looked at her as though she'd suggested a trip to outer space. 'The *zoo*? What brought this on?'

She couldn't bring herself to say that she wanted to try out one of Danny and Grace's carefree romantic escapades, that even though they were well into their thirties there was nothing to stop them from cavorting cheerfully around the zoo like a pair of love-struck teenagers, stopping to kiss and cuddle now and then. They'd had plenty of romantic interludes but never anything quite that playful or light-hearted. She shrugged. 'I felt like breaking out of our usual routine.'

He sat back and looked at her thoughtfully. Then he said, 'I don't understand why you want to be different all of a sudden. First your hair and then …' he stopped abruptly.

'And then what?' she asked.

'Then this,' he said. She had the peculiar feeling he had originally intended to say something else, but had checked himself in time. 'If you want to go out today we could take a spin and have lunch in Powerscourt,' he said smoothly. 'Besides, the zoo will be swarming with hordes of noisy kids,' he gave a half laugh. 'I can't think why you'd want to go there.'

She stayed silent and buttered some toast, turning her attention to that and avoiding his eyes for fear of what he might see in hers, because she couldn't help visualising what it might be like to be strolling around the zoo in the middle of family groups with throngs of lively, boisterous children, their young, high-pitched voices full of wonder and joy and laughter, streaming up merrily into the air.

'If that's what you'd like to do,' Robert said, 'you just have to ask Ruth if you can go with her and her gang of kids some time. That would be fun, I'm sure.'

She looked up then from her toast and glanced at him, feeling it was safe to do so, but she'd been mistaken; not because Robert might sense what she was thinking, but because of the strange look she saw in his eyes. She'd clearly caught him off guard and it took her brain a moment to comprehend that look. Her husband was staring into the middle distance and his eyes were full of something she'd never seen before: a bleak kind of sadness that tugged at her heart, yet made her feel cold at the same time. She attempted to figure out what could have put that there.

'Why don't you want children, Robert?' She was mad to ask him, but she couldn't help herself. It was as though her control was slipping and her tongue was running away from her.

'What are you on about?'

'I just thought you might have other reasons you never spoke about,' she said.

'Like what?'

'That's what I'm asking you. You'll be forty in three years' time,' she said. 'I just want to make sure you're still happy with our decision.'

He didn't answer her question. 'This goes back to the holidays, doesn't it? I knew you weren't yourself. There were times when you seemed miles away. I'm perfectly happy with our choices, aren't you?' he said. 'Or is your biological clock starting to tick loud and clear?'

Her biological clock. Lucia felt an enormous wave of relief building inside her. Surely that was her problem? She was coming up to thirty-five years of age, her weird feelings were pure and simply hormonal. Therefore, there was nothing to be anxious about. Why hadn't she thought of this herself? Her weird feelings had nothing to do with changing her mind or having regrets. They would all pass as soon as her hormones settled back down.

'Maybe it has started to tick,' she admitted, her head light as the wave of relief ebbed away, leaving her drained. 'But it doesn't mean I'm going to do anything about it.'

'Good. Because I certainly haven't changed my mind.'

'And your reasons are still the same?' Why was she prodding him? Why couldn't she tell her husband that her choice to remain childless stemmed from a fear of not being able to provide properly? That her main concerns were financial and nothing else? She'd already experienced the effects of two recessions, the first as it affected her parents, the most recent her friends and acquaintances, including Robert having to go and work in London. She knew how easy it was to find yourself on a slippery financial slope, and how quickly things could deteriorate.

'My reasons?' Robert said. 'Yup, they're still the same.'

She sensed by his vague expression that he was lying, that he couldn't even recall what he'd told her first time out, and that for some reason, he wasn't about to bare his soul to her now. She decided not to push it, but to let it rest for now and move on to a safer topic of conversation. She wondered whether this was safer for her or for him.

He clattered his spoon into his bowl. He stood up from the table, rinsed out his bowl and put it into the dishwasher. In the blink of an eye he was back to the Robert she knew, her Saturday husband in his jeans and soft chambray shirt.

'If you don't mind I'm not sure about going out for lunch after all. The shed needs painting and today would be perfect for that,' he said conversationally, as though nothing untoward had passed between them, and shed-painting was a regular job of his, when in reality the last time he'd painted, it had been that fraught time just before he'd gone to London for the job interview. Soon afterwards, he went to the hardware store to get the paint, and then he changed into an old pair of shorts and a vest top. Out in the garden, he covered the patio with sheets of plastic, stuck in his earplugs and listened to music on his mobile while he spent a couple of hours transforming the dull exterior of the wooden shed into a warm chestnut brown. She stood by the kitchen window and watched him, ignoring a voice inside her head that urged her to join him. Why couldn't she get into her old shorts and T-shirt and join him? So what if the paint splashed like water and went everywhere? Think of the fun they could have later, washing it off each other, in the bath.

She wondered what music Robert was listening to, and what he was really seeing as he swished the brush methodically up and down, round and round the wood panelling. Whatever it was, she'd probably never know. And, she shivered, hopefully she'd never need to know what had caused that strange, dejected look on his face at the breakfast table – because it had scared the hell out of her.

Chapter Forty-nine

Matt twisted his body around, trying in vain to prevent a length of cable from snagging around it. The other end of the cable was attached to a multi-coloured kite, which was struggling and buffeting against the wind. They were in the park on a bright and breezy Sunday afternoon. Perfect for kite-flying, or so he'd thought. But it had been one thing to admire the kite in Grace's kitchen, and another to be inspired to plan a family afternoon in the park, only things weren't working out according to plan and he knew he badly needed some kite-flying lessons.

And Grace was on his mind. He hadn't contacted her yet to tell her what he'd spotted in the reports. It could mean nothing, but then again it could mean everything. Regardless, it would make no difference now.

Danny was gone; the reminder, sobering as it was, made this afternoon seem all the more vibrant and taste even sweeter, especially with Abbie skipping around him, dancing like the breeze in an energetic fizz.

'Higher, higher, Daddy!' she shrieked.

'I'm trying,' Matt said.

'You could try harder,' Janet said.

Was she flirting with him? Or was Matt reading something that wasn't there? He whipped around but by now she was facing away from him, head tilted towards the sky. She looked ravishing today in her slim fitting jeans and pink cotton top. She had a small white bag with a thin gold chain anchored across her body. He didn't remember seeing it before and he wondered if Simon had bought it for her. He had an urge to pick her up and hug her tight, then drive her back to his apartment and hold her close in bed, making love to her all night long. But that wasn't going to happen, not in his wildest dreams. Still, she'd been happy enough to come to the park with him and Abbie that Sunday afternoon, which was a bonus – even though kite-flying clearly wasn't his forte.

Janet was having no problems with her kite. She stood with her back to the wind, spooling the cable out carefully, and it streamed obediently up into the air, drifting gently on the thermal winds. Matt pulled a piece of cable away from his body and manoeuvred the loop over his head, which promptly made things worse. He became even more entangled.

Janet laughed and shook her head. 'Sorry, I don't mean to but you look so funny …'

Even Abbie giggled, her infectious laughter rippling out into the air.

'I'm glad someone's enjoying themselves,' Matt said.

'Come here,' Janet said, reeling in her cable and doing something with her spool so that it was secured against her jeans pocket. She went over to him and told him to stay still. He was suddenly weak and helpless as she got up really close to him, so close he could smell her perfume. When he looked down at her, he could see her individual curved eyelashes fluttering like crescents against the soft skin of her cheeks. Her hands were deft and light as she untangled the cable from his body. Then she looked up the height of him as she traced the last loops of the cable, unhooking them from his body and as she did this, she caught his gaze. It was the closest they'd physically been to each other since he'd left; for a long tense moment, as he stared into the soft dark irises of her eyes, something passed silently between them, strong and true, and as soothing as honey. His blood rippled and his breath quickened, and he imagined that hers did the same.

There was something there, still. He read it in her eyes. Eventually she tore her gaze away, reeled in the rest of his cable and secured it.

'Why don't we try the other end of the park?' she suggested brightly to no one in particular. 'There's more space there and we can go for coffee afterwards.'

Coffee. Afterwards. Promising.

The top end of the park, where the vista opened out to acres of flat fields, was busy; Sunday-afternoon busy, with families out together enjoying the blue-skied sunshine. Matt parked the car and followed a skipping Abbie and Janet across the soft terrain until they found a good spot to fly their kites. Out here, in the big open space under high skies, there were kids playing football against makeshift goalposts, and families having picnics. Beyond the park, the silent blue-grey phalanx of city buildings shimmered, encircled by the Dublin mountains in a hazy embrace.

'You must feel like a child again,' she said to Matt. 'When is the last time you played with a kite?'

'A kite?' he asked. 'Can't remember.'

'Yeah, I bet you had all shapes and sizes. I'd say the fields of Kildare were a fantastic place for kites. You must have had great childhood summers, running wild, compared with where I lived, on a main road in the suburbs.'

Something shimmered in the corner of his mind, an old memory; he saw himself running by the edge of a field, with the breeze in his hair, making a track through the long grass. He had wings on his feet and he was going to run all the way into a magical future. School was out for the summer and he was as free and powerful as a champion dragon-slayer or a warrior knight. His new skateboard was brilliant, and everything, even the warm grass swaying in the glittering field, was radiant with colour and infused with excitement. He laughed and he heard laughter answering behind him. It was all ahead of them; glorious life. He turned around in mid-laugh and he was running backwards through the field, facing whoever had been running behind him, and then the memory suddenly shut down and everything went blank.

'Matt?'

He blinked and the park came back into focus.

'Are you okay?' Janet was looking at him oddly

He pushed something dark away until it was a tiny dot inside him. 'Not a bother, why?'

'You just …' she continued to stare at him. He realised she had put her hand on his arm when he felt the unexpected warmth of it and he looked down at it and frowned. She sprang back, taking her hand away, and he was immediately sorry.

'I what?' he made himself smile, but was horrified to feel his mouth trembling a little.

'You seemed so far away you gave me a start, that's all.' She was still looking at him as though he'd made her feel uneasy, and it unsettled him.

'Sorry about that, I'm right here now. What were we talking about?'

'Kite-flying. Your childhood.'

His childhood. Much of his free time had been spent in the fields of Kildare close to his home, with Liam and their gang of pals – they thought they were the best warriors in the world. 'Oh yeah. Whereabouts can we go for coffee around here?' He didn't care if she noticed how clumsily he'd changed the subject. There was something wrong. Something tight was pressing against his head, causing it to thud, and it seemed to constrict his chest; he had to breathe slowly and steadily to get beyond it. The sunshine of the day was so bright and the colours so intense they were hurting his eyes; he blinked rapidly, feeling an invisible wall between him and everyone else in the park.

He struggled with the coffee, finding things taut and strained. He made small talk, to be polite, but he knew Janet sensed his withdrawal, fixing him with eyes that were slightly guarded. He knew his behaviour puzzled her but he couldn't seem to rouse himself out of a peculiar kind of dark stupor. She was cool with him when he left her and Abbie home, and he felt terribly flat by the time he got home. No way could he have blamed Janet. It served him right in a way. Following the example of Grace and Danny's fun-loving activities in an attempt to wriggle back into Janet's affections seemed to be having the opposite effect and he was thoroughly pissed off with himself.

Dream big? Yeah, right.

* * *

Most evenings, Grace spent an hour or two working on her notes and scripts, with music on in the background. Katie and her kite adventures were taking shape inside her head and on the page. Liz in Jigsaw Press had repeated her interest in seeing a draft manuscript, although she'd also said it sometimes took a while to hear back. Grace just had to get on with the work. It was no longer a pipe dream, she realised, watching her story shape up little by little.

She was surprised to hear from Matt again, who wanted to see her, and she arranged a time on Tuesday evening, putting her notes and laptop to one side when he arrived.

'I was surprised when I got your text,' she said, opening the door to him. 'I wasn't expecting to see you again.'

'I didn't think I'd be here,' he said, walking into the living room.

His eyes flicked to the table. 'I'm disturbing you, sorry.'

'It's fine,' she said. 'Have you found something?' She leaned back against the table, crossing her arms.

'I'm not sure if it's significant, but there was a more detailed report on Danny's file, and … maybe you should sit down, Grace,' he suggested.

'That bad?' she smiled. 'The worst has already happened, Matt. I know whatever you say, Danny is never coming back. So just go ahead and tell me.'

'This report was more comprehensive. It wasn't available the first time I checked, but according to it, Danny had incurred some damage to his internal organs.' He paused when Grace started to nod.

'I know,' she said. 'His mother began to tell me, but I didn't want to hear the details.'

'Thing is, Grace, it might have had a bearing on what happened, but it cannot be established conclusively.'

'Establish what?' She felt a funny lurch in her chest.

'Without going into the details, Danny's heart was damaged. More than likely this was a result of his drug habit as both ecstasy and cocaine overload the heart and tighten the blood vessels. If bad drugs are ingested, it causes more damage. None of us know if Danny took some of the stuff his mate died of. The shock of the impact could have caused a heart attack, but there's a good possibility a heart attack could have caused him to crash in the first place.'

'A heart attack.'

Matt nodded. 'I know it's not something you want to hear, and quite possibly Danny knew this himself, but it seems he was a likely heart attack candidate.'

The words hung in the air and she felt herself absorbing them very slowly, as if they were too difficult to take in all at once. 'Unfortunately some of that makes sense,' she said eventually.

'Danny lived like someone who sensed he was on borrowed time. I think I told you that the first time we spoke.'

'It could explain a few things, or it mightn't explain anything at all.'

'And his family know this?'

Matt smiled. 'They would have been told about the report, but the finer points mightn't have sunk in yet.'

'I can imagine,' she said, Tess McBride's sad face swimming in front of her.

Silence fell between them. 'I won't take up your time, Grace,' he said, 'unless there's anything else?'

'There isn't,' she said. What else was there to say? Matt had done all he could, and she was beginning to accept that some things would never be answered. 'Thanks for calling in and letting me know. Sorry – I didn't even offer you tea or coffee.'

'No worries. I didn't want to drag things up again but it was best to keep you updated.'

'Yes, even if it's something else I have to get my head around.'

'How are you otherwise? There's still the option of a liaison, even a few months down the line ...'

'No, thanks. Honestly, Matt, I'm too busy getting on with things,' she said, looking to where her laptop and notes were arranged. 'It's what Danny would have wanted. I can either sit and cry that he's gone, or make the most of everything in honour of him.'

'I'm glad I didn't catch you sitting and crying.'

'You'll never catch me sitting and crying. How's the girlfriend?' she asked.

He made a face. 'I'm working on that,' he said.

'Good. Keep it up.'

Chapter Fifty

In a hotel in Knightsbridge, London, at the glittering champagne and canapés reception to celebrate a stellar industry accolade awarded to Robert's firm, Miranda Gray leaned forward and kissed the air on both sides of Lucia's face before grasping her shoulders and holding her at arm's length.

'Lucia!' she cried, beaming, her chocolate-brown eyes dancing in her face. 'You look fabulous! What on *earth* did you do to your hair? It's so *cute*!'

'Thanks Miranda, you look great yourself,' Lucia said, admiring the other woman's sparkly black dress and high, spaghetti-thin heels. 'Glad you like the hair,' she said, fluffing up the cropped shape with her hand, 'I don't think Robert was all too keen on it at first, were you, Robert?' Beside her, she felt her husband recoil slightly. Had she really said that? Their differences of opinion were few and far between and she never, ever aired so much as a hint of them in public. This was a first. Which proved to Lucia the way things between her and Robert were starting to fray. She wanted to sink through the floor and be anywhere but here, but Miranda was talking.

'Of course he wasn't keen on it,' Miranda laughed. 'How could he be, when it makes you look at least five years younger and amazingly sexy. He must be terrified of what you get up to, all alone in Dublin during the week. I don't think it's a set-up I'd allow if I were your husband. The men you meet must be drooling and I'm relieved Neil is at home babysitting Sophie this evening.'

Lucia gave a tiny shrug. 'Robert has no worries on that score.' Besides, she felt like adding, with you looking so utterly gorgeous and alluring, Neil would have absolutely no interest in me.

'Hmmm,' Miranda gave Robert a studied glance over the rim of her champagne flute, 'then I hope he knows how lucky he is.'

Lucia watched as her husband stared pointedly at his colleague. 'Oh, I do, Miranda, very much. I do appreciate my good fortune. If you'll excuse me, I need to say hello to the Danish contingent. I see they've just arrived.'

Miranda waved her glass in the air. 'You go ahead, Robert. We could both do with talking to them but I'll catch up later. Right now I want to show some photos of Sophie to Lucia.'

Robert's glance passed from Miranda to Lucia, and then he gave a quirky smile before turning on his heel and marching off. Miranda stalled a passing waiter. She plucked Lucia's almost empty glass out of her hands, and along with her own, plonked them on his tray before helping herself to two fresh glasses. She handed one to Lucia and touched hers to it.

'Much as you love your husband and much as I admire him as a colleague, it's nice to have time alone for some woman talk. Let's head across to that window seat and I'll show off my daughter. To hell with networking for a few minutes.'

Lucia was a bit light-headed as she threaded her way through the gathering of executives and managers, following Miranda to a curved seating area by the window. They had it to themselves, as everyone else was more anxious to be out in the thick of the crowd, busy rubbing shoulders with everyone else, determined to see and be seen, rather than waste a minute sitting to the side.

As Miranda opened her bag, Lucia braced herself. She should be used to this; used to acquaintances and colleagues proudly showing off photos of their tiny offspring, and recounting their amazing little exploits. It had never caused her any bother before, but she felt anxiety spasm in her stomach as she prepared to look at photos of Miranda's baby daughter.

Miranda took out her mobile but instead of passing it to Lucia, she left it on the small table in front of them. 'I had an ulterior motive for bringing you over here,' she said, giving her a wry smile. 'Before I show you anything I need to ask you something. I know I'm driving them mad in the office with my baby chatter. They don't understand what's happened to slave driver Ms Gray and at the coffee break I have to apologise in advance for my baby talk. However Robert ...' she hesitated.

Lucia picked up the sudden tension in her voice. 'Robert what?' she asked, suddenly dry-mouthed.

Miranda fiddled with her wedding ring. 'Robert and I have always had a brilliant working relationship. I really respect his intelligence and I'm fond of him as a colleague, but I think he's deliberately avoiding me at coffee time. He made a silly excuse not to look at the baby photos I brought in. I've tried to apologise to him if I'm bugging him, but he's actually walked away from me a couple of times and left me standing in the middle of the floor...' she looked at Lucia as though Lucia was going to supply some kind of reasonable explanation.

'Walked away?' Lucia felt her anxiety deepen.

'I can't say I blame him, as I said, I'm driving everyone mad, and you can tell me to shut up and I apologise in advance as I don't want to put my foot in it, or upset anyone, or cross a boundary, but obviously I've said or done the wrong thing, somehow, with Robert.'

Lucia shook her head. 'I can't understand that, Miranda,' she said. 'Robert is happy for you and Neil.'

'I don't get that impression,' Miranda's eyes were rueful. 'He seems to be avoiding me like the plague since I came back to work and it's messing up our working relationship. I guess he's afraid I'll take out my baby pictures and make him look at them, which I've no intention of doing. So if he says anything to you, just tell him I'd never intentionally upset him.'

'Why don't you tell him that yourself?'

'He's already walked away and I don't want to bug him by bringing up the subject again. I really value Robert's support and contribution and I wanted this opportunity just to chat with you, and explain myself.'

'Thanks, Miranda, but I can't think of any reason in the world why you might upset Robert with photos of your baby,' Lucia said slowly, feeling she was picking her way through broken glass in her bare feet.

'Can't you?' Miranda's eyes searched her face, but it was such a warm, sympathetic look that Lucia couldn't be offended by the hidden agenda she sensed hiding behind Miranda's carefully articulated words.

'No, there's no reason whatsoever,' she said, keeping the smile pinned to her face.

'I'm relieved to hear that much anyhow.'

'So now, are you going to let me see the fabulous Sophie?' Lucia asked.

Miranda picked up her mobile and passed it to Lucia. 'Just scroll through from left to right.'

'She's beautiful,' Lucia said, admiring the photographs of the pretty baby. 'And she's the image of you.'

'So everyone says. A little mini-me. I'll have to go again and hope for a mini-Neil. He doesn't seem to have got a look in, although I promise she's half of him!'

'Go again?' Lucia couldn't help a forced smile. 'You must have taken to motherhood.'

'I'm finding it the most amazing thing ever. If anyone had told me in advance, how besotted I'd be about a tiny, squalling, puking, little bundle, I'd never have believed them.'

Lucia scrolled through the photos. She tried not to imagine a miniature version of herself or Robert, to coo over and laugh together with, to tickle, to hug and to love. She took a slow breath and did her best to blank it out.

'To say she's the best thing that's ever happened to me is an understatement,' Miranda said.

'I'm not surprised,' Lucia said, relieved to hand back the mobile. 'She's totally adorable.'

After a short while they got up from the window seat and mingled with the throng, Lucia's eyes searching for Robert. He was further down the reception room, chatting to a small group of people, and she watched him unobserved.

Seeing him like this, out with his colleagues in a social environment, she looked at him with fresh eyes. Her husband was beautiful in his charcoal-grey suit, with a crisp white shirt collar setting off his dark blond hair. His smile was charming and attentive, and with his usual modest demeanour, she could see he had the Danish delegation eating out of his hand. This was the man whose bed she slept in and whose life she shared. Looking at him now it was easy to feel she could fall in love with him all over again.

Although, of course, she didn't fully share his life. He hadn't been around for her in those first couple of days after Danny's accident, when she'd really needed him, and she'd found herself getting support from an unexpected source in the form of Aiden Burke. Small things, but vital, practical support. There must have been instances when she hadn't been around for Robert after challenging days in the office and he'd needed some help. And she knew now how easily a shared coffee break or lunch hour could lead to the beginning of an attraction.

She felt a pang in her chest as he looked in her direction and saw her watching him, and then she saw his gaze tauten as it passed beyond her and fastened on the person standing behind her. Lucia didn't need to turn around, even though she felt a tremendous urge to do just that as a way of acknowledging the direction of Robert's stare. It was Miranda who was standing behind her, chatting to some colleagues. Miranda, whose baby daughter was the image of her, and whose baby photographs Robert didn't want to see. Miranda, who had joked about Lucia being alone all week in Dublin. What about Robert, alone all week in London?

Anxiety coalesced inside Lucia like a hard, bright pellet, startling her. Was it possible? Dear God, no. Miranda had seemed friendly and relaxed as she chatted to Lucia, hardly the demeanour of a woman talking to her lover's wife. Yet Robert had been working closely with Miranda until she went on maternity leave. A great working relationship was what he'd said when he'd first talked of her, and their casual camaraderie had extended to include Lucia and Neil whenever the four of them had gone out for drinks or a meal. But now that Miranda was back in the office, having had a baby, her good-mannered, polite and friendly Robert seemed to be avoiding her. As well as that, around the same time, things had slipped sideways between her and Robert in recent weeks. In her fixation on Danny's untimely death, had she misread signals coming from her husband?

* * *

The rest of the evening seemed to unroll very slowly and at a distance for Lucia, and bright laughter and chatter crashed in waves around her as she drank too much champagne and kept Robert and Miranda in her sights. But nothing seemed untoward. Miranda excused herself early and left, smiling brightly and blowing happy kisses at Lucia.

Her imagination was running away with her, she decided.

Her sleep that night was disturbed by the conversation she'd had in the window seat with Miranda. She hadn't been imagining that. It was lunchtime on Sunday before she managed to raise the subject with Robert. They were relaxing on the terrace of a restaurant by the river with the weekend newspapers, and they had a couple of hours to spare before Lucia caught her tube to Heathrow.

'Miranda seems to be very happy,' she began, twirling the stem of her wine glass. She'd stuck to white wine spritzer, needing control of her thoughts and words. It had taken her several deep breaths to open this conversation.

'Yup, she certainly does.' Robert didn't bother to look up from the sports supplement.

'And the baby is gorgeous.'

'I'm sure she is.'

From across the table, Lucia could see he was engrossed in a golf article about Rory McIlroy. 'She's afraid she's getting on everyone's nerves with her baby talk and photos,' she went on, as ultra-casually as she could manage, given the lump of apprehension in her throat.

'She sure as hell isn't going to annoy me,' Robert said, his still eyes fastened on the newspaper.

There *was* something. This wasn't the Robert she knew talking about a respected colleague. Why was he so negative? Where was the laughter she'd expect, and perhaps a friendly quip about his dynamo workmate turning into a besotted mum? The normal, jokey kind of chit-chat they usually enjoyed.

'Obviously not.' Lucia couldn't help the words slipping out.

'What's that supposed to mean?' Robert asked, shooting a glance at her.

Lucia's heart fluttered in her chest at his defensive attitude. 'I'm sure you're so focussed in the office that it doesn't impinge on you at all.'

'Which is the way it should be. Who wants to listen to that kind of silly chatter?'

'Still, as a good colleague of yours, I'm sure you show some interest in Miranda's baby.'

He put down the paper. 'Just what were you two talking about Friday night?'

'Miranda showed me some photographs of Sophie. She also apologised because she's concerned that she might be bugging you all with all her baby talk.'

'And why should that bug me?'

'Exactly. Why should it?' She faced him, her heart hammering. She wanted to ask him why he'd walked away – twice – from his colleague, showing a disrespect that was uncharacteristic for Robert, but she couldn't find the words.

'Lucia, I'm not sure where this conversation is leading or what it's all about, but I don't need to hear shite from the office at the weekend.'

'So it's shite, is it?'

He threw her a challenging glance. 'Well, of course. What else would you call it?'

'I'd hardly call having a baby some kind of "shite". I think it helps to keep good relations in the office if you smile at a few photographs, and then get on with the work.'

He stared at her. It was there again, that bleak look in his eyes. It frightened her.

'Robert? Is something wrong?'

'Not as far as I'm concerned, no,' he said. 'Except I don't understand where my level-headed, practical wife is coming from.'

She couldn't answer. Crazy ideas had tumbled through her head in the middle of the night; had, by any chance, Robert and Miranda slept with each other, a one-night stand, a crazy fling they both regretted? And now he was petrified the baby might be his? Or had he always fancied Miranda but now she was off limits on account of having a child? Or did he really abhor babies so much he couldn't even pretend a passing interest in his workmate's?

Had it been a few months earlier, Lucia knew she mightn't have noticed any of this. She would have brushed off Miranda's concerns and not given them a thought, secure in the knowledge that as far as she and Robert were concerned, babies were not on the agenda, therefore they weren't interested in anyone else's.

She told herself to be focussed on the here and now. She was enjoying a long, leisurely lunch, sitting on the terrace of a London restaurant, with the sun on her face, the bees droning in the flowerbeds, the scent of honeysuckle wafting through the air, the muted, far off sounds of traffic.

All this flew through her head in the space of a few seconds. She heard herself laugh flippantly and say, 'I dunno, Robert. Tell me there's nothing for me to worry about and I'll be perfectly happy.'

His face was set in stubborn lines. 'I shouldn't have to tell you that, and I thought you were perfectly happy.'

She didn't know how to follow his comment and she felt close to tears.

'Robert,' she eventually said, 'is there something happening to us? Something going on?'

'How should I know?' he said, rising to his feet. He took out his wallet and put some notes on the table, not bothering to take his newspaper. She'd no choice but to follow him, gathering her handbag and feeling sick to her stomach as she went out to the car after him. They drove back to his apartment in silence, where Lucia had no choice but to finish her packing and get ready to leave for her flight home.

'Robert, we need to talk,' she said, after she'd wheeled her case out into the hall and came back into the living room.

He was watching golf on the television, relaxing back in the sofa with his hands behind his head as though he hadn't a care in the world. 'I think you've said pretty much enough already,' he said.

'What *is* this?' she cried. 'What's wrong?'

'I don't know, Lucia, you tell me. You seem to be the one with all the issues, wherever they're coming from.'

He wouldn't be drawn, he wasn't connecting with her, and worse, he was fielding her comments, bouncing them back or brushing them off like you would a pesky fly. It took a supreme effort for Lucia to leave him there, to close the door and start her homeward journey, her head fuzzy with the way everything seemed to be collapsing so ridiculously between them.

Chapter Fifty-one

Grace was making an omelette for her evening meal, along with a green salad. She had the radio on and dance music rippled around her while she beat the eggs, sliced tomatoes and onions, and prepared the peppers. She wasn't long home from the office, relieved she'd walked up from the Luas and reached Rathbrook Hall without seeing a black motorbike on her tail, as she did about two evenings a week – though this wasn't annoying her as much as it used to. She'd finally managed to convince herself it belonged to someone who lived in the complex, especially if she was seeing it in the neighbourhood on such a regular basis.

Of far more importance to her was the fact that she'd stayed up late the night before, working hard on her first story until she'd reached the end. She knew she had to go back to the start again and revise and polish, but she felt a huge sense of accomplishment. Jigsaw Press liked the concept of Katie and her kite adventures, aimed at six- to eight-year-olds, they'd said.

At first she didn't take much notice of the banging noise in the background. Someone in a nearby apartment was busy with DIY, she presumed. She had just poured the egg mixture onto the pan when she heard, at a distance, someone calling her name.

'Grace! Can you open the door?'

She put down the knife and wiped her hands on a tea towel. There was another bang, and she realised that whoever was calling her was also knocking on her apartment door. She assumed it was one of her neighbours, as no one had buzzed her to be allowed through the main entrance doors on the ground floor. She went out into the hallway and looked through her spy hole.

Gavin.

She unlocked the door and opened it. 'Gavin? What are you doing here?'

He wasn't as immaculately dressed as usual. His tie was at half mast, the top of his shirt open and his eyes were bloodshot as though he'd been drinking. Her heart sank. She couldn't take anything to do with Gavin on board right now, she'd nothing left to give, yet neither could she shut the door in his face.

'What am I doing here? I'm hoping I can come in.'

'It doesn't really suit.'

He looked at her appealingly. 'Don't close the door on me. Please, Grace. I'm in a bad place right now.'

She played for time. 'How did you get in through the main door?'

'I waited until someone else was coming along and pretended I couldn't find my key. I think she knew my face from when I lived here before. So please, Grace, can I come in?'

She stood back and allowed him into the hall, furious that she'd been caught on the hop, the sight of Gavin walking into her living room making her nauseous.

'Something smells nice,' he said.

'I'm in the middle of cooking,' she said, hoping he'd realise he was interrupting her.

'Good, I'm starving,' he said, rubbing his hands.

He was swamping her. He made it sound like he was still living here, pretending he'd never left. She struggled to break free from under the wave of thick, heavy resentment and annoyance that was tipped with a generous sliver of guilt. She folded her arms.

'I've only cooked enough for one. I wasn't expecting you.'

'Well, no, obviously not.' His eyes narrowed slightly.

'How could I have been expecting you?' she asked, breathing evenly, refusing to be sucked under the dark wave.

'I – look, I know I'm butting in, but I've had a really bad day and you're the only one I can talk to.' He put his hands on the back of a kitchen chair and leaned on it, as though life itself was weighing him down.

She was trembling inside but she spoke as evenly as she could. 'It's nice of you to think of me, but you do know we're over,' she said. She went across to the cooker to switch off the hob, but she twirled the wrong button, turning on a burner instead, and there was an instant smell of gas. 'Oops,' she said, her fingers shaky as she shut down all the burners and moved the pan with the bubbling omelette to one side.

He laughed harshly. 'You don't need to remind me that we're over. It's one of the reasons I'm in this mess.'

He must mean the reason why he was drunk. Especially on a weekday. 'What mess?'

'I was turned down.'

'Turned down? What for?'

'You've obviously forgotten. The promotion. In work.'

'I don't believe you.' She forced herself to look interested.

'I didn't get it. After all the work I put in, the late nights, the licking up to the boss … McCabe Corrigan decided I wasn't good enough to advance to the next level.'

'I'm sorry to hear that,' she said.

'Not good enough. They gave the job to an outsider. Can you believe that? It went to a rival of mine, Dean Reilly.' He stopped, as though that name should mean something to her.

'Dean Reilly?'

'The asshole I knew from college. He whisked it out from under my nose, just like that.' Gavin snapped his fingers.

'That's too bad,' Grace said. 'But I'm sure something bigger and better will come along for you. You know what they say, what's for you won't pass you by. Can I make you a coffee?'

'Can I make you a coffee?' he mimicked. 'Is that all you have to say?'

'What do you want me to say?'

'Let me see … ask me why *you're* the reason I'm in this mess. Why it's *your* fault I missed out on promotion. And what you're going to do about it.' He sat down at the table as though it was an ordinary night and he was waiting for her to serve up the evening meal.

She willed her voice to stay calm and her face to remain neutral. 'I'm sorry you missed out on promotion but I don't see how I had anything to do with it.'

He drummed the fingers of one hand against his chin. 'I was hoping you might say, for instance, "I made a mistake, Gavin, I should never have split us up … would you please take me back? Let me show you just how much you mean to me."'

'Hey,' she gave a half laugh, a horrible kind of embarrassment crawling around her skin at the way he'd imitated her voice. 'We've been finished since last autumn. I'd say we're long past the stage of anyone taking anyone back.'

'Are we?'

'Yes, Gavin and you know that too. I—'

'It's all about you, isn't it?' he said bitterly, slamming his fist down. 'What you want, what you don't want. I wasn't good enough for you either. I didn't want us to finish, Grace. I *love* you. More than anyone else in the world. I wanted us to be together. I was hoping some time apart would have brought you to your senses. Then you met Danny.'

There was a thick silence.

'Don't bring Danny into this,' she said after a while. 'He's got nothing to do with us.'

'Hasn't he?'

'No. You and I had come to a full stop before Danny and I got together.'

'That's something else I want to talk about.' Gavin shook his head as though he was trying to clear it. 'After he was gone I tried to pick up things with you, I said I'd be your friend. I gave you some space, knowing you were upset, knowing how horrible it is to lose someone out of your bed … someone you want so badly that your body is on fire …'

He stared at her. Everything stopped. Grace held her breath.

'See, Grace,' Gavin continued, 'part of the problem is, I thought we were happy together. Maybe we weren't in the first throes of passion but I thought you were happy with me as much as I was with you. I brought you flowers. I gave you presents. I looked after you in every way I could. In bed and out of bed. What more can a man do?'

She didn't reply, her silence an answer in itself. Gavin's face was tight with anger. This was a disaster. How had she let him in and misread him so badly?

'When you agreed to meet me for a drink at Christmas, I had hoped you'd come to your senses at last and that you'd got over your little meltdown. That we could pick up where we left off.'

She shook her head.

'I even had … a ring in my pocket that night, just in case. Then I had to bolt because I felt so sick … some of it was nerves. I was nervous at seeing you again. Can you believe that? I was sorry for the way I'd walked out on you that night, so I even came by here on New Year's Eve. I thought you might be sitting home alone, like me, with no party to go to.'

She shook her head, pin-pricks of anxiety running around the back of her head.

'I didn't think you'd have much to celebrate,' he paused again and she braced herself, 'but guess what, you were out. Out enjoying yourself somewhere.'

Grace found her voice. 'Come on, Gavin, you hardly expected me to be sitting in, waiting for you, having read your mind?'

'Where did I go wrong?' he asked. 'Was it bed? Was I not exciting enough for you?' His voice grew louder.

'It had nothing to do with that either. I'd always enjoyed … that side of things.' It was a lie. She'd even begun to dislike the over-ardent way Gavin had made love to her, scrutinising her face studiously and counting the minutes until she came as if it was some kind of test, then asking her how good it was, but she'd blamed herself for not being appreciative enough – until she'd realised that her feelings were perfectly valid.

'Did you enjoy sex with Danny?'

'I don't think that's any of your business.'

'In other words, you did. Was he better than me?'

She said nothing, feeling tears prick at the corner of her eyes.

'Don't mess me around, Grace.'

'I'm not messing you around.'

'Yes, you are, you're wrecking my head.'

She looked at the man sitting at her table and felt nothing but a cold stab of shock that she'd allowed this to happen.

'I was still hoping that we might get back together and I was going to ask you to marry me, even on New Year's Eve. I gave you plenty of chances, Grace. I thought you and me would have had a different ending.'

'You're joking.'

'So I'm a joke now, am I?'

Grace took a deep breath and spread out her hands. 'Look Gavin, there seems to be a big misunderstanding between us. I'm not sure what you're doing here.' She knew he wouldn't like what she was about to say, but she had no choice. 'I think you're a great person, you're loyal and dependable, and totally reliable,' she cringed. God. It sounded like some kind of job reference. She added, hoping to improve things a little, 'I think you'll have a great career and make some girl really, really happy ...'

Wrong thing. His face dropped. 'But it won't be you.'

She shook her head. 'We've gone through this already. I'm sorry, no.'

'Okay, so I give up. That's it. I've tried, I really have, Grace.'

She folded her arms against a sudden undercurrent of tension. 'Tried what?'

'Tried to make you love me. Tried to make you forget Danny. After he died I even offered you a shoulder to cry on and a night in bed. Even though he's not around anymore I never stood a chance after you met him, did I?'

'You and I were over before Danny and I got together.'

'Were we though? Really?'

Grace felt her heart hammering at the way he stared at her.

'It was bad enough that Dean Reilly swiped my job from under my nose ... I told you he came from a small little dump of an outfit on the fourth floor of a rickety building off Camden Street. Does that ring any bells, Grace?'

He was looking at her so closely she shivered.

'No,' she said, his words filling her with a terrible foreboding.

'Funnily enough,' Gavin continued, 'I have a dirty big feeling Danny was to blame for the way you cut me out of your life. I don't only feel it, I *know* it. I'm really sad about this, Grace. I'm really sad that you filled me up with a big fucking pack of *lies*.'

'I don't know what you're talking about.'

'But you do, Grace,' he said, laughing mirthlessly, standing up and scraping back his chair noisily. As he spoke, he walked slowly across to where she stood by the cooker. 'You've lied to me from the start. I would have forgiven it if you'd taken me back. Or even let me spend the night with you. But no, you can't even bear to hold my hand or let me kiss you. I've seen the look on your face when I tried to get close. The way you slid your hand out of mine, and turned your head away … it cut me up inside. I heard the truth about your little episode in the lift, months ago. I was hoping you might have had the guts to tell me the truth, I was hoping I might have been worth that much …'

He paused. She felt the ground rushing up to meet her, she was so dizzy. He was so close to her now there were only inches between them. All of a sudden she felt trapped. Her back was digging into the cooker and Gavin was looming over her, his face white and taut.

'I met the guys from college for a Christmas drink, the night before I saw you. Including Dean. Remember? We got talking about where he worked and I found out you only told me half the story, Grace. You made out you were alone in that lift when it broke down that day. But you weren't, were you? You met Danny long before Christmas. It was only after you met him that you sent me packing out of your life. I don't know where you've been hiding your guilty little conscience all this time, but it must be as black as hell.'

'Get out,' she said, suddenly scared at the intense stare in his eyes.

'I'm going. Just think of this, if you hadn't sent Danny out to the off-licence that night he'd still be alive, so it's your fault that he's dead.'

There was a thick silence. Then Grace heard her voice coming out in a thin stream, unlike its normal tone. 'What makes you think Danny was going to the off-licence that night?'

A pause. Gavin blinked. 'You told me.'

'Did I? I don't remember.' She'd scarcely spoken to Gavin about the details of Danny's accident, had she? Whatever she'd told him, she couldn't remember.

'Or maybe Lucia did, when I talked to her.'

She had the funny feeling he was lying. 'I can't imagine she would have, because Danny wasn't going near the village when he crashed.'

'Still,' he said, poking her in the shoulder, 'if you hadn't got tangled up with Danny, he might still be alive now.'

'Leave. Just go.'

'You really can't bear the sight of me, can you? This isn't over yet,' Gavin said. With a flourish, he stepped back from her, fixed his tie, jerking it up to his Adam's apple, and he marched out, banging the hall door after him.

Grace stood there, close to tears. She wanted to shout after him that she'd only met Danny on account of *him* – because if Gavin hadn't been so clod-footed as to stand on the hem of her dress, she wouldn't have needed it to be repaired and she might never have met Danny at all...

Chapter Fifty-two

The previous October ...

Because Gavin has stood on the hem of her maxi-dress, she leaves it in to be repaired. Because she's going out for Lucia's birthday that weekend, she rushes to the dressmaker during her lunch hour on Friday to collect it. Because she's forgotten her repair docket, the dressmaker takes a while to locate her dress. Because she ends up running late on her lunch hour from Arcadia, she decides to take the lift down the four floors rather than run down the narrow, slightly warped staircase that clings ambitiously to the walls of the Victorian building.

She pulls out her mobile and checks the time. She *is* late. And her mobile is about to conk out. Great. The lift doors open and she hurriedly steps inside.

'Oh.' Grace makes a slight noise of surprise when she realises there's a guy standing in the lift already. He's tallish and slim built yet he seems to be taking up a lot of space in the small interior. He has unruly muddy brown hair and green eyes.

'Sorry,' she says, moving slightly aside, giving him the space needed to exit. 'Were you getting out here?'

He smiles at her, a warm smile that lights up his friendly eyes, as though she's a very welcome diversion. 'No, I'm supposed to be going down. But I'm here instead.' He looks like it's a good place to be. He has a nice voice. Warm, with a kind of a lilt.

'That must have been my fault, opening the doors again,' she says, feeling foolish. He has a motorcycle helmet anchored under one arm and is holding a large envelope in the other hand. She guesses he must have been calling into the accountant's office across from the dressmaker's. She'd noticed it was closed for lunch. There was a sign on the door; due back at 2.15pm, which was three quarters of an hour from now. He shuffles back a little to make more space for her. She feels his eyes upon her as she presses the button for the ground floor. His eyes are warm and appreciative and he's looking at her as though she's beautiful and the best thing he's ever seen. They have the power of an invisible force field and it makes her run her fingers through her hair self-consciously

The lift doors close rather jerkily, snapping together with a final flourish. Nothing else happens. Feeling jittery all over with the way this guy is still looking at her, she jabs the button again, harder this time. The lift creaks, then it begins to descend and she lets out her breath.

'Gosh,' she says, because she feels the sudden and overwhelming need to say something to ease the tension, 'I thought we were going to be stuck for a minute.'

'So did I,' he says, sounding as though he's disappointed.

The lift descends about five feet when it comes to a juddering halt. She exchanges an alarmed glance with the guy. Grace has the weird idea that he has managed to bring it to a halt on purpose with the force of his mind – a totally ridiculous idea. Still, he seems quite at ease and not the least bit perturbed.

'Hey, I don't think—' her words die in her throat as the lights go out and they are plunged into darkness.

'*Hey!*' Now she is yelping in fear.

'Don't worry, it'll be fine,' he says. 'There's probably an alarm button somewhere.'

'I can't see in the dark,' she says.

'Have you a mobile phone? It might give us enough light to see by.'

'My battery's just about to die, I meant to charge it in the office but I left my charger at home. It's been one of those days ...' She rummages in her bag, feeling around the compartments and finding everything except her mobile. Purse, apartment keys, tissues, Vaseline, pen. Eventually her fingers connect with the smooth surface of her mobile. She takes it out, presses the button at the side, keys in her password, and it flickers into life for a brief moment before making a squawking sound and going blank. 'I do not believe this is happening. What about you?'

'I left my mobile at home. One of those days.' His voice has a hint of laughter in it. Had they been anywhere else, she would have liked the warm, rich sound of it.

'Tell me you're joking,' she babbles. 'Tell me you're going to find it, you're going to call someone and we'll be rescued very soon.'

'We will be rescued soon,' he says calmly. 'I'll try pressing some of the buttons, it might make something happen.'

There is the clinking sound of him placing his helmet down on the floor of the lift, then the rustle of him putting the envelope beside it. She shuffles around in the dark enclosed space, feeling him pass in front of her. She hears him sweeping his hands across the metal side of the lift, pressing various buttons, but nothing happens. She's grateful she's not on her own, trying to keep calm in this situation.

She tries to recall what else is located in the red-brick building. She's not surprised that the lift has jammed because the whole building is in serious need of modernisation. There is a charity shop on the ground floor, a reflexology and reiki clinic occupy the first floor, the second floor is taken up with a printing company and the third is vacant. Up on the fourth floor there are just the dressmaker's and the accountant.

'How long do you think it'll take,' she asks, 'before we're found?'

'Not too long,' he says. 'We could have set off an alarm somewhere.'

'But you don't know, do you?'

'No,' he says. 'Neither do I know how long it will take them to get us out of here.'

'I never thought of that,' she says. 'They'll need to get a repair man out. And ...' she gives a half laugh, 'I don't know who I mean by "they". It doesn't seem like the kind of building where someone is in charge.'

'Someone will soon realise the lift is not working, and they'll tell someone else who'll have a number to contact. '

'This is mad,' she says. 'I'll be late back to the office now.'

'Have you far to go?'

'Nah, the office is just five minutes' walk from here, on the way to Stephen's Green. They won't believe I was stuck in the dark in a broken down lift with a perfect stranger.'

Even in the dark she feels the force field of his eyes upon her. 'I'm Danny.'

'Hi, Danny, I'm Grace.'

'How do you do, Grace? Pleased to meet you.'

'Me too.' Even though she doesn't like the dark, she's beginning to see the humour in this. 'I'm glad I'm not alone. Why don't we make some noise?'

'I think we're caught between floors,' Danny says. 'I'm not sure who'd hear us.'

All the same, they begin to shout, banging on the doors, but they are met with silence. Grace pictures the dressmaker on the top floor with the radio on full blast against the whirr of the sewing machine, the closed accountant's office and the To Let sign plastered across the windows of the third floor. After a while her voice becomes hoarse and her hands hurt from banging the wall of the lift and she slumps against it. Then Danny stops shouting too and he leans against the lift beside her.

'This couldn't have happened at a worse time,' she says. 'I've a busy afternoon lined up and I was hoping to leave the office early this evening. I've a big date on tonight.'

'Oh?'

'Yeah, my sister's birthday,' she gabbled. 'She's having drinks in town tonight and that's why I was collecting the dress, I want to look my best.'

'Sounds good.'

'It's not really,' she says, surprising herself.

'Why not?'

'No matter how hard I try, I feel I'm always in the shade around her.'

'Why?'

She changes the subject. 'Imagine if something went crazily wrong and we didn't get out of this lift.'

'Yeah,' he says in a teasing voice. 'Imagine if we're stuck here forever and we're the last two people we'll ever see. All right for me, having looked at you, but not such a good prospect for you, with my face being the last you'd ever see.'

She can't help laughing. 'This is a weird conversation. Especially if you think it could be our last conversation. Ever.'

'Someone will come, Grace. They'll need to take the lift to the dressmaker's and realise something is wrong.'

When, though? The dressmaker wasn't expecting anyone else that lunch hour. And someone might just decide to use the stairs, even if they are narrow and dipping in the middle, and take for granted someone else has reported a faulty lift. She can make out the dim shape of him in the dark and she realises from the way he is moving around that he is taking off his leather jacket and putting it on the floor of the lift.

'Here, sit down,' he says. 'As soon as we hear any voices we can shout and bang for all we're worth. For now let's get comfortable. We could be in for a wait.'

'This is mad.'

'I know. Life generally is.'

She scrooches down until she is sitting on a corner of his jacket, her handbag on the floor beside her along with her dress, wrapped in tissue in a carrier bag. She draws her knees up to her chest and wraps her arms around them. 'This is exactly what I thought I'd be doing this afternoon, sitting on the cold floor of a lift in the pitch dark ...'

'Telling a perfect stranger your life story.'

'I never said that.'

'That's what happens, though, in these situations, isn't it? Like when you're on a long-haul flight sitting beside someone you'll never see again. Like when you're one of the last people left after a party and it's four in the morning and the few remaining stragglers huddle together for a chat. You drop the usual mask. Secrets have a habit of coming out and souls get bared,' he says in a light-hearted tone of voice and she can't help smiling.

'You wouldn't be all that interested in my life story.'

'Why not?'

She thinks of her job in insurance, her boyfriend of three years and the life she's been sharing with him for six months since he moved in with her. 'It's not all that scintillating.'

There is a silence. She can almost hear his mind turning over her words. Then he surprises her by saying, 'Have you any idea what the odds are on you being here?'

'Well if my boyfriend hadn't stood on the hem of my dress I wouldn't have needed to get it repaired and I ...'

She senses him shaking his head.

'Nah. I don't mean being stuck in the lift with a guy from Mayo. I mean you, being here in this world, moving around, alive and well. In other words, what are the odds on you, Grace, being born as you?'

'You must have been on some great soul-baring plane journeys, and stayed up all night at lots of save-the-world parties. I haven't a clue.'

'You should never, ever feel in the shade, because the chances of you being born as you, Grace, are something like one in a few thousand quadrillions.'

She tilts her head back against the cool wall of the lift. So what if she's late back to the office, she has a perfectly valid excuse. She's beginning to relax into this. She likes the sound of his voice and the things he's saying. 'Is there such a thing as a quadrillion? I was never any good at maths. I can't even imagine what that figure might look like written down.'

'Neither can I, but it just goes to show how amazing you really are before you even do anything at all. Before you even wake up in the morning or lift your little finger or bend your toe. So don't ever say or even think that your life is not all that scintillating. Because it is. Everybody's is. And we're only here once. That's why we should make the most of every single day and live life to the fullest.'

She digests this in silence for a few minutes. There is still no sound coming from outside. They could almost be in a tomb. 'These are very deep thoughts for a young guy like you to be having,' she says. 'You must have been on some kind of monastic retreat.'

'Not quite.'

'And it's a mad conversation to be having in a broken lift in the dark.'

'Mad, but true.'

'Supposing ...' she begins, before hesitating.

'Supposing what?' he says, his voice soft.

'Well, just imagine if we didn't get out of here, which I know we will, would you have any regrets? I mean, I'd just like to know what they are, because it sounds like you must have an amazing kind of life. From the time you wake up in the morning before you lift your little finger.'

He laughs. 'I wouldn't quite say that. And you could be surprised at my regrets.'

'So you do have some.'

'Yes, but maybe not what you'd expect.'

'Like what? Climbing Mount Kilimanjaro? Swimming with dolphins? Name five.' It's turning into a game that is taking her mind off their predicament, as well as his comment about making the most of her life.

He wriggles slightly in the narrow space, making himself more comfortable. 'I want to make a few things up to a few people.'

'I can't imagine you needing to kiss and make up.'

'It's going to take me a while to redeem myself. But other than that, I want to sleep out under the stars in Kerry and count as many as I can.'

'Why Kerry?'

'It's an International Dark Sky reserve, with little or no light pollution. It's possible to see the Milky Way and the Andromeda Galaxy and hundreds of other star clusters.'

'I didn't know that. That's your number one?'

'Yep. Number two, I want to … go skinny-dipping. I've never gone skinny-dipping.'

'Is that legal?'

'It all depends on where you do it. Can you just imagine the fun of it? The freedom? The feeling of natural sea water sliding off your skin?'

'So long as it wasn't freezing cold. What's number three?'

'I want to go kite-flying in the park on a windy day, and build a really decent snowman.'

'That counts as two.'

'Does it? Then I've more than five. I also want to watch the sun rise over Glendalough, have you ever done that?'

'I can't remember the last time I was even there.'

'Tsk, tsk, you're missing something beautiful. And, I want to go up in a hot air balloon over the Boyne Valley at sunset.'

'I've never done any of those things. And I didn't know you could hot air balloon over the Boyne Valley.'

'Yep, you can. In the summer, weather permitting. Now it's your turn. Name five things you'd be sorry you hadn't done if we never got out of here.'

She hesitates. 'Mmm, can you regret something you might be about to do? Like, in advance?'

'How could you regret something you're about to do?'

'I just … might be.'

'You have to tell me.'

'I can't.'

'Why not?'

'It's too hard.'

'Why is it too hard?'

'Because…' she closes her eyes tightly. 'Promise you'll forget this the minute we get out of here.'

'I promise. It will clear off my brain like a melted snowflake. As soon as we get out of here we'll be going our separate ways anyway, like when you disembark the plane. By the time you get to passport control, you've forgotten all about the person you sat beside and the story they've told you.'

'Well then, it's my boyfriend. I'm afraid he's going to ask me to marry him.'

'That sounds all wrong to me. How could fear come into it? Grace, you should never be afraid of anything. Especially if you love the person.'

'I'm afraid because I don't think I want to. Marry him. I'm afraid to tell him that. Gavin is mad about me, I know he is, he's crazy about me, sometimes too crazy the way he falls all over me. We're together three years and he moved in with me six months ago, but I don't think I love him. I think I'm with him for the wrong reasons.' Her words are soft, as if she's afraid to speak them, and they echo like a whisper around the confined space. But she's sitting with her back to the wall, figuratively as well as physically, and they ring true to her.

'Then you can't marry him,' he says.

'At the same time I don't want to hurt him.'

'You'd be wronging him far more in the long term if you marry him in a half-hearted way.'

'You see, thing is, I could be expecting too much? Couldn't I? There is no perfect partner out there, is there? No perfect marriage, and no such thing as bells and whistles and having it all. Maybe I'm looking for too much.'

'In this life you generally get what you feel you deserve. What do you feel you deserve out of marriage?'

She thinks for a minute. 'I guess the usual things, loyalty, love, respect, two-way commitment.'

'Those things should be a given. Let's see. Does your boyfriend make you want to leap out of bed each morning, filled with passion and excitement?'

She laughs. 'Ah, here, Danny, get real. Usually we both grump around throwing cereal into us before we go to work.'

'Are you happy waking up beside him? Does he make you tingle all the way down to your toenails in bed?'

'So we're supposed to have the perfect sex life as well and swing off the wardrobe?'

'I didn't say that. Sometimes a cuddle is enough. To make you tingle. Does he look after you properly and treat you the way you deserve? Why are you with him?'

'He's great at looking after me, he's too kind at times, and considerate and reliable and he wraps me up in cotton wool. I hate saying this, but he's become too overprotective, nearly smothering me. Sometimes I feel I can't … breathe.'

'Does he make you feel glowy and buzzy inside, like you want to do a silly dance with him and laugh a lot?'

'No.'

'What excites you about him? What is it about him that makes your heart beat faster?'

Grace says nothing. To her consternation, she can't answer that question, because there are no answers.

'If you can't make up your mind about marrying him,' he says, 'there's an easy way to find out what's right for you to do.'

'And that is?'

'You just have to imagine what your life would be like if he wasn't in it.'

Grace sits in the dark for a few moments, absorbing his words.

Then, 'Shhh …' she says, 'I thought I heard a noise.'

They both stay silent. There is a clinking noise coming from somewhere above them. Danny gets to his feet and bangs on the lift doors. He shouts out and there is a muffled response and he shouts again. There are answering voices, clearer now.

'It looks like help is on the way,' Danny says.

Lulled into revealing her thoughts and fears in the anonymity of the dark, Grace feels a ripple of alarm. 'Don't forget – you promised.'

"The snowflake has melted. We might never see each other again after this.' He reaches down and ruffles the top of her head. From somewhere above them comes the whine of a drill. 'It was lovely talking to you. Just remember this: you being you, in this world, beats odds of one in a few thousand quadrillions. Make that count, whatever you do. Don't settle for anything less than you deserve. Be the brilliant person you are.'

His touch has warmed her as much as his words. 'One of the first things I'm going to do after I get out of here is to find out how many noughts there are in a quadrillion,' she says shakily.

One of the second things she's going to do is imagine the life she might have without Gavin in it. She waits quietly while Danny talks to their rescuers. She hears the excited voice of the dressmaker. Other voices join in. They've probably been trapped for about half an hour, but it feels longer. She counts down the last few minutes as the noise from outside intensifies, and the babble of voices gets louder. It sounds as if the whole building is outside waiting to see who emerges from the lift.

She's a different Grace to the one who went in, she knows that for sure. There's something diaphanous bubbling up through her veins, something fresh and new that wasn't there before – which she thinks must be crazy considering she's been trapped in the confines of a dark lift with a friendly guy from Mayo, whom she'll probably never see again.

At least that's what she'd thought at the time, little realising that Danny was going to appear back in her life again and transform it completely.

Chapter Fifty-three

Standing in the porch, Matt took a deep breath. It was now or never. 'How about coming over for some food, you and Abbie,' he said.

Well done, Matt. He'd managed to make it sound like he entertained on a regular basis, even though his heart felt it was about to trip right out of its socket, and they were now at the hall door and it had taken him fifteen minutes to pluck up the courage.

He'd popped into Janet's to drop back Abbie's monkey teddy after she'd left it in his car on the kite-flying afternoon. To his delight, he'd been invited in for coffee – *yes, please,* and *thank you, God* – ostensibly so he could admire Abbie's latest treasures brought home from the crèche. For a pleasant half an hour he and Janet had basked together in the glow of Abbie's accomplishments, but now he was at the hall door and he'd be gone in a minute, and he desperately wanted to move things on.

Janet looked at him as though he'd suggested a trip to outer space in a flying saucer. 'Am I hearing things? Food?' she said, lifting an eyebrow. 'What kind of food? Beans on toast? Or have they opened a McDonald's near your place? I know how quickly these outlets can spring up overnight.'

He grimaced. He'd never exactly been all that great in the kitchen, not even when he'd lived with Janet, ham and cheese toasties, the occasional omelette or fry-up being the extent of his culinary skills, relying on convenience M&S foods and pub lunches to supplement his diet and get him through the week when he lived on his own.

'It was just an idea,' he said, trying to look nonchalant. 'Thought I'd save you cooking some evening, and no, actually it's not McDonald's. It's a … wait for it … Matt Slattery special.'

Whatever way those last few words came out he felt mortified. If Janet noticed his embarrassment, she said nothing, preferring to gloss over it.

'And since when did you swallow a Jamie Oliver cookbook?' She looked at him suspiciously. Less scathing than before, he thought. Maybe with a hint of interest. Then again, maybe he was being overly optimistic.

'It's not that either,' he said. No need to tell her he'd been practising with recipes he'd got off the Internet. He'd been pleasantly surprised at the number of sites available giving step-by-step instructions for novices and kitchen-shy folk such as he was.

'So what's on the menu then?'

'Told you. It's a surprise,' he said.

'It will be if it's not coming directly from the chippers or the takeaway.'

'Well, are you up for it?'

'I suppose …' Janet appeared to be giving it a lot of thought. She looked like she was about to say 'yes'. Then, on a softer note she said, 'Matt? What's all this in aid of?'

He tried to look innocent. 'All what?'

'You know …' she shrugged, 'the zoo, the park and now this. And don't tell me you're just saving me from cooking or washing-up.'

He shrugged. This wasn't part of the plan. Images of a romantic kind of meal – including Abbie of course – where he'd impress Janet with great food without breaking a sweat, candles lit, wine decanted, a tea towel carelessly slung over his shoulder, were fast disappearing. Janet was waiting for him, her head tilted to one side.

'Do you still think you're in some kind of competition with Simon? Because I'm not going to be too impressed if you think you're scoring brownie points. I don't care what you get up to, or what you have tucked up your sleeve for us, nothing has really changed. Simon is Abbie's biological father, he'll always be part of her life, and you have to trust me and accept that.'

An awkward silence. 'Are you saying 'no' then?'

'Why are you asking me?' Janet asked guilelessly. 'Why exactly are you asking us to dinner? What's your ulterior motive?'

'Ulterior? Come on Janet, that's a bit strong. Can't I not just invite you over?'

She shook her head. 'Nah – not until you tell me the real, honest-to-God reason.'

This was Janet, soft, womanly, beautiful, but with a core of honest-to-God steel. She lifted an eyebrow, as though she dared him to speak from the heart, but there was something warm in her eyes as if she were ready to listen. She was wearing slim jeans and a soft white shirt, and standing so near he caught the scent of her and could pick out the freckles on her face and the start of tiny crescents of laughter lines fanning out from her eyes. He wanted to crush her in his arms, and kiss each freckle and tiny groove, but he was a long way off from that. He stared at her until he began to feel dizzy.

'I'm asking you because ...' he hesitated.

Because I want to be with you, I want to see your eyes laughing into mine, I want us to be best friends, I want to sleep with you tonight and all the nights ahead, to take care of you and Abbie, to be there for you whenever you need me. To hell with Simon, I know I was a thick eejit for breaking us up but I'm trying to find my way back to you, somehow, even if it's a roundabout way. I keep thinking of someone I didn't even know who was once full of life who's now dead, and someone else who's missing him lots, and it makes me want to wring the happiness out of every moment of precious life and share it with you.

He thought he'd spoken the words aloud, as they seemed to hover in the air around them, enclosing him and Janet in a warm space of their own. Then from the kitchen, where she'd been allowed to watch one more episode of *Puffin Rock* before bed, Abbie squealed excitedly, yelling something about the next-door neighbour's kitten jumping into their back garden. Matt blinked, and the fragile moment exploded into thin air like a burst soap bubble.

'Oh, forget it, we'll come,' Janet said, as if she was doing him a huge favour. 'Why should I pass up a free meal, ahem, a Matt Slattery special, even if your motives are …' she looked directly at him, 'questionable?'

Was he imagining it, or were Janet's words loaded? He could have sworn she was deliberately fluttering her eyelashes. It made him want to shout as excitedly as Abbie.

Chapter Fifty-four

When Grace came back to her desk after a team meeting on Friday afternoon, she had a missed call on her mobile. Lucia. Her sister had left a terse message asking Grace to call her as soon as she could.

No way was she calling her in the middle of Friday afternoon. Lucia was bound to be busy clearing her desk in preparation for getting out of the office after five, as they had planned to meet after work that evening. Grace put her mobile to one side, and was surprised when it rang twenty minutes later.

'Grace? Did you get my message?'

'Hi Lucia, I did, but aren't you in the office?'

'I am, but I need to talk to you. It won't wait. I had an email this morning from Jennifer.'

'Jennifer who?'

'Emer's sister, remember?' Lucia said.

Grace tensed as the image of a very drunken Emer swam in front of her. 'God, yes.'

'Jennifer had something to tell me …' Lucia paused.

'Hang on a minute,' Grace said, knowing she couldn't talk in the middle of the busy office. It was okay for the likes of Lucia, with a private office to herself. She got up from her desk and waved her phone at Karen before she went out to the stairwell. Not very private either, but better than having her side of the phone call echoing around the office. Three floors up meant there wouldn't be much footfall on the stairwell.

'Go on, Lucia.'

'Remember you thought Stacy was harassing you,' Lucia said. 'You were right. She was behind the Indian delivery, the torn-up photo and a couple of other things.'

'Why is this all coming out now?'

'Stacy met Emer for a drink last night. Apparently it had been her own little piece of revenge. Stacy was quite convinced you made Danny leave rehab early and fall off the wagon for some reason. She got your details from Danny's younger sister, saying she wanted to talk to you about him. Then, when you went to Mayo to talk to his mother, word got back to her that you genuinely hadn't known anything about Danny's past. Whatever you said, it impressed Danny's mother no end, who told his sisters, who in turn passed it on to Stacy. She's still crazy with grief over Danny, but now feels guilty over what she did to you. She confessed to Emer, hoping word would get back to you, as she's too embarrassed to contact you directly.'

'And so she should be. Did she not realise that I was grieving too?' Grace's voice rose. 'Sorry Lucia, I don't mean to sound angry with you.'

'It's fine, sis. I understand. I'm just glad it's sorted and over.'

There were footsteps coming up the stairwell, some energetic soul who had decided to take the stairs instead of the lift. But whoever it was went through the door into the second floor. Not quite that energetic, so.

'Stacy doesn't by any chance have a black motorbike?' Grace said.

'You're not still seeing them are you?'

'Now and again. But I know there are hundreds of similar bikes on the road,' Grace went on, running a hand through her hair. 'I'm getting over that obsession.'

'Still on for tonight?'

'Yep,' Grace said. 'I'll be down in the foyer just after five.'

'Perfect,' Lucia said.

Before she went back to her desk, Grace called Matt, expecting to get his voicemail, but instead he picked up the call.

'Hi Matt,' she said. 'I thought I'd have to leave a message because you'd be out doing some detecting.'

'I'm in the station doing just that,' he said. 'Mostly it's very unglamorous, and involves checking detail after painstaking detail at my desk. How are you?'

'Just letting you know I've found out who was responsible for sending me those lovely presents in the post. It was that fervent admirer of Danny's, who was very upset when he'd died and kind of blamed me. She won't be doing it again.'

'Good. That's everything wrapped up so.'

'There was just one other thing …' Grace began, remembering her surprise at the way Gavin had spoken of Danny being in the off-licence that fateful night.

'What's that?'

'Forget it, Matt, it's nothing. Thanks for all the help,' Grace said, hearing the door below her open and the sound of footsteps coming up the stairs towards her. Besides, she must have told Gavin herself. Otherwise how could he have known that Danny was supposed to have been in the village that night?

* * *

Grace came through the foyer of the building just after five that evening when she heard her name being called. It wasn't Lucia, however. Instead, she saw her parents sitting there, waiting for her.

'Mum! Dad! What's up?' At the suddenness of seeing them like this, tears pricked her eyes. They looked good; Mum dressed casually in a pair of blue jeans, white top and striped jacket, Dad wearing grey chinos and a polo top, with a blue jumper slung around his shoulders. They looked happy to see her and they both enveloped her in a hug that felt warm and solid and comforting.

'There's nothing up, Grace,' Mum said. 'We're over this weekend for our friends' fortieth wedding anniversary, but seeing as how you wouldn't come to us, we came a day early to see you. Lucia helped to set it up.'

'Lucia!' Grace smiled and shook her head.

'We thought it would be a good idea to bring you out,' Dad said.

'This is … a surprise all right,' Grace said, dabbing her eyes. 'But a lovely one, thanks. Are we going anywhere nice?'

'Somewhere we can hear ourselves talk,' Dad said. 'We've booked into the Slade Hotel for the weekend, that's where the party is on tomorrow night, so we've reserved a table there for the three of us for this evening.'

* * *

The boutique hotel along the banks of the canal was the perfect spot to linger over a meal, sipping wine and having a chat. The restaurant was on the second floor, with huge windows overlooking the tree-shaded canal. Rain was forecast for later that night, but now it was a calm evening, the placid sky outside tinged with golden-pink light rimmed with cotton wool clouds. The surface of the canal was dappled here and there with the reflection of trees in full bloom. For the first time in months, Grace felt herself relax a little.

With her parents' gentle encouragement, she spoke of Danny and how much he'd meant to her. She showed them the couple of photos she had of him on her mobile.

'Looks like you had some fun times,' her dad said.

'I'm really sorry we didn't get to meet him,' Mum said. 'He sounds like someone after my own heart because he helped you to be happy, Grace, '

'He did.' She didn't mention a word about Danny's past, now wasn't the time. She knew she could trust Lucia not to mention it either. Maybe she could talk about it another time. When Dad went out to the bathroom, Grace turned to Mum and said, choosing her words carefully, 'I didn't think you'd find Danny good boyfriend material compared with Gavin. Were you disappointed I didn't make it to the altar rails with Gavin?'

Mum sighed. 'Grace, I remember that conversation, and I apologise if I gave you the wrong impression. I thought Gavin was lovely, if a bit quiet. Sometimes the ordinary, routine kind of days with someone who is quiet and unassuming are the building blocks of a steady marriage. I thought you might be overlooking that, but I was terribly wrong ... I should have trusted your instincts.' Mum gave her a long, thoughtful glance. 'You might as well know I've been talking to Lucia,' she said, looking as though she, too, was choosing her words extra carefully

'Mum—'

'Just hear me out, Grace, you weren't talking properly to me or your dad so I had to turn to Lucia to find out how you really were behind all the vague phone calls. First, I want to make perfectly clear that you understand where we're coming from. We all love you. We all only want the very best for you, and we're not talking about a glittering career or a high-flying boyfriend whisking you to the altar rails. We're talking about you being you, the one and only Grace, and being happy in your own skin and doing your own unique twirl on this stage we call life, whatever that means for you. We were concerned at the start that you might have hooked up with Danny on the rebound from Gavin, but we can see it was far from that.

Also, from the bit Lucia has recently told me, you were perfectly right to drop Gavin out of your life. We'd all be very upset to think you were in a relationship unless it was filling you with happiness and contentment, and from the sound of it, that wasn't the case with Gavin. Which brings me to my next point.'

'You mean there's more?' Grace felt a smile tremble on her lips.

'I'd hate you to think I was interfering, but at the same time I'm not going to stand silently by this time. Lucia has told me that Gavin has come sniffing around again.'

'That's right. He's offering me a shoulder to cry on. I feel kind of guilty because I can only imagine how much I hurt him.'

Her mother snorted. 'Guilty? Don't be ridiculous. We're not going there. No matter how much he tries to worm his way back into your life again, please, Grace, don't let him. You're in a very vulnerable place now and I'm afraid he'll catch you with your defences down. I was alarmed with what Lucia told me about his checking up on you, about how uncomfortable he made you feel. He seemed to want to control your life, and that's not on. Someone like Gavin, who needs to be in control to cover his own insecurities, will only become more manipulative over time. We only saw the good, mannerly side of him, I'm afraid. I'm really glad you had the guts and the cop on to cut your ties with him.'

'It was a relief. I didn't realise how much he'd been suffocating me until he left. He turned up drunk the other night and caught me unawares, before I knew it, he was in the apartment.'

Mum shook her head. 'That's not acceptable. You'll have to be firm, Grace, and don't open the door to him. He'll soon get the message.'

Her Mum spoke in a no-nonsense voice that made Grace smile.

'If there's any more carry-on from him call me or Lucia immediately. You mightn't like to, but we're fully prepared to threaten him with the police if he continues to hassle you. I didn't tell your father, because he'd be out for his blood. And here's Michael now, so we're talking about plans for your thirtieth.'

'What plans?' Grace said, whirling at the sudden change in conversation, her heart warmed with the love and concern emanating from her mother.

'I hope you'll all come over to Paris – you, Lucia and Robert. We'll book you into a hotel and make a long weekend of it. Good food and wine, a spa. If that's what you'd like.'

'Could we go hot air ballooning?' Grace asked.

'I don't see why not,' Dad said. 'If you want some fun activities I'll check out what's available. We could start with a chocolate walking tour …'

'Now you're talking,' Grace smiled.

Chapter Fifty-five

Janet looked impressed, Matt congratulated himself, when he ushered her and Abbie into his apartment on Friday evening. They'd been here before, dropping in regularly to visit before he'd moved in with Janet, but this was different. He was feeling jittery, and he had been all over the place before they arrived, setting the table out as decoratively as possible with cutlery and glasses, napkins, tea lights in holders and a small jug of flowers. Across the mantelpiece, he'd even hooked up a strand of battery-operated LED lights that he'd bought, along with the napkins and candles, in the homeware section of a department store. It looked as though he'd pulled out all the stops he decided, watching Janet's gaze scan the room. There was a bottle of Merlot on the table, and white wine chilling in the fridge. He had the television switched off and music playing in the background. Best of all, there was a succulent aroma of chicken supreme coming from the oven. All he had to do was pour the wine and cook the rice.

'Are we at a party?' Abbie asked, skipping across to the table, taking it all in.

'Umm, not really,' he said, afraid of disappointing her, not sure of what constituted kids' parties nowadays, apart from clowns and face-painting, neither of which he could manage.

'We must be, 'cos I'm wearing my party clothes,' she said. 'Look.'

She looked down at herself, at her white top with the swirly appliqué, pink velour jeans and white sandals.

'Yes, we must be then,' he said solemnly, meeting Janet's eyes. 'And they're lovely party clothes.'

'Will there be lots of rubbish to eat?'

'*Rubbish?*' This time he threw Janet a startled glance. What had she been saying to Abbie?

Abbie piped up. 'Mammy always says I get far too much rubbish at parties.' This was said in a tone of voice so like Janet's that Matt almost convulsed with laughter.

'Well there'll be no rubbish at this party,' he said.

'Awww. Not even some ice cream?'

'I'm sure Matt has ice cream, but it's for later,' Janet said, giving him a meaningful glance.

'Yes, later,' he agreed. 'I have something else for you for now,' he said, giving her a sticker book and crayons he'd picked up on his shopping trip.

He poured Janet a glass of white wine and poured one for himself. After a while he checked the food, lifting the dish out of the oven, and giving it some seasoning and a stir before putting it back in.

'Smells nice,' Janet said.

'Thanks,' he said, grinning at her, feeling his way cautiously. He could have been on a first date, he was so edgy. He told himself to chill as he switched on the gas hob under the rice and put the plates to warm in the grill compartment over the oven. Then he rummaged in the press for the serving dishes, his back prickling with the realisation that while Abbie was occupied with her sticker book and crayons, Janet was watching him.

He should have left the television on for distraction.

And then it happened.

'Matt, watch out,' Janet said, jumping to her feet.

Abbie yelled. 'Dad, *help!*'

Out of the corner of his eye he saw a burst of flame coming from near the cooker top. The end of the tea towel, trailing too close to the gas hob, had caught fire and Janet was dashing towards it. Matt pushed Janet aside and got there first, wrapping the towel over on itself to help smother the flame before plunging it into the sink and turning on the taps. Immediately there was a hissing noise and the acrid scent of burning as a thin plume of smoke rose in the air.

He was shaking, right down to his fingertips, at the close shave.

'Are you okay?' Janet asked.

He waggled his hands in the air, becoming aware of a smarting in the skin of his fingers. 'Just got a bit of a sting.'

'Here, let's see.' He looked down at the top of her head, the curve of her forehead, the earnest expression on her face as she took his hands in hers and carefully examined their surface. The suddenness of her touch sent a jolt through him. 'You'll live,' she said, glancing up at him, so close he could see the flecks in her eyes. 'But run those hands under the cold tap for a while,' she ordered, pushing his hands under the running water, then scooping out the sodden mess of tea towel from the sink. She shoved it into the bin, just as the rice began to boil over. Deftly she lifted the pot off the hob and lowered the gas, returning it then so that the rice simmered gently.

'Have you any cooling gel? Like for burns? Just in case.'

'I think there's some in the bathroom cabinet,' he said.

'I'll get it, don't move,' Janet said.

He stayed where he was, letting the water sluice over his hands and gurgle down the drain. He was aware of Abbie dancing around behind him.

'Wow, Dad, you *saved* us,' she said, making a sing-song out of her words. 'You rescued us from the fire. You *saved* us.'

Something dark blurred around the edges of his vision. Matt blinked. There was nothing but the feel of cool water under his hands and the sound of Abbie's childish voice. The echo of her shouting for help. Nothing and everything. Inside himself he felt a give of some sorts, like a thin shell being cracked right open, and he was spinning away out of control as fractured images whirled around before his eyes.

* * *

A summer's day with a sky so deeply blue it looked like it would stretch to infinity and last forever, and made you feel all light and happy, the gleam of the cool canal reflecting the sky. He watches on the sidelines, listening to the shouts of laughter coming from the gang that he and Liam hang around with, the thud of running footsteps across warm, scented grass followed by the splash of young bodies dropping down into the canal water. Pale arms and legs and heads with dark slicked hair emerging from the water, bodies sleek and shiny and full of life and dripping wet as they climb back up the gate of the lock with the ease of energetic monkeys shimmying up a tree. Heads shaking, firing drops of water out into warm air. More laughter. More running footsteps accompanied by bloodcurdling whoops of joy.

Suddenly there is a pause, a split second of silence, when time stops under the bright blue sky, when nothing happens and everything shifts. Then a cry for help. Timmy, his mate.

Matt Slattery, thirteen years old, freezes.

Someone comes running up from behind him, in his peripheral vision he sees shoes being flung to one side, a red blur as a buoy is lifted and thrown so that it wheels through the air and falls down into the canal – why couldn't he at least have done that much? – the splash of someone jumping in. Then the splash of someone else diving in: his brother Liam.

He is still frozen to the spot as Timmy is brought out of the canal, his lifeless-looking body flopping down on the bank, his skin shiny and translucent in the sun. More people arrive to help. They lie him down on the warm grass to resuscitate him.

It takes an awful long time for Timmy to cough and splutter, moments when something died inside Matt. He is still frozen to the spot as the ambulance approaches, the noise of the siren shearing away all the fun and innocence of that sunny afternoon.

* * *

'Matt?'

He blinked. Disorientated, he slumped against the sink. Janet was standing beside him with a bottle of cooling gel. Abbie was sitting on a rug on the floor with the paper napkin holder on the rug beside her and was taking out the napkins to make a bed for her monkey teddy.

'I gave Abbie something to occupy herself with,' Janet said in a low voice. 'I didn't think you'd mind.'

He couldn't talk. He shook his head.

'I brought in a towel as well,' she said, proffering a navy towel. 'I think it's okay to take your hands out now.' She nodded at his hands held under the stream of running water.

He took his hands away and she swaddled them in the towel. He pushed his hands, still wrapped in the towel, up to his face and rubbed them across his forehead and cheekbones.

'Are you okay? Matt, what happened just then?' Janet asked.

'I just remembered something, an accident, that happened when I was a kid …'

'Do you want to talk about it?' Janet asked.

'I can't.' Matt's voice cracked. 'I need to get my own head around it. Can we just … go on with things tonight? I'm fine. I'll just stick some of that gel on and we'll have some food.'

'I'll help,' Janet said. 'Can't have you wrecking more tea towels,' she joked. 'I know you said it would be a Matt Slattery special,' she grinned. 'But I didn't expect the full fireworks.'

He was grateful that Janet didn't press him to talk. Doubly grateful that they both moved around Matt's small kitchen with ease, as though they were used to it. Janet was impressed by his cooking. Abbie loved being at Matt's special party for grown-ups. Matt sipped wine and Janet kept up the light, superficial chat, and he was grateful for that too. Then he produced the ice cream and put a movie on the television for all three of them, and Janet let Abbie stay up way past her bedtime, and they sat on the sofa while the evening bleached away from the sky outside and pin-pricks of lights came on in the city. Matt breathed slowly and soaked it up, needing the pure normality of it all; it helped him to cope with the feeling that a giant sticking plaster had come undone inside him and his guts were about to spill out, but not here, and not just yet.

As soon as the movie was over, it was time for them to go.

'Are you sure you'll be all right?' Janet asked, pausing in his doorway.

'I'm fine.'

Janet looked dubious. 'You know where I am if you want to talk, Matt. I thought you were going to faint earlier this evening.'

'Nah,' he said, smiling easily. 'You don't get two party pieces from me in the one night,' he joked.

'Don't I?' she said, with a teasing note in her voice and a look that instantly turned him on.

He risked kissing her on the forehead. It tasted sweet. Best of all, she didn't pull away.

'Thanks, Janet.'

'Bye, Matt.'

He closed the door behind them. The apartment felt more empty than ever now that they'd gone. He looked at the indents made in the cushions placed along the sofa where the three of them had sat and wished he could magic them back somehow. He poured the last of the wine into his glass and went across to the sofa by the window.

He'd forgotten what had happened by the canal when he was thirteen. Nobody had said anything to him afterwards. There had been no one blaming him for freezing on the spot. Not even a whisper of censure. Someone had even patted him on the back as if he'd been a hero of sorts, which he felt he didn't deserve. But somehow, at the core of him, he hadn't forgotten the horror of standing by uselessly, of not being able to trust himself to do the right thing, and hating himself for being found wanting.

An hour later, his mobile buzzed. Janet.

'Hi, Janet, everything okay?'

'Yes, Abbie's conked out and I'm sitting in the kitchen looking out into the garden, wishing it was warm enough to sit out.'

Her voice was soothing. Gentle and low. He relaxed back into the cushions and closed his eyes. He could picture her sitting by the patio door in the kitchen. 'Some evening soon, it will be.'

'I'm calling to say tonight was lovely, thanks,' she said. 'I hope you're okay.'

'Glad you enjoyed it and I'm very okay.'

'Are you sure? I thought …'

'My hand is fine.'

'I didn't mean your hand …'

'Yeah, well, I had one of those weirdy moments when you recall something that happened years ago as a kid. I'd forgotten about it and it surprised me.' No need to go into the details when it didn't matter anymore.

'You used to have nightmares, Matt, sometimes.'

'Did I?'

'Yes, after Simon came home and before you moved out.'

He vaguely remembered Janet mentioning them, but he'd brushed aside her concerns in the heat of everything else.

'I was wondering if you'd like to come for dinner tomorrow evening?' Janet's voice was ultra casual.

'Tomorrow?' His heart lifted. 'I'm on the eight-to-four shift, so that would be perfect.'

'Say around half-six?' she went on. 'Abbie will be seeing Simon in the afternoon but he'll have her home by six o'clock. And maybe you could read her a bedtime story ...'

'Janet ...' his voice broke. 'That would be great. Thanks. Actually ...' A long pause.

'Yes?'

His nerves were gone. The words stuck in his throat. He was the boy standing at the edge of the canal, unable to move, unable to articulate his fear, feeling useless. Now that he recognised it for what it was, he told his younger self it was okay, he was okay, it was fine.

Don't waste a moment, Grace had said, reminding him of the sheer fragility of life.

Tell her you love her.

He took a deep breath and said, 'I'd be very happy to come because I love Abbie and ... I love you.'

'Thanks, Matt,' Janet's voice was warm. 'I never stopped loving you, I didn't like the way you were behaving, but I ...' she paused.

They both spoke together.

'I was a big eejit,' Matt said.

'I love you still,' Janet said.

A pause.

Matt allowed her words to come to rest inside him like a calm, deep pond settling around his heart. 'Even though I'm a big eejit?' he said.

'Maybe you are, at times,' Janet said, with soft laughter in her voice, 'but your party pieces just about make up for that.'

Chapter Fifty-six

When Grace arrived home to Rathbrook Hall later that night, she had the funny sensation that someone had been there, in her apartment, in her absence. It was a faint impression, like the ghostly memory of a lingering scent. She looked around to see if anything was out of place but it was impossible to say. The posters were beaming messages into her living room as a testament to Danny's life-affirming spirit. In her bedroom, the duvet was slightly indented, and not as smooth as she normally left it. And her underwear drawer was slightly open. Then again she'd been in a hurry out to work that morning, hadn't she? And she didn't believe in ghosts.

While she stood there, breathing hard, her phone rang.

Gavin. She'd already had two missed calls from him when she was out with her parents, these had been followed by a text as she was in a taxi on the way home, to ask her what she'd been up to that she'd been unable to take his calls. Her first reaction when she'd got his text had been one of sheer annoyance, but she was so buoyed up after seeing her parents that it took the edge off the sick feeling his words gave her.

Best to get this over with, she decided, accepting the call.

'Oh, so you're home now,' he said.

'What is it?' she said, sounding as firm as possible.

'Well now, that's not very nice and friendly, is it?'

'No, because it's late and I wasn't expecting you to call after the other evening.'

'That's exactly why I'm calling. Have you had time to think about what I said?'

'No, I haven't. I've more important things to think about. Besides you'd had too much to drink.'

'I was right, though, wasn't I?'

'Right about what?' As she spoke to him, the first few spatters of rain were beading the windowpanes. Grace went around the apartment pulling down blinds and closing curtains against the dark night.

'You dumped me because you met Danny.'

'I am not having this conversation. I do not want to talk to you again.'

'Do you miss him, in bed at night?' he asked.

'I'm ending this call,' she said.

'Wait! Seeing as you're on your own, would you like some company? Tonight, in bed? I'm giving you one last chance, Grace. Just the sex. No strings. You don't have to talk to me. You don't have to do anything. I'll do it all.'

'Who says I'm on my own? What makes you think that?' she said. She gripped the phone and her gaze flickered around the apartment as though she expected him to pop up from the behind the sofa, which just showed how jumpy she felt. Gavin had made a little ceremony of handing the keys back to her before he'd left, dropping them into her hand and folding her fingers tightly around them, so that one of the keys had dug into the soft skin of her palm. She wanted to hang up on him but she couldn't help waiting to hear what he'd say in some oddly fascinated way.

'I know by your voice,' he said. 'You're nervous. Nervous of me. Because now you know how awful it is to be all alone without your lover. Wanting him. In a fever for needing him. Crazy with longing. Now you know the kind of torture you've put me through. Only it was worse for me. I was left with pictures of you, naked in bed, fucking someone else, doing what we used to do. Do you remember us fucking, Grace?

'Gavin, I—'

She didn't get a chance to tell him what she thought of him because he'd already ended the call.

* * *

By the time Robert arrived home after the late Friday night flight, the rain had become heavy, drumming against the windows, lowering Lucia's mood, and when he came through the door, bringing a flurry of raindrops with him, she was ready for bed, clad in a lace-trimmed wrap over her cotton pyjamas.

They hadn't spoken since she'd left his apartment the previous Sunday, Robert sending a cursory text to tell her he'd be late that night, and now Lucia's stomach was in a knot, wondering what the weekend would bring. It started as badly as she had feared. She sensed immediately that Robert was frazzled; it was like an aura around him, filling the air as he marched straight down the hall to the kitchen. He splashed a generous amount of red wine into a glass almost as soon as he flung off his jacket, not even bothering to go through to the sitting room, perching instead on a stool by the island counter in the kitchen, the rest of the bottle close to hand, while rain drummed on the kitchen skylight.

'It's been a crap week,' he said tersely, something in his taut face and shuttered glance putting her on the defensive and preventing her from asking him what had happened.

'Sorry to hear that,' she said evenly. 'I've had a busy week as well, so I'm going to bed.' She somehow felt the need to tighten the sash of her wrap and hug herself with her arms. It wasn't so much she'd had a busy week, it had been more an emotionally draining few days. It would be difficult enough to keep a bright look on her face without coping with Robert being in a bad mood on top of the tensions between them. She watched him topping up his wine, thinking of the bottle she'd already polished off between the previous night and tonight, the evidence of which was tucked away into the middle of the recycling box. It was over a half an hour before he followed her up to bed. She pretended to be asleep, wondering how much more wine he'd knocked back before he'd come up the stairs.

On Saturday morning he barely spoke to her, beyond reminding her he was off to play golf for the day. Then as he was going out the door, he told he'd cancelled the table for their meal that evening.

'Why, Robert?' she asked, conscious of her heart beating as though it was caught in her throat.

'We need to talk, you and I,' he said. 'I can't go on like this, last weekend was … the pits. It's better that we have this conversation at home.'

'What conversation?'

'We'll talk tonight,' he said, his face shuttered. 'I have to go out today because I'm making up a fourth. Otherwise I'd cancel.'

He must have seen some of her anxiety on her face, because he gave her the ghost of a smile and said, 'Don't worry, Lucia, it's me, not you.'

Nothing helped. Not all the cleaning or polishing or laundry, or shopping that she tried to distract herself with. *Me, not you …* What the hell did Robert mean? How were they going to start to get to grips with the rift that had opened up between them?

Chapter Fifty-seven

On Saturday afternoon Grace drove south through the heart of the Wicklow countryside. She took a turn that brought her down narrow laneways, where green and gold trees flashed by the window and formed archways overhead, drawing her deeper and deeper into a velvety fold. She turned into a laneway, and up a winding driveway bordered on both sides by a pine forest. The house set in the clearing at the top of the drive was solid, square and Georgian. The windows glinted in the sun, and the ground sloping away to the front gave it superb views of the surrounding mountainside. She parked the car and got out.

Redfern Hill. The place where Danny had learned to pick up his life again.

She walked into the bright, welcoming hall and was brought up to John Gordon's first-floor office. He was younger than she'd imagined. Mid-thirties, friendly and relaxed, wearing jeans and a casual shirt, he was the kind of older brother or cousin she could have imagined Danny having. He shook hands with her and introduced himself, and brought her across to a leather sofa, where they both sat down. Her gaze was drawn to the posters on the wall, carrying life-affirming messages not unlike the ones Danny had hung up in her apartment.

'Well, Grace, what brings you here?' John asked, looking at her with interest.

She felt suddenly shy. 'I thought I explained on the phone … it seemed a good opportunity to meet whoever was looking after Danny. His mentor. Just to thank the person in person, if you know what I mean. I only knew Danny a few weeks, but he changed my life around so much, so whatever you did with him, it was amazing and I wanted to thank you. I only found out after he'd gone that he'd been resident here before I met him.'

She wondered how much time Danny had spent in this office. It had a relaxed, laid-back feel to it. One wall was lined with shelves on which books and magazines were piled higgledy-piggledy. There was a long sash window overlooking the front garden and the incredible view, with a curved desk drawn up to it.

John smiled, his friendly eyes crinkling at the corners, and he shook his head. 'It's not me you should be thanking. Danny missed half of the group engagements and more often than not, skived off his one-on-ones. He played truant a lot.'

'Sounds like him all right …'

'I think you should be talking to my father.'

'Your father?' she faltered. 'Sorry I didn't know there were two Mr Gordons who were counsellors here. I must have asked for the wrong one. My mistake.'

'No, there aren't,' John said hastily. 'I mean my father, Tom, the head gardener. More often than not, whenever Danny skived off, he was helping Dad tend to the gardens, listening to Dad's own words of wisdom. Danny preferred to be out in the fresh air, listening to Dad's stories than being stuck indoors.'

'I can well imagine that.'

'My mother has heard Dad's stories a hundred times over, as have I, so Dad was delighted to have a new recruit and a fresh pair of ears in the shape of Danny.' He said this in a tone of voice that told

Grace he loved his father as much as she loved hers. 'But apart from Dad, the other person you should be thanking is yourself,' John said. 'You gave him something to live for.'

'Did I? What makes you say that?'

'He told Dad he was quitting the programme early because he'd met someone.'

'When was this?'

'Last November. He skived off to Dublin one day to get some posters for me and he seemed very unsettled after that. Then he just took off, and he asked Dad to tell me he was going to look for Grace. I wasn't sure at first whether he meant an actual person or a state of grace. Then he rang me, one day in February, he told me he'd found Grace, and we had a good chat. He sounded very happy.'

'We were,' she said, smiling softly.

'My dad would like to meet you. He said if he was finished cutting the grass, we'd find him in the kitchen garden. That's someplace else Danny used to work, going from one to the other. He was good in the kitchen, too.'

'I know.'

They chatted some more and then John led her downstairs and outside, along a path curving around to the side of the house between rolling lawns and fragrant rose beds. The July afternoon was unexpectedly warm and Grace took a long, slow breath. The smell of freshly cut grass mingling with the roses and a faint scent of the pine forest was the sweetest perfume imaginable.

Last night, she'd completed her submission to Liz in Jigsaw Press, emailing one story across, as well as an outline for two more in the series. Afterwards she'd opened a bottle of wine in a private celebration. Life was looking up.

* * *

Later, driving home, there had been a major traffic accident on the N11 and Grace arrived back in her apartment hot and sweaty after the delay on the sun-soaked motorway. She dropped her bag in the hallway and went straight down into the bathroom.

She was in the shower when she thought she heard a noise above the running of the water. A noise in the apartment. As though someone was there, walking through her living room. She turned off the faucet and strained to listen, standing very still for long moments as soap suds dried on her body. Nothing. She switched on the water again and stood under the spray, turning and twisting until the suds were rinsed clear. After she rinsed herself, she stepped out of the cubicle and dried herself, slathering on some body butter.

Only then did she notice that Danny's bottle of aftershave was missing from the spot on the shelf where she'd left it. She stared at the empty spot, her chest tightening as she tried to remember when she'd last seen it. This morning? It must have been this morning. She'd have noticed it was missing, wouldn't she? Something hummed between her ears. She strained to listen again, feeling unaccountably nervous, but everything was silent, save for a drip of water from the shower head.

Then she heard another tiny creak, swiftly suppressed, as though whoever had made it had halted on the spot.

She pulled on her pink velour bathrobe, tying it securely around her waist. Her phone. It was still in her bag. If she could just call Lucia, or Matt. She padded out to the hallway in her bare feet and looked down to where she'd dropped her bag by the coat hangers inside the hall door.

It wasn't there.

Had she left it in her bedroom? Sometimes she threw it on the bed while she changed after she came home from work. All her instincts on red alert, she crept down the corridor and stood outside the bedroom, her breath rasping in her throat, her galloping heart almost choking her. Standing in the hall, she reached out and pushed open the door. The bedroom was empty and silent. There was no sign of her bag, tossed on the bed. But all the stars had been scraped off the ceiling, every single one of them, even the tiny ones, leaving jagged tears all over the ceiling plaster. As she stood there, silently, she heard a floorboard creak once more.

Dear God.

Her phone. She had to get to it. Somehow.

Feck the phone, she had to get out of here.

She crept down towards the hall door. It was double-locked. She saw herself turning the key in it after she'd come in the door, dropping it into her bag. She couldn't get out without the key.

The bedroom. If she went back in there, she could lock that door, get to the window and shout for help. She thought she was going to suffocate with fear, but she took a breath into her tight lungs and prepared to make a bolt up the hallway. Just as she raced by the door to the living room, it opened and she was caught from behind so that she was sent spinning into the wall, cracking her head against it before she toppled to the floor, which winded her further so that everything went dark.

Chapter Fifty-eight

'This is a conversation I'd hoped we'd never need to have,' Robert said.

He'd come home from golf, and gone straight into the shower. He'd changed into denim jeans and a casual cream shirt and his hair was still damp and ruffled from the towel. Outside it was a beautiful summer's evening, with lemony shafts of sunlight beaming across the garden, and the dazzle of the sun on the windows of a house behind them sent flickering rays onto the walls of their conservatory. It was the kind of sparkling evening Lucia loved the most, especially when she was relaxing in her own home.

She didn't need to be out in a pretentious venue of some kind, or the latest place to be seen, throwing money away just to impress. Everything she needed was right here, although this evening she was anything but relaxed as she sat on a floral wicker chair and looked at Robert. Everything scrambled together in her head as she silently flew through her imaginings one last time before the axe finally fell and Robert spoke. Had it been an affair? A one-night stand? Or had he sensed Lucia's building unhappiness with their lives and the distance between them? And her surprising and amazing need to have a baby of their own – a symbol of new life, their love, a gift to each other – but so totally at odds with what they'd agreed.

'It's something I'd hoped you'd never find out,' he said. 'And that I'd never have to talk about.'

An affair. With Miranda? Somehow though, it didn't ring true. Now that the axe was about to fall, her brain was suddenly crystal clear. She knew Miranda loved Neil to pieces. And she couldn't picture Robert and Miranda in bed together.

'I'm thoroughly ashamed of it.'

Oh, God. Someone else, so. Recently?

Robert stood there, rubbing his face. 'I behaved ... abominably.'

Jesus.

He stared at Lucia, not really seeing her, seeing something else, someone else. 'Funny thing, I felt nothing at the time. It just seemed like the right thing to do, the only thing to do.'

Oh yeah, it was one of those things, it meant nothing at all. It just happened all by itself. So you see, I didn't really betray you. Get real, Robert. If you shoved your dick—

'I think I was in shock,' he continued. 'But I just got on with things and I thought I had put it behind me.'

And now you expect me to put it behind me? After your confession has eased your guilty conscience? You think I'll forgive and forget? Fat chance.

Robert was talking, pacing the floor, pale-faced and uneasy, and as he went on, she realised that she hadn't a clue what he was talking about.

'But I hadn't dealt with it at all,' he said. 'I was quite young. Immature. We both were. That's why it only hit me years later. Funny,' he paused in his pacing and threw out his hands, 'you read lots of articles about the woman who has gone through the pain and trauma of these things, but not the man. Although that's right in a way as she's the one to undergo the most physical as well as the most emotional upset, but the father's emotions are usually ignored in this situation. Not that, in my case, I was a father at all. It's like it's not reckonable at any level. I've no problem with that, because I didn't deserve to be.'

'What situation, Robert?' she asked, feeling goosebumps erupt all over her. 'What are you talking about?'

'Something I never wanted to talk about. Something I'd hoped I'd never have to tell you.'

Robert put his hands in his pockets, and facing her, he gave her a long, unhappy look. In that moment, Lucia realised she still loved him now, before he said anything, but more importantly, whatever he said couldn't and wouldn't change that. He looked like a broken man, and she wanted to take him into her arms and fix that. No matter if she was angry or even devastated by his words, she loved him now; she would always love him. He was embedded in her heart and would forever be there.

'Why don't I pour us both a glass of wine, and then you can tell me, Robert,' she said in a quiet voice, drawing an unexpected strength from somewhere. 'Please don't be afraid.'

Chapter Fifty-nine

'I thought we'd go out into the garden, it's such a fabulous evening,' Janet said.

She appeared at the hall door looking fresh and beautiful, her hair swept to one side and secured with a sparkly clip. She was wearing a plain white T-shirt over a light blue skirt and she had sandals that glittered on her bare feet. Her toenails were painted with pink nail varnish.

Matt's heart swelled.

'Good idea,' he said, stepping into the shady hall, handing her a bottle of wine. 'Where's Abbie?'

As she walked ahead of him down the hall, Janet said, over her shoulder, 'She'll be home at seven o'clock.'

Matt's stride faltered. 'Thought she was due home at six?'

'Well, no,' Janet said, stopping and turning to face him, a hint of apology in her smile, 'I thought it would be a chance for us to talk, uninterrupted.'

'Oh.'

'Matt, don't look so worried or start imagining the worst,' she said. 'We haven't had a chance to chat by ourselves between the comings and goings of the past few months. Why don't you go through to the garden and I'll bring you a drink. Beer or wine?'

'I'll have a beer, please.'

He followed Janet down to the kitchen and went through the open patio doors, and out into the incandescent, summery evening. Sunshine poured across the garden, glinting on the shrubs and flowers, and heady scents rose in the air mingling with the hum of bees and chirping of birds. Janet's decking area was down at the end of the garden, where it caught most of the day's sunshine. He sat on a rattan armchair and looked over beyond the garden fence into the near distance where the Dublin mountains were a gauzy blue smudge under the hazy sunshine. He felt himself relax as calm descended on him. Janet came out, smiling at him, a glass of wine in one hand, a bottle of beer in the other. It could have been this time last year, before Simon had come home, before Matt had started to act like an adolescent, when everything had been perfect between them.

It could be still perfect now too, he sensed, from the way Janet was looking at him. His heart swelled with gratitude that he'd been granted this second chance. He wasn't going to mess it up. So when his work mobile rang, he ignored it and let it go to voicemail. He was off duty and the message would direct any callers to the station.

'So,' Janet said. 'How've you been?'

'I'm good, right now. I love warm summer evenings like this, sitting out in the back garden. *This* back garden,' he said. 'With you.'

Janet smiled at him. Then she looked around at the patch of lawn surrounded by shrubs and flowers. 'Yeah, it's not too bad considering I've been neglecting it …'

The conversation flowed easily, as though there was a secret complicity between them to put to one side the strain of the last few months and simply enjoy the chat. His heart warmed when Janet flirted gently with him and laughed encouragingly at his attempts at a joke or two. He tensed slightly when the doorbell rang just before seven, but there was no need. Janet excused herself calmly, and was gone less than five minutes, returning with Abbie who scrambled out into the garden and launched herself excitedly at him, shouting 'Daddy, you're home!' at the top of her voice.

She insisted on showing him her new sticker book, and then she asked in a clear voice when he was coming back to live with them and sleep in Mammy's bed. Matt's eyes immediately connected with Janet's over the top of Abbie's head and what he saw there made his heart somersault with a rush of love and tenderness. He met Janet's gaze with a tender and hopeful look of his own.

'Maybe … someday soon,' he said to Abbie, feeling a quiet confidence.

When he heard his mobile ring again, he ignored it. What was happening here this evening was far too important to allow anything to distract him.

Chapter Sixty

'Oh dear, you weren't supposed to get that bruise on your cheek.'

Grace blinked. There was a mist in front of her eyes. She became aware that her head was pounding, her throat dry, and the back of her neck was sore from the way she was slumped.

Slumped? She went to move, but her arms wouldn't move with her. Instead her shoulders felt strained. She blinked again and slowly, gradually, the mist began to clear.

She was sitting at her kitchen table. Danny's leather jacket was thrown around her shoulders, over her velour bathrobe. Looking down, she could see it gaped a little. She remembered tying it securely around her with the belt. The belt was missing. Then she realised it was tied around her hands, securing them behind the chair. Her legs were tied to the chair with something else.

Gavin was sitting opposite her. His eyes looked very sad.

'Gavin. What in God's name are you up to? What kind of game are you playing?'

'This is your fault, Grace. You made this happen.'

'Don't be ridiculous. Take this belt off me. Now.'

'I can't.'

'Why not?'

'Because you'd call the police and I'd be arrested.' He said this in a sing-song voice that chilled her.

'But why would I call the police? You're not going to hurt me.'

He said nothing, but merely looked at her with a mock sad expression on his face that chilled her to the bone.

'How did you get in?' she asked. A ridiculous question in view of the way she was tied up. Who cared how he had got in?

'I had keys.'

'You gave your set back to me.'

He said, smiling at her, 'Not before I got a copy made.'

'So you've had keys all along.'

He smiled again, as if congratulating his own foresight. 'Yep.'

'You've been in my apartment before now.'

'Yep to that as well.'

She looked across to her posters. They had been ripped to ribbons, and most of them had fallen in chunks to the floor. A few jagged corners remained, held up by Blu-Tack.

'Why, Gavin?'

'*Why?*' He looked at her as though she was crazy. 'Don't you know?'

'No, I don't.'

'Well, you're a mad fucking bitch. Or else I'm so far off your radar that you don't have a clue where I'm coming from.'

'I'm so mad I know you're about to tell me exactly where you're coming from.'

His fists clenched. She was sure he wanted to hit her, but he visibly controlled himself. 'You're not going to get me that way, Grace. One bruise is fine, where you hit your face off the side of the cooker when you tried to turn off the gas – in vain, I might add – but another one might be suspect.'

'I always knew you were clever,' she said, chills running up the back of her head at the words coming out of his mouth.

'Too clever to be fooled by you. I'm sorry you felt the need to string me along the way you did.'

'I didn't string you along.'

'Yes, you did, bitch. Three years with you going nowhere. Three years of my life down the fucking drain. What a shitty waste of time.'

'It wasn't a waste of time … it was …'

'Fuck off. Have you any idea how much I wanted us to get back together? How much I hoped we'd be spending Christmas together? I bought you a *ring*. You've made a fool out of me and totally fucked up my life. Thanks for fucking me up. Thanks for nothing.'

'I'm sorry if I hurt you,' she said, playing along with him.

'You're not going to get me that way either, you needn't humour me because that won't work. I know what you were up to, both of you. I saw you, that night.'

'What night?'

'At Christmas. Remember? The night I asked you to go for a drink, thinking you might have had a change of heart about us. After I left you, I went up a laneway and got fucking sick, and then a while later I came back down to look for you, in case you were still there, thinking you might be upset. But guess what? I saw the two of you heading up Grafton Street, laughing and joking and holding hands. As though I'd never existed.'

Grace shook her head.

'So then I knew that you'd been telling me a pack of lies, and that prick Reilly had been telling me the truth. He'd told me he'd heard a young woman called Grace had got stuck in the lift in his building along with a guy called Danny, and wasn't that the same name as my girlfriend? So you see, Grace, I knew then that you'd met Danny before we broke up. And that's why you dumped me.'

Grace said nothing.

'You must have arranged to meet him that night, as soon as you'd got rid of me,' Gavin went on. 'It was so handy for you that I had to run off, it must have given you a great laugh.' He suddenly slammed his fist down on the table, alarming her. 'It didn't take you long to let him move into my side of the bed, did it? I saw you on New Year's Day.'

'New Year's Day?'

'I called here on New Year's Eve ... hoping you'd been in, hoping you hadn't really found someone new. Giving you the benefit of the doubt. Maybe it had only been the one night. Maybe by now you'd have realised I was the only one for you. I even brought some wine for us to see in the New Year, but I got no answer. I guessed you were out gallivanting with him. Maybe you were letting him fuck you somewhere. Thinking of you in bed with him ... it made me crazy. Was he good? Better than me? Did he make you come? One of my girlfriends used to say I took too long to make her come. She didn't like the way I watched her. Imagine being told that. It hurt a lot. So when I got no answer from you I sat in my car in the basement and drank all the wine.'

Grace stared at him.

'But I fell asleep. I woke up the next morning in the front seat of my car and I saw you, going through the car park. You didn't see me, but I saw you and him, both of you.'

'We were over, Gavin.' Even with the sparks of alarm charging around her body, she felt compelled to remind him of this.

'Yeah, because of Danny.' He took out his mobile phone. She glanced around the kitchen for hers, but there was no sign of it. Nor was there any sign of her bag. 'This is how you made me feel, Grace, when you blew me out:'

'*A shock like that, you think you're going to seize up yourself, fade away ...*'

At first she didn't know whose voice it was or what the person was talking about. The voice was echoey and slightly ethereal. Then, as phrases jumped out at her, she realised with a cold wave of shock, it was her, talking to Gavin, the day they'd met for coffee.

'*... want to disappear into a dot ... feel you're going mad, but ... living goes on. Your breath comes in and out ... need to eat even if you don't taste the food. You need sleep, so eventually your eyes close and you nod off, and even if you wake up again an hour later ...*'

'You recorded me,' she said.

'You've no idea how much I enjoyed listening to that, all those nights I couldn't sleep,' he said conversationally. 'The only thing that saved my sanity was knowing you were as tormented as I was.'

'Gavin ... what's this all about?'

He ignored her question. 'I didn't even move that far away,' he said.

'What do you mean?'

'I stayed with Trev for about a week, then I moved into an apartment in the next building. Right next door to you, Grace. I can see into your living room from my kitchen window. Clever, huh? I could tell you when Danny moved in. I could see when you were up in the middle of the night, and when the lights were on and off. I can even see the car park exit from my front window.'

'It was you on the motorbike, wasn't it? Following me?'

'I got a motorbike because I thought I might get you back that way. If you had the hots for a guy on a bike, I wanted to be that guy. Then after Danny died, it became a bit of fun. I even got a guy to make me a false number plate – he owed me a favour for fixing up his accounts. I rattled you that day on the motorway, didn't I? I knew when you slowed down and moved to the inside lane that I was getting to you.'

'How did you know Danny was supposed to be going to the off-licence that night?' she asked. 'I didn't tell you, did I? You must have seen him there. What happened?'

She threw out the question on impulse, but when he began to talk, what he said sent shivers down her spine.

Chapter Sixty-one

Lucia took a sip of her wine, glad that Robert had stopped his relentless pacing and was now sitting opposite her in the conservatory.

'Years ago, while I was still in college,' he began, his face set in unhappy lines.

Years ago?

'I went to England with my then girlfriend so she could have an abortion. We were both nineteen and it seemed the only solution for us.'

Something shifted inside Lucia as her heart went out to him. Not an affair, then, not even a recent betrayal. An unfortunate event that had happened years ago, and he was only talking about it now, which meant it had never left him. Yet, knowing her polite, gentle Robert, she wasn't surprised. How could it ever have left him?

'I knew you'd be shocked,' he said. 'Please don't hate me.'

Lucia gathered her whirling thoughts together as best she could. She took a deep breath. She rose to her feet and went across to sit beside him, putting her hand on his arm. 'Robert, please, I don't hate you. Far from it. I just wish you'd told me sooner. Why don't you start at the beginning and tell me what happened?'

She listened while Robert talked, his voice raw and emotional, as the secret that had weighed on him for years was slowly peeled away.

'It's not as if Megan and I intended to stay together forever,' he said. 'It was all very casual except we got caught out one night, when we'd too many Jäger Bombs in the student bar. We were both frantic. Megan couldn't tell her parents, they would have gone ballistic, so it wasn't an option. Mine would have gone mad too. Even if we'd been brave enough to tell them and gone ahead with things – with having the baby – we'd never have managed. We were both nineteen with almost three years in college still ahead of us. We weren't ready, emotionally or financially. Besides, we were just casual friends, nothing more, so we did what seemed right at the time.'

He let his head sink down into his hands. 'Megan made some enquiries ... We topped up our student loans and booked flights to Birmingham. I'll never forget meeting her at the airport. We were supposed to be in Galway on a field trip. We were both in a blind panic in case we were seen. The whole thing in Birmingham was a nightmare, she was just twelve weeks pregnant by the time we got the money together and made our plans. It was a shitty experience, but there was a massive relief for both of us when it was all over. I felt as though a life sentence had been lifted. I don't think we spoke all the way home on the plane. We drifted apart soon after that. No surprises, what happened broke us up, not that we had much to begin with. About three months later, Megan decided the college course wasn't for her so she dropped out. I never heard from her after that. Someone told me she'd gone to America. In a way that was another relief. You must hate what you're hearing.'

'Robert ...' Lucia hesitated, considering her words carefully. 'You can't blame yourself too much for what happened. You were young, okay, but you made a choice that was right for you at the time.'

'I thought I had put it all behind me,' he said, his voice taut. 'I threw myself into college life and things went on as normal. I didn't even stop to think about the baby around the time it would have been born. I didn't want to know anything. Mostly I was just relieved as though I'd woken up from a particularly crap nightmare.'

'I can understand that,' Lucia said. 'But what I don't understand is why you're telling me now. It was years ago, Robert. It has nothing to do with us.'

'It has in a way, because ...' he gave her an apologetic look. 'See, Lucia, that's the reason why I never wanted to have children.'

'Oh. No, I don't see that at all,' she said, mystified.

'I managed to forget all about it, and life went on as though it had never happened. Looking back, I'm amazed at how easy it was to blank it all out. That is, until Ruth announced her first pregnancy.'

Robert paused. Lucia waited, half-fearing, half-guessing what was coming next.

'To say the family were overjoyed when Ruth made the announcement is an understatement. Mum and Dad, Ruth and Jamie, were all thrilled, and I was too, until ...'

'Until what?'

'Until I saw her scan picture, taken at twelve weeks.' Robert rubbed his face. His voice, when he spoke, was hoarse with emotion. 'We were in Mum's house in Carlow, one Sunday, and there was great excitement when she produced it. The first grandchild, and we could see the evidence of it in this little picture. Okay, it looked like a blob of grey, but Ruth was chatting all about it, telling us the midwife had been able to pick out the four chambers of the heart, they were only the size of four dots – *four dots!* – but they were working perfectly, as well as the kidneys and the liver. And she had heard the tiny heartbeat. Mum and Dad and Ruth were all going on about the miracle of life, the tiny perfection of it, the absolute brilliance, but I almost threw up. It hit me with the force of a juggernaut. I had helped to end a small life before it had a chance to be born. I was in a sweat. After a while I made an excuse, something to do with the

office, and I left early. I looked so stressed they believed me. I don't
know how I managed to drive home from Carlow,' he paused.

Lucia stayed silent, letting him talk, squeezing his arm.

'There were more scans of course, in the following months, and
when I saw the baby as a newborn, my heart felt like it had smashed
into tiny pieces. Then there were even more babies. That part has
been difficult, putting on a good face in front of Ruth's babies, trying
to hide the sick feeling I had inside when I saw them coming into
the world one by one, those beautiful, tiny wriggling scraps of life.
I decided I didn't deserve to be a father, having got rid of my first
little baby without giving it much thought, so fucking heedlessly, as
though it were merely a nuisance of some kind to be disposed of as
expeditiously as possible.'

'You have to forgive yourself,' Lucia said. 'You can't allow the
rest of your life to be shaped by a choice you made at the age of
nineteen.'

'I could have had a son or daughter who'd be seventeen by now.
Seventeen! Can you remember being seventeen? All that promise
… all that life …' He bowed his head, dropping it into his hands.
'Instead I was responsible for a life that was cut short and was never
even so much as acknowledged.'

She struggled to find the right words, to make him feel better, to
help him reconcile himself with his past. And it wasn't just empathy
she felt, but it was deeper than that – pure unconditional love.

'That's why I didn't want to have any children,' he said. 'I didn't
feel I deserved a second chance at fatherhood. I was relieved when
you said you didn't want children either. It meant I didn't have to
face up to it and deal with it. Then this year, on holidays, I sensed
you were changing your mind. I saw a difference in you and the
questions you were asking scared me. The look on your face when
you watched the couple with the baby unnerved me. And when I
went back to the office after the holidays, Miranda was there, back

from maternity leave and glowing with happiness. Normally that wouldn't have bothered me, I've had female colleagues coming back from maternity leave before, I've been able to distance myself from it, but this time I kept thinking of the way you might have been, bursting with happiness and love, if things had been different, so I was even more on edge.' His voice trailed away. He sat, staring into space.

Lucia got up and knelt down in front of him. She took both of Robert's hands in hers and faced him squarely. 'Listen to me,' she said. 'You must forgive yourself. Now. From this moment. Let it go. What happened is in the past, and you have to accept that. But please don't allow anything you did to colour your future, or any future we could have together.'

From the island unit in the kitchen, Lucia heard her mobile bleep. She ignored it. 'We can make a fresh start from now, leaving the past in the past – it was half your lifetime ago. Don't you think you've carried this long enough? I don't know much about babies or souls or what happens before you are born. I guess none of us do, we don't remember that far back,' she smiled. 'But I have heard that if a tiny soul's potential life is cut short, it comes back again at another opportunity. So think of that, instead of thinking the worst.'

'Why are you being so kind and understanding?'

'Don't you feel you deserve a little kindness?' When he didn't answer she moved in closer to him, letting go of his hands and putting her arms around him. 'It's not just understanding, it's love. Before you even opened your mouth to speak, I realised that no matter what you were going to say, I still loved you, as both a lover and a best friend. I always will. What you've said hasn't changed any of that.'

'Lucia …' he shook his head, closed his eyes, almost breathed her name. He opened his eyes and looked at her with a hint of regret. 'Don't you feel you married me under false pretences?'

Lucia stared back at him. Everything hung in the balance. Snapshots of their life together flashed through her head. She remembered the first time they'd met in London, and how taken she'd been with the modest, unassuming man. She remembered how happy she'd felt on her wedding day, on their honeymoon, and in the weeks and months afterwards, not knowing the dark secret Robert had been harbouring all this time. How well he'd looked after her, all these years, how much of a best friend he'd been to her. Love wasn't always a big colourful explosion; sometimes the most important love was just being kind to each other, because that underpinned the normal everyday threads of the fabric of life, and held them together.

'Yes, there is that, probably,' she said. 'But so what? Does it matter, here and now, for us? I don't think so. People marry for all sorts of reasons and motives, they come together with lots of different baggage, as well as different expectations. None of us are blank slates. We all have history written across our hearts.'

She paused for a moment. Sometimes it was impossible to wipe a slate clean. Sometimes you had to just move on. She swallowed. 'The big question is, Robert, where we go from here. It's up to us whether this brings us closer together or pushes us further apart. I know what I'd like to happen.' Lucia paused. Once she said what she had to say there would be no going back. It could change everything between them, and yes, there could be mayhem and upheaval, the smooth running of their lives completely shattered with sleepless nights and chaotic days. Then there was the not inconsiderable issue of Robert being in London and she in Dublin, because a baby would need cuddles from both of them, every night.

Ripples of anxiety formed in her stomach as she faced her husband, but she pushed them to one side and took a deep breath. 'Robert, you could still have a son or daughter, and look forward to him or her being seventeen. It's not too late.'

'Isn't it? What are you saying?'

'There's nothing to stop us from trying for a baby, maybe even two. We could have some wonderful times to look forward to. Chaotic years, but wonderful.' She felt tears building up behind her eyes at the very idea of it all.

'But what about … I thought …' he paused.

'You were right, darling, during the holidays, even before them, everything began to change for me. Thing is, I never told you the truth as to why I didn't want children.'

'Didn't?'

'*Didn't*,' she emphasised. 'The questions I've recently been asking myself were scaring me too, because they meant – oh, God –' she blinked back a tear, 'that the comfort zone around us could be gone forever. It could be replaced by something more … scary, but a thousand times more meaningful.'

'Lucia!' There was a glimmer of something warm and hopeful in his eyes. She slid into the warmth of his arms and prepared to open her heart.

Chapter Sixty-two

'Even though I hated his guts and everything about him, I didn't plan anything for Danny,' Gavin said. 'It just happened. It was one of those mad, crazy moments.'

'So he was at the off-licence that night?' Grace said, her stomach heaving with anxiety.

'Yeah. That was a lucky break. I was coming through the village when I saw his bike parked outside it. I pulled up alongside it and waited for him to come out, and I started chatting to him, comparing bikes, the way guys do. He started to excuse himself, saying he had to go up to the takeaway, when his mobile rang. He put down the wine while he took it out of his pocket. Something inside me snapped. I couldn't bear to be there, listening, while he spoke to you …'

'It wasn't me,' Grace said softly. She hadn't been able to find her mobile that night until it was too late. Stacy, though, had called him.

Gavin didn't hear her, caught up in his own thoughts. 'I don't know why I did it … even still. I was so pissed off that something made me reach over and grab the phone out of his hand. Then I drove off.' He fell silent.

'What happened next?' Grace asked, a chilled sense of desperation running through her.

'I don't really know,' Gavin said, blinking rapidly. 'I don't know how it happened. He jumped on his bike and followed me. I drove up past the apartment block and towards the M50 and he was still following me. I went straight through the interchange and took a side road back towards the city, hoping he'd think I'd gone onto the M50 …'

'So you caused it. The accident.'

'No, I didn't cause anything. Danny did it all by himself.'

'I don't believe you.'

'Do you really think I'm capable of killing someone Grace? You'd be amazed how easily accidents can happen.'

She stayed silent.

'He was still following me. I couldn't shake him off. I stopped and turned around, and drove back up the road. I felt a funny kind of calmness, all the rage was gone as though my brain had thrown a switch, even though I hadn't planned any of this. In my head I was like a knight, riding for your honour. But at the last minute, just as I went to drive into him, Danny swerved away and went into the wall … so you see, he did it to himself to avoid me …'

Grace trembled with shock. Instant, the police had told her. A heart attack candidate, Matt had told her. Whatever had been going through Danny's head in those last few seconds, she'd never know. Her voice was a whisper. 'Did you stop? Try to save him?'

'It was no use. We'd passed a van on the road a short while back, so I knew help was on the way. I turned back around again and kept going towards the city. I felt … I don't know how I felt. Weird. I'd tried to kill myself but it hadn't worked. Instead I was still alive and Danny was dead. Like some kind of fate,' he paused. 'But you still didn't want me, I knew by your face you couldn't bear me to touch you.' He stared at her, his eyes bright with resentment. 'So what use was it to me? Being alive? I've tried, Grace. I've given you every chance to love me again. But if I can't have you, then nobody else can. I can't bear to spend any more nights imagining you in someone else's bed. It would drive me insane.'

Grace put on a brave face. 'You can't stop me from living my life. And you won't get away with this.'

'Won't I?' He smiled, but his eyes were empty. 'I bet everyone thinks you're still cut up over Danny. You're wearing his jacket, but in a fit of grief you've scraped off his stars and torn down his posters. That's what it will look like. I bet you've told Lucia you're still seeing his bike.'

'The police are still investigating the accident,' she said. 'I've told them you knew Danny went to the off-licence that night. They'll soon figure out you saw him there and figure out the rest.'

'So? That doesn't bother me, it makes no difference to anything. By the time you're found I'll be far away from here.'

'No you won't,' Grace said. 'Lucia will be over soon.'

He smiled, his calm certainty sending her heart leaping into her mouth. 'Will she now? I bet she's safely tucked up at home with Robert. She sent you a text, saying they were staying in this evening and she might see you tomorrow evening. I've replied to say you're going out tonight. What a pity you never changed your pin number. But I wasn't too surprised to see you have another new guy on your books: Matt.'

'He's someone else who'll be over tonight,' Grace said, wondering where he had put her mobile and frantically trying to remember what she might have texted Matt about.

'There you go again, another lie. I wish you'd tell me the truth, Grace. I know from your texts that Matt is the policeman you've been talking to. He's off duty tonight, or so his voicemail says. Very thoughtful of the guy to keep everyone in the picture. I tried his number from your phone, but I hung up immediately. Then I followed up with a text to say everything's fine and you called it in error.'

'I think it's time to end this ridiculous nonsense,' Grace said. 'Let me go.'

'Have you listened to a word I've said? You don't understand. I never want to go through the torture of imagining you in bed with someone else and I don't intend to.' He was back to the sing-song voice.

'Gavin, let me go,' she said. 'Please.'

'Begging now, are you? It's a bit late for that. Pity you didn't beg me to stay all those months ago. Pity you wouldn't kiss me or let me hold you or fuck you in bed. It's too late now.'

He went across to the cooker and turned on the four burners, bypassing the battery operated ignition so that the gas began to flow out of the ducts.

'It was very handy that you reminded me of this the last time I called. I was wondering how I was going to stop anyone else from putting their hands on you.'

'You're mad,' Grace said, her stomach cold with fear. 'You're insane. You won't get away with this.'

'Yes, I will.'

'Someone will come, Lucia or Matt when they don't hear from me.'

'They'll be too late. I haven't finished my explanation. I've really thought this through, Grace. I'm going to block the door and wait outside and as soon as I figure you're too weak to move, I'll come back in and untie you. There'll be no sign of any marks. So it will look like you brought it on yourself, in your heartache over Danny's death.'

'You won't get away with murder the second time around,' she said.

'Won't I?' he grinned.

'I thought you loved me.'

'I do love you, Grace. That's the thing. I love you so much that I can't bear the thoughts of anyone else having you.'

'If you really loved me you'd let me go.' She could feel the start of a headache already. How long would it take before she drifted into unconsciousness? Minutes? Hours? She hadn't a clue. She was unable to prevent Gavin from bending down to her, grasping her chin, and tilting up her face towards his.

'Kiss, kiss, Grace.'

She kept her mouth closed firmly under the pressure of his and she stared up into his eyes defiantly.

'Oh dear, you didn't look like you enjoyed that.' He held her nose so that she'd no choice but to open her mouth, and he pulled down her chin, widening the opening, but instead of his tongue she felt something different being pushed in until she was gagged; a tea towel.

'In case you feel like shouting for help,' he said.

'I'll wait outside for a little while Grace, and as soon as I untie you I'll be off. I'll make sure to lock the hall door after me. And I have your mobile. I'll leave it where I left Danny's. He was chasing me in vain, you see. I threw it down onto the M50 when I went across the intersection. It was nice knowing you. And remember, Grace: I really loved you.'

She felt strangely chilled when he left. Her stomach was paining her and she was dizzy. She just wanted to let her head rest on the table. She looked across to Danny's kite. A memory glowed inside her of that afternoon, and then how Danny had stayed over for the first time that night, and how, when he'd kissed her awake in the morning, she'd known it was going to be something really special for both of them …

Chapter Sixty-three

The previous January

It's their first morning to wake up together. He has, as promised, kissed her awake. She is tingling down to the tips of her toes. The rain of the night before has stopped. Best of all, it's a Sunday.

'I meant to ask you, how did you find me?' Grace says, turning over in bed so that she's lying on her stomach and leaning on her elbows. Danny is lying on his back, legs stretched out alongside hers. She pulls up the midnight-blue duvet and tucks it around them so that both of them are cocooned together under its warmth. 'I'm still puzzled as to how you "just happened" to walk into the pub the very night I "just happened" to be there with Gavin. *After* he had walked out. I hadn't seen you since the day in the lift. Explain this remarkable coincidence in ten words or less,' she smiled.

'I knew you worked near St Stephen's Green so I stalked you.'

'You didn't! I could have had you arrested.'

'It wasn't quite stalking, it was more keeping an eye out for you. I was in and out of the city centre most evenings so I figured I'd a good chance of eventually coming across you having a Christmas drink somewhere in the vicinity of the Green, which is exactly what happened.'

'How long was this going on? Hardly since the time in the lift. You were supposed to have forgotten about me, like a melted snowflake, remember?'

'I tried, but I couldn't,' he grins. 'You were on my mind. I found myself thinking about you. I hoped you had managed to break up with that boyfriend who was making you feel you couldn't breathe. I didn't like to think of you being afraid to turn down his marriage proposal. I couldn't get you out of my head, but I only began to look around for you about three weeks before I spotted you.'

She traces light circles on his chest with her index finger. 'Umm, I still don't get the bit where you "just happened" to be walking through that particular bar, close to where I was sitting, within minutes of Gavin leaving.'

'My patience was rewarded. See? You should never, ever give up. I was coming up Dawson Street that evening when I saw you both heading into Royal Hibernian Way. And then I almost walked past the bar. I copped it at the last minute, and saw you sitting at the table inside the window, but I got the feeling from the look on your face that you weren't particularly enjoying yourself. I sat outside a nearby café with a coffee. I didn't know at the time that it was Gavin you were with. I took my time with the coffee, ordered a second, telling myself that if the two of you came out looking as if you were an item and going to enjoy Christmas together, I'd forget all about you. Anyway, Gavin came out by himself, I went in, and you know the rest.'

'I only know up to now,' she pointed out. 'I don't know yet what the rest will be.'

'It can be the best we want it to be,' he said. 'I was glad to hear you'd broken up with Gavin.'

'You made me ask myself the questions I'd been avoiding, like could I picture my life without him. Then when I began to imagine what it could be like, how different it could be – after that, I knew I had to find the guts to ease us apart.'

'Did you think about me at all?'

'Yes.'

'Were you going to look for me?'

'I can't be telling you all my secrets, but I was going to go back to the fourth floor after Christmas and pop into the accountant's office to see if they'd pass on a message to you.'

He turns onto his side so he is facing her. He trails his finger down her face. 'Oh, really? What kind of message?'

'I wanted you to know I'd looked up how many noughts were in a quadrillion and that I had decided to make every one of them count.'

'Good. But popping into the accountant's office wouldn't have worked.'

'Why not?'

'I wasn't there that day.'

'Oh, you!' Then, 'Weren't you?'

'Nah. I'd been in the printer's office, on the second floor, getting some posters printed. For a … friend of mine. Just as the lift doors closed and I pressed the button for the basement, the lift went up and you stepped in. And that was it, really. You stepped in. I know we spoke about things we'd regret as we sat there, but I knew from that moment what I wanted to do with the rest of my life, no matter how long or short it was going to be.'

'What was that?'

He gathers her close under the comforting heat of the duvet until their noses are touching. 'Spend it with you.'

Chapter Sixty-four

They ate out in the garden, Janet bringing out plates of lasagne and garlic bread, Abbie insisting on sitting as close as she could to Matt. When his mobile rang again with the station ring tone, he was tempted to ignore it. He didn't want to break this spell or allow anything to spoil the perfection of this warm sunny evening. But when it rang for the second time in five minutes, he picked it up reluctantly. No way would they have contacted him like this unless it was an emergency.

'Sorry, I'll have to take this,' he said, excusing himself to Janet. He pressed the accept button, and picking up the phone, he strolled across to a shady part of the garden, surprised to hear Kevin's voice at the other end.

'Matt ... sorry for disturbing you,' Kevin said. 'It's not an emergency as such but something strange has happened and I thought you'd want to know.'

'Shoot, Kev.'

'We've just sent a squad out to an incident, a motorbike in a single-vehicle collision.'

Something in Matt's head prickled. 'Go on.'

'It's close to where that lady's boyfriend had a fatal accident, remember, the Cameron—'

'Yes, I know who you mean,' Matt said impatiently.

'Funny thing is, when we ran it through the system the registration number of the motorbike is the same number as her departed boyfriend's, Danny McBride.'

'Run that by me again,' Matt asked, unable to grasp what he was hearing. Kevin repeated himself, but Matt still felt he was grasping at straws as it didn't seem to connect with him. 'What condition is the driver in?' he asked. 'Have you identified him or her?'

'It's a male, 30s, no means of identification, no tax disc, no mobile phone, not even a wallet and he's seriously injured. He went up on the verge and into the wall, just like Danny did, but he's survived, I don't know to what extent. He's being rushed to Tallaght as we speak. I thought you'd want to know, it all seems a bit weird. Danny McBride's bike is hardly back on the road again. And even if it were …'

'Not the way that bike was mangled. They have to be false plates. Especially with no tax … But no means of identification at all? Weirder still. Look, Kevin, thanks for letting me know. Keep me in the loop.'

He saw he'd had a missed call earlier from Grace, followed by a text, telling him she'd called his number by mistake and everything was fine. He rang her back, just to be sure, but it sounded like the battery had run out. On a Saturday night like this she was bound to be out on the town with her mates. Or was she? He stood in the corner of Janet's garden and looked at the two loves of his life. Janet was helping Abbie to water some flowers with her little pink watering can to distract her from disturbing Matt's call. Being here now was everything he'd wanted in the last few upsetting months, everything he'd ever want for the rest of his life, and the look on Janet's face was melting his heart.

'I help people,' he'd said to Abbie, knowing he'd joined the force for that reason. Haunted by once being the boy who'd hesitated in the face of an emergency, he knew his job gave him a clear role to play in any kind of crisis that was over and above any personal shortcomings he might think he had. It was bigger than him, and now every ounce of his training and the spirit of that job kicked in as he went back across the garden to Janet and told her a problem had come up.

Her face clouded with disappointment, but only for a moment. 'A problem,' she said, knowing better than to ask.

Janet had had her own special way of distancing him from the gritty side of his job. Sometimes when he'd come home late, drained and dispirited after a particularly bad day, she'd wisely said nothing, just sending him upstairs and pushing him into a refreshing shower, often waiting outside with a big fluffy towel and the warmth of her arms. He'd missed all that so much.

'Yeah, I just need to check something,' he said. 'It could be nothing at all, but I don't want to take that chance.' He picked up his car keys. He'd had less than two bottles of beer so he was okay to go. He tickled Abbie, enjoying the sound of her carefree laughter, and he kissed her on the cheek and told her he'd see her real soon. He left her searching for ladybirds in the flower beds, and Janet walked through the kitchen and up the hallway with him, the nearness of her making him dizzy.

'Sorry about this, it's crap timing,' he said, feeling awkward.

'No worries. Why don't you drop by later, if you're not too delayed,' she said, surprising him.

'Are you sure?' There was a wealth of meaning in his words and in the look that passed between them.

'Yes,' she said, smiling at him. 'I'll wait up.' Then, as he opened the hall door, 'Don't I get a kiss?'

Something flashed between them and he gathered her in his arms; her mouth was soft and sweet, it felt like the first amazing kiss they'd shared and all of his senses were swimming.

* * *

There was no sign of the motorbike he'd seen in the underground car park at Rathbrook Hall. Not that that meant anything. Still, if Grace's instincts had been right all along … He pressed her number into the key pad but she didn't answer. He called her mobile again and it still sounded as if the battery had run out. He had to wait until another resident came along to tailgait her into the apartment block. He stood outside Grace's hall door straining to listen but there were no sounds of life at all. He pressed the bell and knocked on the door to no avail. No doubt Grace was out enjoying her Saturday night somewhere and he should have stayed with Janet.

He called Kevin in the station and asked him to look up Danny McBride's notes for the name and contact number for Grace's sister.

'You don't seriously think—' Kevin began.

'I don't know what to think,' Matt said, walking down to the stairwell and taking the stairs two at a time. It was too much of a coincidence, and he didn't believe in those. Kevin came back to him in less than five minutes and Matt called Lucia, getting through to her voicemail. He left a message, asking her to call him. He checked the car park again for any signs of a motorbike, and he was just about to jump into his car and go back to Janet when he decided to take a last look around outside. He stood at the front of the block, trying to gauge where Grace's living room window was, but everything looked in order. He cut through the pedestrian walkway to the back of the block and the landscaped area. Again, all was quiet.

He glanced around at the adjacent apartment blocks, dull and shadowy on this side where they were out of the sun, and as he looked up and around, he remembered something else. At the entrance to the block adjacent to Grace's, he didn't wait for anyone to come along to open the main door, he just kept pressing the keypad until an occupant buzzed him in. He hurried up the stairs to the second-floor stairwell where he knew he would be almost opposite the kitchen in her apartment. He pressed as close as he could to the glass, trying to figure out which window was hers.

All seemed quiet. He stared again, looking from window to window, not sure what he was searching for, feeling more than a little foolish. In the shadow of the sun, the windows stared back blankly at him.

Then his mobile rang.

Grace, he hoped, returning his call.

It wasn't Grace, it was her sister Lucia.

'Matt Slattery?' she said. 'You were looking for me?'

'Hi Lucia, I've been trying to contact Grace, but her mobile is off. I got your contact details off the police files. I'm the guy who …'

'Yes, I recognise the name. Is there anything wrong?' Lucia asked.

'I want to talk to Grace kind of urgently and I thought you might know where she is …'

'Oh gosh … I don't. But I saw just now when I picked up the phone that she sent me a text earlier … and I thought it was funny …'

'Why?'

'She said she was going out tonight, but I know her friend Karen is away on holidays, and normally she's the person she'd be out with … what is it, Matt?'

'I don't know, it could be nothing at all or …'

'Or what?'

'There's been another motorcycle accident,' he told her. 'In or about the same location where Danny's was, we've no identification yet, but the registration number – shit. *Shit!*'

'What's wrong?'

He was already racing down the stairs. How had he forgotten? He'd been so fixated on the registration number being the same as Danny's bike that he'd forgotten Grace had given him that number as the number of the bike she'd thought was following her. There was no time to lose, to hesitate, to waver on the edge. He ran across to his car, opened the boot, rummaged around and grabbed his wheel brace. A young couple was coming out the main door and they stared at him as he rushed past them and dashed up the stairs. Then he was outside Grace's door.

It felt like forever but he got into her hallway in under two minutes.

He caught a whiff of gas straight away and saw a towel running along by the bottom of the living room door. He whipped it up and opened the door, noticing everything in slow motion, even though it was only a split second; the hiss of gas from the burners, and Grace, wearing a leather jacket slumped across the table, looking as though she was asleep.

He turned his head away long enough to take a deep breath, and then he ran into the room. He lifted Grace into his arms, taking her outside to the corridor where he put her in the recovery position. He took another deep breath and raced back to the kitchen, where he switched off the burners and opened the windows. Then he hurried back out to Grace, and began to make some phone calls.

* * *

The next few hours were fraught. Lucia and her husband arrived at the apartment just as Grace was being rushed to hospital. The motorcyclist with life-threatening injuries was identified as Grace's ex-boyfriend Gavin Molloy. Matt arranged to have Grace's apartment sealed off for examination and Danny McBride's file reopened, all the time berating himself for not trusting Grace's instincts. Funnily enough, only for Gavin crashing into the wall in the way he had, Matt wouldn't have been alerted about Grace, so in a sense Gavin had saved her life. Matt's conscience was only eased a little when Lucia phoned him later from the hospital to say she'd be forever grateful to Matt for saving her sister's life. Grace was stable, she was going to be okay, he'd got there in the nick of time, Lucia said, and she would always appreciate his swift actions.

It was hours before he was back outside Janet's hall door. It was probably far too late to be calling like this, and there were no lights on, but he was so drained he felt blank. Matt tapped lightly on the glass. Whatever about Janet, Abbie would be long tucked up in bed with her monkey teddy, snuggled into the dream world of the young and innocent.

Through the glass, he saw the hallway flooding with light. Then Janet opened the door and let him in.

Chapter Sixty-five

Two months later

There was no sign of Lucia in the check-in area in Dublin airport that afternoon. Grace scanned the travellers, looking in vain for her. It wasn't like the super-punctual Lucia not to be ready and waiting. Grace's instructions had been to turn up at the airport with her passport and her weekend case. Lucia was doing the rest, as it was Grace's birthday treat.

'There'll definitely be a chocolate walking tour,' Lucia had assured her. 'And hot air ballooning. That's all I'm telling you.'

'Sounds very mysterious. Why won't you tell me where we're going? Although I guess it's Paris, because Mum and Dad will be with us. And Robert. I suppose he's flying from London?'

'It's a surprise,' Lucia said. 'Just be waiting by the check-in area at two o'clock. Then you'll find out where we're off to.'

Grace had a surprise of her own. To her utter joy, Liz of Jigsaw Press had finally contacted her. They liked her work. They wanted to meet to discuss a three-book deal for publication rights to *Katie and the Kite*. Perhaps she should consider talking to an agent. The email had arrived earlier that week and she was still on cloud nine, the news spinning around in her head like the glittery disco ball Danny had bought. She planned to break the news to her family when they were all together.

That's if they got going. At a quarter past two, Grace took out her mobile and called Lucia.

Her sister answered with a muffled voice. 'I'm here, Grace, I'm out in the bathroom at the moment.'

'You sound like you have a cold.'

'I'm fine. I'll be with you soon.'

She wasn't fine, Grace decided. Pulling her case behind her, she walked through the Departure terminal towards the bathrooms.

To her surprise, Robert was coming towards her, a wheelie case in each hand.

'Robert? Where's Lucia?'

'She's in the bathroom,' he said. 'I came out to look for you. She said to go on into her.'

'What's up?' Grace paused. 'What are you doing here anyway? I thought you were flying out from London.'

'I've been in Dublin for a few days,' he said, with a gleam in his eyes unlike anything she'd ever seen before. 'Go on, Lucia's waiting for you.'

There was no sign of Lucia in the ladies' bathroom, but from one of the cubicles, there came the unmistakeable sound of someone retching.

'Lucia?' Grace called.

'I'll be out in a minute,' her sister's voice was hoarse. A couple of minutes later there was the sound of flushing, and then Lucia emerged, looking most un-Lucia like, with a shiny, pale face and red-rimmed eyes.

Grace's heart sank. A stomach bug. A virus of sorts. 'God, what's wrong?'

To her surprise, the most incredible smile lit up her sister's face. Lucia shook her head, 'Oh, Grace, there's nothing wrong. Everything is just about brilliant.' She stood in front of Grace, tears slipping down her cheeks, her words tumbling out. 'I didn't expect you to find out here. Robert and I thought we'd be able to keep it to ourselves until we were all together, cracking open the bubbly – not that I could have any of it myself – and I didn't want to steal your birthday thunder either ... but it's happened sooner than we expected and it's still very early days ...'

Something sparked at the back of Grace's head, something wonderful and life-affirming and utterly amazing. 'No!' she said, overcome with emotion, tears beginning to fall.

'Yes,' Lucia nodded, pulling a fresh tissue out of her bag before she fell into Grace's open arms.

* * *

'I certainly didn't expect to be in Rome this evening,' Grace said, shaking her head in wonderment. Lucia had kept up the surprise until she'd had to hand over Grace's boarding pass. Her sister had been fine on the flight over, picking at crackers, the colour gradually returning to her face. Her parents had arrived into Fiumicino Airport just ahead of them, and a people-carrier had ferried the five of them to a plush hotel near the Pantheon. Now they were sitting out on the Piazza Navona in the warm September evening.

'We thought it would be nice to go somewhere different,' Lucia said. 'Exciting, lively, chaotic even.'

'It's magical,' Grace said, her eyes scanning the vibrant square, with its graceful buildings, beautiful fountains, colourful street art, music and throngs of people, set against a dark mauve sky, where a crescent moon was rising, a bright star glittering beneath it. Laughter and conversation rose in lively cadences around them. The late evening air was aromatic and deliciously soft on her skin and the energy of it all thrummed through her veins. Robert had already organised champagne, and they'd toasted Lucia and the new life coming into the family.

Michael Bailey ordered more champagne and everybody toasted Grace on the occasion of her milestone birthday. Her dad made a little speech, telling her how much she was loved, talking of the night she was born and the joy and fun she'd brought to all of them, and Grace had tears in her eyes by the time he was finished.

After a while she said, 'I have some good news of my own. Something else I've been looking forward to telling you all about ...'

'More celebrations?' Her mother beamed happily.

Sitting at the head of the table, Grace looked around, her heart lifting with the sight of the smiling, expectant faces of her loved ones. She wondered what were the odds, in a few thousand quadrillions, of being alive in this moment, on a night like this.

She was going to make it count.

ACKNOWLEDGEMENTS

Sometimes the acknowledgements can be the most daunting part of a book to write, because it's almost impossible to find adequate words with which to thank those to whom I am deeply grateful for immense support and encouragement.

This book is dedicated to Derek, who is always there for me throughout the long haul from the time the ideas begin to form, to the endless days and nights I neglect him in order to spend time with people he's never met, to the nail-biting wait until the edits arrive, right up to sharing the excitement of a finished book landing in my arms. Thank you for the countless hot dinners, the coffee and scones, the dishwasher-emptying, the laundry-sorting, for being a listening ear during the brilliant and not-so-brilliant days, but mostly for taking my dreams under your wing and minding them as if they were your own.

Thanks from the bottom of my heart to my wide circle of family and friends for unwavering encouragement, much love and tons of kindness, especially the nearest and dearest – Michelle, Declan, Barbara, Dara, Louise, Colm, and the cherished Cruz, Tom and Lexi.

Heartfelt appreciation goes to my stellar agent, Sheila Crowley, for her wonderful enthusiasm and amazing support, and to Rebecca Ritchie and all the team at Curtis Brown, London.

A huge thanks is due to Ciara Doorley, my talented and skilful editor, who always manages to bring out the best in my stories, and to the ever-patient Joanna Smyth and all the team who work so hard behind the scenes at Hachette Books Ireland – Breda, Jim, Ruth, Siobhan, Bernard and Ciara C. Thanks also to Plunkett PR, the copy editor Nora Mahony and proof reader Aoife O'Kelly.

It's impossible to mention everyone individually who has helped in some way in getting *Someone New* out onto the shelves, but a big thanks is due to all the booksellers and readers, my writer friends and the online book community, who support me in many different ways and buy my books, without which I wouldn't have this dream job.

I'd like to pay special tribute to all the book bloggers out there, who are so immensely supportive of writers, and who devote large chunks of their time and energy to reviewing books, running competitions, hosting blogs, Q&A's, and cover reveals, and in general helping enormously in putting a book out there to readers all around the world. It means a lot and I owe each and every one of you lots of gratitude for your help and dedication, your enthusiasm and wonderful reviews.

I hope you enjoy *Someone New*.

Zoë xx